5,6,7

THE BOOK OF DAVID

A NOVEL BY

ROSA LEE KLANESKI

For my parents

Stan and Ida

All truth passes through three stages. First, it is ridiculed. Second, it is violently opposed. Third, it is accepted as being self-evident.

Arthur Schopenhauer

This novel is a work of fiction and is not based on any real events—any apparent reflection of actual events, or actual people is purely coincidental. If it appears as if this statement may not be wholly true, this means that the universe is operating exactly as it should: extraordinarily indirectly and consistently challenging objectivity and understanding. Shuffle up and deal!

The Deal

"Things aren't looking too good for you, Mike."

"You're entitled to your opinion." Michael stared back at the State Police detective and grinned like he just ate the canary.

"Don't fuck with me, Mazzone."

"Don't fuck with *me*, Geronimo."

"It's Giordano. And you're the one who's fucked here." He walked away from Michael, who was still sitting in his chair and staring at the pastel cinder block wall. The detective said nothing. His face didn't change.

"Geronimo, listen. You're going to release me once you can't hold me any more. You didn't *arrest* me. You *detained* me. It's a material witness warrant. And I witnessed *nothing*. I don't know shit."

"Mazzone, I know you don't know shit. If you knew what was good for you, you'd be telling me everything."

"And why would I do that, *officer*?"

"It's Detective. You know why? Because I got a person in the hospital in ICU clinging to life that I can directly link to you, and your store. The person responsible for putting them there is *also* linked to your store. And the Feds are telling me that you were in possession of something belonging to them. And that person you gave that stolen property to—they already sold you out. So you know why you're going to talk, Mike? Because you're *fucked*. That's why."

Michael was quiet for some time, performing extensive mental calculations. Poker without the cards. He spoke very deliberately.

11

"Here's what I think. I think that if half of what you just said was true, I'd already be charged. I think you're fishing. I think you want me to do your work for you, you lazy prick. You want me to connect the dots. I'm not your gopher. Fuck you, Geronimo. I'll wait for you to do your thing." Mike leaned back in his chair and smiled.

"You think this is a joke, Fuckface? This is no joke. And I know what you're thinking. I deal with scumbags like you all day long. So let me be very clear with you. Are you listening?"

Michael was still.

"I *know* that someone is in ICU. I saw them. I *know* that the person who put them in there had the *exact same brochure* next to their bed that I found sitting on your counter when I came and picked you up. Tell me you're not connected to that stabbing."

"I'm not connected to…"

"And while we're at it, shithead, why don't you tell me about why you were in possession of federal property? We know you bought it."

"Bought what? Check my records," yelled Mike. "I can't wait for my lawyer…"

"Fuck your lawyer, Mazzone. I'm gonna' do you a huge favor. I'm gonna' lay the cards out really clearly so you understand. You can see how this is gonna' play out. I might just know a little more about you than you think. You wanna' listen to what's gonna' to happen to you if you don't talk?"

Michael looked at him slyly. He liked all information.

"I'll listen," He said flatly. He looked at the detective with the cold empty eyes of a liar. His lids were heavy, irises almost black.

"Here's what's going to happen, Mazzone. If you don't tell me what I want, I will *personally* shut down your business and freeze your bank accounts. You remember a redhead that came in about three weeks ago to sell a Glock? Good looking, nice figure? Well she was a U.C. She sweet-talked your partner Carlo into letting her sell your store a gun. And I know for *fact* that you're missing a piece of paper that's required to transfer that gun's ownership. And I *know* you broke the law by letting her sell you that piece without it. I make *one* call to ATF, and

12

they'll pull up in a dozen cars and trash your place looking for that doc, the one I *know* you don't have because of the little voice recorder in that U.C.'s purse."

Michael squirmed a little in his chair, but his face didn't change. "That's bullshit," he said, a little under his breath. It was the first time he'd felt a bit powerless. He didn't like that feeling—he just got outflopped.

"Oh, but it's *not* bullshit. I already know what you're thinking. You can say you had no idea your man Carlo did that, and you had *nothing* to do with it. And you'll let them haul your boy off to prison. You'll skate, and you'll hire some other shithead to work in your dumpy pawnshop."

Michael said nothing. He was staring at the Detective with a quiet, angry glare. How dare they pick on Carlo, he thought. And sending in a broad to do it, like they already knew his weaknesses. What else did they know? The detective continued.

"Then your friend Eduardo Vasquez came in to sell you that Dewalt drill? He came in with a cracked-out looking woman you'd never seen before? She was a U.C. too. Witnessed the whole thing. Local P.D. caught Eduardo stealing that Dewalt from the Home Depot, and they made a deal with him to bring it into *your* store. Instead of charging him with shoplifting, we were gonna' hit *you* with receiving stolen goods."

"Bullshit."

"Hand to God."

"Bullshit. I don't even know an Eduardo Vasquez."

"Right. You probably know him as Ruben. His middle name. Eduardo *Ruben* Vasquez."

Mike got quiet quick. He remembered the transaction. Ruben had been coming in for years. In and out of the joint. Not a snitch. But he hadn't seen him since. That *could* be true.

"Ruben would never do that," Mike replied, licking his lips. He was buying himself a little time to process.

"Ruben *did* do that, Mike. We already have his statement. You're the one on the hook." Detective Giordano got right in his face. Mike exploded.

"That's fucking entrapment and you know it! You set me up and then arrest me? Just me? There are *dozens* of pawn shops in this state. My lawyer's going to have a field day with you.

13

Even if you do arrest me for receiving stolen goods, we both know it's a misdemeanor. After I post bail, you're getting sued for wrongful arrest. You think I'm a fucking moron?"

"No, Mike. I *know* you're a moron. All we have to do is *arrest* you for receiving stolen goods. Then, we can use our *discretion* to yank your pawn license. You'll have to close your store. You'll need a judge to reinstate it. And you know how slow the courts are, so many delays. We're going to padlock your doors for a year, *at least*, before you ever get a trial. You think you can wait us out? Get fucked Mazzone. They'll *crucify* you in the papers. If you ever work again, everyone in this whole goddamn state is going to know that you're the shady S.O.B. that buys stolen merch. You're fucking *finished*."

He tried to let that sink in. Mike leapt back at him faster than the detective thought he would. Mike was a player. He wasn't scared.

"I'll plead out. I'll take Alford on the larceny. My wife will file for a new license. She'll have the store back up and running in six weeks, max, whether or not I'm in the joint. And I'm still suing you. You can add libel if it makes it into the papers."

"I don't think you want to take a plea here, Mike. Did you forget about your little friend Lexi? The young blonde who sells your merch for you online?"

"Lexi would never even *sit in the same room* as you." Michael was fuming.

"She's not. She's in another room talking to the Feds right now. How fast do you think Lexi's gonna' turn on you when I tell her we're locking her up in the dyke pond for five years for tax evasion? You know all the merch she's bought from you to resell online? All that cash you never declared? You decide to get smart and transfer the business to your wife, I make one call to the IRS, and you're locked up for a *long* time. Granted, it *will* be minimum security. Fucking cakewalk for a degenerate like you." The detective got right in his face. "I will personally make sure that the prosecutor does *not* cut you a deal."

Michael sat in silence. Stunned, was the right word. They had him. He had been outfoxed. He did have one move left—sell out the guy who got him into this mess. He had never seriously

14

considered this as an option—he was no rat. But facing near-certainty of prison? He barely knew the guy he was protecting. But it wasn't about that one guy—it was about his credibility in underground circles. If he ratted, ever, even once, he was finished. No one would ever work with him again after the heat was off. And being a pawnbroker was the only thing he knew. He did the math. He spoke very slowly.

"If I tell you what you wanna' know...what are you gonna' do for me?"

"If you play ball? You tell me what I want, Mazzone. Paperwork can get lost, warrants don't need to be issued."

"What about Lexi?"

"The Feds are questioning Ms. Rini as we speak. I can't save her, but I don't need to look any deeper into your receipts."

"So I tell you what you need, and I walk out of here and you don't bother me again?"

"I can forget about the Glock. That's leverage if you don't work with us in the future. I can forget about the drill. That might come up again if any of your bookmaking friends get any closer to your store's payroll. And we can forget about your little undeclared cash business with Miss Thang. Honestly Mazzone—the second I call the IRS, the Feds get you all to themselves and it looks really shitty for me and my department. I want to keep you close to home. But we can't forget about that person in ICU. If they die..." He stared off into space as part of his act. "I mean, Mike, I'm doin' you a solid here. Just tell me what happened."

"You might find out some things you weren't supposed to know."

The detective's eyes were sober and clear. He responded with honesty.

"You don't have to write it down. No recording. I just need some answers. Man to man. Tell me a story. You're no snitch—I get that. I'm not trying to set you up to die in the joint—I'm trying to keep you *out* of jail. But somebody is *dying* in the hospital. And I need to know why the same evidence was found in the home of the victim's attacker and in your store. The Feds are ready to snatch you up on account of Lexi." He got right in Michael's face. *"I'm your only friend. Do you understand?"*

Mike wanted to spit in his face. That was just instinct though—they were natural enemies in the wild. He calmed himself. He was thoughtful. He was zen. He understood. His speech came from a very distant place.

"Actually, Boss. It's a really long story."

"That's okay."

Michael inhaled slowly. He needed a cigarette. He stared at the man across from him.

"It all started with Danny V."

"Go on…"

Small Blind

The music coming out of the mailman's earbuds was so loud Michael could hear the tinny high-pitched sounds from behind his desk as the mail fell. Turning on his toes out the office to the door, he left Michael to flip through bills, solicitations, and a couple glossy fliers. His gaze stopped on a hand-written #10 business envelope. He didn't recognize the handwriting, but he saw the return address.

"Carlo, get over here," he yelled in a raspy voice. Giancarlo was busy at a computer where he could keep an eye on the store. Busy was a relative term—he was updating one of several of his online dating profiles after his last one got him lots of winks from women in their forties. He didn't understand why it was so hard for these broads to believe that at thirty-nine, he deserved a woman in her early twenties, max.

"Kinda' busy here, Mike."

Michael lit another cigarette and was looking for the letter opener to not destroy the envelope.

"We got another letter from our friend," he said with a grin.

Carlo didn't flinch. He was trying to figure out how to write "ten and thick" in the least offensive way possible. Brow furrowed, his attention was not wavering from that computer.

"Carlo…"

He looked up. "Michael, I'm not comin' to the office. Who's going watch the store?"

"Isn't Morgan here?" asked Mike.

Carlo looked over to the jewelry counter. Morgan was filing her nails and did not look up. "She's doing her nails."

"What, she can't do two things at once? She can't file her nails *and* watch the store?"

"She's all the way over at the jewelry counter."

"Do I *pay* you?" Michael's tone moved Carlo.

Michael popped a breath strip in his mouth and examined the return address: "#14065916 Poquoddonock, Twin Lakes, Connecticut 06001." He wondered why Dan put his inmate number instead of his name. Carlo came back and handed Mike a fresh pack of Marlboros from the freezer.

"Mike, I have to show you this broad. She just sent me a pic and it's fuckin' hot!" Carlo started to walk around the desk to Michael's computer.

"No," he said. "Lexi's comin' down to fix the computer today. It has some sort of virus. I called Lexi. She said disconnect it from the internet and she'd come down this morning." Michael handed Carlo the letter. "Read this."

He unfolded the paper and started laughing softly.

#14065916
Poquoddonock Prison
Twin Lakes, Connecticut 06001

Michael Mazzone
Premium Pawn
Franklinville, Connecticut 06105

Hi Mikey,

It's been a long time. How's business? Everything here is fine. I know, I know, I am away again but I got three hots and a cot. At least they didn't give me persistant offender so I'll be out in probly 2 or 3 more months. Say hi to Johncarlo and tell him to be careful with that sausage of his. Hi to Morgan and tell her I will have a pearl necklace for her when I get out. And hi to Lexi and any other broads from the store. I'll call you when I get out. I might need like 5 or 600 to get a car to set up shop again. If you send me a money order in here I can have some cash that would be sweet. You know I'm good for it. I'll see you all soon.

18

Carlo gave a big belly laugh. "That son of a bitch. How come I can't get away with what he can? I mean, he makes 100K a year boosting, gets caught, then sends a letter from the can trying to get a date. I gotta' give it to 'um—the dude's got balls." Michael didn't look up. The ash on his cigarette was long. He was reading the schedule for the next set of poker tournaments at the Borgata—he really missed Atlantic City.

"Carlo, that's what you don't get—the guy made a hundred thousand last year and now he needs to borrow 500 for a car. That's sick."

"It's how we stay in business," Carlo said under his breath, lumbering back to his seat.

Lexi sauntered in at 11:45 with two coffees from Dunkin' Donuts. She was twenty-three and pretty. Every time Carlo saw her, he thought she just didn't belong in this place.

"Michael, I'll be with you in one second," she said as she dropped off the coffees in the office. He immediately started drinking it while he checked out the buy-ins for the deep-stack events. Lexi moved easily through the store down to the jewelry counter. "Hello Miss Morgan Chandler!" she said with a smile.

Morgan looked up from her nails. She hated that she called her by her full name. Who did that bitch think she was? Morgan hated her.

"Hi there, *Alexis*. How's our tech support girl today?"

Morgan realized she was being a little passive aggressive, but she was just pissed because she had smoked the last of her weed the night before and then her hook-up didn't pick up his phone. His name was Victor and his weed was really good, so she could overlook his laid-back phone etiquette. She had been over his place and had seen the little plants that he grew and trimmed with a pair of little nail scissors. She had never really gotten over the joy of handling cannabis—it was just a magical thing. That slight sticky texture, the delicateness of her fingers touching it as she placed it on its sacrificial altar for cremation. She missed it. She wanted it in her body.

Lexi snapped Morgan out of her reverie.

"You want coffee?" Lexi asked smiling. Morgan perked up. No matter how much she couldn't stand the fact that this bitch probably didn't smoke pot at all, she didn't want to let on that this was the reason for her sullen face. She nodded.

"Now, Missy. You're late." Michael smiled at Lexi like the Cheshire Cat.

"I'm not," said Lexi as she dropped in the chair across the desk from him. "How many times do I have to come down here and take care of your computer problems? Just stop fighting me. Move over." She elbowed him out of the way. She started typing furiously and checked the history—he hadn't deleted the porn sites. She started to scroll and saw such a variety—black girls, BBW, ass-to-mouth, cumswapping, shemales, the list went on.

"Well," Mike began.

"This is going to take me awhile. Go do something else."

While he left to get a haircut and Lexi worked fast, Morgan opened her laptop to shop for some new clothes. She was definitely a shopping addict. And an alcohol addict. She had woken up in different clothes, in different places. She lost three phones. She didn't want to remember the last time she drank SoCo: she woke up in the backseat of an Escalade with tinted windows, and had no idea who the other two guys in the car were who were putting their boxers back on.

To fill her days, she had started a side project—she was going through different transactions in the store to see if she could save them money. She noticed was that the same people came in over and over again. Some of them came in every single day. And there was a record of all this in the computer. And the merchandise appeared stolen. And no one stopped them. It was almost as if it were okay.

"When is Michael coming back?" she asked Carlo.

"Haircut," he said distantly. He was looking at a photo of a hot blonde, early thirties, nice rack. He imagined that she had really big areolas though. He thought, how did you politely ask a girl how big her nipples were before you started dating? I mean, why waste the time to iron a shirt and put on cologne if he would want to gag when she took off her bra? God, he thought, it should be easier to see a girl on a non-adult dating site and be able to find out what her breasts looked like. Maybe he was just too shallow.

Lexi came out of the office. "Computer's fixed," she said. "I don't want to wait around for him. Just tell him to call me later." She strutted out the door.

Several minutes later Michael returned. He never looked better than right after a haircut and a shave with a straight razor. His skin was smooth and soft, not wrinkled yet though he was nearing forty. Morgan motioned to him.

"Are we buying stolen items?" she asked him purposefully. He went to slap her face but she stepped back and he swatted at the air.

"There could be customers in here!"

"There aren't any customers." She paused for effect. "Are we buying stolen merchandise? I just want to know for myself. I mean, I really think we are, but I don't know why if that's true we can exist as a real business."

Michael stared at her. He had known her since she was a baby. Her mother was an addict and mentally ill. Her mom had been in and out of prison and halfway houses, and Morgan had spent most of her time at Michael's on the couch. Back when he was a bookie, before the store, she didn't even know that all those people coming and going were all due to gambling. She was a really good kid, but it was his policy never to speak about such things.

"Morgan, the merch isn't stolen. Why are you asking me that? You grew a conscious all of a sudden?"

"It's *conscience*. Not conscious." She pitied him.

"Whatever. What's the matter with you today?"

"I just want to know if I'm breaking any laws."

"You? You break laws all the time! Your car is unregistered and you smoke pot every day!"

"Whatever. At least my mouth doesn't taste like an ash tray. What do you smoke? Three packs a day?"

"Shut your mouth Morgan."

"Why? You smoke so many cigarettes it's cheaper for you to drive to Virginia and buy cartons and freeze them than to just buy them here. Just buy them online."

21

"Never." Mike was smiling as he walked up to Morgan and got closer. "Let me tell you what those guys do. They buy those cigarettes wholesale and then they undercut everybody. Then the government comes in and shuts 'em down, and they solve their legal problems by giving up their client lists. The Feds make more money going after all those schmucks for evading taxes than they do off the actual taxes! No thanks."

"You're deflecting me. Tell me the stuff we buy isn't hot."

Michael stared at her with cold eyes and said nothing. The back of his neck itched a little from the haircut. What was *this* game? Of course the merchandise was stolen. Most of it. Except for the old guys bringing in stuff they'd bought for a couple dollars at tag sales, and the addicts that framed houses and did roofing that couldn't hold on to their tools 'til the next season because they wanted to get wrecked.

"Morgan, my dear, let me explain something to you." He motioned to the cash register. "You see these slips of paper? The ones the customers sign before we pay them?" She nodded. "Have you ever read one?"

She thought for a minute. "No. What does it say?"

"It says that the customer has 'legal title to the goods' they are selling. So, they have to sign something that says that they legally own it and therefore have the right to sell it to us. You understand?"

"Wait," said Morgan. "But what if they lie?"

"Actually, Morgan," said Carlo, "The law says that in order to be found guilty of larceny, we must be able to reasonably assume that the goods are stolen when we buy them. It'd be pretty hard to find a jury that would convict us of receiving stolen property when we produce a form signed by the person that says he owns the stuff."

Morgan was getting miffed. This was not the direction she wanted the conversation to go. Laws. Rules. Technicalities. Michael knew, Carlo knew, she knew the stuff was stolen. I mean, who would sell a brand new vacuum cleaner for a third of the price? Who would sell a meat slicer if they didn't own a deli? The stuff could only be stolen. But she didn't really want them to admit it to her—she wanted a raise. She decided on a more direct tact.

"I need a raise."

"You don't need a raise. You *want* a raise."

"Okay. I *want* a raise."

"Well, you're in bad position. It's hard to raise from the small blind—it's easier to just call."

"Stop it with the poker analogies Mike. I don't know how to play. I just want a raise. I just think with all I know about how this business works, I should be paid more."

She doesn't know the first thing about how this business works, he thought.

"You're blackmailing me? When you're asking for a raise? You know what? I think maybe you need to just go home. I'm not going to pay you today. Just leave." She stared at him and didn't move.

"If you make me leave, I'm going to tell them that you're paying me under the table and you're going to be in big trouble." He smiled.

"Okay, Missy. Then I'll tell them where that little glass pipe is in your car, and have them arrest you when you leave the parking lot." She smiled—she really loved this place. There was nowhere like it.

"Fuck you, Mike. What are we having for lunch?"

"I don't know." He smiled at her. She must be hell in the sack, he thought. "Carlo, what do you want?"

"Henrietta's," he said. "Get me a chicken parm."

"K. And I'll have eggplant rollatelli. Extra garlic bread." He pulled out a twenty and handed it to Morgan. "Call it in and pick it up."

"Why can't we get Jimmy's instead? Henrietta's has nothing that I like."

"A tossed salad's a tossed salad, Morgan." She gave them the finger as she walked out the door.

An old man walked in as Morgan was leaving carrying a large old DVD player. He walked in small steps and wore a mesh baseball cap with an embroidered battleship on it.

"We're not taking those any more," coughed Michael. He looked at the unit and then at the man, who it appeared wanted the human interaction more than anything else. He was very sad all of a sudden—the man reminded him of his dad.

"Does it work?"

"Yes sir," he said.

"What are you going to do with it if we don't want it?"

The old man was not expecting that question. Probably give it to the Ladies Auxiliary at church. Then he remembered where he was. "I'd cut the cord off it and strip the wire. They're paying good money for copper one at the scrapyard. Then I'd scrap the rest as steel. It's mostly plastic, but they don't really give a hoot if you throw it in with a bunch of sledge heads and angle iron." The old man chuckled and coughed. Michael nodded with respect.

"Test it, Carlo. If it works, give 'em a fin."

Outside, Morgan looked at her dashboard where every light was on. She just thought about how much easier the day was when she got to start it with a couple pulls on her pipe. Pulling out of the lot, her CV axles clicked, power steering pump whined, and struts moaned, but she heard none of it. She slipped on her visor sunglasses and touched up her makeup for the cute guy that worked in the kitchen at Henrietta's while the music blasted through the car's aging tinny speakers.

*   *   *

David Evans ran a comb quickly through his dirty blond hair in the mirror of the men's room off the lobby at the Westin. It was only recently that he had started growing it longer in a frat-boy rebellion against the onset of middle age. His hair wasn't long enough that anyone at work had commented yet, but he knew those days were just around the corner.

His meetings were running long, and East Coast delays tended to ripple through and push everything ahead. But whenever his vendors needed their meetings, he was at their disposal. With his roller bag at the bell desk, he was just waiting for the car service that was caught in traffic. He hadn't really needed to pee—he just wanted to get away for a minute. Every now and then when he was travelling on business he would long to be home. It wasn't so much that he wanted to be back and see his wife at their lovely home and sit in *his* couch and watch *his*

TV—he wanted to be alone with his thoughts, and not need to be on.

He didn't even want his wife Allison any more. He could no longer focus on her good qualities. They were always bickering over something. Did he call and schedule the cleaning lady? Why couldn't *she* call and schedule the cleaning lady? It's not like she was spending her time cleaning, right? Her job was to sit around and surf the net and watch TV and go to the gym? Had he moved the boxes of Easter decorations up into the attic? Why were they only on the stairs and not *in* the attic yet? What was he doing besides earning a nice fat salary that he didn't have time to do that? And why did he even have to care what she made for dinner? He loved her—he always had. But he'd never felt so distant from her.

And there he was, standing in the men's room for just a little too long, long enough that someone else came inside. He washed his hands while he looked in the mirror at the man's back standing at the urinal. Greasy hair, hunched over a bit. He noted the bad posture, cheap leather belt. Please don't come near me, he thought. The man turned toward the sinks and glanced long enough at David for him to spy that he was Arabic, and had a birthmark on his forehead. David couldn't help but glance at the birthmark, and then, embarrassed, left the restroom.

Walking out to the lobby, his phone vibrated at the same time the bellman told him the car had arrived. As his roller bag was being put in the back of the Lincoln, he thought about how much they'd be able to charge clients to eliminate a mole or a birthmark with an oral medicine. Would a drug like that amortize the R&D costs with a reasonable time left on the patent to return a profit at a higher rate than other drugs in the pipeline? How could we get repeat customers? Scratch it, he thought. Insurance won't cover it, and even if they could come up with the perfect drug, it'd probably get appropriated by the cancer people. It would just be studies and scrutiny—what a fucking headache. So hard to make a profitable drug any more. David ripped the doodle off the mental sketchpad and threw it in his virtual trash. He had long since accepted his perspective—money and consumption were the only two things that ever made sense to him while he was on this big blue ball hurtling through space.

David was an executive vice president at a company called Durham Pharmaceuticals, one of the larger international drugmakers. He'd just finished a barrage of exhausting meetings about increasing the distribution of one of their flagship drugs called Duscantia for sufferers of migraine headaches. He was just sick of sitting there in these rooms and in virtual rooms with other people just like him who were trying to squeeze every dollar out of each other. They were all sharks, and there was no new prey.

The only way he could make money any more was to withhold information from other people so that it appeared that he'd exceeded his goals, in order that he is rewarded with a bonus. Then he gives that bonus to his accountant (doing the same thing at his firm) to advantage as many loopholes as possible in the tax code to give his wife more money to spend at Neiman's. His company is using the same technique among other companies to increase their income and insure a healthy future for itself. The health of people taking their drugs was not on anyone's radar. He didn't care about people in the slightest.

David had to come back from these big marketing trips ahead. And he always did. But his mind was elsewhere. He was thinking about this other project in the company (that he would be directly supervising) taking place in their offices in Germany. The only other person in the company that knew anything about it was his old friend Viens, an American research chemist who took the bump up in pay to relocate to Europe and work in the office overseas.

Of course, for purposes of plausible deniability he was simply the liaison in the American office, and was not directly overseeing the project. While he had to keep the whole thing very hush-hush, this was his brainchild. During an earlier visit to the neuroscience lab at UCSF, he had a wonderful conversation there with an old friend Peter Pickering about a class of chemicals that radically alter consciousness to the point where it is unrecognizable in terms we understand. Peter had really blown his mind and changed his thinking about chemicals he'd only ever heard of anecdotally.

David was definitely *not* an early-adopter. He was calculated. Rational. He still remembered what his dad taught him: the early bird may get the worm, but the second mouse gets the cheese. So when Peter told him about the chemicals, while he would personally never consider ingesting anything resembling those compounds, he knew an opportunity when he heard one.

David thought about his conversation with Pickering and realized how far into the mainstream, cookie-cutter, suburban life he actually was. Peter always had a wonderfully simple explanation for even the most complicated knot, which he always delivered in some sort of multi-leveled analogy. In this case he told David that it was a simple question of fear. Peter explained that because of his educational pedigree and life experiences, David was conspicuously aware of being a mere kindergartener in his understanding of ontology. Thus, he was so afraid that his results on the final exam proctored by the Grim Reaper could possibly be an "F," that he would never strive for an "A," and instead would settle for a "C." And the C student ruled the world.

David thought about what Peter was telling him with respect to the power of the chemicals he'd stumbled upon. He wouldn't *ever* want to experiment with some sort of crazy drugs. What if he never came back? He remembered taking painkillers when he broke his ribs playing lacrosse. He wasn't awake. He wasn't asleep. He closed his eyes and it was the winter sky during snow—the darkest shade of red instead of black. He still saw the room he lay in when he closed his eyes—his brain was producing and erasing the writing on those walls faster than he could read it. He remembered thinking the pain-killers didn't dull the pain in his ribs as much as they made him forget he was breathing altogether.

But Pickering wasn't describing opiates. David didn't have any experiences he could compare with what his friend was talking about. He had asked David if he'd heard of a plant called Salvia divinorum. He *had* heard about people smoking salvia—he'd actually had a conversation with his step-daughter after photos of Miley Cyrus smoking salvia surfaced on the internet. He did the whole concerned dad routine, telling her how bad drugs were for her, and how she shouldn't think that smoking salvia was okay just because that little skank did it. She basically

27

ignored him, and David abandoned that whole discussion when she went back to her phone.

After he told Pickering he knew of salvia, Peter told him to think about the type of compound that would be found in its leaves, a naturally-occurring chemical in some rare but legal plants found in the Amazonian rainforest. He was given a lot of details about that end that went over his head, but David only ever focused on returning to the decision-makers with the bottom line. However, after a more detailed discussion with Peter, he had decided not to turn this information over to his bosses just yet—he'd begun to hypothesize that the value of this chemical could be much larger than Peter surmised. In fact, he believed this compound had the potential to have more worth than the fair value of his retirement account if it were auctioned to the highest bidding company on the open market.

The specific compound was called "5,6,7-trimethoxy-dmt," or, "5,6,7," for short. The grad students in Pickering's neuroscience lab had discovered that the chemical had been found to link certain people's consciousness together for short periods of time. Peter's notes were vague with respect to details, but David remembered him saying several things very clearly during their meeting. There was a lot of anti-government and anti-establishment ranting.

"This is too fruitful of a research area for our lab...I don't want this project ending up being commandeered by the government...my libertarian views may have gotten me in trouble before, but this is not something that those idiots in Washington need to have dropped in their laps...there *is* a small problem. The chemical is *technically* illegal because of an antiquated Draconian law that treats it similarly to some illicit drugs, simply because a certain part of the chemical structure is the same. But, David, it's as similar as the serotonin and norepinephrine in your own brain are to this same illegal morphology. I think it would be *very* easy to fight in court, if you even could get a judge who wouldn't need a month of expert witnesses to explain what this thing is. And by that time, as soon as the prosecutor heard the case, whisper here, whisper there, it's already shut down. Remember, David. This is the same government that classified cocaine as a 'narcotic' in the

28

jurisprudence. Cocaine! The definition of 'narcotic' *is* 'sleep-inducing'! Who do *you* know who has ever fallen asleep on cocaine?"

"Peter, I understand everything that you're saying, and I appreciate your dropping this into my lap, but I still don't understand why you're not keeping this in-house. I've just never known an academic to willingly turn over research to a private corporation, even if it's one of your best friends' companies."

"David," he responded, "It's just that I've accepted the eventuality of this project being co-opted. I run the department, and eventually, those with oversight are going to want to know what it is we've been working on, and I'll have to tell them. This is better in your space. It's for the good of the quest for knowledge that I give this information to you—no other reason."

Their conversation was much longer than that, but colorful anecdotes aside, they set upon a plan. David would have his German team working on the R&D of the compound. There would be no more talk about the chemical in Pickering's lab—he would tell his students that they did not receive clearance from the government to continue its research. He would turn over all his data and materials to David's company, and turn the reigns over to him in exchange for a new sponsored fellowship at the college. David literally had to push this idea on Peter, that his company could find room in their budget to create a merit-based scholarship for a post-doc.

They both agreed that they could not afford fighting the bureaucrats right now over R&D of a drug that was technically illegal in America, however ridiculous and outmoded the arguments were over its legality. David laughed at Peter's inability to accept the reality of consumer capitalism in America in the 21st century. Peter attempted to explain to him how they should just conduct the research in the States, and that the government wouldn't even know what they were doing. Then, even if they found out, a cogent argument could be made that this was the sort of chemical analog that was outside the umbrella of the law. Peter would be more than willing, he said, to go to a court hearing and explain the chemical structures, and on and on. David was zoning out.

Finally David just broke it down for him—federal oversight is a hassle. He didn't want any hassles, he didn't want scrutiny, he didn't want to be on any government agency's radar for any reason. Forget academic integrity. Forget if the law had a nuance they could massage. This was *not* about taking a principled stand. This was about making money. And the best way to make money was to use every tool in your toolbox as well as possible. Since Durham had the corporate structure set up in such a way that their office in Germany could do the research off the radar of the FDA, this would be the best way to circumvent the problem. No confrontation. No headaches. He had made his point, they had agreed on the terms, and David was on his way out to his next meeting.

"What does it take in this country to change the laws?" asked Peter as he was leaving. "Why won't you challenge the law here? It's the perfect opportunity."

David turned back to face his friend. "Peter, it might be an opportunity for you, but not for me. You made a decision to try to change the world, and shape minds, and challenge the boundaries. You're an academic. I want to find success in my industry. I want to be powerful. I want to be part of this swell we call America as it washes over the rest of this planet. I am more than content with my decisions."

"Well you shouldn't be so happy with them. This is what is wrong with this country! When I met you, you weren't so jaded. You still had idealism. Youth."

"I had stupidity," replied David.

"You weren't stupid. You were a broke kid working in the cafeteria doing dishes to help pay for school."

"The dirty end. I remember. But Peter, it was just that I was unaware of the power of capitalism. I understand it now. I work for it. I provide for my family. Big pharma does a lot of good. I'm happy with my choices."

Peter stood erect. "It's *not* capitalism. That's what you don't grasp. Capitalism I can understand, but this is something more sinister. This is what fascism looks like. It's what fascism is! It's the complete entwining of government and capitalism. It's worse than crony capitalism. It's this sick slow dance to the tune of the Devil's fiddle." He exhaled and shrunk a little.

Go take a ride in your Prius, you homo, David thought. But he didn't say it. In fact, he could never be mad, or hurt Peter—he was his freshman roommate back in college. Randomly drawn together. "There's a reason you called me—you knew I could handle this. And we're going to do good things with this information. I wouldn't ever let you down Peter."

The men embraced quickly and smiled. "If your next meeting is in the city, tell your driver to check the traffic," Peter said. "They've been doing construction all around the Embarcadero and the traffic patterns are totally different."

David smiled. He still thinks logistics. What a great mind wasted trying to keep over-privileged hippies out of the workforce for a few extra years, so they can rent tiny apartments and run teahouses for their hippie friends. He would've been so good in business. Then he looked at his clothes—a shirt so old the seams were starting to fray, shoes he couldn't believe didn't have holes in them, unruly eyebrows and sideburns. He would never make it. He's not a shark. More like a disheveled panda, but angrier.

David swam away and got back into the Lincoln.

"How was your meeting, Mr. Evans?"

David pulled out his phone. "Good," he answered as they started driving away.

"Are we headed back to the Westin?" the driver asked.

"Yes," said David. He was processing the implications of Peter's thoughts around 5,6,7. He had been vague. Intentionally. Almost as if on purpose. But David trusted no one more. Peter had never lied or led him astray. And yet, the ramifications were almost overwhelming. Sharing consciousness with another human being? Were that even possible? He felt the car gently downshift and the motor whine at a slightly higher pitch as the driver passed a truck up a hill. Sharing consciousness? What exactly would that mean? Then the waves of thought flowed over David—he pondered the practical implications of 5,6,7.

If he and others were sharing consciousness, he wouldn't have had to wait because there was traffic on the Embarcadero. He would have already known it without seeing it because someone else saw it, and then he could adjust his route accordingly. But it went further than that—imagine instantaneous psychic communication. It made phone calls and emails in an office obsolete—it would mean if they could tap into this they could have almost no waste and infinite productivity. It could mean a whole sports team working in unison against their opponents. What this chemical promised was something nearly priceless—and David loved money. This was too valuable to share with anyone. He decided right away that this was the most valuable research chemical that had ever come across his desk, and he could quite possibly sell it to the highest bidder and not even keep it at Durham. It was larger than Durham. It was the future.

David thought about sharing consciousness with this man—what would that be like? His brain was spinning so fast. He had to slow it down. Say something, he thought to himself.

"How many miles are there on this Lincoln?" he asked, licking his lips and bringing back his mind.

"Two-hundred eighty-three thousand," the driver said deliberately. Nonchalance.

David was surprised. "That's quite a bit. Don't you ever think about how amazing that is?"

"How amazing what is?" asked the driver.

"That after 283,000 miles there are all those little precisely-timed explosions going on under the hood that move those cylinders up and down billions of times and it all just works?"

"No," he chuckled. "If the motor's going to go, it's going to go. I'll bring the car to the auction and sell it and get another one. I'm just happy that with all the people coming to work drunk and high on the assembly line in Flint, that nobody missed a weld on my U-joint. I don't want my driveshaft falling out while I'm doing eighty."

David had never even thought about that. All of the union auto workers at the assembly line making cars, things that he just assumed were safe, and how many were intoxicated on any given day just letting parts go through? It sent a shiver down his spine. And with that, he wasn't sure about sharing consciousness. What if it were too long? What if he didn't like it? Could he opt out? And what did Peter mean "for a short time?" This man's sense of time was *clearly* different than his—

he thought that 283k was an appropriate number of miles to have on a car. David frowned a little.

The driver glanced in the mirror and saw his face. "Don't worry, Mr. Evans. You're almost back to your room. Just hit the mini-bar and 1-2-3, your problems will disappear."

One, two, three, he thought. No, Five, six, seven. That's where the money is going to come from. He went back and looked down at his phone. It was on silent, but the second he looked down he saw an incoming call from his wife. He took the call as the Lincoln whooshed down the wide stretch of pavement.

Big Blind

Morgan opened the painted wooden window in her living room, held it up with her right hand, and took the small piece of wood off the sill to prop it open. She was just taking a couple hits before work while she checked her email.

She went back to this link one of her acquaintances had sent her. She had never seen anything like it. It looked like a real website—it didn't look like a scam. And she trusted the guy who sent it to her. She had bookmarked the site. It was called "The New Liberty Church," and had a very cryptic sort of message on the front page. The reader clicked on a waving American flag with a single large dollar sign instead of stars on it in order to enter the site, which made you state that while there was no pornographic content, there was adult content and you needed to be eighteen to enter. Truth be told, she only clicked on it because she liked the flag icon.

When she got in the site, she found some pretty complicated stuff. Something about IRS form 1023, and 501(c)(3) and a bunch of other stuff she didn't understand. It talked a lot about freedom from government intrusion into consciousness, and that the church was a way for an individual to preserve one's right to "augment, decrease, or abridge one's mental state," using "traditional and non-traditional methods." She got caught up on the idea of "abridging" her mental state. She had to look up the word to be sure she knew what it meant. She thought she knew, like an abridged book or an unabridged book, and she was right. So, she couldn't figure out what the site meant by, "abridging her mental state." It sounded like drugs. Maybe it was reiki or yoga or some yuppie bullshit? The guy who forwarded it to her definitely liked ganja. She was just too high to really pay attention to it—she popped in her old South Park boxset, bookmarked the page, and went to sleep.

So here it was, the next morning, and it made a little more sense in the light of day. It appeared that membership in the church gave you the benefit of being able to possess these particular "research chemicals, alkaloids, and plant precursors" for the purposes of religious rites and ceremonies. She looked up alkaloid: "naturally occurring chemical compounds made up mostly of nitrogen." Chemistry was all Greek to her. She didn't understand most of what the site was talking about, but she got the gist—it looked like a church where the "rites" and "sacraments" were getting high.

She was actually really curious about these chemicals. Was pot one of them? She wasn't someone who followed any of the legal stuff with pot—she just knew that in Connecticut it was not legal under any circumstances. Morgan was way past thinking that pot should be legal—she was just waiting for the day when it would happen.

The website mentioned how The New Liberty Church was definitely not affiliated with other organizations, but it did have some linked pages about some church for Indians who still got to use peyote and a couple other fringe groups. She didn't really want to do anything else besides pot—she had no interest in peyote or mushrooms or acid or anything. She looked at the girls that did that and she just didn't get a good vibe from them—none of them took care of themselves. They all had bad hair or bad skin or bad style. But she loved marijuana. She was a better person smoking it. She searched every bit of the website for more information about pot, but couldn't find any. Morgan wasn't stupid. Every sentence seemed to be leading right to it: "church members often find that ceremonial use of natural plants in the shamanistic tradition can lead to a more stable and happy life." She read a different section:

"Humans were created to be in tune with the environment. So much of that natural harmony has been lost as we continue to slave inside, working at desks and in buildings, in tandem with machines of our own design. We are slaves. These machines keep us apart from our natural world. They fix our concentration on a single goal—productivity for its own sake. We at The New Liberty Church are not Luddites, and we are not advocating anti-capitalist, anarchistic, or nihilistic sentiments. We do believe, however, that it is our right to experience the benefits of certain natural compounds in a religious setting outside of the realm of necessary and healthy work. When we play, we should be able to play with the toys that we choose, not those that are given to us by others. We believe in our own minds and in our own bodies, and in our own abilities to make good choices."

The page continued, but Morgan got the idea. This was some sort of scam. It had to be. The only way to get more information about the church was to send a $5 donation to a post office box in New York State, and they would mail you back a packet. Five dollars? What kind of scammer asks for $5? The site said that the money was to cover the cost of printing and shipping, and that they made no money off of it, and it was simply to help get the word out. The material you received would have information about church membership, which was a separate yearly donation.

It seemed ridiculous. If you were scamming someone, why you would only ask them for five dollars, she thought. She had heard of online panhandling but this was a different sort of thing altogether. It definitely had the air of a genuine site. The person or people who wrote the content for the website were definitely smart. She had to look up what a Luddite was, and then when she read it she vaguely remembered hearing something in history class about people that smashed the looms and weaving machines in order to fight against machines taking their jobs. She remembered liking the story—people breaking into work and smashing their employers' new machines so that they could keep their old jobs. Sometimes she wished she could smash stuff at the pawn shop. But they would kill her. Literally. She would be dead.

So if the people were smart enough to make these references to Luddites and stuff, weren't they smart enough to run a scam that would actually make them money? How many people could actually respond? How many would even want to? Maybe it wasn't a scam. Maybe these people were really trying to make a church that let you get high. Maybe they really were

36

going to try to make pot legal that way, like they were doing with the medical marijuana laws in other states. Maybe they just didn't mention pot specifically because then it would be on police radar and stuff. Did the police even watch stuff like this? Could she be in any trouble giving them her info?

She needed to think. She packed another bowl and fired it up. Coughing, her face turning red, she decided she would send them five dollars. What's the worst that could happen? She would lose five bucks? If they took her money and sent her nothing, she was going to have a little chat with her friend Denis and tell him not to forward her that type of trash. She addressed an envelope to the post office box, took a five from her wallet, wrapped it in a piece of typing paper, wrote her contact information on it, and sealed it. She got in her car to drive to work at the pawn shop.

*   *   *

Josh Grenier wasn't sure how he first got the idea to start a church, but now that the idea had taken shape, it had grown a life of its own, and was threatening to engulf him. For awhile it was all he could think about. Studying at Williams College, there wasn't a lot for Josh to do *except* get high. Granted, that particular potted Ivy offered plenty of sports and clubs and organizations, but Josh was so set and fixated on his goals that he could see little else. He knew deep down that this was more likely than not a distraction from the reality that he felt inside himself—fears that he was afraid to share with anyone. He found this reality only went away when he was at a level of intoxication so great that it could stuff those feelings away, but then his drug use got in the way of his everyday functioning.

There wasn't a name for what Josh suffered from. For him, attempting to even name his "illness" would be to accept the Cartesian mind-body duality that most every Westerner except Josh took for granted. He also didn't like conceptually that an individual with an outlying non-traditional viewpoint had a "disease," rather than an "eccentricity." But Josh's eccentricity went deeper than being quirky. The best way to verbalize what he felt was that his life force extended farther outside of his body

37

than other people's, like a pickup truck filled with hay or tree branches that stuck outside of the bed. And the load kept hitting things. And Josh could feel it. He wanted to numb it.

He tried to compartmentalize his life—he pictured putting different pieces of himself in boxes, arranging those boxes in his cellar or attic, and just not touching them so he could go out and enjoy the sunshine. But he couldn't do that. He didn't really know if others could, either. Maybe they just *said* they did to justify the maintenance of power structures, misapplying Judeo-Christian religious beliefs to a variable morality. All these drugs he was taking—the hallucinogens, dissociatives, painkillers—they were all part of his grand design to take apart his material reality brick by brick. He kept thinking that if he could take apart that wall and leave himself enough bricks, he could remake himself in his own image. But he kept breaking bricks, pulverizing them into a fine red dust.

Paranoia got in the way. What actually happened was that he had ingested so many potent chemicals that his brain was no longer interpreting reality to the point where he could cogently interact with others. In fact, there was a twelve-day stretch where he didn't sleep. When he looked in the mirror, the person staring back at him was not him. It had to be some sort of projection of his own mind designed as some sort of avatar for him to interpret the planet.

The school had sent Josh to a full-service hospital, where he was admitted to the psych ward and given a shot of Haldol to quiet his mind. He woke up with a hangover, but not from alcohol. He had never felt anything quite like it before—his mind was more still. It was as if the background noise were set at a lower volume. But he hadn't even realized it was background noise—he thought it was the foreground. I've been driving this whole time by looking in the rearview mirror and glancing through the windshield, he thought. Josh rested.

After a short regimen of Seroquel, his life returned to normal. He didn't like the drug—it wasn't really making him sober. It was fucking with his head. He could feel its power. It was his first exposure to this sort of chemical. A legal one, okayed by the powers that be. His actual material reality was changed. He wanted to go back and study. What was it that he cared about again? Something to do with ethics? And philosophy?

Josh wasn't taking any meds any more after his sleep returned to normal. He went back to his old perch—looking ahead at the future and focusing on contingencies and risk assessment. He was planning for the future. He knew that soon, anyone could know anything they wanted at any time without cost. The end of information scarcity. What would that world look like? Josh imagined America would still be on top—our momentum would take us through to the end of the race. And one of our explicit freedoms in our Constitution was a freedom of religion.

So he was going to found a church. A new church. And the holy sacraments of his church were going to be the use of a laundry list of chemical intoxicants that were legal at present. If they were legal to use now, once that information asymmetry disappeared and the powers that be knew they could be used recreationally, they would be made illegal. But if he protected their use by making them religious freedoms, he could grandfather them in as legal for church adherents. Simultaneously, those church dues would create a nest egg for him, which would make it so he would never have to work a day in his life. He could travel and live life without being tied down to some concrete building with a cubicle and a W-2. It was the perfect plan.

But he wasn't protecting addictive behavior—he wanted nothing to do with drugs that fed addictions. He only wanted to deal with entheogens, that is, drugs that humans used in a context of a religious, spiritual, or shamanic setting. He hated that people said things like alcohol were addictive: it was addictive to people prone to addiction. Addicts could be addicted to anything. Josh felt that addicts suffered from compound ignorance: they don't know that they don't know. That's the reason he was founding this church. He was going to get these non-addictive spiritually-enlightening chemicals protected under a religious exemption. All of them. He had a grocery list. All the tryptamines, the natural alkaloids, the research chemicals, all the ones people were currently using. He was going to protect the raw materials and the chemicals inside. He was casting as wide a net as he could. Anything unscheduled by the Feds.

He had done his long-term business planning. He knew it was only a matter of time before the scientists came up with a way to test for an "addict gene" or equivalent. Inevitably, after a bunch of fighting, there would either be a "cure" for the "disease of addiction," or there would be a new set of laws made that would control the behaviors of those more likely to hurt themselves when compared with everyone else. Josh could never figure out where this disease concept of addiction came from in the first place—he just thought it had to be a moral issue.

He had remembered a long time ago being taught that the AMA had made alcoholism a disease in 1956, but he had no idea how that could even be possible. It was only those people that gathered in church basements at night who said drug addiction was a disease, right? The Bible-thumping creepy Christians who thought that if you found God then you were somehow cured by divine intervention, right? That this luminous God who covertly floated over all of us could just remove our desire to use drugs? It sounded like trickery. Tomfoolery. Josh never saw God fixing broken arms or multiple sclerosis or muscular dystrophy after someone said, "I no longer want to have this problem." Addiction had to be a moral deficiency. But for now, in our culture, under the purview of our decision-makers, it was only a matter of time before "science" came up with a way to identify the footprint of an addict.

So, he knew in the foreseeable future, there might be a completely different method for the federal government to schedule chemicals. Even so, there would definitely be a window of time where things were the way they are. So he was going to take advantage of that window of excess profit before it closed. He was going to prop that window open with his church, and let that money blow in.

*   *   *

"Mike, I need a stamp," Morgan demanded as she walked in. There was a cloud of smoke in his office.

"Is that how you say hello?"

40

She grabbed a stamp from his desk and dropped the envelope in the outgoing mail pile. He didn't bother to look up at her.

"Hello," she said, stomping her feet as she went over to her area. She spent the new few hours filing her nails and staring against the wall. It was a slow day.

"Mike."

"Yeah?"

"Where are we ordering lunch from?"

"Nowhere. Buddy's bringing food."

Morgan didn't know a lot about Buddy. She knew he was one of Mike's friends that they played poker with. She was pretty sure that wasn't his real name.

"Is Buddy bringing *me* any food?"

"He's bringing pizza and grinders." Mike went back to his online poker game. Buddy came in a short time later carrying pizza boxes, with his cousin Eddy holding two-liter sodas and another bag.

"Mikey," he said. "One pepperoni. One sausage, hot pepper, and garlic. And chicken parm grinders." He put the food down and almost as soon as it stopped moving the men descended on the table. They couldn't eat it fast enough. They folded the pizza slices in half lengthwise so they could inhale them quicker, the oil dripping off the sides.

They're animals, thought Morgan. She watched them eat. They sat in the back room, hunched over the paper plates that were drenched in oil. They didn't look up, and they didn't say a word. Just powering through that food. They literally looked like gorillas or apes. Their shoulders were up and out, and they hunched over their food, protecting their share from the others. Morgan learned later they ate like that because they'd been to jail—old habits died hard. Morgan was looking around for some paper towels, and by the time she found a roll of Bounty they had finished eating and were all leaning back. Buddy was picking at his teeth.

"Good work, Buddy," said Michael. "Who's going to make the demi-tasse?" The guys rumbled with laughter. Someone belched.

41

Morgan had learned that "demi-tasse" meant espresso. She also had learned that it meant "half-cup," because the traditional Italian espresso cups were so tiny.

"I'll make you some coffee," volunteered Morgan.

"Young lady, I didn't say I wanted *coffee*," growled Michael. "I said I wanted *demi-tasse*. Are you going to go get us all espressos?"

She held her palm out. "Okay."

"Actually Mike," said Buddy, "Do you have any Sambuca?" Michael lit his last cigarette and threw the pack into the gaping trash can.

"Yeah. There's a bottle with some left in the back room."

Buddy reached into one of his pockets and pulled out a wad of cash with a thick elastic band around it. He looked at it, and then put it back into the pocket, then dug in a different pocket and found a *different* wad of cash with a skinnier elastic band on it. He peeled off a ten from under the stack of ones to hand to Morgan.

Michael had tried to teach Morgan to always carry two bankrolls—your real bankroll and then your fake one. In your real bankroll, you carry your hundreds with a single one-dollar-bill on the outside, and always with an elastic around it. Then in the fake one, you put your small bills, and wrap that one the same way with your ones on top. Then, if you ever get mugged and there's a gun in your face, you hand the guy your fake bankroll and you're out a few dollars, instead of getting your whole wad lifted. Morgan tried to explain to him that she never even had enough money to fill her gas tank, but Michael just liked to feel like he was teaching her something somehow. He always told her that someday, if she kept working for him, she would have so much money that she'd have to start wearing cargo pants to hold all the different wads of money. *Accounts*, he called them. She called them pockets. Morgan watched Buddy, and how he had two bankrolls just like Mike said. She stared at Michael, who was standing up and bent over at the waist.

"What's wrong?" asked Morgan. He moaned.

"That sausage pizza." He reached for his cigarette. "Buddy, I asked you to bring me lunch not kill me. What the fuck?"

42

"Well what do you think was going to happen when you ate five pieces of sausage and hot pepper pizza in two minutes?" said Morgan.

"Morgan, shut up and get us some espresso."

She flipped them the finger and bounced out to her car.

"All right Mike. Setback until she comes with the espresso?" asked Buddy. "Dollar a point, double in spades?"

"Sounds good," said Mike as he shuffled. "Listen, what's the news about our friend?" They kept dealing the cards and playing while they talked.

"The washers and driers that Marty dropped off last week should be fine. They're clean. They came from Sears, and since the warranty is separate from anything point of sale, there is no way to connect the buyer to the particular serial number on the unit. So, if you bought that appliance at a garage sale and it died the day after you bought it, you can still call LG, give them that serial, and they have no way to see who the original buyer was."

"Good," said Michael. "Now does that go for just the LG units, or the GE units too?"

"The GE ones are the same. I told our boy Stevie-B. not to go to Home Depot and Lowes. I told him the heat was on, and he told me not to worry, that they didn't know who he was and it wasn't a problem. Well guess what, he got fucked."

"Was it him personally?"

"No. I heard there was an internal memo circulating about a crew going around and using fake business checks to make purchases, and not to accept those checks after 4pm on Saturday when the system was down and they couldn't verify them. I mean, Mike, they pretty much knew what was going on before Stevie-B. even got there." Michael coughed hard and couldn't stop.

"But they don't know about, you know, the big man."

"No!" exclaimed Buddy. "He's fine. But Stevie B.'s gonna' have to do time. He's got a record."

"That's bullshit," Mike said as he pulled on the cigarette. He sat back and thought for a minute. "So I don't need to worry about the merch?"

"Right," said Eddy. "That's why we're here. To let you know this stuff's fine. But there may be a little supply chain issue here until we get someone else out there. Remember, we still got the gift cards and the prepaid VISAs. We'll be retooling a little. Home Depot and Lowes knew too much. There may be some people talking a little too much about how things work. I mean, it just takes one too many drinks at the wrong club for the wrong someone to hear and you're fucked." Michael put out his cigarette and shuffled the cards.

"But," Mike said, "Stevie B.'s been on the inside. He'll be fine. We got plenty of guys to take care of him in there."

"Misdeal," said Carlo. He held up seven cards.

"You asshole!" said Buddy. He turned over A-Q-J-8 of diamonds. He threw the cards down. Michael brought them all back in and started shuffling again.

He had to admit that the system was pretty good despite its flaws. There were guys he never met (and didn't know who they were) who printed up fake debit cards and fake retail gift cards. He'd seen the cards. They were perfect. You would have absolutely no idea. Then, using a system of distributors, they sold them massively discounted to the street-level guys who would go and buy the merchandise. Expensive, big-ticket items. All clean. All with receipts. No heat. The trucks would come once a week. Unmarked. Or rentals. Michael paid 25-40% of retail depending on the items. Cash. Everyone knew where to go to get an appliance. And it wasn't the crazy bald guy yelling on the TV that he had the best prices, or the used appliance store on the old main road that was now the back road. It was Mike. It was Premium Pawn.

But he was mad that they had tried to go too big and hit the big box stores. It hurt everybody. He was protected if they ever came after him, but the more information the legit corporations and law enforcement learned about how this particular system worked, the more it hurt his bottom line. He knew a lot of it never even made it on to the tube, and it went that way on purpose. He always thought it was like how you almost never saw people killing themselves on TV with a long vertical cut from the wrist up the forearm. They always just made a short cut across the wrist horizontally. Hollywood didn't want you knowing that if you actually wanted to die, you'd make the long cut so that you'd lose the most blood the fastest and maximize your chance of success. So he hated that they knew some of the details about the way they were running their scam. Whatever. He was off the hook. It wasn't his problem. The rest was semantics.

"As long as what I have here is clean," said Michael with finality.

"Absolutely," said Eddy, crushing the end of his Lucky with the pad of his thumb. "Business as usual. Clean serials. Receipts. Everything's fine. How's Lexi working out?"

"She's fantastic," said Michael.

Just then Morgan walked in with their espresso. She had gone to Dunkin Donuts and had the girl there fill an extra large coffee cup for her. There had to be twenty shots in there.

"Have you been talking about me the whole time I was gone?" she said. Carlo snickered.

"Actually, I was talking about Lexi."

"Sure you were. Asshole. Here's your espresso." She almost threw the cup at him. Buddy kept talking.

"You know Mike, the government is the biggest bunch of crooks. Just remember that. They tax everything, and for what? I don't see a thing. You think Medicare and Social Security are going to be solvent when *I* retire?"

"You don't work, asshole," laughed Carlo. "And I don't think you've ever paid taxes."

"I'm not talking about for me. Personally. Necessarily. I mean for all those other idiots out there spending their days doing some shit that they hate to get a paycheck and have Uncle Sam take a big chunk out. And then they get hit at the gas pump. Even buying clothes. It's a scam on such a huge level."

"But you see Buddy, you get it," said Michael. He started pouring together the coffee and the anisette liquor like a Roman Catholic priest mixing the water and the wine. "They don't get it. They don't want to get it. They won't admit it, but those jobs give them meaning and purpose. I mean think about it. What's the first thing someone asks you in a social setting when you first meet?"

"How did you get so ugly and not ever have anyone tell you?" laughed Carlo. His fist bumped Eddy's. Michael kicked Carlo.

"Asshole. They want to know what you do."

Carlo asked, "What do you actually tell them Buddy?"

"That depends," he said. "Sometimes I tell them I'm self-employed. Or I'm a consultant. Or a contractor. Sometimes I say I'm a property manager—that usually shuts them up."

"Property manager?" asked Carlo incredulously. "What the fuck are you talking about? Property manager. Now I've heard everything." He laughed.

"Hey, I paid that kid to mow my mother's lawn. Isn't that property management?"

"Yeah," said Michael, "And I'm an ad for Marlboro. You're such a shithead. You just don't want to pay *any taxes*, that's all. You know, those are the ones they go after—the ones that pay nothing. You should pay them just a little something."

"You're damn right I don't want to pay taxes. My money's going to a whole bunch of shit I don't want to pay for. I'm not payin' for peoples' welfare and food stamps." Carlo started laughing again and slapped his knee.

"You *sell* food stamps, you asshole," laughed Carlo. All the guys started laughing. Eddy's face turned red.

"Well, once they put them on cards instead of printing them like money, what did you expect me to do with them? They made them that much easier to sell."

The men smiled and left. Carlo went back to his computer to check the online dating action. Morgan went back to looking at this website, her belly full. She really wanted to know about the people that ran the church's site. Was it just one person? A whole group? Was it like a commune that lived on a farm somewhere? The mailing address was in eastern New York State. That was a couple hours away. Maybe she could check them out. Maybe they had some really good weed.

Michael walked over to Morgan's area. He knew she got high when she went and got the espresso. He didn't want her doing that when she had to work with customers.

"Morgan," he said with a raspy voice.

"What?" She tried to scowl and then made a noise that sounded like half a hiccup.

"Excuse me, young lady?"

"What do you guys talk about back there? You always send me away when those guys you play cards with come down." There was whining in her voice. "I like to know what's going on in the store."

"This is *my* store."

"Yeah, well you don't work. All you do is tell *us* to work."

"That's what being the boss means. You just stick with me, young lady. You always get paid. You're fine."

"Thanks. Really though, what were you talking about?" Michael looked at her.

"Sambuca. We were talking about different kinds of Sambuca." He edged away from her.

"I tried that stuff, Mike. I think that's called 'Arack.' It tastes like licorice, right?"

"Listen, Missy. Sambuca is anisette liquor. It's made from anise. Fennel. It's like licorice-flavored celery."

"Yeah, Mike. I know what fennel is. And I know what that drink is called. It's called Arack. It's Middle Eastern. And it tastes just like that. Stronger maybe. I've had it before. What's the difference between Sambuca and Arack?"

"You listen here. We don't drink any shit from the Middle East. Fuck that camel-fucker for blowing up those buildings on 9/11. Fuck *I-raq* and *A-rack* and *A-rabs* and all those other towelheads. So the difference is, in this store, we only drink Sambuca, got it?"

"Whatever Mike. Leave me alone. You're so racist." Michael walked away.

"I'm proud to be an Italian-American!" He went back to his office to resume his online poker game.

47

Call

Josh created his church. It wasn't brick and mortar—it didn't have to be. It was created for the purpose of protecting altered states of consciousness. He had compiled a short list of chemicals to start off of a British website, with a plan to supplement it with others found in Sasha Shulgin's work. He began by making a primary list of sacramental chemicals and raw materials for inclusion in what he called the "corpus vita," which he would later amend:

- Atropa belladonna (belladonna, precursor to atropine)
- Banisteriopsis caapi (yaje, or, "vine of the soul", precursor to DMT, 5-Meo-DMT, and bufotenine)
- Datura stramonium (Jimson weed)
- Digitalis purpurea (foxglove)
- Peganum harmala (Syrian rue, precursor to harmine and harmaline)
- Phalaris arundinacaea (reed canary grass)
- Psychotria viridis (Chacruna)
- Scolopendra subspinipes (Giant centipede)
- Spheroides testudineus (Checkered pufferfish)
- Virola pavonis (epena, or "yopo,")
- Alpha-methyltryptamine (IT-290)
- 5-Methoxy-Dimethyltryptamine (5-Meo-DMT)
- Dipropyltryptamine (DPT)
- Diisopropyltryptamine (DIPT)
- 5-Methoxy-Diisopropyltryptamine (5-Meo-DIPT)

It was Josh's final intention to include every single possible chemical that could ever be found to induce a hallucinogenic state. He knew his list would never be complete, but he had a good starting point, knowing he was going to keep adding to it.

The next thing he had to do was to walk the very fine line between telling people that their right to use a chemical was protected, without actually telling them that they *should* use it, or *how* to use it. Josh wasn't too worried about the nuts and bolts of it—his next door neighbor growing up was Mr. Reynolds. Now though, he called him Corbett.

Corbett ran his own consulting firm called Omicrone. He was a former federal employee who had worked for the DEA before retiring to start his own business. He had a lot of juice. He had been with the agency for his entire career, and had friends in high places. He took a well-padded early-retirement package, started his own NGO, and collected his pension. "What a country!" he always said. Well-educated, well-connected, a great networker, and he loved Josh like a son.

When Josh first told him he wanted to talk to him about starting a new project, Corbett assumed it was your typical liberal arts undergraduate college bullshit nonsense. He'd seen so many of his friends bragging about the work their kids were doing at their schools, and Corbett just thought they wanted to justify the obnoxious prices they paid for a particular Latin name on a diploma that was near worthless in the workforce anyway. Corbett always had this mental imagery of that famous 1923 photo of a German man pushing a wheelbarrow full of money after hyperinflation rendered the deutsche mark worthless. He pictured a wheelbarrow full of private college diplomas.

When he had actually talked to Josh, though, he realized Josh was on to something different, and this seemed like a good pursuit for him. Corbett knew quite a bit about drugs from his earlier work, and he also knew Josh was probably better behind a computer creating a virtual business—conversations with him tended to be tedious. He was also very well aware that Josh was approaching a very large pool of quicksand, but since he appeared more interested in the academic pursuit rather than the end use, Corbett liked that Josh had found himself a niche. When he asked Josh about how exactly he was going to explain to people that these chemicals were protected for religious use but were not to be consumed, Josh showed him a written disclaimer he had found on another website called JLF.

"What does JLF stand for anyway? It's some sort of acronym?"

"It's an initialism," said Josh.

"I'm sorry?"

"It's an initialism. That's a group of letters where each letter stands for another word."

"Right. An acronym."

"No," said Josh. "When people use the word 'acronym,' it's typically a malapropism."

"I'm sorry. Malapropism?"

"A misuse of a word." Josh sounded annoyed having to define what he believed was a universally-understood notion.

"And why is 'acronym' a 'malapropism'?" Corbett asked patiently and very deliberately. Josh annoyed him.

"Because JLF isn't a word. So it's an initialism." Josh was getting impatient.

I pity the woman who is going to marry this kid someday, thought Corbett.

"So…"

"So, when you say a Navy SEAL, 'seal' is an acronym because 'seal' is both a word and an initialism. Its letters each stand for something, but they also make a word."

"I get it. An acronym is a special type of initialism."

"Yes, like in mathematics a matrix is a specific type of array. All matrices are arrays, but not all arrays are matrices. Just like all acronyms are…"

"Oh, I loved that movie!" Corbett smiled and looked off. He was trying to change the subject. Josh must be fun at parties, he thought sarcastically. Why do these smart kids always have no social skills?

Josh started to fume. "Oh my God don't even get me started on that movie. They're describing an array, not a matrix. A matrix is a very specific type of array where all of the cells are filled with numbers or numerical expressions. This is basic linear algebra…"

"*Josh,*" he said forcefully. Corbett had to cut him off. I want to wring this kid's neck, he thought. He's just such a smart kid with such undirected brainpower, and Corbett felt bad about his father. He was always extra nice. He took a deep breath and continued.

"You know Josh, they probably didn't call it 'The Array' because it wasn't grabby enough."

"Yeah," he laughed, "the 'X' in 'Matrix' makes it sexy."

They both laughed.

"So, what does JLF stand for anyway?"

"Hell if I know. My buddy tells me it's the Jesus Lives Foundation."

"Huh." Corbett needed to mull all this over. This kid was definitely going to make something happen, he thought.

"Thanks for your help in advance, Corbett."

"Yeah." His reply was syrupy.

The wheels were in motion.

* * *

Laida Stafford was on probation. She found that so ironic. She was on probation and Dan was in jail for the same charge *because* she had a penis. Had she been a natal female, she most likely would have been arrested, held, then forced to serve a similar sentence in the women's prison by the shore. For once, being a transwoman helped her out. She was idling the black Mercury Marauder in a lot right near the prison with her phone in her lap, waiting for him to tell her his paperwork was finished and to swing by and get him. Dan fucking Vauxhall, she thought. She didn't dare carry any shit with her to pick him up. She had a sealed handle of Captain Morgan spiced rum in the passenger seat and Dan's favorite sweatshirt. He could get high later if he wanted.

A tan Cadillac DTS with dark tints pulled in to the same lot, very gingerly entering the driveway to be kind to the rims and the low profile tires. He pulled in a slow half-circle and parked a polite distance away. She realized that she didn't even care what wheels came on her car, but that would have been such an important thing to know if you were one of the young men she used to know in Pennsylvania before she transitioned.

She thought about that life she could have had if she had stayed an unhappy young man in that shit town in PA. Hanging out in parking lots. Vandalizing shit. Going nowhere slowly. Those guys knew what wheels came stock on a Marauder. Or a Crown Vic. Or they could tell you a pretty good estimate on the value of a Tahoe or a Trailblazer or Grand Cherokee, not that any of them drove anything but shitbox rice. Or worse, shitbox American trying to look Japanese. Why? Everywhere. Souped up little Mitsubishis, Civics, Neons, Aleros, Paseos, Supras. Everything had 250,000 miles on it and had no suspension and bad exhaust. Those heaps couldn't get out of their own way. Keep dreamin' guys.

She didn't even remember where they had gotten this car—in their line of work she couldn't count how many cars they had to ditch. She liked the Eldorado in dark metallic green. It had a big trunk, a lot of power, and it was nice and smooth. She still remembered taking the plate off that car the last time—she was sad. They had tons of plates. But always two sets with the car. The real plates and the fake plates. They always drove around with the real plates on the car that matched the registration. Then, when they were going to hit a mall or a big box store, they'd pull over, put the fake ones on, do their business and leave. That way, if they had to make a hasty exit, or a security officer from the store followed them out to the car to take down their info, they'd speed off and change them back in the next open parking lot before the cops could find them.

They had done it so many times with the Eldorado Dan said there was too much heat and they had to dump the car. She had watched Dan abandon the car, but not before he cannibalized it. She remembered how horrible of a sin it seemed, to take a perfectly good working car and pick pieces off it until it became a carcass. He had jacked the car up and put it on stacks of wood so he could get the rims and tires off, but the process didn't stop there. He took out the radiator too. She remembered the argument. He was going to cut the radiator hoses and let the antifreeze leak out on the ground. She told him not to do it.

"Why the fuck not?"

"Because you can't just spill that antifreeze all over the ground!"

"Why the fuck not? We're not here to save the fucking Earth. We're stripping some easy shit off the car."

"That stuff is really bad for the environment!"

Dan thought about a special he had seen one night about estrogen in the groundwater. What about all that estrogen in your piss that kills the fish, he thought in his head. But he didn't like saying anything too complicated to her. Instead, he just said, "Fuck off."

"Dan, come on, what the fuck?" He grabbed the knife and went over to the front of the car. "Dan, at least…"

He cut into the upper hose and the green goop shot out on to his sleeve and then dripped on to his leg.

"Fuck!" he exclaimed jumping away and looking dumbly at his limbs.

"At least cut the *lower* hose first so everything drains out." Laida shook her head with disdain. Why did she have to think about these things? The drugs were messing with him. They had to be. Who would cut the top radiator hose first? She hated *knowing*. It made her feel like a man.

Then he had to use the Sawzall to cut the bolts on the radiator because he had stripped them. It was no longer worthwhile from a cost-benefit perspective, but he just didn't want that Caddy to win. When he finally got the radiator out, his shirt was covered in grease and antifreeze. He handed her the Sawzall.

"Go under the car and cut the cat off."

Laida looked at the Sawzall blade. Most of the blue had been worn off the outside of the blade and the teeth looked beat. It would be just her luck to have the blade snap off and impale her arm. Or worse, her face. Her eye. She didn't need an E.R. visit.

"You do it." He glared at her.

"I can't fit."

Can't fit easily, she thought. Laida didn't feel like getting dirty. She disappeared under the car and carefully held the saw and cleanly severed the two sides of the pipe. She rolled out from under the Caddy pushing the catalytic converter along the ground. Dan picked it up.

"Nice. I love the big cats in these old American cars. And the platinum price spiked. We should just scrap out tomorrow with the other shit and pick up a couple bundles." He held the heavy radiator in one hand and put the catalytic converter under his opposite arm. The grease ground into his fingerprints and under his nails. They walked away from the wet spot on the ground sprinkled with shiny metal zest.

She always wanted to keep the used up plates as trophies—they could be mementos of a past she sought to one day leave behind. She could picture them on the wall of the garage in her future house. EEC 262. IAV 401. And on and on. And that wasn't going to happen. It just wasn't going to happen. She was a drug-addicted shemale who would end up getting knifed in some alley after sucking off some guy whose balls stunk like cheese for a bag of dope. Right? Who was she kidding? A garage? A house? She was a shoplifter. Those dreams weren't for her. She had long since stopped being able to cry.

*   *   *

Josh was reading the letter he had written some time ago—he hadn't wanted to remember what happened next. He began to think about it when he went into his tiny lockbox. He didn't have a shadowbox the way a woman might, or even a fancy hand-carved chest or jewelry box for his sentimental things. He kept his letters in a straight-up fireproof lockbox for keeping important papers in. Car titles. Deeds to homes. Wills and codicils. Those were the types of things that belonged in a box like that. Not poetry. He moved the yellow ten thousand dollar bank wrappers to one side and pulled out a letter that he had written to his ex-girlfriend. She'd broken up with him and had given Josh the letter back.

He unfolded it and read it again. It was almost committed to his memory:

Dear Love,

I was watching a television today and flipped through the channels. One channel was a cooking show, and the next was only static and white noise. I just was flipping back and forth between them. I remembered when I worked in the computer lab teaching kids how to use graphics software. I remembered that it took less memory to store and reproduce a picture of say, a person smiling, than it did to store a picture of just random static. (It's because of the way file compression works – not super complicated, but a concept whose explanation is unnecessary here.)

The take-away is that it actually takes more memory, more space, and more energy to view and participate in disorder than in order. I had a true moment of clarity this morning. I had a true glimpse of God's infinite wisdom and beauty. In that split instant, I realized that the Fibonacci sequence that determines how plants grow, the golden mean we see in something as beautiful as a nautilus shell, all of the order we see in nature is perfect.

What's more is that I realized that such order completely continues into our civics, and into our interpersonal social intercourse. That order is natural. I had this amazing sense of peace and happiness. Think about it: if it takes more energy to represent chaos, the universe's natural resting state must be order. If I accept that, then there must be a God.

And that God has brought you into my life. And I do not need to know how, or why, but just that it is all part of this order that has a natural momentum. I do not want to fight. You are my soulmate. You are the one I'm supposed to be with. I accept God's will.

Please be gentle and delicate with me. If I let you in, if I open my heart to you, you need to promise to love and accept me and realize my fragility. I am not afraid, but I do have limited time on this blue ball hurling through space.

Please love me. Please believe in me. I will try to take you places you never dreamed. And I promise I will not disappoint you. I love you Love. I love you. Please love me back.

Me

A tear rolled down Josh's cheek. It wasn't because he would not be able to spend time with the one human being on earth that seemed to understand him—he had never again felt that level of emotional intimacy. He feared he never would again. This was not a left-brain/right-brain thing: he thought the noblest pursuit he could engage in was the rational deconstruction of the irrational part of his brain. This was the driver. This was the impetus. This was the reason that Josh decided that the best way to actually solve his problem of not being understood was to look at the bigger picture. An experiment had yet to be created that could prove that consciousness emanated from our very brains. It was equally as likely that consciousness represented a static steady state all around us, and our brains were merely receivers of the information that *is*. Josh decided he would take on consciousness.

He was going to map it, brick by brick. He was going to start to rappel down the sheer rock face where others dared not traverse. He knew where some of the pins were that other climbers had left—LSD, shrooms, PCP, Dex, 5-Meo, DMT, DIPT, muscarine—and he would just keep mapping. He didn't have a death wish. This was the frontier. How could you claim to live without exploring it? And he was doing it for a purpose. He didn't want to hurt himself—he wanted to help himself. He wanted to understand his psyche from within so that he could understand his mental evolution and not be doomed to live alone. Not life without communication, but life without meaningful exchange. He didn't even want to live if that were going to be his static reality.

The church was his own idea. His own spin. His own English on the cue. His own signature added to the age-old problem of self-discovery. He was going to have everyone else want to whitewash the fence, get them working, then bill Uncle Sam. It was perfect. He already had his startup money from some friendly Albanian investors...

* * *

She and Dan had been using the Marauder for awhile. It wasn't as a comfy as the Caddy, but it fit a lot of merch in it. She glanced up. The DTS hadn't moved. She couldn't see the driver. She looked down at her phone and wondered what was taking Dan so long. She saw another car slowing down with its left signal on to pull into the parking lot—a Buick Riviera like her father drove. She looked down at her chest and tipped the rearview mirror down to look at her cleavage. Eat your heart out, Dad, she thought. Her new tits were perfect. She had a rough go of it when she was younger—after she flunked out of school at sixteen, she had a car and a lot more time on her hands, and just started shoplifting all day to earn her keep. She became a full-time booster.

She thought it was simple—society owed her because she was transgender, and fuck them for bullying her out of high school. That, and she had picked up a nasty dope habit after realizing that while her family had always told her not to do heroin, it did what the Oxycontin did better and for a lot less money. She took everything that wasn't tied down to sell to the fences. Razor blade refills, packages of batteries and dietary supplements were easy. She would just check for an inventory control tag, and stick them down her loose pants. There were plenty of drug stores and grocery stores to rob. The fences resold the merch to other fences or to the shops, where most of it went away online to some wretches in North Dakota or Wyoming who had to drive an hour to their nearest Walmart.

When Dan called to say he was ready, her phone's buzzing jolted her out of her memories. She put the Marauder in gear and pulled out of the driveway into traffic to go get Dan at the entrance to the correctional facility. Laida held up the handle of Captain to show him through the window. He didn't walk any faster, but it put a big smile on his face.

Now that she rolled with Danny V., she had grown her business the best she could. She had met Dan at the Club. He wasn't gay, and neither was Bump. But his boy was a drug dealer, and he told Dan that no one paid better prices than the homos, and those fags always had money. So here Dan and Bump were, hanging out, drinking beers and shooting the shit in Dan's Chevy Malibu (back when he drove that Malibu) when Bump gets the call.

"Yo," he said. "Bring me to Club 12-20." Dan laughed.

"You a faggot now, Bump?"

"Fuck you Danny V. Just bring me there. You don't have to go in. Just wait outside."

"You deliver to them?"

"They're my best customers. Top. Dollar."

Once they had gotten there, Dan decided to go inside to have a beer after Bump said he'd buy him a drink while he did his business. So there was Dan, and he looks around at this foreign place. The music was pulsing and throbbing and the lights were flashing. It just had too much energy. He liked a dark bar with pool tables and sports on the TV. There were no sports here. He looked up and saw rainbow flags and streamers and disco balls. Not his crowd. He had never been there—he wasn't homophobic, but he was just all about business. The only business he wanted with the gays was for them to help him try on a suit while he was stealing a tie. He asked the big dyke behind the counter for a Bud, and sat and looked around. That's when he spotted Laida. He didn't even see her new fake titties. It wasn't sexual—he looked at her eyes and they were the same as his. Dope fiend.

From that point on they started running together, and it worked well. Dan gave Laida an education. He taught her all about booster bags—he took a big heavy store bag, like one from J. Crew that looked kind of like thin cardboard and wouldn't crinkle. Then, he'd layer the inside with pieces of aluminum foil, then put a liner inside that looks just like the same color as the bag. Dan used double-stick tape to seal the top, and unless it were closely inspected, it looked just like a regular J. Crew bag. You just walk right out. No sensors. No alarms. Nothing. Brand new shit with tags. Anywhere.

She and Dan drove *everywhere*. New Jersey was best— there was a big concentration of malls there—but they'd hit Westchester county, Pennsylvania, and greater Boston. Sometimes they would just drive up 91 or down 95 and just hit outlet malls. They always changed their routes. They'd go for a couple days at a clip and literally fill the trunk. Laida was getting schooled. She used to think all she could steal was what she could fit down her pants. Dan showed her that she could steal anything that could fit in a big shopping bag, and it didn't even stop there.

Dan was the best in the business. He crushed Nordstrom and Neimans and Bergdorfs. He looked pretty straight. He would wear a French blue collared shirt and a nice pair of slacks and shoes with nice socks. No holes, no stains. He didn't look like an addict. He looked like a man shopping on his day off from work. He took it all, and like a pro. Limoges. Lalique. Riedel. Lenox. Jay Strongwater. Judith Lieber. Faberge. Anything within reach. He didn't care if it took two hours of talking to a clerk. At some point he or she stopped paying attention. At some point the façade weakened. And Dan knew the spot to strike. Laida watched and learned.

She liked going to Crate and Barrel, Sur La Table, Pottery Barn, Restoration Hardware, anything home-related and high-end. It was all part of this elaborate fantasy she had for herself of just living in some nice big house in the suburbs and sitting by her pool with a cleaning lady and a gardener. She truly enjoyed looking around at everything before she made one final safety check and her heart skipped a beat as she slid something into her bag and covered it with a sweater or pair of leggings. Nothing felt like that. Nothing made her feel more alive than boosting. Excitement. Chemically. She left the planning up to Dan, and just practiced her trade. But it still left her with questions.

59

At first she didn't know why they were going there. What kind of person is going to buy this sheet set or this duvet cover? It's just ridiculously overpriced. That's when Dan explained to her how not everything went to the same place and that was part of the business. That was where Laida came in. She was the one who returned everything. Without a receipt.

"Follow the script," Dan would say.

"Hi. My name's Laida, how are you? I got this as a gift from my mother and it just does not go with our décor. I'd love to have a look around here for some other things. Can I get a store credit for the difference if I pick out something for a little less money?" Testing. The clerk was either going to say that she could give you a refund right now for store credit for the whole thing, or she was going to give you a hard time about what your mother's name was and where she bought it.

"Your mom's name is going to be some very generic name like Elizabeth McDonald. There's going to be a million in the computer. If they ask where she bought it, you say that your mother works for a design firm or a law firm or for some fashionista or garmento. Use your judgment."

Laida learned that the garmentos were the super gay guys that ran fashion, the incredibly snotty, snarky twits that made her hate the gays and made the blacks in the South say they were on the down low instead of saying they were gay. She learned the art. It was poker—it was reading people. She would look at the clerk. Did she have any tats? How was her hair done? Read the person. What was the best way to engage? What was the best back story to use with this particular individual to minimize the chance of conflict? Dan taught her to always tell the clerk your name up front.

"It looks trustworthy. You are selling yourself as straight. You are saying to them, 'I'm *Laida*. I'm a *person*. Just like you. I'm not trying to scam you. I'm trying to make a connection. You have something I need, and I am willing to appear as concerned about you as I need to be to complete this return.' Trust me, Laida. It's the big black bitches and the Puerto Rican cunts with the neck tattoos that start yelling at the clerks when they won't take the return, and make a bigger and bigger scene that cause the problems and get nowhere. They don't know the

60

game. Whether or not the clerk thinks the shit is hot doesn't matter. If they like you enough, they always make an exception. So, you're likeable first. 'Not a criminal' second. The worst case scenario here is that you have to walk out with nothing and try again at a different store. You never make a scene. You never make a fuss. Stick to the script. Stay in character. Get bitchy if you want but don't yell. If you think you crossed the line, you get a freebie. You just tell them you're on the rag and they'll cut you slack. That's a bonus *I* can't use."

"I feel like I'm always on the rag, Dan." Dan was like a Dad to her. She wasn't attracted to him, and that seemed just fine with everyone involved. She knew that *he* knew she had a cock. It didn't really faze him. He didn't treat her like a man or a woman. She was a business partner. A running partner. For Dan, the merch, the driving, the vehicles, the clothes, it was all just to get high. There was nothing else for him. That was life. And he never even talked about it—he just nodded out.

Sometimes Dan had bills to pay other than for the dope man, like when he needed another car or truck or he wanted a new TV. That's when they got brazen. That's when they went to Home Depot, Lowe's, Staples, Office Depot—away from their familiar territory. An away game. Laida would be waiting in the car, always. She didn't like this type of boosting. It wasn't even boosting, she thought. He would put something big in the shopping cart—an air conditioner, an air compressor, a Dewalt tool kit, a business printer/copier, a computer—and just wait for the right time to walk right out the front door as if he had already paid for it. He always had something in his hand—a receipt or something that looked like an invoice—and would be talking on the phone when he walked out so if anyone said anything to him he would point at a clerk all the way across the store and just walk out. Cool as a cucumber, he'd load the car or truck and Laida would drive him away.

From time to time things went south, but nine times out of ten it worked fine. Personally, Laida didn't like it because she couldn't feel it. After all the drugs she'd done, she could feel very few things, but she could feel the rush of boosting. She could feel the danger. The pounding of her heart as her mind calculated the consequences of placing a dyed piece of fabric from Vietnam with a little tag on it into a bag. The blood rushing to her ears and face. Knowing the makeup could cover anything but her eyes. And her eyes could see nothing. She loved boosting. Loved it more than she could love any man, or any woman. She loved it almost as much as the drugs she needed to take to come down from it.

But with this, it was more like they were buying something and she was pulling the car around to pick it up and make it easier to get it home. There was no action. And the few times there *was* action, they didn't get the merch. No payoff. She could see it from a distance. She'd see Dan walking briskly toward the car, usually with a security guard or store manager on his ass, and once he even sprinted out. It was her job to look as nonchalant as possible for as long as possible to not raise suspicion, and then to start the car, throw it in gear, and floor it and get them out of there so they could swap the plates off down the road and go home to lick their wounds.

He always told her not to worry—no one was going to get arrested. *There were no cops.* The store personnel had all been trained to just let them walk out and call the police. After a few cases where boosters sued the stores when employees had tackled them and broke bones and won monetary settlements, they just lived with the shrinkage as part of their bottom line. So, when the two of them got arrested, it was not part of the plan, and it was not about boosting.

*   *   *

Morgan had been watching Alexis come and go quite a bit this past week. She knew Lexi worked with computers, knew her way around networking and troubleshooting, and seemed to do more that Morgan didn't follow. That is, until she started paying attention. Her little visits talking to Michael, going in and out of the office, merchandise going in and out of the store. Michael was very tight-lipped about everything that went on between the two of them.

One day, Morgan decided to just stop in the office when Alexis was there. Michael had a standing policy that when his door was closed, you had to knock to enter under any circumstances. So, when the phone rang and this little fucker Moshe kept demanding to talk to Mike right away, Morgan made a decision. She walked right up to the office and just burst in through the closed door. When she blew in, they were both very startled. Michael was counting a lot of money. (Well, *she* thought it was a lot of money.) Maybe seven or eight thousand dollars in hundreds. Lexi was just standing there looking at her like she was this huge bitch for interrupting them. Michael remembered his catechism: God is slow to anger and quick to forgive. Fuck the Catholics, he thought, as he grabbed the 18k Virgin Mary medal around his neck.

"What the fuck are you doing here, Missy? You know you never come in the office when the door is closed. Period." Lexi smiled at Morgan and crossed her arms. She knew they wanted her to go. But she saw what she wanted. Someone was paying and someone was getting paid. And a pretty large sum of money.

"Moshe's on the phone for you. He says it's *urgent*." Morgan turned and walked away, leaving the door open. Michael yelled after her.

"Close that door!"

She said nothing and went to the jewelry area. Lexi stuck her head out of the office and gave a long look at Morgan before she closed the door. After a couple minutes, she left quietly. Michael stuck his head out and motioned for Morgan to come and see him. She slunk over.

"Close the door," he said.

"What's your problem, Mike? You're such an asshole."

"My problem is that you know better than to come in when the door is closed."

"Then fucking lock it."

"What did you say?"

"I said, *then fucking lock it!*"

They stared at each other silently, both with claws out. After a moment Michael spoke first.

"What do you want from me? What do you want Morgan? No one else would put up with half the shit you do around here if you worked for them. What is it with this, this, arrogance?"

"I'm not arrogant," she said. She was fuming.

"Oh," he chuckled. "But you are. You do absolutely nothing all day, come to me at the end of the day with your hand out expecting to get paid. You get paid in cash. And you get lunch for free. And you don't listen! In fact, I don't even know why I keep you here!"

"Was she giving you that money or were you giving it to her?"

She took Michael aback. He paused for a moment. Morgan had been working there a long, long time and probably knew much more than she let on. His poker instincts kicked in. Feeler bet.

"What do *you* think?"

Morgan was surprised at the frankness of this response.

"I think she was paying you. I don't think she does enough for this store to get paid that much. Which means she was paying you."

He had been felt.

"That's true." He had felt this conversation coming. For some time.

She looked at him. She honestly wanted to understand Michael. She saw a man who appeared to just float through life so effortlessly while she struggled at every turn. He was always flush with cash. She was always struggling to fill her tank. She knew it couldn't be the drugs, the booze—Michael had done all of that when he was her age too. There was just something about him. Some sort of energy that she couldn't put her finger on that was always on the tip of her tongue, and she never had him like this, just the two of them, both straight, no one else around.

"Can I see it?"

Michael smiled wryly, tipping his head to the side while squinting his eyes.

"You little…"

"The money, Mike," she cut him off. He looked at her. Without breaking eye contact, he reached into the drawer and pulled out a bulging business envelope and threw it to her. She opened it and fanned out the money. It always smelled the same.

"Have you ever held that much cash, Morgan?"

"Not cash, no." She liked it.

"There's a lot more of it in the safe. But if you go near it, I'll shoot you."

And he would, too, she thought.

"Michael, do you trust me?"

With my life, he thought. I just don't trust those losers you hang around with.

"Yes."

"Well then would you just explain how this works to me? I think if I knew, I could make the business more money."

Michael was always interested in making more money. Maybe the girl could use a little lesson in business. She was street-smart. He knew she sold pot. It could be time.

"If you ever tell anyone what we do here, I'm going to deny that I ever told you anything. You understand me?"

Morgan nodded. "I do."

"And on top of that, I will fire you. I will then have the police search your car and arrest you, and then search your house and take all your paraphernalia, and then you can make love to some big black bitch named Latisha for the next year in the pen."

The thought of being locked up scared Morgan and Michael saw the fear flash over her face. There was always power in fear, and leverage from that power. Michael never liked to use it, but this girl was ready to be taught. Morgan sprung back.

"I'm not scared of Laqueisha. I'll slap a bitch!"

Michael laughed. What a stupid cunt, he thought.

"Morgan." His voice lowered. "There are a whole bunch of boosters that go out every day and rob everybody. Some run solo, like a cheetah. Some run in pairs, like, uh, I don't know, some animal that works in pairs, and some travel in packs, like wild dogs or rats. They go every day. *Because every day, they need to get high.* You see them here all the time."

"Yeah. They're here, like, every day."

"That's why Monday morning they're lined up outside the door at 10 a.m. These people are sick. They have a disease. They steal so that they can get high. Stealing is the only job they can do. Sometimes they go on the clinic. Sometimes they go to the can. We don't see 'um for a little while. Otherwise, they're here every day. You understand?"

65

"Yes." Morgan was starting to get depressed.

"Now, when they come here, we pay them for their merchandise, and then we put that merchandise in the store. You know how that works. That's your end. So, we buy an item that retails for $100. Carlo'll give the guy $30. If he puts up a stink I'll come out and give him $35. He's my best friend for life for that extra $5. Trust me. Then, we price that item for $75 out in the store, and if someone comes in and we know them, they can have it for $60. We double up."

"We double up." Her mouth mimicked the wording, but her brain was spinning fast.

"Mike, I know how *this* business works. What does Lexi do?"

Mike smiled.

"Lexi makes sure that we don't pay taxes." Morgan looked at him quizzically.

"I don't get it."

"Lexi pays us cash for the extra merch we'll never sell in the store."

Morgan's brain caught the ball.

"Like the vacuum cleaners," she said.

Michael started to nod.

"Yes, like the vacuum cleaners. We're never going to sell ten vacuums in here. That's going to take a long time. But, we can't turn 'um down."

"Can't we just tell the guy we don't want them?"

"No. We want him to keep coming here instead of going to a different joint down the road or in another town. So, we have to take everything to maintain the relationship. Even if we don't really want the merch. Then, Lexi comes and sells the stuff quick."

"Is that why she's here all the time?"

"Yes. The longer those vacuums sit here, the more time the cops have to make those vacuums as the same ones that went out the back of the Target down the street. You understand?" Morgan nodded. "So Lexi comes and buys the Dysons from us and gets rid of 'um."

"Well, right, Mike. But what if some booster steals ten vacuums and you give him $100 apiece?"

66

"That's probably happened."

"Okay. So he steals ten vacuums and then the cops come. They just take the vacuums and we get nothing right? Then why buy them?"

"Because if Lexi comes down an hour later and sticks 'um in her SUV and drives 'um off the property, when the cops come *two* hours later for the vacuums, I can just say I sold 'um and don't have 'um any more. They can search the place if they want. They're *just not here*."

"And you can do that? That's legal?"

"Absolutely."

"You have to tell them you sold them to Lexi?"

"The law doesn't require disclosure."

"But don't the cops understand how this all works?"

"Cops are as dirty as anyone else."

"But there must be some time when the cops actually come looking for stuff. Like, they know that the stuff came here. Like, what if they arrest the booster, then what?"

"There's a constant line of communication, Morgan," said Michael. "As soon as someone gets pinched, everybody knows."

"So, selling the stuff to Lexi means it's less likely for us to get in trouble?"

"No, we're not going to get in trouble either way. Lexi just brings us cash. Lots of cash."

"And what does Lexi do with the stuff?"

"Beats me. It's not my business. But she pays cash and I don't give her a receipt." Morgan got it. It all came together.

"I get it now."

"You do?"

"Yeah. You spend $1000 on merchandise. You put on your taxes that you spent $1000 on inventory. Then, Lexi comes in and gives you $1500 cash, which goes in your pocket. Then, when we sell stuff in the store, that $1000 offsets our profits we make on the books with credit card purchases and stuff."

"Bingo."

Even Morgan thought it was a good idea.

"So Lexi is basically washing money for you. And she does it with the help of the boosters."

Michael got quiet and looked intently at her. He reached for his cigarette pack but there were no more. She had grown up. He chuckled.

"It just sounds so dirty when *you* say it, Morgan."

"So. I want in. I want to make more money. I can work with that. It's better than selling weed. It's a racket."

"What's the class you're taking in school?"

"Accounting and finance."

Michael smiled. "No wonder all the questions. Don't you worry about the books. Just study and make something of yourself. You don't want to end up like me." Morgan got up. "And give me back that money." She threw the envelope of hundreds back at Michael and went back to her area.

*   *   *

Laida and Danny got arrested together when they were literally sitting at a traffic light. There was one car in front of them and one behind. She still remembered it was when they had that old Infiniti. They had no merch in the car—they had just sold a bunch of Kitchenaid electric mixers, and Dan had made a quick stop to pick up a couple bundles. They hadn't even gotten high yet—they were on their way back to his place. Out of nowhere, a rented moving truck from where else but the Home Depot slammed into the car behind them, crunching their backside and sliding the front end of the Infiniti under the bumper of the pickup in front of them. There wasn't a huge amount of damage, but they couldn't move if they wanted to. And it didn't matter.

By the time they'd figured out what had happened, the driver of the truck in front of them jumped out before they could hide their works. He was a fireman off duty, and as he's calling in the accident on his phone, he's literally standing with his head in their car checking on them. It only took a couple minutes for them to be in handcuffs. The cops found a spoon that they claimed (correctly) had residue on it, a syringe, and the heroin baggies they just bought. After searching the vehicle, they found a bunch of other discarded empty baggies under the seat and stuck under the console, and they could see from the different stamps and designs on them that these were not just addicts, they were pretty serious addicts.

It all added up to a pretty grim situation for the two of them. Dan was fucked. He had priors—he was going away. Laida had gotten away without a record, but that was less of a problem than the cock between her legs. She thought about telling the beat cop who put her in the back of the car but decided against it. If there were one thing she always knew, it's that if people thought you were born a female, it was best to keep it that way. She kept her business private, and never let anyone know that she still had any of her male parts.

She had been able to change her identification when she got her breast augmentation surgery—a couple letters and a quick trip to Motor Vehicles and voilà! A new license marked "F" for female. So, no one needed to know that she had been born a man except for anyone she let know. She knew this had the potential to cause her trouble if she were arrested, but once she had picked up such a nasty drug habit, she didn't really have a choice about the world she inhabited. She was always incredibly careful. She trusted Dan with the boosting that they would never get caught doing that, and Dan was always the one who had the hook-up or went and copped, so she was not in danger of getting arrested there. She had such a fantastic run of good luck that she started attributing that luck to some sort of superhuman force that was watching out for her, rather than just a good run of luck. She thought she was Wonder Woman. She thought she was untouchable.

As the guard led her into the holding cell, she wasn't really fearful. She knew she was going to get out. A pretty little thing without a record. However, after they booked her a new fear crept in and rose up the back of her neck.

"Why do I have $1000 bond?" The officer looked at her.

"'Cause you're a lousy drug addict."

"But I don't have that kind of money on me. Can't Dan bail me out?"

"You're talking about the, ahem, *gentleman*, you were in the car with?"

"Yeah. I'm sure he has $100 on him. Then I can get out and get him out." The officer laughed.

"It doesn't work that way, Sweetie."

"What do you mean? I know he has $100."

"No, he doesn't." Laida's eyes narrowed.

"I *saw* the money in his wallet."

The officer chuckled.

"Oh, the money's in his wallet, but he can't reach his wallet from his cell." Laida saw where this was going.

"Okay. Well, can I get the money out of his wallet to bail myself out, and then get him out?" The cop got right in her face. She saw his name tag. Greeley.

"Sweetie. It's simple. His wallet's been put in a bag with his other personal belongings that he'll get back when he leaves. He doesn't need his wallet. There's nothing to buy in the cell. So, if you need to get out of here, you need to call someone you know and have them bail you out. You get me?"

Laida glared at him.

"Why was I not given a promise to appear? I've never been arrested."

"It's standard. You're considered a flight risk." He walked away.

Laida's brow furrowed. She was prepared for this. Her sister Nicole had always told her to call if she needed anything. Nicole would bail her out. The real dread set in when she realized that her sister was in Europe at a conference. Well, worse than that—leaving Newark and flying on a plane right now to France. She was not going to be able to reach her. And she'd been talking about this trip for so long. Why did this have to happen when it did? She felt so powerless. Helpless. A hot wave flashed over her face. She called the officer back.

"I'm...I'm so sorry, sir. I was just a little off guard. This has never happened to me." She started to cry. The officer softened.

"It's going to be okay, Sweetie. We'll give you some time to come up with the money. We're not going to move you for a little while."

"Move me?"

"Well, it's Friday afternoon and it'll be after the close of business before your paperwork is done. Monday's a holiday. So, the first day of court isn't 'til Tuesday. We can't keep you here 'til then. So, if you can't post bail, we'll have to put you in population until you can be arraigned."

Laida got dizzy and grabbed the bars. Her head spun. She knew what would happen. She'd had this conversation before. In population all the women wore prison jumpsuits. Some woman would be checking her snatch to make sure she wasn't sneaking bags of dope into the joint. And wouldn't that woman be surprised when she found a cock. Whisper here. Whisper there. A phone call. She'd be taken to the men's unit. And she could only imagine what would be done to her there. She thought she was going to pass out.

"But, I...I mean..." She stuttered and tried to find her words. "I need to make a phone call." She gripped the bars. The officer sensed her distress—he saw it was not an act and softened more.

"I *can't* get you his wallet. They already took that away. I'm not even supposed to do this, but you can call however many people you want. I don't want to see you have to get sent to population over the weekend. Especially over a lousy $1000 bond. It might teach you a lesson to get off the junk, but my dad was alcoholic and I know what he was like without a drink. You should get out of here and check yourself into rehab. You hear?"

Laida heard him as if it were a dream. What was she going to do? She was going to be dope sick on a men's unit. Someone was going to smash her head in there as a hate crime, or she was going to get raped and left to die. She needed to get out of jail— this was a life and death situation.

"Yeah. I just need a phone."

She called her father, whom she hadn't talked to in years. He had excommunicated her. He didn't pick up.

"Did you call his home or his cell?" asked Greeley.

"I don't know his cell." Greeley looked around to see if anyone were listening.

"Sweetie, if you want, I can get your cellphone and let you get the number out of it. I'm not supposed to do that, but you shouldn't have to get moved because you don't have his number memorized. We're not animals." Greeley laughed. "Hell, I don't know almost anyone's number anymore. Don't worry. I can get your phone."

71

Laida bit her lip. How could she say it? Her eyes started to tear up.

"I don't have the number," she mumbled.

"What?" asked Greeley. He hadn't heard her. She started crying.

"I don't have the number. He didn't give it to me. And my sister's out of the country. Fuck. Fuck." She started hyperventilating. Greeley stepped back and sighed.

"There's no one else you could call?"

There was one other person Laida could call—Chris. But how could she? How could she debase herself like that? Chris was the one who paid for her tits in Miami. He was the first man she'd been with—a lawyer, an upstanding guy, and she had screwed him over. They had *not* parted on good terms—after he'd paid for her surgery and she was recovering, she had stolen one of his debit cards and cleaned out one of his bank accounts.

"Sweetie, is there anyone else you could call?" Greeley snapped her out of her daydream. Back to reality. She looked down at her tits. They were still a little too firm and up a little too high from the surgery, but were healing nicely. The dirty men who were going to be holding her down by the neck in jail and covering her with thick, ropy, smelly cum were not going to care.

She grabbed the phone and punched in Chris's number without looking at the keys.

Raise

Greek Timmy was on tilt. He had raised pre-flop to $60 in late position because the kid in the big blind was weak. The small blind was this old guy who was tight as a motherfucker—he figured his $5 is going into the muck. The only one he's worried about is the guy under the gun who limped. It didn't seem like a limp with kings or aces expecting a re-raise—he would've probably had the same read on the blinds and raised himself. Timmy just didn't know if that guy was going to call the $60. He had never played with him—he thought his name was Dave. Dave Edmonds? Evans? He seemed pretty tight. The old guy snap folded. Then that kid in the two-seat with the big blind. He looked Arabic or something like that. He was definitely the fish. Overplayed his ace-queen of diamonds out position and got fucked.

So here Timmy had raised to $60 with ace-nine offsuit, which was loose, but good poker, and the Arab is thinking, thinking, thinking, and he finally calls. Timmy was surprised. He honestly didn't know if the kid was deciding if his hand was worth the $60 or not, or if he was going to re-raise. He actually had a hard time reading those people—he wasn't used to their facial expressions and body language. Then that guy Dave called—he's a solid player, but Timmy didn't have a good read on this hand. He could be marginally priced in with three to the flop and no possible re-raise. Six-seven suited maybe? Pocket threes hoping to hit his set? Ace-jack suited? The guy was pretty tight.

The flop came jack of clubs, nine of clubs, eight of spades. The Arab kid paused for a split second before he bets $600 into the pot. David stared at him. All the thoughts about the drugs in the pipeline went away. There was no wife—Allison just sucking down those boxes of wine. She didn't even buy Franzia any more—they were just generic double-wall boxes that he had to cut with a utility knife into pieces to hide them in the recycling and not have the whole neighborhood thinking they were a bunch of lushes. There was no house. No car. No 401(k). Just analysis. Reading. He looked at his opponent for a long time before he finally spoke.

"Good bet," he said slowly. "That's a...that's a good bet." He paused. "You know there's only $200 in that pot, right?"

Kasim tried to keep his cool after the overbet. He was nervous. It wasn't really the money—his family had always had that and he didn't think he cared about it the way anyone here did—it was just that he didn't feel that comfortable in an illegal poker room. He also attended Williams, and he had told Josh that he wanted to play poker because he liked the mathematics of the game. Kasim had thought they were going to go to one of the Indian casinos in upstate New York or maybe southeastern Connecticut, but Josh brought him to Stamford, CT, a town just outside of New York City. Apparently, Josh's father used to take him there when he was a kid. Kasim loved being a voyeur into that world.

It was a little private game in Stamford—nothing but an unmarked door with a single light over it behind a seedy lounge next door to what looked to be a piece of a crumbling industrial building in a marginal class C commercial block. Inside, it was actually nice, like a decent sports bar with a wall of nice flat-screen TVs all showing different games, some comfy overstuffed leather couches, a fully-stocked fridge and bar, and a kitchenette. Five poker tables, some neon beer signs, some autographed sports memorabilia, and a bunch of framed cuesticks on the walls were all the decorations inside. But it felt complete.

He looked at a camera in the entranceway when he arrived with Josh and needed to be buzzed in after they saw who was there. They were greeted by a grey-haired Italian man in his mid-forties named Johnny-O who wore a short-sleeved collared shirt with a cigar-cutter hanging out of his pocket, and who shook Kasim's hand with a firm grip. Josh had insisted that while the place was technically illegal because they raked the pot, the cops already knew about it and not to worry. Kasim questioned his judgment a bit—Josh never seemed to understand that regardless of his family's connections that he was in this country on a sort-of semi-permanent trial basis and could be deported for a criminal activity—but he had wanted to play poker in America. And here he was, betting $600 into a $200 pot, just like Dave had said. He didn't want action.

David watched the boy. He made a move to his checks as if he were going to count out a bet and started shuffling them, watching Kasim. The young man had thin, long fingers with big pads on the end of them, and when David went for the checks, he instinctively moved the tip of his index finger off the table and put it back down ever so slightly. David knew he had a hand: he didn't think he was on a draw. He either had hit a set of nines, or maybe pocket tens with a big draw, or he already had the queen-ten for the nut straight.

"Fold." He tossed his cards into the muck.

Greek Timmy looked at his cards. His ace-nine was still there. Middle pair with an ace kicker. This kid could have a jack, maybe ace-jack, but it's *such* an overbet. There's no way he bets like that if he has the straight. Unless he had ten-seven and hit the shit end. But then there's no way he's calling $60 out of position with ten-seven. He had to have caught part of the flop. If he had an overpair he would have raised to get Dave out of the hand pre-flop. I don't think he makes that kind of overbet with top-top or even king-jack. I don't think he's calling me preflop with any smaller jack. Would he bet a set of eights like that? Maybe. If he hit a set of eights may Allah bless his sorry ass. If he has jack-ten I still have outs. I still say he's on a club draw. My money is the club draw. I'm going to re-raise his overbet. I think he's going to fold. Timmy's mind was made up.

"Fuck it. I'm all in," said the Greek.

Kasim snap called and flipped over jack-nine offsuit.

"Top two," mused Dave. "Wow."

"Shit," said Timmy. "I didn't know you were that strong."

A seven fell on the turn.

"Fuck me," said Dave. "I folded ten-eight. I make my straight on the turn. Good fucking bet." The river bricked out.

Timmy was counting out chips to match Kasim's stacks and was cursing himself. He only had a couple hundred left. "How do you do that?"

"I'm sorry?" said Kasim.

"How do you overbet the ace-queen of diamonds and play jack-nine the same way? Really?"

"Well, I wanted you to…"

"Oh shut the fuck up. I fucking wasn't asking you. Arab piece of shit."

Kasim shut his mouth and counted his chips. Even with the double-up he was still down for the night.

David looked at his watch. He had worked a half-day and just wanted to blow off some steam. He checked his stack. He was up $600. He put his chips in a rack and went to cash out.

"Okay, I'm done. You guys have a good night."

While he was standing at the window to cash out his chips he saw the young man that had come with Kasim. He had been playing at the 2-5 game rather than the 5-10. David liked that game—there was a $1000 cap so it played pretty much like a 5-10, but when he saw the hoo-has at the 5-10 he changed his approach. Counting his bills, he glanced over, Josh had turned to look at one of the other televisions and David could see his dirty white Williams baseball cap and its frayed brim.

"You go to Williams now or did you graduate from there?" David felt like he couldn't tell how old anyone was anymore.

"Who wants to know?" asked Josh before he turned his head around to meet David's gaze.

"David Evans," he said sticking out his hand.

"Josh Grenier." They shook hands, sizing each other up. "Yes, I go there. I'm a junior. Are you an alumnus?"

"No. I was just wondering. It's an awful long drive.

Josh decided to change the subject rather than talk about school after the terrible semester he had just experienced, with its quick jaunt to a drug rehab facility that simply taught him more creative ways to break laws and get high. Time to poke at David, see what he was holding.

"Are you up today?"

"Yes," said David.

76

"What'd you make?"

"Six hundred."

"Not bad for a couple hours work. Probably more than you make at your regular job." Poking. This guy was definitely a suit. His outfit was too nice to be a charade.

"No, I just got lucky. I mean, not that I don't make that much, or, not that I do, I just..." David lost his thought. Josh made him nervous somehow. It was the way he looked at you. Like he had lost all hope. It was his eyes. They were blue, and too deep. They were pure blue water in a limestone quarry, two pits that resulted from past systematic destruction, surrounded by chalky white.

Maybe he has Asperger's or something, David thought. Better to just leave it alone. But he remained intrigued. There was something in Josh's eyes, something like an information burn rate or a processor speed he had never seen before. He wasn't exactly sure why, but he just wanted to know more about this young man.

"I just had a good day today," continued David. "Had some money in with a suited 8-9 and hit a straight on the flop."

"5,6,7?" asked Josh.

"What did you say?" David was surprised.

"5,6,7?"

"Five. Six. Seven?" David repeated Josh's words slowly and methodically.

"Yeah. Did the flop come 5,6,7?" For some reason David looked like he wasn't following him. Josh squinted and reframed. "I guess it could have come six, seven, ten or seven, ten, jack. I was just guessing."

David started laughing and actually looked relieved.

"It came ten, jack, queen." For some reason he truly believed for a split second that this young man just *knew* somehow about the project he was working on. It was bizarre. Creepy. Goosebumps rippled across his arms under his ivory shirt. He wondered if this is what it would be like to share consciousness with someone else—noticing something, then noticing something from the other person's perspective, and then seeing it for yourself again. It was just the way Josh looked at him, like *he knew* somehow.

He thought about how crazy that would have been if Josh had heard of this particular experimental chemical. The odds of that. I mean, there were grad students in Pickering's lab. Theoretically, one of them could have told another about the compound, or maybe it was on a blog or website somewhere. Maybe this was not just a chance meeting in a back room of a sports bar in Stamford. I mean, what *were* the odds?

Odds were what David hated to think about most in poker. He remembered he was at the Golden Nugget on vacation in Vegas just wasting some time in the 1-2 no-limit game. He usually stayed on the Strip and didn't venture out to Downtown Vegas, but his wife Allison had found a bar on a little side street with half-price Happy Hour drinks that were strong as hell, and was very happy there with her girlfriend. Her daughter was enjoying the pool—it had a water slide where you slid down past sharks swimming in an adjacent tank. She couldn't get enough of that pool.

So there he was at the Golden Nugget in their dumpy little poker room. He remembered watching a black guy at his table flop quad threes. They gave him some pittance for the high hand of the night. Literally, ten minutes later, the same guy flopped quad threes again. The identical hand. The odds of that defied calculation. He would have never believed someone telling him that story unless he saw it himself.

He knew the odds of flopping quads with a pair in your hand were around quarter of a percent. Mathematically, around one in about four hundred times, you would statistically flop four-of-a-kind while holding a pair. To have that happen within ten minutes is sick, and then with the exact same cards is just disgusting. David was totally convinced that there were no coincidences. Josh didn't know about 5,6,7. He just happened to say those numbers based on what David himself had said. He felt as if he had shivered a little bit, but believed that his façade remained unchanged.

"Wow," said Josh, ingesting all the data he had just observed. "So you flopped the bottom end of the straight. That's a tough hand to get value out of. It would have been a lot easier if you flopped the top end."

"Yeah, I got lucky. I'm pretty tight and it was a loose table." Josh wanted to know more about David. Josh had a mathematical mind, and that reaction when he said those numbers was uncanny—he didn't think he'd ever seen a guy react so deeply to describing the cards on the flop in a poker game. He'd never seen someone react so deeply, to his core, and then so vehemently try to cover it up with nonchalance. Ever.

Kasim announced he was just ready to go—they had to drive all the way back up to Williamstown. As they started to walk out, the Sicilian man yelled to them, "Josh, bring your friend back real soon!" The men all laughed.

Josh went over to the bar area and mixed himself a screwdriver with just enough orange juice to color the vodka, poured it into his Big Gulp plastic cup, and capped it. David waved goodbye to them, and the young men walked out the door to Kasim's Escalade.

* * *

"You get in here right now, Missy!" The smoke from Mike's cigarette was hanging in his office. Morgan stomped over.

"What."

Michael was holding what looked like a brochure and was leafing through it.

"Do you know what this is?" he asked.

"No," Morgan said flatly. She really had no idea.

"Well, at first I thought it was junkmail so I tore it open. Then I saw it was addressed to you."

"Mike! What the fuck!"

"And then I saw it's from something called The New Liberty Church and I didn't read the whole thing but it looks like some sort of shit about drugs. This is trouble." Morgan's face turned bright red.

"I can't believe you opened my mail!" She lunged at the piece of paper. He put it over his head to keep it away from her.

"Since when do you think it's okay to get mail here? Addressed to you? This ain't your apartment. Ain't your parents' house. You are *not* allowed to do that. Period. I don't care what kind of mail it is. I don't wanna' be responsible."

"Give me a break, Mazzone. You're not responsible for anything. Give it to me. I paid for that!"

Michael's eyes got big. "You *paid* for this. *This?* This looks like some sort of pamphlet the homeless people hand out on the corner. Are you serious? I don't want any shit coming here, you understand?"

Morgan said nothing and was skimming the newsletter.

"*Morgan Chandler*," said Mike strongly.

She looked up, annoyed.

"Okay, Mike. I won't have anything come here again."

She walked away and over toward Carlo's area. He motioned her to come over.

"Morgan, don't say anything," said Carlo. "Why don't you do everyone here a favor and don't challenge him on this? He doesn't want anything to do with drugs associated with this store. He can't deal with that sort of heat. Got it? This is a legit business."

"I know."

"Why did you have that sent here? Were you trying to piss him off?"

"No. I just didn't want them to have my address."

"Who?"

"I dunno'. The people who write this newsletter."

"Why not?"

"Just because."

"All right. Seriously. Morgan, you should just get a post office box. They're pretty cheap and you don't need to tell anyone your address. You comprendé that?"

"Yeah," she said as she walked back to the jewelry counter. She looked at the newsletter. It was fascinating—she'd never seen anything like this before. There was a bunch of stuff in the newsletter, some columns about some laws and stuff about U.S.C. and C.F.R. and words she didn't understand at all, but she skipped right to the main article. It was titled, "Rongorongo: why we can't decipher the native script of Easter Island." Morgan started reading the article, which was attributed to an author by the name "J.G." At the first sentence she opened her laptop and clicked to an online dictionary to begin deciphering some of the words. She found it slow going.

Rongorongo: Why we can't decipher the native script of Easter Island

The fundamental confusion arises from the epistemology of the Christian Church—its autocratic hegemony profoundly limits the knowledge of the adherents of the Church, to the extent that its current followers could never be thought of as similar to the original followers of Jesus. In fact, the original followers of Jesus would be as incoherent in today's world as the current Christian Church would be unrecognizable to the Christians of that era. The fundamental cause of the rift that once separated Protestants from Catholics (and then later cleaved the evangelicals) was this attempt to interpret the static book that remains from Jesus' time with exegesis, eisegesis, or both.

No one can possibly know who is right or wrong. Of course, I do base this statement on an assumption of subjectivity of reality, as opposed to a kind of Kantian objectivism that popped up in academic circles well after these ancient books were written. The take-away from that is simply that if we look at our ideas of ontology as a spring that expands and contracts with time in a gentle oscillation, we still cannot get away from the fact that it is, indeed, a spring. Expanded or contracted, we're still agreeing on the shape of the mechanism that defines the structure of the ordering of our reality.

My argument is that it is simply not a spring. The early Christians understood this. I mean, who *wouldn't* think of reality as subjective—these people witnessed miracles firsthand! We need to look at their work not as one describing Jewish law or Jesus and a chronicle of his work and the work of his followers. I don't want you to think that this means I am fully accepting either interpretation of the actual words. Rather, we need to look at the written word as a type of partial recording of the visual language and unspoken language of the times.

Think of how things changed. Consider the fact that the current symbolism of a priest carefully dispensing a single drop of water into a cup of wine used to mean something wholly other than a single drop of humanity in a sea of divinity surrounding us on this Earth. We are so quick to forget that these very priests used to be the ones who were in charge of managing the powerful hallucinogenic mushrooms that grew in Eurasia, specifically, the fly agaric. This Amanita muscaria was so vividly pictured in the cartoon *The Smurfs*, and in all sorts of fairy tales and children's stories.

This mushroom (legal to sell, possess, and harvest in the U.S.) contains the powerful chemicals muscarine and muscimol, which are potent biotoxins that alter our central nervous systems, leading to powerful hallucinations. One of the amazing facets of these chemicals is that they pass through urine unchanged, meaning that were one to drink the urine of another who had ingested this fungi, their urine would be psychoactive as well.

Imagine these cardinals and priests, draped in red and white like the very caps of the mushrooms they were ingesting. Imagine them drinking each others' urine until the chemicals were correctly titrated such that they could put a few drops of the urea into the wine and pass along just a small bit of their mass hallucination into the minds of the new willing converts. Then, they immortalized their very saints and spiritual leaders in iconography and painting and artwork with halos on their heads. They too resembled the very mushrooms whose visions on which people could collectively agree that they had all just witnessed some mysterious traveling carpenter who healed the sick.

There are some that would say that there is no basis for this blasphemy. However, if this were in fact the material reality during the time of the transcription of those sacred documents, why would that information be included? When a widget company prints up its annual report, it doesn't include the age, gender, ethnicity, religious affiliation, health conditions, hair and eye color, sexual orientation, familial status, net worth, home addresses, Schedule A deductions, and car insurance premiums of each of its employees. It's not because that information does not exist, but because it is inorganic to the message. Likewise, there was no need to mention the role played by the mushroom—that was a given.

Imagine then, the confusion that arose when the Bible was translated into Greek. (This was the prevalent language at the time of the writing of the New Testament, after one of many historic Jewish diasporas.) Picture the passage that was written, saying, "…and Jesus was resurrected, and it was Easter." Now, for some reason, a new high holiday comes into existence. Easter. The resurrection of Jesus celebrated annually by Christians. And what was "Easter"? Nothing more than a bastardization of the pagan holiday known as "Ostara," the celebration marking the vernal equinox. This confusion is akin to the name of the city of Buffalo, New York—the early settlers heard the French trappers calling the town "Beau Fleuve," or, "beautiful river," and thought they were saying "Buffalo." The city of Buffalo has absolutely *nothing* to do with bison. Jesus was raised, and it was Ostara—the man has nothing to do with Easter.

Easter, then, has nothing to do with Jesus. Well, it has as little in common with Jesus as it does with the name of Easter Island, the remotest habitable land on Earth, which is what this article is about. Easter Island is a small, triangular-shaped volcanic island a couple thousand miles west of present-day Chile. It was colonized by Polynesians traveling by boat over thousands of miles without the aid of compasses, maps, or any other known navigation tools. How is it, then, that these early Polynesian settlers could have made the voyage to Easter Island from either the Marquesas archipelago or Mangareva in French Polynesia sometime before 1200 CE? Probably over a thousand years ago?

These are distant island groups separated by huge spans of water—the Marquesas archipelago (French for "Land of Men") is 2000 miles away. Closest neighbor Mangareva (or, the Gambier Islands) in French Polynesia is 1600 miles away. That's equivalent to traveling from Maine to Florida without a map. When researchers recreated the type of boats these Polynesians used to travel (using the kinds of materials found on these islands) the journey to Easter Island from the next closest land took nineteen days. Nineteen days with no map. In a wooden boat. No GPS. How could they have done this?

They did this because they were exceedingly advanced people whom we simply cannot understand today because our fundamental notion of measuring intellect is different. These people navigated by the stars. To those individuals, this would have been called "Ostara Island," not "Easter Island." To them, the solar and lunar calendars meant something. Being in tune with the Earth meant their survival. Easter was a Christian holiday. Christians were the people who came and colonized the Land of Men with a mission in 1834, killing their native population. The decimation was so incredibly hard to explain away to those back home in Europe, that the priest in charge of this genocide, Honoré Laval, was sent away to Tahiti and treated as criminally insane until he died in 1880.

So why Easter Island? Because the Dutch explorer who "found" it in 1722 sailed by it on Easter Sunday. Not unlike Jesus happening to being raised from the dead on Ostara. I spied a man raised from the dead, and it was Ostara. I spied a new land where I thought there was none, and it was Ostara. Don't you see—it's, Ostara, the vernal equinox, that's the constant all along. And what better a name given to these people on this tiny triangular-shaped rock jutting out of the Pacific Ocean than the name of the high holiday of the religion whose followers would slaughter its population? And why did the Christians feel the need to set up missions there at all? There was no gold for chalices for priests to keep while the nuns took their vows of poverty. There were no natural resources to plunder. These people hadn't heard of Jesus Christ. I mean, how could they have?

The natives of Easter Island were pagans, as evidenced by the huge stone heads (called "moai," these giant heads lined up looking at the island with their backs to the ocean). Probably the most well-known items attributed to Easter Island, researchers have now discovered 887 stone heads (one of the largest weighs eighty-two tons and is nearly thirty feet long), each of which is a carving of one of the ancestors on the island. Disregarding the type of tooling and equipment needed for the design, execution, and transportation of such enormous pieces of rock sculpture (estimated to be around 800 years old), one must ask why they exist at all.

The same reason we don't know why they exist is the same reason why we cannot read their writing, called Rongorongo—we killed the majority of the people on the island. Their writing remains one of the few undeciphered languages left on the planet. It has consistently defied many attempts at translation. Interestingly, the only records we have of the writing are on pieces of non-native woods. It's almost as if they didn't want to use written language on their native flora. Aside from the rare petroglyph—I would argue, the "graffiti" of the time—rocks were used to carve the giant heads and not for writing. Most of the writing is on pieces of wood that appear to be pieces of broken European oars that washed ashore.

Igor & Konstantin Pozdniakov were the first to collect up all the symbols on all the pieces of writing we still have and attempt a synthesis of only the main characters. Amazingly, they found exactly 52 "letters," aside from a few "rare" symbols that popped up from time to time but as a whole were *incredibly* rare, making up only a tiny fraction of one percent of the total glyphs. Since they were so statistically rare, the researchers did not feel that deciphering them or even understanding them was important to the translation process. The number of letters, fifty-two, of course, is the exact number of cards in a deck of standard poker playing cards. And why is that number important? Why isn't it?

Remember Ostara? The day the island is named after? Remember the stars these people used to navigate by? The solar and lunar calendars used for centuries to understand planetary motion and earth's cycles? 52 Cards = 52 weeks. 4 suits = 4 seasons. 13 cards in each suit = 13 yearly lunar cycles. 364 / 7 days in the week = 52 cards in a deck. And add up the spots on all the cards. Ace is one, two is two, jack is eleven, etc. The entire deck added together is 364. All we need to do is add in that joker, add in the bunch of symbols that we don't understand to add that last day. (I assume it would be Samhain, the Wicca celebration coinciding with Halloween, when the world of spirit and the world of flesh are closest.) So the people from Easter Island were using a proto-language that had fifty-two different symbols, just like fifty-two discrete playing cards.

And why has this system not been deconstructed by people with all the resources of breadth and speed and the blindingly fast binary calculation potential of present-day computers? Initially, the conclusion was that this language was not actually a language. It was just designs. Random. Meaningless. But what if it's simpler than that? When people first began to ask where playing cards came from, there was a book published in the late nineteenth century wherein the author claims that the cards originated on the lost civilization of Atlantis, and were then propagated around the earth after the demise of that civilization. Those fifty-two "symbols" are readily understood and traditional, right? But they don't equate to a language.

The reason we cannot decipher this script is the same reason why we don't know what most of the grey matter in our brains does. It's the same reason why there is such a huge percentage of "dark matter" and "dark energy" in the universe that takes up all this space but we can't account for it. It's the same reason why we have to sleep every night and cannot recount our dreams. It's that fundamental epilepsy. We have had our brains split in two, cleaved as a result of our own hubris.

Remember the Tower of Babel in the Old Testament of the Judeo-Christian Bible? The story is simple. Apparently, the framers of the long-distant roots of our society needed a story to tell their children at night to explain why there were other cultures out there who spoke different languages. (After all, if the stories in Genesis were true and we were all descended from a single pair of humans, wouldn't we all speak the same language?) The point of the Tower of Babel story was less about building a tower up to heaven, and more to underscore the fact that in order to build a tower to God, we would need to not only be speaking and hearing the same language, but also that we would need to be on the same page. We would need to be thinking with a hive mind. Without autonomy. In that story, Yhwh struck down the tower and scattered the workers, making none of them able to understand anyone else's language. So why can't we decipher the Rongorongo language of Easter Island? One of only three or four known inventions of writing on the entire planet Earth?

BECAUSE THEY DIDN'T WRITE AND DIDN'T NEED TO SPEAK. THEY SPOKE TELEPATHICALLY.

86

The inhabitants of Easter Island didn't need to read or write—what people would if they could all speak without talking? Reading or writing would not be something that would need to be invented. Mouths were for eating, the gateway to the esophagus, with teeth for chewing to make for easier digestion. Mouths were never designed for talking. This is the same reason why they carved the giant stone heads, and moved them (and act that would take 150-200 men, and one which we don't really know how it was accomplished) to face them from the ocean. It reminded them of their ancestors who had died. And remember, if you were all part of a hive mind and thinking together, everyone would know when someone was going to be born and someone was going to die. People gathered together to celebrate the transitions.

It's why we can't decripher Rongorongo. It's also how the Great Wall of China was built, the Pyramids, many wonders of the world, constructed in a manner that could only take the efficiency of a system of humans working all together. These Polynesian islanders were far from stupid. They knew that just like the sun and the moon always had cycles, so did they. They saw the proverbial writing on the wall. They knew they were going to end up dead, they just didn't realize that the devil would be arriving on a ship with a European flag. So, they started trying to write things down.

It seemed ridiculous at the time. They made a very orderly system of 52 characters matching the 52 weeks and the 52 cards in our deck, but the way they put them together means nothing now because we are not using those other parts of our brain. The telepathic parts. They are turned off. But there will be a way to turn those parts back on. All we can tell you is, be ahead of the curve—early adopters can stake out their place in that upcoming new state of consciousness.

The New Liberty Church is processing applications now—your donation helps us get the word out, and helps our work protecting certain non-traditional consciousness states through any means available to us without lobbying politically, or engaging in any other behavior that would be contrary to our tax-exempt status. Membership in our organization neither requires nor precludes membership in any other. We cannot make any promises of future returns on your membership dues—in the world we envision, our system of interlocking currencies will be nothing more than a relic of interest to historians and numismatists.

It will be a place where gold, silver, platinum, palladium, and rhodium will once again be heavy materials with a beautiful shine that occurs in a fanciful dance of the sun's photon-electron wave bouncing off chemically stable metals. We at The New Liberty Church actually believe that in the future, the most precious metal will be osmium, and not because its chemical symbol is "Os," which is Latin for "bone." Rather, along with iridium as one of the heaviest metals, osmium is not native to the earth. It is extremely rare, and the only reason it is even here is because it was deposited here very slowly, over millennia, by striking meteorites. What could possibly be more valuable than an elemental compound on earth that requires more heat than our planet can produce, and is too dense to be forged in the furnace that is our Earth's core? One that can only come from outer space?

Because we do not want to be sued for making promises we cannot be legally bound to keep, all we can tell you is that it's a good idea to join. Just think about why even with today's vast computing power, we can't read the writing of indigenous people whom we "discovered" in the 1800s. These are the same people who were able to travel across thousands of miles of open ocean without maps, and who were able to create and store nearly a thousand stone heads weighing tens of thousands of pounds apiece. Perhaps, their hive mind made a collective decision when those white men came, and they knew their fate was sealed.

Think of our organization simply as holding your place in the future, a future where scientific study of the brain will be hurtling toward restarting the telepathic pieces through the study of certain chemicals and their "interesting" interactions. Let's just say that those chemicals and their interactions may have been misinterpreted by entities that traditionally maintain a monopoly on coercive force. Hence, some of these bio-agents may have had their ability to aid in communication "overlooked." Everyone and their uncle is a researcher, but we want to ask you, are you a "searcher"? Why re-search when the search has already been done?

With respect to our fundraising, let us pose this question to you: what do you think it was like for people who were pitched the first radio advertising? Can you imagine? The people at the company who owned the radio station told people, "You're going to pay money for us to broadcast your message out to your potential customers."

Can you imagine what the advertisers were thinking? How do I know anyone out there is listening at all? I can't see them or hear them—it's a one-way radio. How do I know how many people are going to hear the message? How will I know if anyone buys my product because of it?

Or better, consider the first to invest in the speculative field of domain names. There's going to be this thing called the Internet. It's going to be huge. You need to stake your claim now on a name that will correspond to the IP address of a computer that could be in Iceland or Palestine or Tasmania, a name that people will someday be able to find with something not invented yet that will be called a "search engine." You should pay actual money you have in your wallet right now that you could spend on chicken feed or motor oil or municipal bonds for these names that in the future, will be bought and sold and traded. And hurry before everything's gone. And guess what—it's *all gone*. Now all we can do is make new top-level domains.

Your donation to The New Liberty Church confirms your membership in an organization that has made its goal to be a pioneer in the new hyperspace developing as we unlock the potential of our own minds. We not re-searchers. We're not searchers. We're finders. It's going to happen—it's not a question of "if," just a question of "when." We are staking our claim, and you are invited to join our guest list for the party of the millennium. Do you really need to think about it? You already know the answer...

Morgan bit her lip. This was too much. This was just crazy. This wasn't about pot at all. I mean, she had tried mushrooms, but she didn't think that they were the type in this article. But this? The group that had written this was just miles ahead of her in terms of how they processed their world. She was not expecting this. She needed to clear her head. She had to go light up a bowl.

* * *

Josh was sitting in the poker club again, grinding it out at the 2-5. The door buzzed open. That man David walked in again. No coincidences, thought Josh. He smiled and threw his pocket tens in the muck. They bounced a little against the other cards and ended flipping face up. The others at the table looked aghast.

"You fold tens?" Moe couldn't believe it.

"You don't even limp?" asked Carrick, this skinny drunk.

"He's waitin' for aces," said a man named Bruce.

"Guys, I mucked the hand," said Josh. He was certainly not going to speak aloud about his proprietary system for playing poker, one that had served him well.

"Seriously," said Bruce, "I can't believe you mucked those tens. The best hand I've seen all day is suited king-queen. And I ran into a set of eights with two pair."

"Maybe it's just not your day," said David as he joined the table and sat down in the eight seat.

"Hey, Boss," said Bruce to David. Dave didn't know if this man had ever remembered meeting him before. At least he didn't call me Chief, David thought. He remembered seeing Carrick, but he was always so drunk.

"I'm in for five hundred," said Dave as the dealer flattened out his money and counted out chips.

"You're not playing the big game today, Mr. Evans?" Josh stared right through David.

"No, Mr. Grenier. As a matter of fact, I wanted to play the 2-5."

He remembered my name, thought Josh. Business guy. Good with names and faces. Did he sit here because of me? The dealer was shuffling and dealing hands.

"So David, who are you named after? Are you a Junior or 'the Third' or 'the Seventh'?" asked Josh. This David guy looked really WASPy, he thought. His family could have been here forever.

90

"I don't know," he replied. "My father's name was Michael and I'm the oldest. I guess my mother just liked the name."

"That's a good name," piped in Moe. "A good Old Testament name."

Josh laughed.

"What's so funny, Josh?" poked David. "Joshua is an Old Testament name too."

"Well I'm named after my Dad, not the prophet Joshua." The other men at the table got quiet. David didn't know anything about Josh's father. He felt a little uncomfortable, like he had just fallen outside of an inside joke.

"Well," he said, "I don't mind being named after King David. Jesus came from the House of David. That's not really a bad legacy to be named after."

Josh stared through Dave.

"The story of David is a story of forgiveness. He was kind of an asshole before he straightened out."

"Excuse me?" David didn't know how to begin to react.

"Have you ever actually read the story of King David in the Bible?" asked Josh. Josh had read the entire New American Bible and the King James Bible when he was in high school. He was trying to look at the critical differences in the books. Not for a school assignment—for fun. He didn't realize until much later how precocious he was.

"Well, it's been a long time..." David was trying to remember a picture book his mother had given him as a child that told the story of King David. All he remembered were palm trees and camels.

"David and Goliath," interjected Moe. "David killed Goliath with a slingshot."

"Yes," said David, regaining a bit of his composure. "That's true."

"That's not what I meant," said Josh. "After he defeated Goliath, years later David became king. He was married, and then he met this woman Bathsheba. He fell in love with her, took her as a mistress, and then got her pregnant. The only problem was, she was already married to a guy named Uriah who was in the army."

91

"Nice," smiled Moe.

"Shut up, Moe," said Bruce. "Josh is telling a story."

Josh continued. "So, David calls Uriah home from duty and tells him to take a week off and spend it with his wife. This way, Uriah will sleep with Bathsheba, and no one will need to know that David was the father of the child. Well, Uriah says no way. I'm a soldier. I can't have sex before a battle—I have to save all my energy and have it pent-up so I perform better."

"My football coach used to tell us that," said Bruce.

"He used to tell you not to have sex before a game?" asked Moe.

"Yeah. He said, 'No pullin' your pud before the game. Wait 'til afterwards. If you have a girlfriend, she can wait.' He really said that."

"Like you ever had a girlfriend," chided Moe.

"Guys, shut up." Carrick awoke from his drunken daze. "So what happened with the Queen of Sheba?"

"*Bath*sheba," said Josh.

"Bathsheba, Queen of Sheba, whatever," said Carrick. "Wasn't that a cat food?"

"There *was* a Sheba cat food," said Bruce. "My ex used to feed it to our cat Kitty. I remember it because there was a black cat on the can and our cat was black too."

"You had a cat named Kitty? You're such a homo," said Moe.

"My ex-wife had the cat. Douchebag."

"*Anyway…*" said Josh, waiting for the other voices to quiet, "David told Uriah to sleep with his wife, and then he refused out of his military duty. So, David showed *him*. Since David was the general of the whole army, he sent Bathsheba's husband back into battle, and told his commander to put Uriah on the front lines so he would get killed."

"And what happened?" asked Carrick.

"He got killed. David kept the kid and married Bathsheba."

"Wow," said Moe.

"Wow is right."

"That's in the Bible?"

"Yes," said Josh. "Your little King David committed adultery and then committed manslaughter. Then he married his mistress. I'm glad *I'm* not named after him." Josh looked up at Dave and smiled. Dave was staring back incredulously. Josh had won the round.

"I never knew all that," said David pensively.

"Lots of crazy shit in the Bible," said Moe.

Josh mucked another hand.

"I gotta' take a piss. Deal me out." Josh walked away toward the bathroom, staggering a little when he got up.

After he was out of earshot David asked, "Is he usually like this?"

"Usually like what?" said Bruce.

Manic, thought David. We have a drug for him. Incredibly intelligent but just sitting here drinking and playing cards in a dimly-lit back-room poker game instead of living life, he thought.

"Like, does he usually talk so much about such complex stuff?"

The men all laughed in low tones.

"That kid is *crazy*," said Carrick, pulling a tiny folding drink table over to him with an ashtray on it. The men all nodded.

"*Cra—zee*," said Bruce.

"But we're all a little crazy," piped in Moe.

"Not like he's crazy," said Bruce. "He's, like, certifiably nuts. But he's a good kid."

David really resented that. He resented that saying: "but he's a good kid." It was as if you could just add that on to your description of someone, and no matter how horrible it was, it's all okay, because the person is "a good kid." He puts cats on hoagie rolls like ALF and eats them, but, you know, *he's a good kid*.

"Well I know he's a good kid," said David. "I like him. I just wonder why he hangs around here. I mean, we usually talk about sports and cards and he always seems to be off on some wild tangent."

"He's always been that way," said Bruce. "He's been comin' here since he was a little kid. He's really fuckin' smart."

93

I got that, thought David.

"So, then how do you know him?"

"His father," said Bruce.

"His dad plays here?"

The men all sat in silence.

"His dad's in jail right now," said Carrick. As he completed his sentence, Josh closed the bathroom door and headed back to the game. David's face softened. He didn't know that. That's a tough lot for a twenty-year-old kid. He didn't want to ask any other questions. That explained a lot to David. He vowed right there he would try to help Josh—David believed that everyone deserved a solid running start.

*   *   *

Morgan alternated between trimming her cuticles and rubbing in scented nail oil while she sat behind the jewelry counter. Mike was talking loudly up front with some other Italian guy, and Carlo was at his computer. Everything was in order.

"Did you ever get that P.O. box?" Carlo asked her.

"No," she said, working those nippers.

"I knew you wouldn't."

"Fuck you," she said quietly.

"Michael told me about that newsletter you had delivered here. Can I see it?"

"Here," she said and threw it on the counter. He was quiet for several minutes. She hadn't thought too much more about it—she didn't want to admit that a lot of the stuff in there was above her head, and she wanted to avoid any uncomfortable conflict at the store.

"The person who wrote this is *very* dangerous," said Carlo finally.

Morgan said nothing. She looked at all the engagement rings and it just made her sad: how many men brought these in after buying them for their special women. Or, how many women brought them in when they needed cash, or when they just couldn't stand the sight of them anymore. The guys thought they knew about color, cut, clarity, and carat because of a

94

television ad, but they never knew the kind of setting their girlfriends wanted. And so many of the women were unaware of the pricing structures and the grey-sheet and just wanted something to look nice on their hands. It was a delicate balance.

Morgan didn't care. She already had the ring she wanted picked out. White gold 18-karat, antique setting of a 1-1/2 carat princess cut that was VS1 with two small rounds on either side. She knew the guy she had been seeing on and off was just such a douchebag—that ring was not coming from him. She sighed. Her job wasn't to pine over a ring. Her work was to strip the emotional capital off of pieces of jewelry, reducing them to scrap metal with intrinsic value that moved up or down depending on the swings of world markets trading future values of real goods in the present. She looked at Carlo lumbering back with her newsletter.

"Did you hear me? I said…"

"I heard you. Dangerous."

"Yeah. This guy's dangerous."

"How do you know it's a guy? It just says 'J.G.'"

"Have you ever met a woman that would write anything like that?"

Morgan thought back through the last ten years of her life. Did she know anyone who would say things like that, even in jest? I mean, she wasn't religious, but priests drinking their own pee and then giving it to people in the holy wine? Something about that was just not right. She looked pensive.

"No, I don't know anyone who would write like that. Man or woman."

"Are you going to join?" asked Carlo.

She looked up. "I don't know. I really…I really don't know. That letter made me think about a bunch of different things."

"That's why this guy is dangerous, Morgan. And I'm not just talking about the blasphemy, which I personally don't care about. He's synthesizing a lot of different things together in ways most people don't talk about. And for good reason. And the way he connects things together? I mean, a whole rant against Christianity and then connecting that to Easter Island because of the name? That's a little crazy. Like, lock-me-up-crazy. Or, I'm off-my-meds-crazy. Just because some priest messed with this guy a long time ago doesn't mean he should suck everybody else into this crazy world of his." Carlo turned around and went back to his computer.

She was tempted to start an argument, but saw Laida and Dan in the doorway carrying in a bunch of cardboard boxes. They were back from one of their fishing expeditions. Mike came out of his office, and Laida walked back to see Morgan.

Morgan didn't know Laida all that well. She knew Laida was a tranny—Mike had made sure to tell her *that* juicy bit of gossip. But it was old news. A tranny, not a tranny, it was all just money. The first few times Morgan saw her she tried to catch glimpses at different parts of her body that might let on that she had been born a man, but it *really* was hard to tell. Her skin was soft and feminine and her voice was a little lower than an average woman's, but it wasn't *manly*. Almost nothing about her seemed masculine—though Morgan did have to admit that she sure carried boxes like a guy. She guessed that she still had the musculature of a man.

"Hi, Morgan," she said. She knew her name, but had only interacted with her a couple of times.

"Hi, Laida. Can I help you?"

"Yeah. I want to scrap this out." She pulled a gold earring out of her pocket. She had found it on the floor in the ladies room at Club 12-20. She had checked it—it was stamped 14k.

"You lost the other one?" asked Morgan, trying to be friendly.

"Huh?" Laida was distracted.

"Nevermind. It's gonna' be $50. Tell Mike I told you and he'll write it up."

Laida looked at the counter—Dan and Mike were busy. She didn't want to get involved. She would get her cut, and that earring was a bonus. She glanced behind the counter.

"Can I use some of your nail oil?" she asked.

"Oh my God, yeah," said Morgan. She put a paper towel down and Laida started the slow process of dropping the oil on and rubbing it into her fingers. She was looking at all the rings.

"You have some really nice stuff in here."

"Yeah, we do." Morgan liked Laida. She thought she was cool. She thought that it took a lot of strength to stand up for what you believe in and just do what you thought was right. Morgan had never really been passionate about anything—that's why she had paid for that newsletter in the first place.

"If you wanna' see anything in the case, just let me know," she told Laida.

Laida looked a little surprised.

"What do you mean?"

"Well, you *know*..." Morgan motioned at Danny V., who was still talking to Mike with his back to them.

"Oh, we don't date. We just hang out."

"Oh." Morgan had no idea why she thought they slept together, but she just did. She thought any two people, if they spent enough time together, would eventually start to have sex.

"That's okay," she smiled. "Lots of people think that and I don't care. I haven't had a boyfriend in awhile. Relationships with men can be pretty complex, and throw me in the mix and it gets worse!" The two girls laughed together.

"Which one do you like the best?" asked Morgan.

Laida scanned the case quickly. There were all sorts of rings. The older style emerald cuts, marquee cuts, princess cuts, brilliant cuts, a couple pears, white gold, yellow. Her eyes rested on one.

"That one." She pointed and Morgan smiled.

"That's my favorite one!" said Morgan with glee. "That one! The princess cut with the antique setting in white. Oh my God that's awesome!"

"It's the nicest one in there. Can I see it?"

"Yeah!" That was so neat. She never thought she'd have the same taste as this tranny. She pulled the ring out.

"One second, Laida, I need to clean it. It gets dirty because I try it on all the time." She disappeared around the corner to the steam cleaner. There were a few puffs of steam, and the ring shone brightly under the lights by the jewelry counter. Morgan wanted it to look perfect for her. When she came back out, she found Laida looking at The New Liberty Church newsletter—Carlo had left it on the counter. Morgan didn't interrupt her, and watched her eyes move quickly back and forth, skimming the page. She finally looked up to see Morgan presenting the ring to her.

"Is this yours?"

"Yeah."

"It's pretty cool," said Laida.

"Yeah. I thought so."

"I kind of want to meet these people."

"Me too," said Morgan as she connected with Laida.

*   *   *

"You wanna hand, Chief?"

"Naw, deal me out," said David as he watched the game. After Josh's comments about the Bible he'd taken a break from the cards and sat on the couch. A few minutes later Josh came and sat next to him.

"Listen, man, I'm really sorry about all that shit about King David and all that."

"Oh, it's fine," said David, thinking about Josh's father. "So, how did you start coming to this place?"

"I used to come here a lot. My dad's been friends with Johnny-O. for my whole life. I've been coming here since they opened the place when I was just a kid. How about you?"

"My wife and Johnny-O's wife were next door neighbors. They grew up together. I've known Maria since before she married John."

"That's cool. So, what do you do?"

"I'm a vice president of a pharmaceutical company called Durham."

"Durham?"

"Durham Pharmaceuticals."

"What do they make?"

"We're probably best known for Duscantia, which works to curb the effects of migraine headaches. We make Neadom, which is a pretty new antidepressant. There is also Gestacin, which is a new hormone cocktail given to women going through IVF. Then a bunch of oncology drugs given for late-stage cancer you've probably never heard of…"

"I feel like I've heard of your company's name before."

"Well, you might have. It's an international firm."

"And you're a vice president?"

"Yep."

"Then what are you doing here?"

"I could ask you the same question." They both smiled.

"No, really," said Josh, "why do you come here?"

"Honestly, Josh..." David hesitated. "Do you have a girlfriend?"

"No."

"Well, I come here to get away from my wife. She can just be such a naggy shrew that I need a place to get away. If I make money, I make money. If I lose it, I lose it. But I have a good time. Plus, my step-daughter usually yells at me for watching the TV too loud at home. Here, I can watch what I like."

"So, what do you actually do at Durham?"

"Well, I'm in charge of a team that oversees the development of new drugs. So, before a new drug like Neadom or Duscantia comes on the market, there's a lot of work that goes into the front end before it's ever brought to the public."

"Is Neadom an SSRI?"

"Yes. Do you know about SSRI's?" asked David.

"Well, I don't really like medicine. I like philosophy and civics, but I've done some reading about selective serotonin update inhibitors."

"So you know what they are then?" asked David.

"I do. Can I ask you something?"

"Fire away."

"Do you believe that you are the same as everyone else, or incredibly different?"

David laughed. "That's a really strange question. I guess I believe I'm both the same and different than everyone else."

"Okay. So you're the same as everyone else because of your biology. Right?"

"Right..."

"That's why the drugs your company makes work for people, because there's a lot about our brains that are the same."

"Right."

"So, we all have these brains, and they all have neurotransmitters in them. There's acetylcholine, dopamine, serotonin, norepinephrine…I can't remember all of them."

"Wow, I'm impressed. Go on."

"Anyway, so we have all these neurotransmitters, and then these drugs your company peddles to us changes them in a very specific way to alter our behavior."

"Well, yes, Josh, but a neurotransmitter is just a chemical that when artificially administered acts identically to those chemicals in the brain that are naturally produced. These drugs aren't really altering your behavior. They're changing chemical reactions in your brain that your brain could actually do on its own. We just don't know how to do that yet."

David had definitely reached the end of the pier of what he knew of the science of his work. His background was in sales: he could sell Raid to a roach. If Durham closed tomorrow, he could work for a Big Three automaker, an energy firm, or manage a retail chain. He was staring out into the vast abyss of information he didn't know that stretched out in front of him. Josh continued.

"Well, anyway, we had a guest lecturer who was a neuroscientist, and I asked him after class about the experience of taking illicit drugs. I wanted to know if this feeling of dying but then coming back to life on account of that drug experience were different from *actually* dying. I wanted to know if there were an innate mechanism in the brain that told oneself that 'everything was going to be okay and there was nothing to worry about' when it was getting shut off and in the process of dying and death. He told me that the brain can never know how to feel like that. So, my question is, if your company keeps pumping everyone full of these SSRIs to alleviate their depression in lieu of dealing with reality, could we collectively hit a tipping point? Could we reach a critical mass where there existed a new and improved steady state of consciousness which would then become actual reality?"

This kid is crazy, thought David. Crazy. But super-intelligent.

"You're asking me if I think a large enough number of people simultaneously using Neadom could exist that such a group would create a new reality for themselves?"

"Not for themselves. For everybody as a whole. Like, if our consciousness became glued together a little more. Like we shared a little more in that reality."

David felt the blood rush to his ears and tried his very hardest not to show it. He started to sweat. He thought about his new project. He got the same feeling he got the first time he saw Josh, like, somehow he just *knew*.

"I…I don't know what you mean."

Josh saw the fear in his face. He had freaked him out. He knew David was freaked out, even though his expression stayed the same. He just wanted David to like him—this man just seemed to like him more than most people. He decided to bring the level of discourse back down.

"I don't know. I was just talking out my ass," said Josh. "It sounds like a cool job." Josh glanced at the television to see the game. David's adrenaline level was back down but he was guarded. He thought that Josh was smarter than anyone else he could think of at Durham. Just with absolutely zero social skills. He knew Josh could never succeed at a company like his without being groomed. And even then, kids like Josh were never ready to settle down for awhile. They wanted to always find a better offer.

"Here's my card," said Dave.

"Thanks," said Josh.

They both walked back to the table. David had a flash—he just thought how crazy that would be if the cards on the flop were 5, 6, 7. For a second he thought that, then glanced over at the men in the hand and saw picture cards on the flop from a distance. The tiny amount of sweat evaporated off his back and disappeared. Thank God for poker. Poker always grounded him. He waved goodbye to the men and walked out to his car. He always parked in front of the lounge and never by the entrance to the club—he thought his car was safer there.

Walking by the front door, he saw a short Mexican man with a moustache wearing a white apron lugging in a folding sign that had been placed near the door. It read, "5 for $6 'til

7pm." The numbers were in a very large bold font. His heart landed in his throat and his hair stood on end. The sign said 5,6,7. He stopped dead in his tracks.

The other man stared at him, as David tried to pull himself together.

"It's all over," said the man to David.

"I'm sorry?" Dave was starting to freak out. "What's over?"

"It's all over." The man looked back at David with black eyes. "The 5,6,7 deal."

David felt sweat erupt from his pores.

"I don't..."

"The 5,6,7 deal is over. It ends at seven o'clock. Five appetizers for six dollars each until seven o'clock. We have $2 well drinks now 'til close."

He carried the sign inside. Dave could use a drink. But he was just a little too freaked out. He needed to go home. He was going to call Pickering once he'd gotten back from his conference in Amsterdam. He got into his car.

What were the odds of that sign being there...

*　　*　　*

Morgan thought about the guy who founded The New Liberty Church—she wanted to meet him because he seemed like he would be a pretty cool character. She pictured some old hippie that looked like a retired professor, or like the Unabomber. He was probably living on some farm up in rural upstate New York growing all sorts of mushrooms. He was probably a pretty cool guy to share a bowl with. She didn't know if Laida smoked pot or not, but she assumed that she did. Watching Laida try on the engagement ring, Morgan was struck by how much she seemed just like a traditional woman to her, the way she held her hands, the way she admired that piece.

"What do you think of the ring?" Morgan asked.

"I love it. Don't know when anyone's ever going to *get* it for me. But I love it." She turned her hand ever so slightly so that she saw it from all sides.

"Lai. Let's eat. Pizza just got here." They heard Danny V.'s voice across the store. Laida was hungry—she hadn't eaten yesterday.

"Thanks for the nail oil," she said as she handed back the ring. Morgan put it back and hid the newsletter by her laptop. She was not going to forget to bring that home today. The two girls walked to see two pizzas on the table that were already half gone.

"What's on those Mike?"

"This one's hamburger-bacon, and this one's barbeque-chicken-bacon-ranch," he said, mouth full of food.

"Oh my God, Mike, that's disgusting." The girls frowned.

Carlo was busy finishing his piece. Laida looked at the chicken pizza, then at the hamburger one.

"Mike," said Morgan, "does that one even have sauce?"

"Yeah. It has sauce. The sauce is ranch dressing, and then they put mozzarella and barbeque chicken pieces, and then bacon pieces on top of that."

"How can you eat that?" asked Laida.

"The ranch dressing makes me shit."

"God, Mike, you are so disgusting!" said Morgan.

"That pizza's slammin'," said Dan already with his mouth full, shoving the end of the piece in his mouth.

At that moment Alexis walked in.

"Everybody's here! Come and have a seat my dear," Mike said as he belched. Lexi waved hello to everyone and sat with her legs pressed tightly together next to Michael. The two of them spoke in low tones.

"They all come when it's time to eat," said Carlo. Morgan went to pee. When she returned, Laida was telling Michael about reading the church newsletter.

"I couldn't understand a word of that," said Mike. "All I know is, it's talking about drugs, and we don't like to hear anything about that in here." Danny grinned.

"It's more than just drugs," piped in Morgan. "I mean it's about freedoms and chemicals and philosophy and stuff."

"I actually agree," said Laida. Carlo's eyes got big. He had never really heard Laida talk about anything. He was always just so confused by her, since she was attractive, but he knew she

103

was a guy. She continued. "He's talking about how we fundamentally look at things wrong. I definitely understand that. I mean, all that stuff about Easter Island? That's pretty out there."

"I think I heard something like that before on Discovery Channel," said Carlo. "It was something about unsolved mysteries. But there are these different groups of people all over the place that believe all sorts of kooky things. And that's what they are. Kooks."

"You know, Carlo," said Morgan, "just because people don't agree with you and you find what they do objectionable doesn't mean they're wrong. Nothing he says in there is illegal. I actually kind of want to meet the guy."

"Me too," said Laida. The girls looked at each other and smiled.

"Well did you guys ask Lexi what she thought?" asked Carlo.

Neither of them had. They both got the same vibe off of Lexi—stuck up, not interested in getting high. Would probably be a drag if she were high. Probably never gets drunk because she's afraid of some guy taking advantage of her. Just not down for dope or pills or shrooms. They would never ask her.

Lexi heard her name and turned around from her conversation with Michael. She didn't feel like engaging Morgan, and she had met that tranny before but didn't really follow what was going on. She turned back to Michael.

"Lexi," said Carlo. Lexi looked annoyed that she was being interrupted.

"Yes?" she said impatiently.

"What do you think of this church?"

"What church?"

"Morgan wants to join a church that's trying to protect altered states of consciousness from government intervention," said Carlo.

"That's a mouthful," said Mike. He didn't even know what Carlo had just said.

"They probably *are* the government," replied Lexi without hesitation.

"Huh?" said Morgan. Her fears were beginning to be realized. Why had they dragged Lexi into this?

"I said, they probably are the government. You know. Like DEA agents. Or they work for the NSA, or something like that. There's no way that's legit. You got this off a website?"

"Yeah, a website," said Morgan as her brain started processing what that could mean. Was this what it was like to be a victim of a scam? She hadn't given anyone anything except her address at the store.

"You have your computer?" asked Lexi. Morgan nodded and went and got it. Lexi did a whois search on the domain name. "It's a post office box in upstate New York." She Googled the town of Leadville. "There are only about fifteen hundred people in that town. The post office is probably only one room, and they probably know everybody already in the whole area. I'm already bored with this, but I'm sure with some disciplined web homework you could figure out who this 'person' is. But I'm telling you right now, it's the government."

"Well that would be disappointing," said Laida. "I was excited. It seemed like a cool thing."

"I don't think it's the government," said Morgan. "I just don't think that the guy who wrote that is someone who could work for the government. It sounds really *real*, you know."

"I actually agree with her," said Laida.

"Well," said Lexi, "If it's not the government, then I wouldn't give them anything. That's going to get shut down, trust me. They don't really need a reason. That site won't be up for long."

"But if it's the government it'll probably be there a long time," said Morgan.

"Like a lobster trap," piped in Carlo. He laughed at his own imagery. He pictured those women as lobsters literally just walking into those traps to eat that bait. They were just so dumb.

"Morgan," said Lexi, "I really think it's just a way to consolidate opposition in one place in order to crush it."

"I don't get it." Lexi sighed. She realized she'd be better off just telling her story and moving on. This was a drop-in business stop for her—she had a hair appointment in a little while and didn't want to waste extra time, but she enjoyed putting people in their place.

"I was visiting a childhood friend at her college, and we were spending the day together. She told me she had the whole day free except for this one hour block of time. She had told her friends at the women's center she would go to see some guest lecturer they were sponsoring. At first I wasn't going to go, and then she told me that the faculty dining hall was catering the thing and we'd get a free lunch that was actually really good."

"What was the lunch?" said Michael. "Tuna? Clams? Was it fish?" Mike fist-bumped Carlo.

"Nice," said Carlo.

"Shut up," she said, annoyed. "That's not what's important. Anyway, the speaker was this girl, Rosa Lee something, and she had written a book called *Why Feminists Are Wrong*. The book was all about how feminists think that they're rebelling against the establishment because they don't dye their hair, or they don't wear makeup or whatever else they do philosophically. But then it's worse than the paradox that's already implied—how can you say 'I'm a non-conformist' without conforming to the opposite point of view? Instead, Rosa said that the *establishment itself* has actually created feminism as a way to see the shortcomings of its own power, for the sole purpose of increasing it. She said there is nothing outside of the establishment. And anything that says it is? That's just the research arm of the establishment studying how the strongest of the most disenfranchised people try to escape, so that they can patch up the holes they didn't know were there, and keep an eye on the troublemakers. Those feminists are like a diagnostic test—they tell the machine about its weaknesses so the machine can repair itself, and be stronger. Feminists, by their very existence, serve only to strengthen the power they, by all rights, are intending to fight."

Everyone sat in silence, chewing their food. Finally, Carlo spoke in a deliberate and thoughtful way.

"So, if society is like a person, feminism is like the colon of the person. And the feminists are like the shit inside?"

"Wow," said Laida as she got up. "Wow. This place is crazy."

106

"You said it," said Michael. "They should make a reality show about *us*! Now clean up those pizza boxes." Morgan knew that job was intended for her.

"Who wants the last piece of this chicken pizza that makes me throw up just thinking about it?" she asked quickly, hoping she could throw it away, box and all.

"That's chicken-bacon-ranch, Missy, and I'll take that," said Michael. He looked at Lexi and held the piece in front of him, ready to shove it in his mouth. "This is for the feminists...I wanna'...I wanna'...I just wanna' help the movement."

Re-Raise

"It's not a formal job offer, but I definitely want you onboard my team," said David. "You would be working directly with me."

"I mean, you know I'm still in school," said Josh.

"Well I know that, Josh," he replied. "But I know what this is like. We have some different guys here from the top tier schools, and believe me, we know that you get scooped up pretty fast. You need to start thinking about your future."

Josh was about to put up a mild protest when he heard the phone beep.

"Josh, it's my wife. I'm going to call you right back."

"Go ahead." Click.

Josh is the one who had called David. The cable news had been on at one point, and he heard a soundbite that Durham Pharma was scrapping its plans to release a drug that was colloquially being referred to as the "female Viagra." He had immediately gone to his computer, Googled it, and read the press release from Durham:

While Durham believes in the efficacy of pirozatum to treat women with HSDD, we are ending clinical trials and will not release the drug.

Durham Pharmaceuticals announced today the end research on *pirozatum*, one of many chemical solutions for the treatment of Hypoactive Sexual Desire Disorder (HSDD). According to American Medical Association research, this psychiatric condition affects upwards of 20% of the population, and HSDD has significant impacts on millions of women in this country and abroad.

"It's an unfortunate decision," said Madeline North, Vice President of Research and Development and spokesperson for Durham's Risk Assessment Team. "We have been running repeatedly into procedural hurdles on account of the sheer number of unique pathologies that are bundled into this particular diagnostic code. While we believe in the efficacy of the chemical, it will not be our prerogative to shoulder the financial burden for exploring the entirety of the complex etiology of HSDD at the bequest of the regulatory agencies, which continue to raise the degree of scrutiny on our proprietary research."

Durham routinely reviews products in its pipeline, and because efficacy is not the only component of a successful new drug application, the company has decided it best to reallocate resources to existing drugs and other research compounds currently in process.

"We believe we have created something which can potentially change women's lives on a scale we have not seen in decades," said Mitchell Potter, Vice President and Pirozatum Team Leader. "It's hard to let something like that go. It's a bad regulatory climate to introduce a drug like this, and we are confident others will build on our knowledge base created during the research. Perhaps after the new DSM is released along with its markups and clarifications of HSDD, we can revisit this incredibly effective compound."

He just had to call David after reading that to razz him a little—he seemed so confident about everything he did, and here was his own company stating publicly that they were scrapping the next big thing. Josh definitely had never wanted to actually work for a pharmaceutical firm—he had always thought that licit drugs were just fundamentally misused in the American culture. He remembered a poem he'd written in high school about that very subject—he still had it committed to memory:

Note to My Significant Other

When it comes time
For me to be given
My sleigh ride to heaven,
Please don't make me do the
Drug dance
At the hospital.
I want to die outdoors,
In the crisp, cool, clean,
Frost,
Where Mother Nature can pull over my head
Her clean white sheet.

He continued to think they were misused. But there was something about David that made him feel like it didn't matter what he chose to do: it was all just business. So, if big pharma was business just like anything else, it couldn't hurt him to learn a bit more about the nature of corporate America generally.

The membership in his church was growing. He hadn't told David about that yet. He figured David wouldn't be especially cool with him running this church, and then working for a company that sells licit drugs. But he had done his very best not to publicly attach his name to that church on the web. He also hadn't told David that he wasn't graduating in June with the rest of his class, but in December on account of that lost semester when he ended up in rehab after not sleeping for almost two weeks. There was a lot David didn't know about him, but there was a lot that he did. For some reason David perceived he had some sort of superhuman intellect, which he thought was odd because he was in the middle of his class at college. He let David feel that way because he really did look up to him like a father figure.

Josh's father was a businessman as well. He ran a little antique store in Sunderland, NY near the rolling fields and forests by the Hudson River. His father was involved with some very bad people—in the endless greedy American quest for more and more yield, he had hooked up with an Albanian crew to make cash on the side. These guys knew someone, who knew someone, who knew Johnny-O., and his father was taking trips to buy antiques in California almost every month.

Antiques were just a cover: on these trips, he was picking up old dressers and roll-top desks and armoires that had been packed full of high-grade cannabis in sealed bags. Joshua Sr. was the perfect cover—he'd been in the antiques business for years and years, and had contacts all over the country that he'd met at auctions. He made sure to stop at his different spots all along the way, maybe buying or selling a few silver coins, or dress-making fixtures, or mallard decoys, but without ever letting on to anyone straight that he was actually hauling drugs. He avoided any inspection issues by using his F-250 to haul a converted vehicle trailer that he had custom-painted to say it was a rental. With his New York license plate not visible and a rental trailer from Michigan going slowly in the right lane and full of furniture, he was hiding in plain sight.

He avoided rest areas and never stayed at hotels, motels, or campgrounds. When he needed to sleep, he would find a small town off the highway, park in their local post office during office hours, and get some shut-eye. He knew that post offices were federal property, and that local police did not have jurisdiction to hassle him there—only a federal marshal could bother him. And everything worked like a charm. Four days home in the truck going on I-80 since I-70 was so hilly and harder on his vehicle (and, he hated driving through Kansas) and he would deliver his load to the Albanians. He got paid cash money.

So, once or twice a month he would leave his little store on a "buying trip" to the West Coast and return. Everything was fine. Until one day it wasn't. He was pulled over on the interstate in Colorado after the Feds had wiretapped one of his business partners' offices and arrested the proprietors. They were looking for his trailer, which they thought belonged to the Albanians. The Feds were looking for him, and when they found his cache, they cuffed and stuffed him and seized 120 pounds of the choicest marijuana out of several large pieces of old furniture. He took the rap and didn't give up his partners—that would have been a death sentence for his wife and son. As a thank you for him not ratting, the Albanians paid Josh's mother a stipend every month to cover her bills, and they had given Josh a chunk of cash for himself as an apology for his father's detention. Josh had a bankroll for poker, and his father been in jail ever since.

* * *

Lenz really did have a dumpy apartment. He knew it. He was perpetually single. Single to the point where he was asking out women in just an absolutely enormous demographic range because he had been so unsuccessful. He wasn't really sure why he had such problems attracting a mate. He had been with his ex Laura for about two years, but that was years ago. She had short, severe hair and squirrelly eyes, and always wore pearls. She was wound so tight, like a ballerina with ADHD constantly worried about that single free strand of hair that was going to slip out of her bobbypins and slice her cornea during a furious twirl.

Now he was forty, alone, starting to see grey in his beard and on his temples, and without a woman. He wasn't even sure why Laura had been with him in the first place. She was so tidy and he was always such a mess. And she was *cold*, just so plainly unaffectionate to everyone, not just him. She didn't like to hug or be touched. When they broke up, she basically did it by phone. After two years. Despite that, Lenz didn't feel like a loser—he was accomplished and made money and ran his own blog called "The Zoom Lenz." He had been so proud of being so punny. He remembered Laura telling him that was the kind of wordplay you saw on hair salon signage, and it was nothing to be proud of. She never had a kind word. She was always so critical.

Lenz's name was actually Ric Lenz, but no one ever called him Ric. When he was younger, he had gotten so tired of having to tell everyone that it was Ric without a "k," that he found it easier to just slip into his last name. Even then, he still had to tell people that it was pronounced "lents" like the plural of the Christian holiday, rather than "lens" like a camera. At least it helped him separate the telemarketers and solicitors. Nice of my parents to do this for me, he thought. Give me two different names that both require additional information for every person I meet. But the name did fit him well.

Lenz was doing a second piece on tax loopholes for the blog. Specifically, he was looking into the IRS allowing new potential non-profit businesses conditional tax-exempt status while their applications were in process. Lenz calculated that in

112

essence, anyone could open a phony "organization" that was never intended to produce anything that could ever be construed to be a net positive on society. That entity did not need to be affiliated with any other organization, could collect "donations," and could keep a tax exempt status because it was a pending application. Then that entity could claim the money was spent on marketing activities or was given away to other charities, and with a little Book-Cooking 101, could file a final return, owe nothing in tax, and close up shop ahead of the game.

Were there ever a legal challenge undertaken by the government into these organizations, the burden of proof would fall on the government's lawyers to convince a judge that it was the company's intent to defraud, which was a difficult job indeed. Clearly, this sort of thing would be incredibly hard to do on a massive scale. However, Lenz was looking for the type of person who would do this type of thing over and over again, being tied to one failed non-profit startup after another, that could all be written off as failed businesses if viewed individually.

Lenz had a very non-traditional way of perceiving the events he blogged about—he was constructing fake, archetypical people in his mind, and then he imagined, what would a person like this do? Then, he looked for patterns of behavior that matched this construction, and, voilà, he broke a number of very stunning, non-traditional stories. He had gotten the idea after eavesdropping at a sushi bar.

He liked eating at Niseko because he could eat alone, sitting and looking at the cooler full of different raw fish, and one of the thin-lipped Asian gentlemen whom he assumed were Vietnamese (what Japanese would debase himself to be a sushi chef in that dump?) chop the fish into small pieces. Lenz didn't think they spoke a word of English, which was good, since he didn't want to have to explain why he was there so often, alone. He still remembered that particular night—he had ordered eel and was expecting the unagi (freshwater eel) he was accustomed to, but he was served anago (sea eel). When he asked his server, she simply said, "New chef," and walked away.

While he sitting at the sushi bar alone eating his anago, a couple of men around his age sat down. They had been drinking.

They ordered angry dragon rolls and red snapper sashimi and were talking about their recent trip to Atlantic City. The man was describing how he played poker, which Lenz was able to hear without issue because they were carrying on so loudly. He was talking about playing in tournaments with the same individuals for hours on end, and said that he only played well when he was stoned. He would smoke pot on the breaks, and then when he came back, he would construct these elaborate storylines in his head about his opponents without ever speaking to them. He'd imagine where they were from, what they did for work, everything all inside his own crazy mind, and then apply a strategy of play to them based on these "assumptions" about their characters he invented in his head. And these were not simple stereotypes. They were involved personal narratives about grandparents and icefishing and trophy cases and bulletproof vests. Lenz thought that the guy was definitely nuts, and definitely drunk.

But it was on that day that he tried doing the same exact thing. Instead of looking at criminal activity or new public policy, Lenz would invent a character in his head that he believed to be a live person, and then would pretend his little avatar was interacting in society. What would his little avatar do? He never told Laura about his little system. He never told anyone. That was proprietary—a trade secret. So what would a person do who thought that society owed him something? Someone who was smart enough to know he knew nothing, but not smart enough to know he couldn't get away with anything?

Lenz looked at the tax-exempt scam like it was legal stealing, and doing so by using that particular loophole. In all fairness, he knew that the government already had their hands full with all sorts of actual malfeasance and impropriety on the order of multi-billion-dollar Ponzi schemes and bankrupt local governments with corrupt officials. He knew that the types of stories he was breaking and looking into were small potatoes, small fry, not really worth prosecuting. However, for Lenz it was all about the human interest aspect. He firmly believed that after awhile, the news all looked like which people were shot where, what companies were doing well and which were not, and what sports teams were ahead of the curve. It was only the niche

114

pieces that actually grabbed attention, and that was what he intended to focus on.

Lenz re-read part of his first article that he had published to the blog earlier in the year:

The setting: The Tangiers Casino in Fabulous, Las Vegas, Nevada. No, not a real place, a fictional one, in Martin Scorsese's epic crime drama *Casino*. In this sharktank, we are introduced to Robert Deniro's character Ace Rothstein, a convicted criminal running a casino. And how was he able to do it? A simple loophole: the law said that you did not need a gaming license to be employed by the casino, only that you had *applied* for one. Approval not required. Only application. DeNiro's character is advised that because of an enormous backlog of applications, it would be months or years before he is rejected, at which point Ace could simply pick out a different position in the business and the whole process could be started again. Always a bridesmaid, never a bride. And never intending to marry. This is what we saw in *Casino*.

It's exactly what I saw when I traveled just south of Atlantic City, NJ to a small community called Surf City. Picturesque beach houses along bike-friendly main streets dotted with small stores and smiling faces. It's a family-friendly little borough as far from the brick and wrought-iron slums of Atlantic City's Mediterranean, Baltic, Adriatic, and Caspian Avenues as the distant squares on a giant Monopoly board. I had been researching a charity called "Atlantic Pet Rescue," which claimed it accepted "tax-exempt donations" to support the cause of saving cats and dogs.

I happened upon the website by accident—I was looking into a place to board my dog Snooker for my next visit to Caesar's Palace for an upcoming journalism convention, and I guessed if I called an animal rescue they would be able to point me in the direction of a friendly business that could oblige Snooker's special dietary needs. I was surprised when I called and the woman who answered sounded drunk, was rude to me, and hung up.

After a little more digging, it turns out that Atlantic Pet Rescue is a total fraud, and consists of a middle-age couple living in a mobile home with about fifteen cats running around their feet. The husband had lost his court case where he was suing for past disability—though he looked able enough, and was able to take care of pets and take donations, he hadn't worked in eighteen months. He said that if he had taken a job, it would have proven to the State he was able, and he would have lost his disability case. So he didn't, fought the denial of his claim, and lost the appeal. To make up for the difference, he started a website accepting donations to help strays and abandoned animals. His online panhandling had netted him $3500, on which he paid no taxes.

Lenz looked up. The article continued, but he didn't want to read any more. After it went up, the first call he got was from Laura. They hadn't talked in a year.

"You're such a liar, Lenz. Your dog, *Snooker*?"

"Yeah, Snooker."

"And what kind of dog, might I ask, is this *Snooker*?"

"He's a pug. I mean, a boxer. Wait. Which one is bigger?"

"Lenz, you really are an idiot. You don't have a dog named Snooker. You have no dog at all. You could never keep a pet. You killed my spider plant, my Christmas cactus, and my hens and chickens. That hens and chickens is a succulent, Lenz. *A succulent!* You don't have to water it. It just sits there and looks pretty. But you couldn't do that. That was too much for you. You *killed* it."

She's still mad about that stupid plant, he thought. "I…"

"And what if someone does an exposé on you, huh? And they find out you don't have a dog? What then?"

"Laura, I…"

"Lenz, I swear to God I would make up a screen name and post to your comments that you're a lying S.O.B. who could never have a dog because he's a guy who kills plants. God forbid someone entrusted you with a dog, or a child! But the way you are, you'd find some way to turn it around on me."

She knows me too well, he thought. He liked that after she broke up with him he could still get a rise out of her.

"Oh Laura, where did the magic go?…"

"Goodbye, Lenz," she said and hung up.

116

Josh's phone rang again. He was looking forward to continuing their prior conversation. "Hi, David."

"Hi, Josh."

"Listen, I just have to ask you about that female Viagra drug."

"Pirozatum."

"Yes, pirozatum. Did you guys really think that would work?"

"It works, Josh. It was clinically shown to stimulate female arousal."

"Yeah, but what does that even mean? I mean, there are lots of ways for women to get aroused that are not sexual." He sounds like my wife, thought David.

"Well you're right. Allison seems to get aroused when she nags me about doing the chores and I actually do them." David laughed at his own joke. Josh said nothing. David was getting more accustomed to Josh's lack of social skills.

"But this drug is pointless. A woman just needs a Jacuzzi jet or a vibrating back massager to get aroused if she wants to. It's a worthless drug."

"That's not really true, Josh. This drug actually speeds up the lubrication of a woman's body to ready her for intercourse."

"But if a woman really wanted the man she was with, she would be aroused anyway."

"Well, yes, she would be aroused, but this quickens and deepens the process to make the whole thing more pleasurable."

"No, you're not following me. A guy takes Viagra because he can't get aroused no matter what. Like, it doesn't matter if he's looking at an ugly girl, a pretty girl, you know, he just can't get a stiffie. So, taking the pill gives him a stiffie, right?"

"Well, right."

"But with this pill, if a girl takes it but she's emotionally not into it with the guy, it's not going to matter if she's wet. She's still not going to enjoy sex any more. She's just going to have a leaky cooch. It might even annoy her. It's a total scam."

"Well, Josh…"

"It's a total scam, and you're just mad that the regulators called you out on it."

"Josh, it's…"

"I mean, that's just a messed up drug. How much money did you guys spend developing it?"

"That's not public information."

"I'm not the public."

"That's proprietary."

"Well, do *you* know?"

"Yes. But I can't tell you. All I can tell you is that it was not one of the drugs that I worked on at all, and the other people working on that drug saw appropriate treatment by management, and the project is on hold indefinitely."

"Well, okay."

"Josh, did you get a chance to email me back that NDA I sent you? I can't talk to you without you signing that non-disclosure agreement."

"I just sent it back to you. Check your mail." There was a pause.

"Oh yeah, there it is. Anyway, did you read the NDA carefully?"

"Yeah. It looked pretty standard."

"Huh. So you've seen one of these before?"

Josh thought quickly.

"I don't believe I have to disclose that."

David laughed. "Well played."

"Thanks."

"So, here's what I wanted to talk to you about now that we have that paperwork out of the way. I'm heading up a new team that's working on a drug that's in its early stages, and that has shown some real promise. It's a new drug that our American team has been working on it for almost a year now, and there is a trial on the horizon. We don't even have a name for it yet. I know that you've already made it clear to me that pharmaceuticals were never really your main interest, but I truly believe that watching this process of the design of a new drug from research to market will be an amazing experience for you. I believe that no matter what you decide to do with your life in the

118

future, this experience will be a net positive. Now, I'm not at liberty to discuss everything with you, just enough to find out if you want to work on the project. Is that clear, Josh?"

"Yes."

"Okay, well, Durham has been experimenting with the area of the brain that's involved with sexuality. We had come up with a drug like Viagra that we never took to market because we were beaten out of the gate, and you know how certain things have brand loyalty and certain things don't? That type of drug has it."

"Like cigarettes."

"Yes."

"A guy smokes his brand and that's it," said Josh.

"Exactly," said David. "If he smokes Marb reds, that's what he smokes. He doesn't smoke Camels or Newports. Or Parliaments." David didn't smoke at all.

"Or Chesterfields."

"Chesterfields? They still make those?"

"Yeah. I only know the brand because they were the first cigarette maker to come out and say, 'Yeah, our product causes cancer. But we're going to keep selling them. They're smooth and mild.'"

"I know, isn't that actually amazing, Josh? They make a product that's proven to hurt people. And yet, if we release a drug that's carcinogenic in even the smallest percentage of the test group, we scratch it and can't sell it."

"David, I think that all these people with tobacco-related illnesses are why we don't have socialized medicine in this country."

"Hey, easy there Kucinich. That would probably put me out of a job. It's best to keep those kinds of thoughts to yourself too. Especially if you're going to be working with me." Grooming was beginning, thought David.

"Sorry," said Josh.

"It's okay. Anyway, we researched a Viagra-type drug, but by the time we could get everything through there was already a Big Three of Viagra, Levitra, and Cialis. We don't want to be the fourth. Durham would rather focus our resources elsewhere. Then, we were coming out with pirozatum, and that release got scratched too because of some procedural issues."

"I know. That's why I called you. I read the press release. It sounds like you're trying to treat a disorder that affects 20% of the population. It's called *I'm not horny any more*."

"Very funny."

"Or, I'm not attracted to my husband any more, but I like him paying for me to live, and I don't want to step down my lifestyle…"

"Josh. *I get it*. Just listen. Think about if you had a big cut in your arm. What are your choices? There are basically two. You could take an anti-inflammatory like Advil. That type of drug decreases swelling around the inflammation, taking pressure off, and allows more blood to flow to the site to speed the healing process and relieve the pain. Think of the Viagra drug as Advil."

"Except that it increases the swelling," he laughed.

"Yes," laughed David. "It *increases* the swelling. Your second option is to take a painkiller like an oxycodone or a hydrocodone. You take a narcotic, and it does nothing for the actual site of the pain. It's just masking the brain's ability to feel the pain at all. It tells your brain that you have no pain, but doesn't speed the healing. The body does that itself. Think of the pirozatum that way. It tells the brain to lubricate the vagina. Does that make sense?"

"Yes."

"Well, what if there were a third possibility. Your arm is cut. You can take Advil to relieve the swelling, you can take oxycodone to forget the pain is even there, or you can take a third option that would actually cause the cut to heal itself."

"Well, that sounds like science fiction, Mr. Evans," said Josh sarcastically. He paused. Then he added excitedly, "You mean like a pill with tiny nanorobots in it that would go and repair it or something like that?"

"Wow, Josh. No. Wow. No. No one has that kind of technology yet. No, Durham is experimenting with a different part of the brain, one that deals with cognition."

"Go on." Josh was very interested.

"It's a chemical called DP-153407."

"Huh. Why is it called that?"

"Well, the 'DP' stands for Durham Pharmaceuticals, and the number following it is an internal number that every chemical we research gets. So, the chemical we looked at before is 153406, and the next one is 153408, and so on."

"That's just weird. You put my two favorite numbers together."

"I'm sorry?" replied David.

"You actually appended them."

"Appended?"

"My two favorite numbers are 153 and 407," said Josh.

"Really?"

"Really."

"Dare I ask, why is that?"

"Well, they're the only two numbers that are the sums of the cubes of their digits. $1^3+5^3+3^3=153$, and $4^3+0^3+7^3=407$. That's so crazy that this drug has that number. I mean, it's a sign."

"That *is* pretty amazing. The sum of the cubes of their digits. Huh."

"David, are no coincidences," Josh smiled through the phone. "So, tell me about this drug."

"Well, we don't call them 'drugs' at this stage. They're just 'chemicals' or 'compounds.'"

"Okay. Tell me about this, 'compound.'"

"Well, first you have to understand the concept of sex of object choice..." began David.

"I know this one," said Josh.

"You already know what I'm going to say? That's not really possible."

"Well, I have a pretty good guess."

"You can't know," said David.

"I do know. Not too many things make sense after 'sex of object choice.' It's like if you said 'one, two, three, four...'" Josh paused. "I mean, I kind of know what you're going to say next."

There was silence on the other side of the line as David caught his breath. It's just a coincidence that Josh said that, he thought. David had never mentioned 5,6,7 to anyone else outside of the German office. No one in America besides Pickering knew about it. It didn't have a DP number, and it never would. And he wasn't talking about 5,6,7. For all intent and purposes, that didn't exist. It was a special side project. Some new workhorse intern like Josh would never catch wind of it. And yet, he didn't stop counting at three. He said one, two, three, four. Anyone could have said that. At any time.

David's hand started to shake. He started to think about the poker game when Josh had asked him if there was a five, a six, and a seven on the flop. That was the bolt of lightning that hit him and put Josh on his radar. But twice? What were the odds of that? Then he thought about that black guy in Old Vegas hitting back to back quad threes. It was just in the cards. Accept it. There is a reason why you are talking to Josh right now. Just go with it.

"David?" Josh couldn't hear anything. David swallowed and collected himself.

"I'm here, sorry." He exhaled slowly and quietly to not reveal his elevated heart rate. "I accidentally hit the mute button. What were we talking about?"

"You said, 'sex of object choice,' and I said 'I know what you're going to say.'"

"Yes, yes. Now what was it you thought I was going to say?"

"Well, that's like Women's Studies 101. You have sex, gender, and sexuality, which are three separate and distinct things. Sex is the biological 'male' or 'female' that you are born as, 'gender' is the social role you play on account of your sex, and 'sexuality' defines the sex of object choice that arouses one sexually. The key is that they are all separate and distinct."

"Wow. That is *not* really what I was going to say, but it's a very interesting insight. Who claims this to be true?"

"Modern feminist scholarship."

"Like, bra-burners and lesbians?" David laughed at his own joke. Josh was silent.

"No, it's pretty mainstream. Pretty widely accepted. I mean, look at Chaz Bono."

"Right. Mainstream. Right. Anyway, I was going to go a little more basic than that, but we should talk about that some other time. So, one's sex of object choice means that if you are heterosexual you like the opposite sex, and if you're homosexual, you like the same sex."

"It's actually a lot more complicated than that, I mean, what about bisexual people?"

"Honestly, Josh, I don't want to open a can of worms right now. Let's just focus in on what we're looking at. So, if you're hetero or homo, this means that you need to be able to look at yourself and conceptualize that you are a man, and you desire either 'one like me,' or 'one different than me.' And I know that's reductionist and oversimplified, but the point is, there's a pretty complex piece to this whole attraction thing. It requires awareness of self and of others, which requires a meaningful system for the brain to interpret reality.

"So, we're investigating an area of the brain that we think is responsible for the construction of our reality. Instead of looking at sexual orientation through the lens of pheromones, or body language, or the way you look at a girl or the way she looks at you, we're looking at sexuality as the actual fundamental basis for interpreting reality. Think about it—the reason why you think some girls are out of your league is because you have a particular self-conceptualization that you then weigh against what you perceive as 'the other person.' So, if we fundamentally and materially alter the manner in which the brain perceives reality, including your own view of yourself, we can boost libido that way."

"Like an anti-depressant for your penis?" asked Josh.

"Yes, that's a very good representation. Rather than Viagra, think Paxil for your package."

"That's clever, Dave. You should use that in the marketing collateral."

"Do you want to play, Josh? Does this sound like your cup of tea?"

Josh couldn't think of anything more appropriate for himself.

"Absolutely."

"Well, good then. I'll be in touch. Get back to the books." David knew this kid didn't really study.

"You know I will," said Josh, having absolutely no intention of busting his ass, especially now that he already had a job offer lined up.

Josh decided that telling David about his church could wait. I mean, it was still in its infancy; it hadn't done any additional outreach, its spread was viral, and hadn't reached a point where he thought it could be on anyone's radar. It was more of a pet project, like restoring a car in a garage. There was no motor in it yet. It was just a particular collection of pieces of metal with certain morphologies and specific gravities. It wasn't a car. Just parts. No license plate or registration certificate. No inspection required.

David decided that he was not going to tell Josh that he didn't care about DP-153407 at all. In fact, looking purely statistically at how many compounds they researched before one got through the pipeline, it was unlikely that DP-153407 would ever move through and become a moneymaker for the company. No, he wanted Josh because he was the goose that laid the golden egg. He was going to have Josh process a massive amount of information around this experimental drug, and then he was going to use that analysis to apply to the data coming out of the German office where they were working on his pet project with 5,6,7. And Josh wouldn't have to know. He was like a big battery—it didn't really matter where his brainpower went. David was going to claim any of the work that he did toward his own numbers anyway—Josh should be happy I'm even getting him a job, he thought.

Because Durham was a privately-held pharmaceutical firm (one of the world's largest) there was no collection of shareholders that needed to vote on anything, and hence little accountability outside of the corporation. With respect to the origins of their pipeline, they were a black box company like Enron. Nobody needed to know, and unless something required damage control, no one ever needed to know. He was just looking for that payoff.

*   *   *

124

Lenz still remembered that conversation with Laura over his article. She was right about everything. On all counts. He didn't have a dog named Snooker. He didn't have a dog at all. She was right—he'd probably kill a pet, and he had killed her plant. He hated that hens and chickens plant—he didn't know why it was named that, and it reminded him of these votive candle holders that his mother had. Ugh. Why did Laura have to be right all the time?

What was Lenz supposed to say? He had no dog? He didn't "happen" to stumble on this phony charity? He had been searching and searching at night, alone in his bed with his tablet, for some sort of company that looked like a scam? And that even with all that searching, that's not how he'd found the McMorley family and their cat house? That didn't make for good copy. He could never write the truth in print. If he did, it would have gone something like this:

He didn't even want to cough up the registration fee for the journalism conference. He was leaving Brooklyn and going down to Atlantic City to try to hit it big on a slot machine to break out of his tiny shithole apartment, where his human neighbors were all Polish or Ukrainian families living with six people in a one-bedroom, and his only other neighbors were warehouses and huge garages to store out-of-service buses and cabs.

The area in Brooklyn where he lived—Greenpoint—was like the community college of the Hipster University system. It was as if the kids that didn't make it into Williamsburg or into DUMBO might settle there while trying to decide, is wearing ironic clothing and pretending I care about this slew of left-wing progressive social issues for me? Am I willing to take 3-5 years of my life to live in abject poverty with only a bike and thrift-store hand-me-downs to show for my decision to reject corporate consumerism, and the coercive force of capitalism? Greenpoint was only supposed to be a green room, a holding cell, a temporary stop, and Lenz got stuck there. In a Brooklyn he barely recognized.

So, while he was traveling to AC, he happened to be in Surf City because he had met a realtor at a bar at the Tropicana who seemed cute and into him. Of course, after he drove to Surf

City, he found out that she was a lesbian and just assumed he was gay, and was interested in showing him some gay-friendly properties to rent over the summer in the otherwise traditional community. He got so flustered when he left her that he got lost and ended up in front of a mobile home at the end of a dead-end street with cats wandering around everywhere, and made a mental note to follow-up on that property.

He just didn't think that was as grabby as the story he told for the blog. Dog named Snooker. He liked it because it wasn't just the game of billiards, but because it meant to dupe. Drunk woman. Pow! Stepped in shit accidentally. Wanted to tell you all about it. Not, predator-posing-as-a-housepet-dyke, whose chunky silver jewelry and flowy J. Jill clothing he misread as "realtor" instead of "lesbo" thought he was a homo, and ugh! Stepped on a cat turd. And it would be just like Laura to call him on it. At least she's still reading the blog, he thought.

After that first accidental exposé, he was working on this side project of trying to identify other examples of this in the real America, where people were starting non-profit companies, accepting money from donors, and then closing the companies. He had done a lot of research. He wasn't about to name names— if he did that he opened himself up to a lot of retaliation. It was one thing to suspect someone of wrongdoing or malfeasance. It was another thing to hurl assertions out on the web that could open him up to slander and libel suits, which could not only shut down his website but also spoil his reputation.

So to this point, while he had his suspicions, he was content to inform the public of this loophole, always with the thought in the back of his mind that one time he would break a real story, get spotted by CNN, and have a national audience for his investigative research. It would be his song out to the universe to attract a smart woman who wanted to take a chance on ol' Ric Lenz.

It was no surprise why The New Liberty Church caught his attention. As soon as he saw it he smelled blood. It was an information broker's wet dream. He was wondering how many others were watching this impending storm. It had all of the elements of your classic First Amendment case—when it all went to hell the author was going to claim that he was merely presenting information in a fair and direct way that could be easily gleaned from a number of different websites. On top of that, he could say he was not telling anyone to use illicit substances to get high, and that everything on the site was simply for informational purposes.

But Lenz saw through all that. He saw what this site was doing. This website was claiming to start a religious organization whose sole purpose appeared to be making the ceremonial use of presently-legal intoxicants protected. This way, in the future when they were scheduled or controlled, adherents to this "religion" would be grandfathered in to use those chemicals as sacraments in the worship of their church. He appreciated the trickiness of the whole thing: just because these chemicals were legal didn't necessarily mean that it was legal to use them as intoxicants, or even cause them to interact with the body internally. In some cases it was even worse than that.

This reminded him of an article he had written where he had exposed some companies who were selling mushroom spores "for research purposes" online. There were companies that were selling what they called "sporeprints" of varieties of hallucinogenic Psilocybe cubensis mushrooms. Since mushrooms reproduced through spores, those spores were like mushroom "seeds." So, these seeds were technically legal, even though the only thing they could ever grow into was patently *illegal* to possess, sell, or ingest. Apparently, the reasoning behind this loophole was that because the spores required a specific temperature range, growth medium, and amount of light to grow into "adulthood," they required a human's intentional interaction to become something harmful. Plus, the spores didn't fall under the statutes in the same way the government controlled "noxious weeds." They were, after all, fungi, and not flora or fauna.

It wasn't that Lenz was necessarily anti-government or pro-government, or wanted more laws or fewer. He was a whore—he just wanted more hits on his blog. He wanted his blog to be controversial, but not so controversial that it tumbled out of the mainstream. He had to be blue seaglass—standing out and oh so much rarer than the common clear and green glass. But he had to be worn down and soft enough to be held, and kept, and displayed. If he were *too* edgy, *too* sharp, he would be tossed back to the sea for endless pummeling by silica and quartz.

He just wanted to be able to say to all the other bloggers that he was a success. It helped him justify his existence in that little apartment in shitty Greenpoint. And he felt as if he had succeeded—because of his prior article, the state of Georgia banned the sale of mushroom spores inside its state lines. He couldn't *prove* it with *evidence*, but the timing was unavoidable.

This church idea was a wholly different notion—the arguments for it and against it were rooted firmly in semantics and not in science. Lenz did appreciate that it was a very smart idea. People would get all of their future drug use protected under freedom of religion, and it would be remain legal as the courts duked it out in appeal after appeal. Surely, some radical left-wingers like the ACLU would get involved, and the whole thing would reach a boiling point.

On this subject matter, Lenz had done his research. He knew Native Americans could use peyote in this manner, but he always thought that this was because the Indian reservations were technically not part of the United States. He had heard of the Church of Santo Dominæ, who appeared to have done the same thing with the drug dimethyltryptamine in a hallucinogenic concoction called "yaje." He remembered it being mentioned on the long-running FOX sci-fi drama *The X-Files*.

However, Lenz had read enough new-agey post-modernist pulp like Terence McKenna to know that the whole thing was suspect. Apparently, this illegal chemical in yaje that these druggies got a pass on was actually a naturally-occurring serotonin analog found in very tiny concentrations inside a normal human brain. All of our brains.

He remembered reading in an article that it was like finding carbon-14 molecules inside of regular carbon, or four-leaf clovers mixed in with three-leaf ones. He did find it fascinating. It was the only case he knew of where a chemical we had in our own bodies was actually found in a bioidentical form in nature. Yet, were one were to possess it (outside of one's body of course), one would be guilty of a serious drug charge. Imagine—you could be locked up for possessing a chemical that naturally was found in your own brain chemistry. And it was all a result of the amazing power of the juggernaut that is the Earth's evolutionary biology.

It was a gutsy play, thought Lenz. However, he was glad it wasn't him who served up his neck on the guillotine. He never even published the article about the yaje because he thought it lacked merit—the fundamental argument that would be read into his piece would be to make drugs legal, and Lenz was very happy with their controlled status. He never really understood the appeal of trying to alter one's reality—aside from being single, he pretty much liked his life, and he certainly didn't think that getting high was going to help him find a quality life partner.

He was watching The New Liberty Church site very carefully. He knew it was only going to be a matter of time before it imploded. He was going to be there when that moment happened, if not virtually, because he knew that there was a great story in all this. It had all of the makings of a feature article for the *Times*: there were constitutional freedoms of speech and religion, government intrusion, privacy laws, and drug policy. Of course, one could also not ignore the potential plethora of criminal activities that could be attributed to the website: Lenz estimated they could be as benign as some minor tax code violations, to as large as a potential second-degree manslaughter charge if anyone actually died ingesting one of these chemicals whose use this church implied it espoused.

He had already done his research on the organization, which, with regards to everything he could uncover, was actually a lone man artfully utilizing technology to appear much larger than he was. A real Wizard of Oz pulling strings behind the curtain, and Lenz wanted nothing more than to find him. The church had not made his domain registration private—the boss was attempting to hide in plain sight by providing a toll-free phone number that was nothing but a voicemail from a telecom provider specializing in call forwarding. That was a dead-end.

He had slipped up on the address, though. He had listed the address as Box 9998 in the town of Leadville, NY. It was not a bogus address—legally, it couldn't be. It was, however, an extremely clever ruse. When Lenz looked into the town of

129

Leadville, he found that it had a population of under two thousand. He looked at some other post office box numbers of others in the town he could find online: Box 15. Box 70. Box 81. Box 3. No doubt this was a small one-room post office that was just a dinosaur, a relic of an era before email when the first class letter reigned supreme.

So he did a little more snooping. Turns out, whenever a Zip+4 code ends in 9998, that designation of "9998" is for the post office itself. This guy's clever, thought Lenz. That's even better than using a private mailbox company where people could get at an employee and find out that information. A Mailboxes Etc. was easy: slip the clerk a hundred and he'll just allow the computer screen with the boxholder's information on it swivel out into your line of sight. Not as secure as it seems. But hiding behind the actual federal government while printing up a nihilistic newsletter espousing the use of intoxicants that alter perception to the point of undermining that very government's power? That was bold. Lenz liked this guy already.

*　*　*

Josh had been trying to plan out the next newsletter and was having a difficult time compartmentalizing his thoughts. He tended to find fodder for his articles in the thoughts he'd gotten accustomed to swimming through right after his periods of extensive use of entheogenic drugs. It made sense to him. Those chemicals were his muse, and so he was charged with protecting their use for future generations. He thought back to college, when his infirmary had sent him to a large county hospital.

They'd sent him to a hospital in Pittsfield, MA. Josh had always hated Pittsfield—he thought of it as this dying industrial town so indicative of where New England was at in this point of its history. The whole area had gone through its life cycle. The first settlers gave the Native Americans blankets infected with smallpox to decimate their population, so they could clean house when white people moved in. Then, it was a booming city of industry. Then, the wealth moved farther and farther outside from the dead wood in the pith of the tree to the part still growing. Now, it was just insects dining on the bark and woodpeckers going after them, and fewer and fewer leaves springing forth from the top branches. The slow death of an old tree.

Pittsfield reminded Josh of what he'd learned in the single Women's Studies course he'd taken. He learned that the Industrial Revolution changed the nature of work. Men and women used to work together on family farms, sharing the duty of labor. Then, factories and automation arrived, pulled men away from their wives to work in the cities, and then work became compulsory as the demand for factory goods drove up wages, and farmwork became less lucrative. A man had no choice—in order to support his family, farmwork no longer paid the bills. He had to work in the factory. And that's what Josh saw when he looked at Pittsfield. Factories. Or more precisely, he thought, boarded up and abandoned factories, home only to rats and spiders. And drug addicts.

Some had become inexpensive apartments and artist's collectives, and cheap studio space. However, even that was just way for the big national banks that came in and slaughtered the small ones to pretend that they cared about reinvesting in the local community. It was all just a big ruse. PR. Spin. They only did so to posture for the next wave of big-box chain stores that were always imminent as part of the homogenization of America. The urban renewal following the previous suburbanization, which was a direct result of the urbanization of the rural farms long ago. The fractal, repeating itself. The spring expanding and contracting. Josh believed the pattern to be just like the ice ages.

He heard the talking heads kept ringing out the alarm for a move against "global warming," but Josh thought it seemed like a way for an overly-intrusive government to move money from some private companies to others. Nonsense, he thought. The Earth was just doing her kind of breathing, her kind of in and out. So what if we were adding to so-called "global warming" by driving SUVs? The volcanic eruptions of Mount St. Helens and Krakatoa alone put more pollution in the air than would come from 150 years of driving cars and trucks. So the media that earned money showing Prius commercials to husbands with clipped-off balls was confusing causality and correlation. Yes, we were driving more cars and using more gas, and yes, the temperature was going up, but you couldn't connect those two things. That volcanic ash pollution did make for nice-looking sunsets, though.

Josh always recalled that we didn't have cities, government, even agriculture during the last Ice Age. There was no government blaming the "global cooling" on some scapegoat social group back then. There was no government, and we were fine. And yet, that same government that pretends to fix a problem that is not actually a problem unless one happens to build a hotel on an atoll is going to tell us that we can't get high? Fuck them, thought Josh. Fuck that government that bails out big banks that go in and pick the carcasses of those abandoned and reclaimed factories just to exploit others.

That was going to be his next article, he thought. It was going to be about causality and correlation, and how we so easily confuse the two. He would write about how the banks periodically dumping toxic assets into the ocean of world currencies was actually very negligible with respect to the level of those oceans. Dumping a little wastewater off the side of a pirate ship waving the flag of an American bank did nothing to the bottom line. Fuck the government and fuck Occupy Wall Street. They're both wrong, thought Josh.

*   *   *

Lenz's research pointed to the fact that the founder of The New Liberty Church most likely lived in the town of Leadville. After several times calling the post office and getting no answer, Lenz took advantage of one of the nice days and took a ride up there. He was off to see the wizard. It was, in fact, a small white post office that was one room and looked like it dated back to the 1800s. The clerk was this sweet old woman named May. Lenz asked her about using that addressing standard, and May sweetly explained to him that when mail came addressed like that, it was the equivalent of writing "General delivery, Leadville, NY."

"Of course, no one uses General Delivery any more. I remember those times—that was when people made a trip to come to the post office."

"It was like getting an operator when you dialed zero on the phone," he responded, trying to turn on his charm and relate to the old woman in a way he thought she could. Even his attempt to connect with the old woman fell as flat as his interactions with the young ones.

"Yes," said May. "It's not a method we really use any more, but the computer is set up to accept mail that way. It's a legal addressing standard."

"Could you be so kind as to tell me who it is?" asked Lenz.

"I'm sorry, but we're not allowed to give out that information," said May. She paused. "Are you a detective?"

"No, ma'am. I'm just curious. I'm very interested in speaking with this individual, and his phone number didn't work."

"Well, I'm sorry to hear that."

"You wouldn't happen to have the form he filled out when he applied for the box, would you?"

"Oh, I'm sorry, Hon, I'm just not able to release that information. I could get fired for doing that! But legally, we have to have one on file."

"Well, May, I've driven a really long way. From the City, actually. Manhattan," said Lenz.

"Oh my!"

"Yes. I had quite the time finding this little town. This really is a beautiful area."

"Well, I am sorry," said May. "And I feel terrible that you wasted so much gas to come here, but I can't release any of that information."

"No, no, no. I'm sorry. Can I just ask you, did this person ever live in this town? I mean, it seems like a really small community. Maybe someone else here knows him?"

May looked at Lenz. He just seemed schleppy to her. And like he would always be a little sweaty if you touched him. She frowned. She would never break the law—in all her years there, she had never crossed a single line. She liked order. She liked discipline. She liked respect. She paid all of her bills early. She had her original passbook savings. She was most certainly not going to tell someone from Manhattan about her people. On the

133

other hand, he had driven a very long way, and seemed like a genuinely kind man. Her perception of him was that, though kind of a sad case, he had no negative energy and raised no alarms. She always trusted her instincts.

"What did you say you did for work?" she asked.

"I'm a blogger."

May looked at him and her expression didn't change. Lenz continued.

"A blogger is someone who writes a blog. It's short for 'weblog'…"

"I know what a *blog* is," she said matter-of-factly. "My granddaughter is blogging about her trip to Europe, and I've been following her and looking at all of her pictures." She lowered her head and looked at him over the edge of her glasses. "I even use Skype." She stood up tall, very proud of herself.

"Well," said Lenz, smiling with respect, "I can see you know the ways of the world. I don't want you to break any of your rules. I have journalistic ethics myself. Maybe you could just direct me to someone else in town who might have had business with him, you know, just something you might have noticed, you know, informally, and I can talk to them?"

May thought about it. She didn't mind doing that much— it could never be construed to be illegal. "Oh, well that I can tell you. He stayed over at the Peace Pagoda for awhile, that's how I met him. I think he was a carpenter. They might be able to help you."

"Peace Pagoda?"

"It's a big monument next to a monastery. Head up County Road 25 and bear left at the stone church."

"I'm sorry, a monastery?"

"Yes. I remember he was staying there for awhile and he came to me and said he needed a place for his mail to go because the monks and nuns don't speak English there. He didn't want them misunderstanding and opening his mail."

"They don't speak English?"

May lowered her gaze and looked at him.

"They're Orientals," she said softly.

Lenz smiled to himself and thought about sitting at Niseko across from the sushi chef, and how different a place he came from.

"Is there a sign for this place, this, 'Peace Pagoda'?"

"Yes. There are some prayer flags by the entrance. Head north from here up County Road 25, stay to the left at the fork by the stone church, and if you get to the river, you've gone too far."

"Okay, I'll stop and say hello."

"Do you need any stamps while you're here?" she smiled.

"Oh, no, May." Lenz couldn't remember the last time he'd bought stamps, or even been inside a post office for that matter. "But thank you for asking."

Lenz's phone was not getting any service up in the hilly, backcountry terrain—he had no way to look up the information she had told him, and if there was one thing he was unaccustomed to it was not having the internet. Lenz drove through the rural roads of the Taconics looking for Tibetan prayer flags, which were the absolute last thing he surmised would be out there in the woods. The road was winding and he seemed to be going up and up a very large wooded hill. He started cursing May: how could that sweet old lady have fed him such a load of baloney? He was supposed to be looking for a traveling carpenter who lived at a church? What was his name? Jesus? Did that simple country woman play him? When he started heading down the hill, he saw a small dirt driveway on the right-hand side of the road, and a tiny sign that said "Peace Pagoda." He stopped short, and turned in. Wonders never cease, he thought. He slowed to a crawl—the driveway was badly rutted.

The road continued forward, and there was a sign for a parking area on the right. He pulled into the desolate dirt parking lot. There was an old Subaru Brat parked there. Also, there was a Volvo 242 turbo with a sticker that said "Peace" on it, and a second sticker that was just a black "W" with a red line through it. Lenz was surprised to see that car—they made very few turbo 240s, and he'd never seen a 2-door model. The Subaru had a "Space your Face" Grateful Dead sticker on it. Guess I'm in the right place, he thought.

He read a sign that said no alcohol or drugs, no overnight parking, no hunting, and to keep noise at a minimum. He locked the car and started walking up a steep dirt path. It was heavily wooded and poorly maintained. It seemed odd—it felt like there should be people here, living here, but he didn't see anyone. He started to sweat as he trudged up the hill—it was a bit of a hike. He kept heading up the hill. When he turned the corner he almost couldn't believe his eyes.

There was an enormous white concrete dome on the top of the hill. It was at least eighty feet high and over a hundred feet across. Lenz stopped in awe. He walked all around the dome, which was inscribed on the outside in an Asian script he did not understand (he found out later it was Cambodian) and topped with what looked like a gold-plated stationary weathervane. There were statues inlaid into the sides of the dome. He ran his hands all over the side of the structure—it appeared to have been made of concrete, and had no doors or windows. If it were a temple, he didn't understand how that worked—you couldn't get inside.

He found out later through his research that it was not a temple, but it was actually a type of grave marker for a monk. Apparently, when the monks died, they were cremated, and then the others poked through the ashes, looking for colorful crystal relics. These relics are thought to be the material form of the very essence of the spirit of the monk, and contained the energy of all his prayers and deeds. The others would remove those sacred relics from the ashes, and then bury them in the center of the dome. The dome was like an Egyptian pyramid, and it was called a stupa. Lenz had no idea such a thing existed—and he considered himself a bit of an academic.

After wandering around the dome for awhile, he still had not seen another soul. He walked a bit further away and saw what looked to be a rock garden for meditation, and a koi pond, both with prayer flags draped all above them. There was a beautiful vista point overlooking the rolling hills of the Taconics. He sat and looked at the sky for a minute—it really was good to get out of the city, and get some fresh air, and just be. Even if he found out nothing on this trip, he surely found a very interesting place he would have to learn more about.

Just as he was about to give up, he heard a kind of humming that grew louder. It began to modulate, and he realized it was chanting in a language he didn't understand. He waited and saw them, five human figures draped in white, walking in a line out of the woods and down a path away from him. They didn't look in his direction. The chanting got louder and shriller, and then they passed. He didn't get a good look at them, but by their small stature and high voices he guessed that they were nuns. He waited for them to go by and be out of his line of sight and then he followed the different path down the hill that they had taken. This is all so fascinating, he thought. He would never have guessed that he was in rural New York.

As he walked down the path, he began to see signs of human development. There were two sheds with long orange electrical extension cords leading down the path, and connected to the little houses. He looked in the window of one and just saw a rice mat and a pillow for a bed and a tiny chest of drawers. No people. He continued down the path. Now he could follow the electrical cords—there had to be someone at the end of that. He made his way past several very large statues—there was a seated Buddha and a reclining Buddha that were ten or twelve feet long at least and made of concrete. Unbelievable to see art on this scale in the middle of the woods, he thought.

Finally the path opened into all he could think to describe as an old dirt main street of an Old West town. There was a row of trailers on either side of the "road," and then at the end of the road on the right was a Buddhist temple. He could tell by the shape of the roof and the designs out front. The women in white had disappeared. He saw chickens walking around freely. He'd been in Brooklyn too long—he couldn't remember the last time he saw that. He felt like the birds were sizing him up. He kept walking slowly down the road toward the temple until a woman in white poked her head out of the trailer. She saw him and stared.

"Hi, Ma'am?" His voice went up at the end of the question.

She went back inside and he heard the woman speaking to another woman. The two of them came outside and pointed to the temple, saying, "Um-noi." He didn't know what that meant, but he walked toward the temple. Shortly thereafter, a man with very dark skin and white hair dressed in what appeared to be canvas pants, and a loose-fitting white shirt came outside from around the back of the temple. He had a large smile and happy eyes. Lenz continued toward him.

"Sir? Um-noi?"

"Yah!" the man said with a big smile. He looked like a koala that had eaten too much eucalyptus.

"You're Um-noi? That's your name?"

"Yah!" said the man. Lenz had no idea if he understood a word of what he said.

"Um-noi, my name is Lenz."

"Yah. Come."

Lenz understood that. The man led him to the temple. They walked up the stairs.

"No," said Lenz. "I'm not a Buddhist. I…"

"Come," said Um-noi. Lenz was already involved in this little adventure, so he thought, why not? He walked up the rest of the stairs and was ready to go inside. Um-noi stopped him by putting his hand on Lenz's shoulder. He was strong for an old man. Um-noi looked at him in the eyes, and then pointed at his shoes. Lenz didn't understand. Then he saw the other shoes outside. He wants me to take my shoes off before I go in the temple, thought Lenz. He started to take them off and Um-noi smiled.

Shoes off, the two of them went inside. Lenz was not ready for what he saw. It looked sort of like a Christian church, except there were pillows lining the whole side of the place for people to sit on, and mats laid out on the floor where the pews of a church would be. The altar was the centerpiece: there was a gold Buddha statue in the middle, and it was surrounded by hundreds of candles, and Christmas lights, and brightly colored cloth. Um-noi walked up to the altar.

"Hey," he said. He then proceeded to kneel in front of the altar, bow to the ground three times, then remain kneeling with his hands in front of him. He motioned to Lenz, who got the hint that he was supposed to do the same. What a story I'm going to have for those hipsters in Williamsburg, he thought while he was kneeling. Then Um-noi disappeared. Great, thought Lenz. What else is going to happen?

* * *

Josh didn't play cards the way most people did. Or, at least he had never met anyone else that played them the way he did. In order to understand his perspective on cards, and reading what cards came up and when, he had constructed a very complicated system of interpreting and parsing information. Josh did not believe in accidents. And he didn't believe in faith. What he actually believed was this:

He had studied physics, mathematics, the law, and had observed human nature since he was very young—his feeling of his soul being too large for his body did not really affect his being precocious. Nonetheless, he had a very particular way of understanding reality. He believed that humans, as a race, would definitely have the future capacity to travel through time, even if we could not do it spatially at this particular moment. It seemed clear as day to him—the rate of human population growth, the rate of industrial output, the rate of increase in the speed of our communication, the rate of growth of our ever-increasing knowledge base—everything he observed signified an exponential growth rate. Yet, plotting time along the bottom axis of the graph, his tendency was to plot time in a linear way—we measured time in discrete units of measurements based around planetary orbits.

His instincts told him that if time moved along linearly, but output moved along exponentially, at some point the graph of output would have to reach infinity, while the time line would continue to progress. (Some people he'd met called this point 'singularity,' but Josh didn't agree with their viewpoint.) Apart from his own meanderings through consciousness with the use of hallucinogens, he believed that as part of this infinite exponential output we would reach the scientific point where we could travel in time. Since this was a *given* that we could eventually do so, he merely thought that the reason there were no coincidences was because the game had already been played out. It was the *time* that was an illusion.

139

Accepting the fact that time travel would one day be possible, Josh then surmised that he could not *disprove* that an avatar of himself from the future was able to pause his present, go in and fix the deck a certain way, and disappear without anyone the wiser. (Mathematics had taught him that provided you could not find one example that disproved a hypothesis, there was no reason to believe that the hypothesis was false.) And that other people would be able to do the same thing, provided they lived long enough to pass that singularity, a point Josh preferred to call "unity."

He had never told anyone this because he didn't want his observing something to change it. Josh truly believed that the game of cards he was playing was not with the other individuals in the room. Rather, he believed he was playing a game of tennis with himself from the future. Every time he looked at his hole cards, that was his future self giving him a "hand." (He thought of that hand as an extension of his own consciousness.) How he played that hand sent the volley back to the other world. He didn't know how to touch it. He didn't know how to get there. But he knew that the cards came in such a perfect way so often that this could be the only way he could understand it. So when he played, he was a very unpredictable player who was hard to read, because he would lay really hard on certain hands and would fold others that were excellent.

Josh's brain was like a computer, and he could remember in at least a distant way, almost every single hand he'd ever been involved in. His brain kept track of all the two-card combinations and made little notations next to each one in this giant visual database he had of what hands he liked, and what hands he didn't. And that made total sense to him. Some people loved red cars or black cars. Some liked trucks or vans or station wagons. There were innate preferences.

Certain hands he knew were losing hands: he had been taught those by losing large sums of money. Whenever he saw those hands, he interpreted them as his silent tennis partner saying, "danger," "avoid play," or "loss is imminent." Queen-ten offsuit he would fold into the muck any time. It was the worst hand. He had other terrible hands. Ace-nine. Ace-ten. Ace-jack.

140

Ten-nine. Deuces. Ten-seven. He wouldn't play them. He just knew.

Other hands he loved. Five-six of clubs was his absolute favorite. He also loved three-four of diamonds. Eight-nine of hearts. Pocket sixes. On top of that, the way he decided to play his hands had as much to do with how the cards had hit the flop earlier. He read them like tarot cards. The middle card in the flop was always the most important, whether it was upside-down or right-side up indicated to Josh whether his "luck" or "ability to earn money" on that trick if he were in the hand, or the next trick if he had folded. He read that up or down information in conjunction with the rest of the information, ran it through his proprietary system of interlocking databases, and voilà! He sat quietly in what appeared to be a standard war of attrition with the other players.

In his mind though, he was only playing with himself from the future in an imaginary set of tennis. These were tarot cards. They were a fluid Ouija board that was being moved and changed. He was there to practice his game. Whenever he dosed himself with those potent drugs in the past he felt himself jumping over that net. Just like in tennis, he wasn't allowed to touch it. But he always jumped back.

Josh always hated when he got dealt pocket tens. He never knew what to do with those. He always thought of tens like deuces, which never did right by him—the number "10" was just the binary representation of the Arabic numeral "2." There had to be a correlation.

There was a part of Josh that really hated computers. Counting with only zeroes and ones? How arcane, thought Josh. And they can't understand a space in a web-address? There's no space at *all* in that Cloud? Is the Cloud really that dense? That Cloud that started as many little unconnected cirrus wisps in the Arpanet, tipping off the powerful governments of some massive upcoming changes in humanity. The Cloud that became cirro-cumulus at the advent of the Internet, then cumulus as powerbrokers directed capital as water vapor between the naturally-occurring thermals on the Earth's surface. And now out of control, a force all its own, the cumulus clouds were coalescing into one fantastic cumulonimbus. One giant

Computer Cloud hypermind poised above Earth, the electrical charge building on both surfaces until that bolt of lightning inevitably hits. The singularity. Unity.

And Josh had his wits about him—he was preparing for that strike. He knew that if his hypothesis were true about his future-self pulling levers behind the scenes, the only way that time travel were going to be possible was with massive amounts of computing power. And you know what that meant. Companies who made computers and engaged in the R&D for those computers (and investors in the tech companies that made those computers) were all going to have their hands out. They were all going to want money or credits or whatever would be the future equivalent of money. Computers were going to be toll-collectors. Why wouldn't that be starting now? When he saw tens, he saw tolls. And he'd been seeing lots of pocket tens lately at the poker club.

*   *   *

Um-noi had left for what seemed like an eternity, and Lenz thought he had been forgotten, a feeling he seemed to get often throughout his life. Finally, a pre-teen boy came up the stairs and walked over to Lenz.

"Hi. Um-noi doesn't speak English. My name is Vy." The boy stuck his hand out.

Lenz got up and shook his hand.

"Hi. I'm Lenz."

"Hi, Lenz. Is this your first time to our monastery?"

"Oh my God, yes," said Lenz. "I didn't even know this was here."

"A lot of people don't. Let's not talk in the temple. The monk doesn't like that."

"The monk?"

"Yes, the monk. This is a monastery. There is the monk, and then the nuns, and then the staff like Um-noi, and Don-noi. And me."

They walked out of the temple and outside. This boy has got to be only twelve or thirteen, tops, thought Lenz. I don't know how much information I'm going to get out of him.

"Are you training to be a monk?" he asked.

"Are you crazy?" asked Vy. "I'm here because I've been bad in school. I have to come here every day after school so I stay out of trouble."

"Oh."

"My dad makes me. He tells me to do what the monk says or he'll hit me."

"Well that seems pretty violent for a Buddhist. Does he hit you?"

The boy smiled. "I was just kidding. He doesn't hit me."

Oh boy, thought Lenz. This kid is lying to me right off the bat. But at least he speaks English.

"Do you like it here?" asked Lenz.

"Yeah, I'm the only one who speaks English though. Except for the people like you who come visit. Did you bring us food?"

"No, I wasn't planning on it. Just stopped by."

"That's good," said Vy. "Do you know they don't let me have a computer here?"

This kid is totally ADHD, Lenz thought.

"Well that's too bad."

"There's a computer in the monk's office, but that's just for him. And I can't use his keyboard anyway. They said it's because they're punishing me for being bad. But I'm not bad. Do you think I'm bad?"

"Well, I mean, I just met you..." said Lenz. You're a pretty annoying kid, he thought.

"Why did you come here?"

"Oh, well that you may be able to help me with. I'm looking for a man that lived here for a little while. He was your carpenter?"

"Oh, Josh."

"Okay. His name is Josh. You know who I'm talking about then."

"Yeah. Josh. He was all right. He got mad at me though. He told me I stole his phone charger, but I never did."

"Okay. So, there was only one guy who was a carpenter here?"

"Yeah, I told you. Josh."

143

"Do you remember his last name?"

Vy drew back.

"Wait, are you the police? I didn't do anything wrong."

"No. I'm not the police. I write a blog."

"Oh, that's cool. I wanted to write a blog once. But then they sent me here."

"I'm sorry, Vy. I really am."

"You know Josh isn't here any more?" continued Vy.

"Yes. I know that. Do you know where he went?"

"I thought he went back to school."

"School? Is he a teacher? A professor?"

"I don't know," said Vy.

"Is there anything around here that would have Josh's last name on it?"

"He told me before," said Vy. "It was like, 'grenade.' Or, 'Grand Marnier.'"

Lenz chuckled. "Do you even know what that is?"

"Hell yeah, I know what that is. That's all I drink when I'm in the club. I got my bitches, one on each arm. And I'm drinking my Grand Marnier." Vy laughed.

This is probably why I kill hens and chickens, thought Lenz, because I could never deal with a teenager. And he's living with actual hens and chickens running around that he probably eats. This kid's never been to a club. He's probably never even had alcohol. This is a particularly painful interview.

"So, his name is, 'Josh Grenade'?" asked Lenz.

"Yeah," shrugged Vy. "It's like, Yo, we got grenades!" said Vy crossing his arms to imitate the Italians on the *Jersey Shore*. It *was* comical. But Lenz wanted something a little more substantive here. Either this kid was a sociopath, an imbecile, or Lenz had not been interacting with enough teenagers.

"Okay, Vy, do you have anything that would have Josh's name on it? Did he ever write you a check or anything?"

"No. He stayed here for free and then he did things for the monk."

"Like what things?"

"He fixed that door in the basement." Vy motioned back to the temple.

"Oh, like carpenter things."

144

"Yeah. He had tools and stuff. A pickup truck."

"He had a pickup truck?" asked Lenz.

"Yeah. A red one."

"Okay. Do you know how old he is?"

"I don't know. How old are you?"

"How old do you think I am?" smiled Lenz.

"Fifty?"

Lenz stepped back. "You think I look fifty?"

"No." He paused. "Are you thirty?"

"That's fine," said Lenz, shaking his head. "What can you think of that would have his name on it?"

"I don't know…" Vy was looking off into space.

Lenz was losing patience. He opened his wallet and pulled out a twenty. Vy's eyes got big.

"If you can find something that has his name on it, I'll give you this twenty."

"Okay," he said. "Come with me." They went down the side stairs to the temple through an unmarked door to a finished basement. There was a bathroom, a closet, and a spare room. Vy started going through a stack of boxes in the spare room.

"So, Vy, what are you looking for?"

"When he was here, the monk gave him this card that you can go to the store and they don't charge you tax."

"A tax-exempt certificate?"

"Whatever," he said. "It belongs to the temple. Josh gave it back. But when he bought stuff at Home Depot he had to sign when he used that card. I think there's a receipt."

Vy stopped and looked at him and got very serious all of a sudden.

"Don't tell the monk I'm doing this."

"Okay," said Lenz, confused. "I don't want you to get in trouble."

"It's not trouble." He started to go through the boxes. Lenz got uncomfortable standing in this strange place with a pre-teen boy. He nervously kept up the conversation.

"So, are you Vietnamese?"

"Cambodian. I'm not Vietnamese. And I'm an American. I was born here. My dad was born in Cambodia. He delivers vegetables to restaurants."

"That's nice. Are all the people here Cambodian?"

Vy stopped what he was doing. Does he always have to stop every time he wants to say something? Lenz was getting annoyed. Maybe this is just what teenagers were like.

"Yes. We're all Cambodian. Don't you know anything about Cambodia?"

Lenz was embarrassed.

"Not really. I know where it is on the map. I think I've had Laotian food."

"Laos and Cambodia are totally different. Cambodia was under Communism. Buddhists were illegal, and they could kill the monk. The monk and the nuns all are safe here. If they go back to Cambodia..." He looked at Lenz, then pretended to get shot in the chest about a dozen times and fell over. "They'll kill them. So they're here and they pray."

"Huh." Lenz found it amazing that he was getting a geography, civics, and history lesson from a child. Perhaps he was getting jaded. "And what about that dome?"

"That's the Pagoda."

"What's inside?" asked Lenz.

"The monk's bones. Not our monk. A different monk."

Truly fascinating, thought Lenz.

"And that rock garden?"

Vy stopped again. This time he looked serious. Why can't this kid just multitask?

"That's not a rock garden. That's the old temple."

Lenz was intrigued.

"What do you mean, the old temple?"

"When the monk first came, they built a temple there. Then, a really bad man came up here and said he hates Chinese people and he didn't want us living in his neighborhood and he burned it down. With gasoline. He burned it to the ground. Can you believe it? He thought we were Chinese."

"Wow, that's painful. Did anyone get hurt?"

"No. No one was there. They caught him though and he went to jail. Everyone in the town felt so bad that they donated money to help us rebuild the temple. So, they built the one we're in now. We leave that one there to remind us of life."

How poignant, thought Lenz, and such a lesson for even a young kid to understand. "How long ago was that?"

"Before I was born."

"So the monk told you that story?"

"We all know that story." Vy looked up and to the right as if he were reading a story off a teleprompter. "We came here because people in Cambodia were trying to kill us for our religion, so we came to America where there's religious freedom. It's in the Constitution. And then they tried to kill us here because we weren't white. But they didn't kill us. We made it. And then all the white people felt so bad, they donated money and now we have the new, big temple. And we keep the old one to remind us that pain exists, but we can't let it beat us."

"Wow," Lenz said. He was truly moved. He tended to take his rights for granted.

"Here it is," said Vy. "Give me the money."

Lenz mechanically removed the bill from his pocket and handed it to the boy. He handed Lenz a receipt from the Home Depot—it was stapled to a copy of a tax-exempt form, and on the bottom of the receipt was a signature and then a printed name under it: "Josh Grenier."

"I told you," said Vy. "Josh Grenade."

"Right," mumbled Lenz. "Josh Grenier."

"You better watch it," said Vy. "Josh Grenade is gonna' blow up yo'! Ka-bow!! Blow up that grenade!!"

There's more truth to that statement than you know, thought Lenz.

"Can I make a copy of this?" asked Lenz.

"You can have it. Just don't tell the monk."

"I won't tell the monk, I promise. Don't spend that all in one place."

Vy laughed. "Do you want to eat with us? It's almost time."

"Oh, no, I couldn't, but thank you."

"All they eat here is fish head soup," Vy said. "Three meals a day. Fish head soup and vegetables over rice. They get the fish heads donated from the fish place up the street, and then they cook it and eat the fish faces. I hate it. Who eats fish face meat? I want McDonald's. I want a Big Mac instead of a big fish face. Can you take me there?"

"No, no, Vy. I can't take you to McDonald's. Why don't you find Um-noi and help him clean up or something?"

"Eh. Um-noi is boring. He's old."

Lenz heard some high-pitched Cambodian tones. Vy cocked his head sideways. "I have to go Lenz. It's time to eat. Say hi to Josh Grenade for me. Tell him I'm sorry I took his phone charger." He ran recklessly out the back door of the temple and around to one of the mobile homes, after which he disappeared, leaving Lenz standing alone in the building staring at a little dust still stirring from where the teen had gone.

I better go, he thought. What a strange place. He started walking back down the dirt driveway to the parking lot. The whole interaction had been strange—the whole place had just been so strange. It just begged for more scrutiny. There was so much going on here. Fish face meat soup. A monk's bones in a big white breast-shaped dome on top of a mountain. A burned-down temple where arson was committed by a townie as a hate crime against Asians. And Cambodians living here to avoid the oppression against their religious freedom. How fitting that this would be the endpoint of his quest to find out about The New Liberty Church—searching for answers to a question online, he found a tiny, secluded colony of living, breathing people trying to protect their religious freedom. And they had nothing to do with Josh. Just parallel. It was just too good of a story. He was going to have to blog this one serially.

He got back almost to his car, and put the folded piece of paper in his back pocket. The Volvo was gone, which was too bad—now that he had gotten what he wanted, he kind of wanted to check it out. In its place was a banged up Volkswagen Jetta station wagon with a faded bumper sticker that read, "My country invaded Iraq and all I got was this expensive gas," and one of those equal signs. The driver must have walked up the other way. Lenz heard another car approaching. He turned to look.

It was a Mercedes. S-class, AMG package. It was driving very slowly up the road—the low profile tires did not take kindly to the rutty dirt. It was shiny black, just washed. The windows were not tinted—Lenz looked at the four young Asian men in the car. The one in the passenger seat looked back at him. His stare was blank and cold. Short, spiky hair, leather jacket, pale face. Something about the way he looked at Lenz caused him to shiver, especially in contrast to all the happy, positive energy he had just experienced with that young boy to whom he was a total stranger. The car kept going out of view.

There is something not right about this place, thought Lenz. That car did not fit. Something just does not add up. This might require another visit back. He decided just to make a short little posting to the blog.

He wrote, "Working on a new story for all of you. A very big one, the details of which I cannot divulge right now, but it is going to be one with all the intrigue and breadth you are accustomed to. Just visited the Peace Pagoda in Leadville, NY. Very hard to find anyone who spoke English, but picturesque vistas of the countryside. I live in the best city on Earth, but I'll tell you, a beautiful experience. It's all connected to a story I'm working on now about a man whose path crosses here. Can't divulge too much right now—have some more digging to do. Peace. Lenz"

He uploaded the post. At least now he had a starting point. Here's what he knew: The man behind The New Liberty Church was named Josh Grenier. His ways around dealing with the equivalent of standard "911-addressing" issues on the internet were creative to say the least. He used the fact that he had lived in a tiny town to get a general delivery mailing address, where access to his personal data was blocked with federal privacy laws, and then forwarded his mail from there to another town where he actually lived. That was shrewd, and a new idea to Lenz. But it wasn't as incredible as actually visiting the town and find Josh's trail ending at a group of Cambodian refugees living in asylum to escape a tyrannical government that was attempting to eradicate them, in the name of destroying their right to free worship of religion. You couldn't make that stuff up. That religious community had been there since before the internet.

Lenz was definitely going to need to plan another trip up to this location—there was definitely a bigger story going on there. That Asian man in the Mercedes. He was cold. Cold as death. What had he stumbled into? Anyway, the service was terrible as he was driving back, and he gave up trying to read if there were any responses posted on the blog. That would have to wait until he was comfy cozy back at home in his little bed, alone in Greenpoint.

*　*　*

"Software picked this one up. New guy. You wanna' look?" Philip had walked up to Anthony Clark's office and took half a step back—it smelled like a little too much Axe body spray in there. Anthony leaned in.

"You couldn't have emailed it to me?" He popped a pistachio kernel in his mouth.

"It's your game." Philip handed the paper to Anthony, who scanned it quickly. "Besides, I needed a walk. Knee's still sore."

"Who is this guy, Ric Lenz?"

"Didn't look too much at this until you give me the thumbs up. Didn't know how interested you were."

"Interested. Find out what you can about this Lenz. He's a blogger? We have a file on him?"

"No. Typical waste-of-space hipster as far as I can tell. Not on our radar."

"Why did the computer flag it?" asked Anthony. He glanced at Philip and ate a handful of pistachios.

"Peace Pagoda."

Anthony looked up at him, annoyed. "Phil, we've been getting nowhere trying to trace the money, and then the heroin just disappears…"

"Tony, listen, I'm telling you, our problem is that our agents can't get near these Cambodians. It's too tight. We're still working on it."

"So, this guy Lenz. He's researching some story? You think he's looking at the same shit we are?"

"He's gotta be. 100%. Cambodians running heroin inside hollowed-out pieces of art heading for that temple. Says it's big. Doesn't want to talk too much about it. Who the hell else could he be talking about? It's gotta be Phan."

"Right. Go through everything this guy Lenz has written. See what we can cross-reference to Phan, or any of his associates."

"You got it boss."

"And I want surveillance on everything going in and out of his phone and computers."

"Done."

"He have a car?"

"Yep."

"EZ-Pass?"

"Yep."

"If he leaves the city again drop me an email."

"Got it."

"And Philip?"

"Yep?"

"Can you bring me some more pistachios?"

He smiled. "You got it, Tony."

* * *

"David, I'm just not that sure about this DP-153 project. It just seems like the kind of thing that could get a lot of people in trouble." Josh was no think tank, but having slept on it, he knew that the type of work David's company was doing seemed dangerous.

Josh was sitting at his computer surfing and talking on the phone to David. He decided he wanted to spend more energy on the Church—he wanted that side project to become his main focus. That meant talking to David about his job offer.

"Well, Josh, I'm not saying that this particular chemical would be the only one you'd be working on. I only brought it up to you as a suggestion because the interest you showed in SSRI's. I wanted you to see the types of opportunities that were open to you here at Durham."

"Don't lie to me David."

"I'm sorry?"

"You and I both know that a drug like the one you're working on would have the power to change people's actual understanding of their worlds around them. This could be made

151

out to be some sort of brainwashing pill. Sexuality? I mean, the way you're talking about sounds like it gives you a little back entrance into people's minds. I mean, think about how often guys think about sex. If the power to change those thoughts fell into the wrong hands? I mean, it's fascist. It's the same kind of shit the establishment's been trying to do for a long time, just more efficiently. But that kind of medical endeavor never works—the universe just never lets it happen. That should show you that this is not a question of methodology but of philosophy. This is not a good drug."

David felt that he had hit a nerve. He guessed that this wasn't a question of actual sexual preferences. He remembered Josh mentioning an ex-girlfriend before. He believed that Josh had just been overliberalized through his college education. He almost sounded like his old friend Pickering. But Peter didn't play poker.

"Josh, I think you're getting ahead of yourself." David knew that Josh was very intelligent, and decided to speak directly to him. "Do you understand what Durham does?"

"Yes."

"I'm not sure you do, Josh. We're a business, just like any other business. Yeah, sure, at some point, maybe in our early history there were individuals involved who really wanted to help people, but you have to understand something. We don't care about the people that take our products. We just want them to keep buying what we offer."

"Now that seems a little oversimplified."

"Josh, my mentor when I first started at Durham told me his biggest innovation at his last company was to call China and have them make all new toothpaste tubes with a slightly bigger hole at the end. He told me that people aren't really looking at exactly how much paste they're squeezing on to the brush. They've done it so many times that they don't see it. What they're used to, it's the act of squeezing the tube. So, if the company made the round holes at the end of the tubes just a tiny, little bit bigger, each squeeze of the tubes that was done unconsciously, by rote, meant bigger blobs of toothpaste on all the brushes. And no one would keep track, because no one dates their toothpaste. They just buy toothpaste when the tube is low.

152

Now multiply that times millions, or even billions of people squirting toothpaste on brushes every day. That's free money, Josh."

There was a slight pause. David thought he had impressed the boy and gotten through to him. He didn't expect Josh's response.

"I disagree David. That's just inflation. It's not true growth."

"But what's the difference, Josh? This man made the company millions by, pardon the pun, squeezing more profit out of a business model that already appeared perfect. It already seemed as efficient as it could be. And if someone uses ten or twenty percent more toothpaste, it doesn't hurt them. It's not a net negative."

"But it's not a net positive either. It's a hidden tax. The company may have made more money, but they did it on the backs of everyone else without them having a choice. That's coercive."

"No, Josh, it's not coercive. It's reality. A hidden tax is a two or three percent merchant fee on every single credit card transaction in the country. That's a hidden tax. Making the hole in the toothpaste tube a few microns wider? That's genius. Josh, no matter how you slice it, not just us, but anyone in the health care field only comes up with new drugs to generate revenue. That's the bottom line."

David breathed deeply. He didn't want to have to be so direct with Josh, but he figured if he were already playing poker in the illegal clubs at twenty, he probably had as jaded a view of humanity as David did. There was a long pause, which was odd for Josh, who was usually very quick to converse.

"David. My father told me that the reason that we have 1.75 liter jugs of booze is because they used to be a half gallon, and then one of the companies cut the size of the bottle just slightly and kept the same price point. And it worked. And everyone else did the same. I believe him. Why else would we have such a funny unit?"

"Your father's a smart guy. Haven't you noticed that in other things?"

"Yeah. Orange juice."

153

"Right. Orange Juice," said David.

"And Lenny down at the club. He always says, 'a 2x4 isn't a 2x4 any more.'"

"Right. It's not. Josh, I had a chance to meet an equity analyst once who told about Connors Brothers. Have you heard of them?"

"No. What do they make?"

"They made Bumblebee tuna, Josh."

"Oh, I've heard of that."

"So, this man tells me that after they sell the company, the first thing the new owners do is change the size of the tuna can from six ounces to five ounces and keep the price the same. It's an instant sixteen percent markup. People don't even really see the difference. Less tuna in each can. Less steel to make each can. People buy more tuna in an economic slowdown because it's a low-end basic consumer staple that's high in protein. It's recession-proof."

"Everybody eats tuna," said Josh.

"Right. Everybody eats tuna. Do you know why I'm telling you this, Josh?"

"Not really."

"I want you to think about this. It's just what you said. 'Everyone eats tuna.' There's truth in that statement. But it's not just tuna. It's everything. Every commodity. Every service. We're all caught up in this huge system of epic proportions. It's the whole *thing* that's coercive. I don't care if you're a vegan. Where do you think that shoe leather came from? You drive a car? You got leather seats in it? It's all self-reinforcing. It's America. You can either play, or be played. I'm giving you a huge opportunity here. I'm offering you work right out of college for a major firm working directly under a decision-maker. You're ahead of the game. Don't blow it for some misplaced idealism. The chips have already all been placed. Be on the winning side. Honestly Josh, I don't even care if you want to work on the 153 project. Forget it. It's off the table. I just want you at our company. Period."

David was breathing heavily again. He saw a younger version of himself in Josh. Idealistic. Probably still a Democrat. But he had gotten a little later start because no one had actually explained all this to him as directly as he was attempting to. He truly felt like he was helping him, not ruining him. Josh's reply was distant.

"Okay, David. I appreciate everything you just said, and thank you for speaking to me like an adult."

"You're welcome, Josh."

"Anyway, I just think that maybe my talents might be better utilized by a smaller firm. In fact, I was thinking about maybe even opening my own organization, you know?"

Poor, misguided boy, thought David. But then he remembered that this was *his* first response to being told that the ocean was full of fish swimming in schools, and each of those schools was a company, and being part of a company gave you strength and power. There were so many fish trying to swim alone out there. And nine out of ten got eaten. No, he was going to have to let Josh figure this out on his own. He would stay close.

"I respect that Josh. I never had the balls to try to open my own business. Always liked that paycheck at the end of the week. Or, I guess now that direct deposit receipt."

Josh laughed. "I know. It's like, you don't even get a paycheck any more. Who uses those?"

David laughed. "Josh, I…"

"I think for my birthday I'll just say, 'Grandma, here's my account number and my nine-digit ABA routing number for when you want to make the ACH deposit.'" Both the men laughed.

"I'll be in touch, Josh. Will I see you at the club anytime soon?"

"No, I have some stuff to take care of."

"Okay. Take care." He clicked off.

Josh stared at his computer screen. He had been doing a lot of reading about something dubbed "Operation Web Tryp," which was a DEA covert operation that ended in 2004. The government had gone after a bunch of online retailers of very specialized chemicals, mostly unregulated compounds that were discovered or researched after the scheduling of some of the better-known hallucinogens years before. These chemical supply houses were selling these "grey-market" drugs that were not *technically* illegal, but could be probably be prosecuted under something called The Federal Analog Act.

Josh was extremely interested in studying the early history of the movement he was effectively injecting himself into. He had ingested so many different "research chemicals," that he knew these to be powerful enough to be on the government's radar. And it wasn't that he wouldn't have loved to be one of these online sellers himself. To the contrary, he read that many of these companies netted tens, even hundreds of thousands of dollars. But he wasn't being driven by the money—his father had accidentally given him that. He wanted to make a statement. And he didn't want to end up in the federal pen like his dad—he could never do that to his mother.

He was working on the second-order, the derivative. He was attempting to create the first "derivative" product to sell "shares" of a pool of information, whose value would come from the future worth presently legal grey-market research chemicals. He was betting the "share price" of his derivative investment vehicle would significantly increase over time as those legal drugs were made illegal. For Josh, as the fund's creator, it was just going to be a matter of deciding a sell point. It was his own IPO, his own initial public offering of a hedge bet against fascism.

He was going to make all that business about skirting the law by calling these things "research chemicals" instead of what they were, "drugs," a moot point. He was going to push the issue. And what's the worst that could really happen? His girlfriend had left him. His dad was in jail. How, really, could this get any worse? Fuck David, he thought. Fuck David, and his fucking Mercedes. And his house in the suburbs. He was taking it all down. He popped on to Facebook and clicked on Corbett Reynolds.

He's so gay, thought Josh. The first thing I see on his page is that he "likes" his own company. Of course he likes Omicrone. He made Omicrone. He *is* Omicrone. He messaged him.

"c. u there?"

"Hi Josh. Long time."

"c. worried about nlc. want to publicize the church more. don't want any heat."

"Josh I think if you don't do too much, everything will become clearer. Just sit on it. It'll grow. You have a real good thing there. Keep writing more articles. ☺"

"k. ty." He clicked off of chat. He looked at his status.

Josh Grenier is...

He looked at the empty bar. Josh Grenier is a lot of things, he thought. He typed into the bar: "Josh Grenier is going to start selling pirozatum to bored housewives."

Almost immediately, one of his friends from high school who he never talked to any more (and didn't even care for) commented, "what's pirozatum?" Before he could respond he saw that David Evans liked his post.

He's watching me, thought Josh. He's watching me.

Call

Morgan had just gotten off her phone and was putting on makeup—she always wore some, but was taking just a little extra time today to put on a tad more than usual. She looked in the mirror and attempted to work with her hair, which was just not behaving.

Laida was supposed to come over her apartment and the two of them were going to watch a movie together called *Being John Malkovich*. They were talking about it the last time they were together at the store—both of them had only ever seen parts of it when they were really high, and neither of them had ever watched the whole thing all the way through. It would be the first time Morgan was going to see Laida outside of the store.

"It's crazy," said Morgan. "They crawl through this little hole in this weird little short floor with low ceilings in this office building designed for midgets, and then they end up falling out of the sky on to the side of the New Jersey Turnpike. That's some tripped out shit, oh my *God!*"

"I never saw *that* part," said Laida. "It must've been in the beginning. I just remember seeing the part where Cameron Diaz wants to sleep with the other woman, but only when she's inside of Malkovich and operating him like a robot while taking over his body." Laida twirled her hair.

"Oh my God that's nuts. Nuts." She paused. "I mean, do you really want to come over?"

"Do you not want me to?"

"No, no, it's not that. I just never have people come and see my apartment. It's a total mess." Morgan was actually excited—she didn't get too many visitors and had always wanted to get to know Laida. She seemed cool.

"Honey, I don't give a shit. You should see where I live."

They both laughed.

"You're sure Danny V. doesn't care?"

"Fuck him. We've been working a lot lately. I need a break. I'll come over after dinner?"

"That's awesome. How about, like, at eight?"

"See you soon," Laida said as she walked out.

She and Dan had just sold them a few Dewalt multi-tool combo packs, a half dozen electric razors and electric toothbrushes, and a whole bunch of memory cards including the original store display, all of them still inside the theft-resistant hard plastic packaging usually removed at the register. After they left, Michael had made Morgan take each of the memory cards and flash drives out of the plastic so they didn't look stolen—there was no tool to do it, so she was using a utility knife in the back room. She called it "men's work," and she hated it. He told her to put the destroyed security tags into a black plastic trash bag, and then toss the bag into the neighboring Asian food store's dumpster.

"Ugh. Mike! Don't make me do that! That dumpster stinks!"

"Exactly," he replied. "No one's gonna' go in there and fish that shit out. Just throw it in."

She carried the bag out and had to cover her nose when she opened the dumpster door—it looked like someone had piled about a thousand pounds of rotten mangoes inside. The stench was horrifying. She cursed Michael and threw the bag inside, making her way back to the store. Danny V. and Laida were gone when she had gotten back.

She was looking forward to spending a little time with Laida. She actually had a lot of questions for her, about being transgender and stuff, but she never wanted to be rude and just ask her things in the store. She knew Laida appreciated that and respected her for it. Morgan didn't have many female friends. She was the type to maybe have one really close girlfriend that she did everything with to the exclusion of everyone else. And right now she was alone.

The knock on her door was a little louder than she expected. She wondered if Laida still did things like knock on a door like a man would, or if she just automatically started doing it a little softer and gentler after she became a woman. Imagine, "becoming a woman," but not ever being a girl. And did men even knock on the door differently than women? Her thoughts moved back to words.

"Come on in!"

"Hi!" said Laida with a smile. "Sorry. I didn't bring anything."

"That's okay. I wasn't, um, really expecting a hostess gift or anything."

"Uh-huh." Laida looked a little high. Her eyes were just not responsive. The lids looked like they were sitting just slightly lower on her eyes than they should. Like a big sedan packed down with five adults—just a little less room between the wheel wells and the tires, but something you only noticed because you've seen thousands of those same sedans with only one person in them. And her consonants were just slightly slurred, but at the same time coming out slightly faster. Her skin looked taut.

"That's cool. I think there are some American cheese slices in the fridge and some Bugles in the cupboard. There are a couple frozen pizzas in the freezer but my toaster oven's broken."

Laida looked around the scantily furnished apartment. It was a one-bedroom with a dumpy little dim kitchen, and dull walls that had lost their sheen with what looked to be like years of cigarette smoke baked into the walls without the smell. In the living room, there were just two chairs and a lobster trap with a piece of glass on top of it for a coffee table/ottoman. There was no television in the room.

"Is there even a TV in here?" asked Laida kind of incredulously.

"Oh, yeah," said Morgan, slightly embarrassed. "We can watch on my laptop." She had a pretty nice, pretty large laptop that she proceeded to plug into the wall.

"Well don't worry about that now. Can I have a glass of water?"

160

"Oh my God, I'm sorry, I'm a terrible hostess. You want a beer?"

"Yeah, that would be awesome," she said as Morgan disappeared. She looked nicer than usual, thought Laida. Morgan handed her a beer and went back to fiddling with the computer.

"Who drinks Killian's?" asked Laida.

"What do you want, a Sierra Nevada?" replied Morgan. "This isn't a bar." She laughed and went with it. "No really, Lai. You want a Beck's? A Fat Tire? We got Magic Hat on tap, Stella Artois, and Dos Equiis."

"Stay thirsty, my friends," said Laida, dropping the register of her voice.

"Oh my God!" Morgan laughed and snorted. "You sounded just like the Dos Equiis guy! That's amazing! You sounded totally like a man! I didn't even know you could do that! I've never even heard you talk like that! I mean, your voice. It's not low. Oh my God!" She continued laughing.

"I like those commercials," said Laida sheepishly.

"No, I know, it's not *that*, it's just, I didn't, um, I didn't know you could talk like a man."

"Well, I'm a girl, so I don't want to sound like a man."

"But I didn't even know you *could*." Morgan was nervous.

"You know Morgan, the hormones don't change your voice." Laida paused. Morgan was nodding eagerly, and was waiting for her to continue. I guess she wants to know, thought Laida. She went on. "So, once your voice changes, it changes."

"So, your natural voice is low, like a man's?"

"Yes."

"Say something to me. Like a man."

"*Why don't you go make me and my friends some jalapeño poppers and grab that 18-pack of Bud Light—Jets kick off in ten minutes. And make it fucking quick!*" said Laida, her voice clearly in the masculine register. Morgan was laughing hysterically—the disconnect was just too profound. That pretty face, those perky breasts, and that man's voice. It was just too much. She felt like she was watching a Japanese film dubbed in English, and the characters' voices didn't line up. After her fit of laughing she looked up and saw Laida smiling too, but with sad eyes.

"Oh, I'm so sorry Laida!" Her gaze softened. "I didn't mean to laugh at you. It's just funny. I mean, I didn't mean to..."

"No, it's okay, Morgan. I don't mind—I like you."

"Thanks, Lai."

"I just don't talk like that. Ever. I mean, I actually have to stay really vigilant about it and never let myself slip into that. I had to train my voice to be higher, and then talk like that all the time."

"So, you have to try to talk in a higher voice, like a woman?"

"Yes."

"So your voice doesn't just change once you *become* a woman?"

"No," replied Laida. "It's lower because my vocal chords thickened before I started taking hormones. When I had my growth spurt and my voice changed, that was it. That's irreversible, unless you want to have surgery where they scrape your vocal chords."

"That sounds really bad." Morgan shivered. "It sounds like it would hurt like hell."

"It does. That's why I haven't done it. And it's expensive. And if they make a mistake, or you have any complications, you could lose a lot more. It's just easier to talk a little higher."

"But you always have to consciously do that?"

"You heard what my voice sounded like when I did nothing."

"Yeah. You're the fuckin' Dos Equiis guy." Morgan laughed.

"Right."

"Wow. That means you can never let your guard down."

"No. Never."

"Wow. I'm sorry."

"No, it's okay. I let my guard down with you because I feel safe here. I mean, you invited me to your house. And you seem cool."

"Thanks. Seriously, Lai, I'm sorry. I didn't mean to embarrass you."

"It's okay. It's hard to explain. It kind of brings up complex feelings. My parents really don't approve, and they don't talk to me."

"Oh."

"It was hard growing up. Especially knowing what I know now. I mean, if my parents had let me take hormone blockers before I got to puberty, my voice would have never changed at all. I probably would've been able to grow up with natural breasts and rounder hips too. There's a lot to it."

"Wow, I mean, I just didn't know it was that complicated. The voice was just funny, you know?" said Laida.

"When I talk like that, it actually reminds me of being 'Larry.'"

"Oh my God! Your name was Larry? I didn't *know* that! Are you serious?"

"Yeah, I was a Larry." She looked up and far away. "Larry. It's like that person doesn't exist any more. Like, he was my brother who died in a car wreck or something. Like, he used to be a person but he's not any more. Just gone."

"Wow," said Morgan. This was heavy, she thought. No wonder Laida got high so much. But she had so many questions.

"So, do you feel like the boy part of you died? Or like, I mean, I don't get it. I mean, you really *were* a person named Larry."

"Yeah. My parents named me Larry, but I never really felt like that was my name. It was really confusing growing up, and growing up is really confusing anyway."

"Tell me about it," shrugged Morgan. "I mean, I don't really want to go back to being in high school. But I still don't understand. I mean, you were born a normal boy, and everyone treated you like a boy growing up, right?"

"Well the crazy thing is, I never felt like a boy. That's the weird part. It's like, I looked in the mirror and saw a boy when I was little, and I looked at other boys. And I knew I was supposed to be like them. But I just wasn't. I knew I was a girl."

"But, like, did you play with trucks and stuff, and footballs and stuff like boys, or did you play with girls' toys growing up?"

163

"You don't understand. My parents didn't accept this. So, they gave me boys' stuff to play with. My father's a macho guy. He's *real* traditional. And he wore the pants in the house. I played with whatever he told me to."

"But did you want to play with dolls?"

"Well, yeah. But I wasn't allowed to have them. I remember I stole a Barbie doll from one of my friend's houses when I was little. It was his sister's and I was over there playing in the dirt in the backyard with him, and when we went inside and had to pee, I saw it on the floor in the living room. Before I left, I told my friend I think I'd forgotten something. I went in and grabbed the doll and put it down my pants and brought it home."

"Wow."

"I know. And I got her home and I played with her and, you know, I brushed her hair and pretended I was her, and pretended to go to the mall and stuff. I mean, I only had one set of clothes for her so there wasn't too much I could do. And then I remember the phone rang and my heart was just in my throat as soon as I heard that ring. And it was my friends' mom asking my mom if I had taken the doll."

"What did she do?" Morgan looked at her expectantly.

"She asked me and I started to cry and gave her the doll back. My mom was so nice about it. She tried to explain that I had probably done it because I had a little crush on my friend's sister. I still remember the sister. Her name was Marissa and she was repulsive. She was fat and her face wasn't symmetrical and it was a little crooked and I hated her. I don't even think her mom believed me that I had a crush on her. She took the doll away from me and I cried. And after that they started calling me little faggot or fag and told me I was gay. I was seven."

"Wow," said Morgan. "I just…I don't know what to say."

"It's okay. I'm fine now. I'm just saying that it was really hard. Really hard growing up the wrong sex."

"That's crazy."

"It is. It's like, I close my eyes and look in the mirror and I see a pretty girl, and then I open them and I see a dumb boy. You have no idea what that's like. I mean, there's a total disconnect

164

between how you feel inside, and how you look on the outside." She paused. "Morgan?"

Morgan was just staring at her. She had no idea of the complexity of this. It was amazing to her. She had never even thought about stuff like this before. She just thought Laida was the most interesting girl she had ever met. She felt that Laida probably had a very deep understanding of her world around her because of what she had to go through to get to where she was.

"I'm sorry, Lai. It's just amazing. I mean, I really respect you. I never wanted to ask you this stuff because I respect you a lot. I know it's private and I know you don't know me that well, but I'm not going to go and tell this to everybody. I'm just really curious. In a good way. Like, I want to learn. I always just wanted to know."

"I understand, Morgan. I like you too. There are a lot of assholes out there and you are *not* one of them." She smiled.

"So, you said you think of yourself before as like a boy that died?"

"Not really. It's a little different than that. I never felt like a boy at all—other people told me that I was a boy, but I just never believed it. It made me not believe anything that anyone said. Honestly, I thought that this life just had to be some bad dream and I was going to wake up from it someday."

"I hear that," countered Morgan. "I mean, sometimes when I smoke pot I think that this whole life I'm living is just a dream, and in real life I'm just in a bed somewhere, or in like a pod, like in *The Matrix* and none of this is real. Or that it's like *Inception* and I'm just dreaming and can't wake up like that guy."

Laida laughed. "I hear *that*. Except that I felt like God had made some sort of big mistake and I was supposed to be born a girl, but that I was a boy instead. When I was younger I used to think that I had had like, twenty past lives that I couldn't remember, and in each one of those past lives I was actually a woman, and had lived life as a woman. Like, my soul is a woman's soul no matter what. And like, I had gotten through the maze and gotten the cheese. Or, I had been successful, and so God gave me more and more of a challenge each time. And this time, I was given the ultimate challenge—to switch and start off as a boy. But my soul is a woman's."

"That's neat," said Morgan. "My mother used to always tell me that the Greeks thought we were all hermaphrodites before we were born, and then the gods cut one half and made a woman, and the other half and made a man. And then those two halves tried to meet each other on earth and that's what soulmates were."

"That's really beautiful."

"Yeah, I guess it is, and I have absolutely no idea why I just said that. I don't think I've thought of that for years and years." Morgan laughed as she remembered fondly.

Laida paused. "I don't know how that would apply to me."

"Well you're both already. That's the best," said Morgan. "And honestly, if I can say this, you're beautiful Lai. Seriously. There's just no way that you were supposed to be a man. I mean look at you. You have such smooth skin and your hair is so shiny and your breasts are amazing. I'm so jealous."

"Stop. That's really nice. Honestly, it's the hormones."

"Really?"

"Really. It's the same as birth control."

"No way." She paused and thought about it. "Really? So, you're telling me that if a guy takes birth control, he'd look like you?"

"*No!*" she laughed. If only it were that easy, she thought. "No, I take, like, ten times the amount of hormones a woman would take for birth control."

"Ten times? Like, you eat ten birth control pills?"

"Well, I mean, they have stronger pills."

"And when can you stop taking them?"

"I can't."

"You have to take them forever?"

"For the rest of my life."

"But Lai, aren't you worried that it's not safe?"

"Well, yeah, there's always that. But I don't care."

She does take other drugs, thought Morgan, but I'm not going to ask her about that. And I smoke a lot of pot. I kinda' just want to keep asking her about being trans. It's pretty neat, thought Morgan.

166

"But how can you not care? So they're safe to take? I mean, what would they do to me?"

"Well, your breasts would get a little bigger. And your skin stays clear so you break out less."

"Um, what's wrong with that?" asked Morgan.

"Nothing."

"So why aren't we all taking these hormones?"

"Because of the health risks," said Laida.

"You just told me they're safe."

"*Relatively* safe."

Morgan looked at her with a bitchy face. Why was it so hard to get a straight answer out of her, she thought. Laida's so passive-aggressive. Then it hit her—Laida is such a girl. No wonder she changed—she was *definitely* not a guy. Guys must not have known what to make of her as a him. Morgan's face softened and she laughed.

"What?"

"Nothing, it's just funny. Lai, you're such a girl."

"I know I am," she said matter-of-factly. "Can I have another Killian's?"

"Oh my God have all of them. This douchebag guy left them here and I don't want them."

"He your boyfriend?" asked Laida when she got another one. She heard no response. When she got back, Morgan was sparking an old dirty glass bowl. She uncapped her beer and sat back down. Morgan's face was all scrunched up as she held the pipe out to Laida. Laida put her hand up to refuse.

"I'm good," she said. "Pot makes me paranoid. I'll just have some more beer."

Morgan breathed out a long, smoky exhale pointed toward the floor, and then started coughing. Laida handed her the open beer and she took a swig. She handed the beer back.

"I'm sorry—I didn't wipe it. I'm not sick or anything."

"I know that," laughed Laida. "I'd share a beer with you anytime." She smiled and Morgan's face slowly returned to its original color.

"Well, thanks. I'm glad you finally came over. It sucks in that store. I'm there all the time."

167

"Well I mean, it *is* a pawn shop. You don't really go there when you're doing really well, you know. Don't you get depressed working in there?"

"No, not really. It's funny and the guys treat me nice. Mike and Carlo are good guys, they really are."

"I don't know them that well in there. Danny takes care of most of the business. I'm just there with him."

"So, Lai, where did you meet Danny?"

"Club 12-20. You know where that is?"

"I know the place. The gay club."

"Yeah."

"He's gay?" asked Morgan. "I mean, I guess that makes sense if he runs with you."

"He's straight."

"Oh." Morgan got confused. "Sorry. I mean, you met him at the gay club."

"If a guy likes me, he's not gay. I'm a woman." She sounded a little defensive.

"No, I understand that Lai. I'm sorry. Really, I'm sorry, it's just confusing."

"It's okay, Morgan. It *is* confusing. Honestly, whether I'm with a man or a woman, people could call me gay once they know I'm trans. I mean, think about it. If I'm with a man, people would say, well, they both have penises so that's what gay is. And if I'm with a woman people would say, well, they're both women so they're lesbos."

So she has her penis still, thought Morgan. I wasn't going to ask her that but I really wanted to know, she thought. Morgan began speaking.

"Yeah, I mean, I remember a guy called me a lesbo once and he got me really mad. I like cock. I just didn't like *his* cock. It was crooked and he wasn't clean and he had tiny balls. So he thinks that because I don't like him I must be a lesbian."

"That's so typical," responded Laida. "Like, they're too proud and arrogant. You must just be a dyke."

"I know, right? But I'm not a lesbian. I don't know what I'd do with...I mean, another woman's thing in my face? That's just disgusting. I just...I don't know. It kind of freaks me out..." Her voice trailed off.

168

"No. I know. I like guys too."

"Is that normal?" The irony of that question was not lost on Morgan. She caught herself. "I mean, do most trannies like guys?"

"Well, first of all, I don't think of myself as a tranny. I'm a woman who was born a man. Or a woman who was mistakenly raised as a man. But never a man, or anyone who is part man. I'm just *a woman*."

"*With a penis*," laughed Morgan with a snort. She was overwhelmed by the ridiculousness of the whole thing.

"Yes. A woman with a penis. I know. It sounds kind of dumb."

"Not *dumb*, just a little weird," laughed Morgan.

"Well, it's normal for me."

"Right. It is normal for you," smiled Morgan. "So, Lai, I mean, can you tell me how that feels? I mean, when you look at yourself in the mirror, does it look wrong? Like, you should have a vagina there?"

"Can I tell you the truth?" asked Laida.

"Yeah," said Morgan. She was pretty stoned.

"When I was younger I just looked at a lot of porn. A lot of porn with shemales in it. I mean, it's really one of the only places to see someone like me on the internet. So I just made it normal. Some women have penises, some women have vaginas. But they're all women."

Morgan was just staring at her. What a mindfuck, she thought. She couldn't imagine having to do that sort of thing to feel normal. She reached for her pipe and started packing another bowl, almost unconsciously.

"That's, uh, *interesting*. Laida. You're very *interesting*."

"Thanks Morgan. I'm gonna' pee and get another beer." She got up and Morgan started fumbling with the laptop. She had the movie and was trying to get the disc in, and then the drive wasn't reading it. She took it out and wiped it on her shirt to get any fingerprints off it, and she ended up dropping it and it rolled under the couch. Laida walked back into the living room a little drunk, only to see Morgan on her knees reaching under the sofa.

She has a really nice body, thought Laida. It was the first time she had ever thought that about a woman. Then Morgan stood up with her back to Laida and in her stoned daze, stuck both her arms up in the air to stretch, with the center hole of the disc on her finger, tipping it slightly like the rings of Saturn. Before she turned around Laida figured it out—she had broad shoulders and a narrow waist and narrow hips like a man. Like a man with breasts and a pretty girl's face. Morgan turned around—she was high, high, high. Her eyes felt like they were open really big but they were really small.

"So, Laida. I mean, can you show me what you're talking about? I mean, I don't want to make you uncomfortable. I'm just really curious. My ex used to have all sorts of porn, but never anything with shemales. He'd say that was gay."

"Oh my God, you don't make me uncomfortable. You've never seen a shemale on the computer before?"

Morgan looked at her dumbly. "No. I mean, I think there was some video I saw on someone's phone, I think, where the camera moved down all the way over a woman's body and then she had a penis. I don't know, my stupid friend was laughing the whole time."

"Can I use the laptop?"

"Yeah."

Laida started typing and the background changed. There appeared to be all sorts of thumbnails on the screen.

"Lai, I'm not going to get a virus or anything, right?" It would kill her if she had to have that bitch Lexi come and fix the computer. That would just be the turd icing on the shit cake, she thought.

"No, this site is okay. I go on it. Look."

Laida handed her the computer and put it on her lap. She sucked down the last of her beer until it was just foam sliding slowly down the inside of the bottle. Morgan couldn't believe what she was seeing. It was an entire web page of naked and half-naked women, most of them with cocks visible. Most of them looked a *lot* like women who were women at birth. Morgan started scrolling through.

"This is unbelievable. These are *all* transwomen?"

"Yeah. Pretty amazing, huh?"

"These aren't just regular women with penises Photoshopped on?"

"Not on this site."

Morgan was silent and kept scrolling through. She clicked on one of the links—it showed a dark-haired woman with a penis with two men. She clicked the movie—it came on for about ten seconds with sound. She was enthralled. She could *not* look away. She even sounds like a woman, she thought, and totally looks like one. Except she has that cock flopping around. That's nuts. The video stopped playing. She put the laptop down on the floor.

"That's crazy, Lai." She paused. "I mean, I'm sorry, not crazy bad, I mean...I mean...I've just never seen anything like that before." Laida smiled.

"That's okay. You don't offend me."

"Wow. Wow. That's all I have to say. Wow. And I was really looking forward to watching the John Malkovich movie. Seriously, that clip was just so much more interesting than anything else I've ever seen."

"Well, shemales aren't really something you see every day."

"No, that's true," said Morgan. She paused. "Can you fix the computer, Lai? I'm having a problem with it."

She packed another bowl, sparked it up, and stared off into space. There's a woman with a penis in my house, thought Morgan. I could totally hook up with Laida. I mean, I never slept with a woman because I like cock, but she has one of those. I mean, her breasts are really nice, and her face is pretty. She glanced over at Laida, who was fully focused on the laptop. She closed her eyes for a moment and envisioned grabbing a full, firm, breast and rubbing her clit. She felt a little stirring inside of her. She snapped out of it, but not before feeling warmth wash over her face and down her spine.

"It's not reading the disc," said Laida. "I think it might be the drive. Like, the eyeball on the drive could be dirty? If you have some computer duster to spray in there it might help."

"No," she said from a far away place. "I don't have any of that. It just stopped working, sorry. You know a lot about computers."

"Cars, too," she said.

"Huh?"

171

"Well, when you're raised as a boy you learn about cars and tools and computers and stuff. People just talk about stuff like that to you."

"What do you mean?" asked Morgan.

"Well, what do girls talk about?" asked Laida.

"I don't know. Hair. Clothes. Style." She paused. "Other girls."

"True."

"But yeah, clothes, stuff like that."

"Right. Like a sale at the mall or a new line of housewares or paint colors, interior design, throw pillows, you know, our stuff. Guys don't talk about stuff like that. They talk about miles per gallon and taxes and insurance. They really want to know how much you pay for pellets for your stove. Is that flooring laminate? What type of primer required fewer coats on that wrought iron furniture? Does that router really deliver the megabits per second it advertises?"

"Sounds boring," interrupted Morgan.

"It *is* boring. But what I'm saying is, I had to listen to all that stuff for years, and so about computers and stuff I know some things. I think the worst case is that the whole drive is no good. You could get a used one online for not that much money. Best case, you buy a five-dollar can of computer duster and spray it in there and it should work." Laida paused. "I drank almost all your beer."

"I told you not to worry about that. You're so polite."

"If the worst thing someone can say about me is that I'm too polite, I'm doing okay."

"Yeah, you're right," said Morgan. "I'm the impolite one. I invite you over and then the computer broke. I mean, we could just watch it in the bedroom. It's a queen size bed, and there's plenty of room, and there's even a comforter on it." Morgan was wondering if Laida were feeling her. Laida seemed to be holding eye contact with her longer than she was before, but Morgan couldn't really remember how much pot she'd smoked. It could just be a trick of her mind.

"Oh! That's okay. I thought that this was the only thing you had to watch it on."

Morgan led her into the bedroom and snapped on the light next to the bed. She had a queen-sized bed with a white down comforter on it, and a 42" flatscreen television mounted on the wall. Morgan grabbed the movie and put it in the player, and fiddled with the TV.

"That's a really nice TV. It's big."

"Pawn shop," Morgan said quickly as she hopped on top of the bed.

The girls arranged the pillows to prop themselves up against the headboard, and kept moving their legs around to get situated on top of the bed. The comforter was getting all bunched up, and so were the pillows. Finally, they found a comfortable position to lay still, both on their backs looking up toward the screen. After resting there for a minute, Morgan felt what she thought was the bunched up comforter move from under the sole of her foot.

"Oh my God, I thought that was the blanket, I'm sorry."

"It's okay," said Laida. She paused for the most miniscule extra amount of time. Her voice dropped in register just a hair, and got just a tiny bit breathier. "You can touch me."

Laida stayed lying on her back looking up at Morgan. Her breasts sat firm on top of her chest. Morgan moved and turned on her side. She was laying on her side staring at Laida's face. She really has a beautiful face, she thought. You can see hints of masculinity in it, but it's definitely feminine. It's like looking at someone who's biracial or half-Asian. They're just beautiful. Their eyes locked.

I'm not going to kiss this girl, thought Laida. I'm still a little high from before, and now I'm almost drunk, and I don't know anything about Morgan. Maybe she's this crazy person. If she wants me, she can make the first move. I've already come over her house, gotten into her bed, and showed her porn on the computer. I've done my part in this whole thing that I didn't even know was happening on a conscious level, and I only got this idea in my head after looking at her stretching and realizing she looked a little like a man. I've just never been with a woman and maybe I just need to get this out of my system to know I want to be with men. But I don't want to use this girl as an experiment—I won't try to turn her out. I don't really want to be pushing myself on her. If she wants me, she'll take me.

Morgan was staring at Laida's face for what felt like the longest time, saying nothing and not moving. She felt like she wasn't even breathing any more. She started to envision the act, and then what it meant for her. She wasn't gay. She never felt gay. Was that what was stopping her? Her hang-ups about sexuality she had always thought that she didn't have? She had never even kissed a woman, except that one time when she was drunk and she made out with that random chick to get this hot guy's attention. But this person before her, she wasn't *really* a woman. Was she? She had a penis. How could she be gay if she were having sex with someone with a penis? Yet, here she was, her legs entwined with another woman's in her bedroom. No one has to know. She's drunk. I'm high. It doesn't matter.

I wonder why she doesn't kiss me, thought Laida. She's been staring at me for so long. I'm not going to move. I'm not kissing her. No matter what. If she kisses me, that's a different story.

I wonder why she doesn't kiss me, thought Morgan. Then it hit her—*she* was the girl. Morgan was "the man," and Laida was "the girl." At first, the thought was a little disgusting to her. She didn't want to be like a man, she wanted to be *taken* by a man. Then she started thinking about the different men she'd been with, and how after they were laying next to her after sex she had wished that they were women so that then they could talk and go shop together. Like, sex with a best friend, instead of sex with some douchebag guy. So, she was going to have to be the man. Maybe she could do this.

Morgan gingerly leaned in and kissed Laida gently on the lips, softly and quietly. One, two, three, four little kisses on her lower lip without parting her own. Then she pulled back and licked her lips. Laida paused. This is happening, she thought. Laida closed her eyes and put her hand on Morgan's ear, pulling her head toward hers. Their lips met in the middle.

They lay on their sides, just gently kissing for a few minutes. They each rested their hands on the others' cheeks. Laida gently caressed Morgan's hair and moved her hand down, gently squeezing her broad shoulders. Morgan did the same, caressing Laida's shoulders as their lips locked. Laida took Morgan's hand and gently moved it to her breast. Morgan gently squeezed it and felt the blood rush between her legs. She never thought she'd be aroused like this from another woman. She wanted that breast in her mouth.

She moved Laida on to her back and pulled her V-neck shirt down. With her other hand she dug the breast out of her bra. She had small areolas with small nipples, just beautiful and perfect. She licked the tiny nipple a few times and then started sucking. Laida arched her back and unhooked her bra, sliding the straps off and taking her top off. Laying there topless in the bed, Morgan saw the dark scars under each breast. Laida grabbed her breasts from the bottom and held them close together. The skin was perfect.

"Suck my tits," she said softly into Morgan's ear.

Morgan grabbed the outside of her breasts and pressed them roughly together. She was thinking about how men had touched her—she could do that to Lai. It was a new adventure. She started sucking and gently biting the nipples. She wished she could have both of them in her mouth at once. She buried her nose in her cleavage and took a deep inhale—her skin smelled like traces of perfume, but her natural scent was beautiful. She smelled wonderful. Like both man and woman at once. She went back up and started kissing Laida's beautiful full lips again. Laida squeezed her breasts together and pressed them against Morgan's chest. Morgan inhaled sharply—she was starting to get wet.

Morgan sat up and got on her knees and took her shirt off. She was kneeling on the bed in a balconet bra with a lace fringe in a salmon pink color. Laida grabbed up at her breasts.

"No..."

"What, no," responded Laida, who started tonguing her ear.

"No, yours are so perfect."

They kept kissing, speaking in hushed breathy tones.

"They're fake."

"I wish mine were fake."

"Just be quiet. I love your body."

"You do?"

175

"Oh my God, Morgan, you turn me on."

"God. You turn *me* on." Morgan knelt over Laida. Laida put her arms around her and unhooked the back of her bra and pulled her close. Their breasts fell on top of each other and the flesh rubbed together. Morgan felt herself getting wetter. Laida reached up and squeezed her breasts—they were soft, real D-cups. They felt amazing. Morgan reached and squeezed Laida's breasts. She stepped outside of herself and saw this act, these two women on a bed caressing each others breasts—it turned her on even more. She furiously began kissing Laida.

Sitting up for a second, she looked deep into Laida's eyes. Morgan wanted her. Morgan wanted Laida inside of her. She leaned down and whispered in her ear.

"I want you *in* me," she said in a breathy whisper, and then kissed her ear. More blood flowed into Laida's organ. She reached down and moved her panties out of the way. It was getting harder as she moved it. Morgan unzipped her pants and dug her hand inside her lacy undies. She brought out two dripping fingers and shoved them into Laida's mouth, who began sucking and licking her juices off of them.

"See how wet you make me?" she whispered. She took her fingers out of Lai's mouth and licked them, tasting a little bit of herself. She returned her fingers to her panties, pulled out her wet index finger and rubbed her juices all over her right nipple, which stood to attention as she rubbed it gently. She returned her fingers once more, and coated her left areola with her juices and then shoved her breasts into Laida's mouth. She sucked and sucked and started moaning. She freed one of her hands and brought it down to her cock and started rubbing. Morgan watched her hand, and she started rubbing her clit.

Laida took one hand and held Morgan's breast, sucking on the soft skin and the large nipple and rubbing her cock with her other hand. Morgan got up and took her pants off—all she was wearing was a tiny pair of lacy hiphuggers. Laida could see the shape of her swollen labia through the moist panties. Morgan looked at Laida's left breast. The little nipple stood to attention. She spread her legs and started to ride Lai's breast, rubbing the nipple against her clit. She didn't even know why she was even

176

doing it—she'd never done that to a guy, but she just instinctively moved there. Her panties were soaking wet.

"Take them off," whispered Laida into her ear. The girls each paused to take off their panties. Morgan continued humping Lai's breast, her clit getting more swollen. The nipple flicked past her clit over and over in an increasing rhythm.

"I'm gonna' come," she said. She moaned twice and Laida felt her legs shudder and squeeze against her rib cage. She rolled off the breast and was breathing heavily, laying on her back next to Lai.

"Lick it off," whispered Laida, rubbing her erect cock. "Lick it off like a good little dyke."

That turned Morgan on again. She looked at the nipple, that one so red and angry and glistening with her own juices. She started sucking it and tasted herself. She closed her eyes—she wanted that cock. She finished licking and looked into Laida's eyes. Laida grabbed her wrist and guided her hand down to her cock. Morgan grabbed the shaft and started rubbing it. Laida's back arched up slightly.

"Suck it," whispered Laida. "Suck my cock, slut. Do it. Come on skank. Suck that cock." She pushed her head down and closed her eyes and smiled. Morgan was slobbering away, thick ropy saliva dripping down the side of her mouth and on to the comforter.

She holds my head like she's a guy, thought Morgan. And a cock is a cock. Hers is actually pretty nice—she keeps it shaven, it smells good. No wonder she didn't get rid of it—that would be such a shame. Morgan felt another wave of arousal begin to build inside of her.

"Do me," she said, rolling off Laida and on to her back next to her. As Laida got on her knees and moved over toward her, Morgan spread her legs and waited for Laida to start licking her clit. Laida used the tip of her tongue on her clit and gently used her fingers inside. Laida's tongue alternately moved from her clit to moving deep inside of her, tasting the salty reward as she found the right rhythm for her tongue, lapping at that salty fountain. She pulled her lips back and sucked her clit while she rubbed her cock. Finally, Morgan couldn't take it any more.

"Fuck me. Just fuck me. Please. Put it in me."

Laida steadied herself and slid herself inside Morgan. It took Morgan's breath away. She clung to Laida's body, mashing their breasts together and caressing Laida's hair as she moved in rhythm in and out of her. When she didn't see Lai's face, all she saw was her beautiful smooth womanly back and smooth, hairless backside, and her beautiful hair. She couldn't stand how much it turned her on. Laida rested her hands, palms down on the bed, and continued working. Morgan reached her neck up so that she could reach Lai's breasts. Sucking on her breasts while she penetrated her was amazing. Morgan could feel her get bigger and fuller the harder she sucked on the nipples. It was incredible—their bodies were wired exactly the same, except she had a cock. Sex with her was better than anything she'd ever imagined.

Laida flipped her on her side and slid inside of her from behind, the inside of her thigh rubbing against Morgan's swollen clit. Morgan took her right hand and started squeezing Laida's breast. She couldn't take it. She felt Laida's pace quicken, and knew she was going to come.

"Come with me," said Morgan as their breathing coalesced. The two locked eyes. She felt Laida's cock ready to burst. "Come with me. Come with me. *Put a baby in me!*"

Laida's mouth opened just slightly as the thrusting stopped and the two of them clung to each other, and they both sighed in ecstasy. Laida's organ pushed up against her cervix, and she felt it throbbing all through her. Bodies still connected, they moved slightly apart. Laida kissed her gently on her forehead several times, moving down to her temple, and then finally kissed her lips gingerly. Neither of them spoke for what seemed like an eternity. They just stared into each others' eyes. Finally, Laida's organ was soft enough that it started to slide out. Morgan coughed a little and helped it.

"You're *amazing,*" whispered Morgan. She smiled and squeezed Laida's soft body.

"No. *You're* amazing," she replied.

"That was the most *amazing* experience," said Morgan. "That was...that was the best sex of my life." She touched Laida on the arm.

178

"No, you're just saying that. But I thought that was amazing."

"No, you don't understand. That was the best sex I've ever had."

"Me too."

"What? Really?"

Laida turned to look right into Morgan's eyes.

"Morgan, I've never had sex with a woman. I didn't even know I liked women. But you, you're incredible. Just, how you smell and feel, and your breasts and your face and...you're perfect."

Morgan's eyes started to tear, but she didn't cry.

"Lai, you don't understand. Those guys I've slept with, that wasn't what I wanted. I want you. Making love to you was the most amazing thing I've ever done." The two lay next to each other on the bed.

"Did you know you wanted to sleep with me when I came over?" Laida put her arm across Morgan's chest and held her close.

"No."

"You swear?"

"Yeah," she said. "I thought we were going to watch the movie. I mean, I was glad we were getting to be better friends before. Like, that we were talking more at the store."

"I knew you wanted me."

"You did not!"

"I did," replied Laida. "I could tell when you met me. You were intrigued."

"Well, I did have a lot of questions for you. But I didn't want to..."

"Don't lie to me. You wanted to fuck me."

"Oh my god," said Morgan. "Egomaniac."

"Morgan, *you* kissed *me*."

Morgan shut her mouth. She *had* kissed Laida. And now, with this woman lying in her bed, all she wanted to do was kiss her again.

"Lai, what does this all mean? I didn't think I was gay, but after that, I don't know what end's up."

"There is no 'gay' and 'straight.' It's just not that simple."

179

"I mean, your tits, your cock…you're perfect."

"That's sweet, but I'm not perfect."

"No, I don't think you understand. That's a really nice combination. You're just a custom body. Like a custom car. You're custom. That's hot."

Laida looked at Morgan. She didn't know what she was getting into. Laida already wanted to get high again, and certainly not with the pot. She needed to see Danny V. again and needed to get some more junk. She didn't need it this minute though—she was nicely buzzed from the beer, and she was so relaxed from the release.

"Morgan, I don't know if you understand. You don't know what you're getting into."

"No, Lai, I get it. And I'm not going to talk about it with those stupid guys at the store. You just made love to me better than any man has in my life, and you have a great cock, great tits, you smell wonderful, and I think you're beautiful. I hope I can see you again."

Laida softened. She liked this woman too. She had never pictured herself with another woman, but the whole part of that was that she wanted so badly to be thought of as a woman herself, that she felt being with a man validated her. Being a straight woman was being a woman. Being a lesbian was…what *was* being a lesbian? Maybe she *was* a lesbian. Maybe she was just bisexual. In any case, it didn't matter. She was attracted to Morgan. Morgan had that boy shape, with the addition of the big boobs that she liked. She worked with all men, and spent all day with men. She was as feminine a woman as she was going to find that was for all intents and purposes a tomboy. So what did it matter about the details in the bedroom? She liked making love to Morgan more than getting fucked by any guy. This was something she was going to have to look into further.

Laida held Morgan close to her.

"Yes, we're going to see each other again."

"When?"

Laida stared at her. She could see that Morgan wanted more.

"When do you want?"

Morgan stared at her.

"Can I ask you something, Lai?"

"Yeah."

"Are you ready to go again?"

Laida moved toward her and gently started rubbing her breast.

"I'm ready."

"You're incredible," said Morgan, as she started kissing Laida again, tossing her on to her back and diving in.

The Flop

"Corbett Reynolds, please." Anthony Clark was annoyed that he had to wait. He'd run out of pistachios and the act of cracking them and eating them calmed his nerves. He did have Corbett's cell number somewhere, but after his phone got fried, he had to wait for the secretary at Omicrone to transfer him to voicemail. He just wasn't used to waiting.

"Corbett. Anthony Clark over at DEA. Call me back on my cell when you get a minute. Need to talk to you about a little something that came across my desk. The number is..." As he was speaking his cell buzzed, and he saw a number that looked vaguely familiar.

"Hello?"

"Tony, how are you?"

"Corb, nice to hear your voice."

"Tony, if I had known it was you I would have picked up the phone. Just call me on my cell."

"Ugh. Long story. Wife dragged me to the beach. I didn't want to take off my shirt. I'm kind of preoccupied. Next thing you know, my cell ends up in the water, fried, and your number's gone."

"Wow, I've never known you to *not* take off your shirt. Remember that trip to Vegas? That was always the first thing off!" Corbett thought back to that time. So much younger, so many fewer cares.

"Oh man, how I miss those days," said Anthony. "To be young and clueless again. I *have* let my abs go. But wow, you know, the women out there were just amazing."

"I agree," said Corbett. "They *were* amazing."

"And that was the time before every woman had silicone tits. It was a nice treat, you know. Now a girl turns eighteen, and it's just part of growing up."

"True," said Corbett. "So what was the problem? Have you put on a few pounds since the last time I saw you or what? Why the business with the shirt?"

"I confess, Corb, and I only say this because it's you and you *know* me, but it's because I had some scratch marks on my back from you-know-who from a couple nights before that hadn't really healed yet, and I didn't want to deal with the fallout with the wife standing right there."

"Wow. You're still seeing what's-her-name?"

"Kimberly," said Anthony.

"Yeah. Kimberly. That's still going on?"

"Yeah," said Anthony. "Now and then. You know, she calls *me*. I don't call her. I don't know if she's so crazy she thinks I'm gonna' leave my wife for her or what. Like, set off an atomic bomb in my nice peaceful little life to move in with some whore? She's nuts."

"That's…that's been going on for awhile," said Corbett.

"Almost three years now."

"That's awhile, Tony. Does she actually love you?"

"Love me? She swears she's *in* love with me. But I couldn't give a shit at this point. She knew my feelings going into this."

"Well, I mean, you are married. She knew that going in." Corbett was agreeing, but refused to cosign the behavior.

"Exactly. She just wanted something on the side, and it's never supposed to be anything more than that. The problem is, the harder I pull away from her, the closer she tries to get to me. It's like she's on this big elastic band. But not that I'm complaining. I don't think I need to tell you that emotionally fucked-up women give the best head. And that's what she is. My girlfriend. A little something on the side. You know. My wife is still my wife. That's not going to change."

"I hear you, Tony." There was concern in Corbett's voice. "She probably knew that this was just a fling going in. But feelings aren't facts—they change. I mean, this seems to have gone on for a long time. Don't you feel bad, Tony? Like, you're hurting the girl? You should just leave her. You'd probably both be better off."

"Corb, I just don't see it that way. She knew upfront that I was married. She was okay with that. It's not my fault if she'd always thought I'd leave Mary for her."

"Well then you need to tell her that," said Corbett. "You need to tell her that you're not leaving Mary. Tell her you love Mary. I still don't know why you're doing this. What's the upside for you?"

"Honestly, I mean, just between you and me Corb, the sex is fucking phenomenal."

Corbett had heard that one before. This wasn't the first one of his friend's trysts that he'd gotten caught up in.

"The sex just can't be *that* good. There just can't be a big enough difference between what you have with your wife and what you have with this girl."

"Corbett, I'm not going to say you're dumb as a stump because clearly, you aren't. But when it comes down to sex, somehow, you just don't get it. I understand—you met your wife, you love your wife, you can't ever even imagine being with someone else, et cetera, et cetera. Am I close here? In the ballpark at least?"

"Well. Yes, Tony. I do love my wife. You know that. I don't really understand how..."

"And that's exactly what I mean. You don't even understand what I'm saying, even though you're a really bright guy and women like you."

"Well, thanks for that, at least. I guess."

"You're welcome," said Anthony. "Anyway, let me break this down for you so it's simple for you to understand. It's Kimberly's self-loathing that just translates so well into the bedroom. The fact that she's not married and wants to fuck a married guy—it's that very detail that makes her so good in the sack. You should see all the self-deprecating shit she does. All the ass-to-mouth, DP'ing her...and I piss on her...and, Jesus, fuck *me* Corb, I could just never ask my wife to do anything like that. How do you fuck your wife 'til she pukes? Like she's gonna' puke on her own rug? Then she's gonna' have to clean it up too? No. Kimberly...Kimberly claims she does it because she's so in love with me that she'd do anything for me, but if you ask me, the bitch is just a little fucked in the head, you know? Otherwise she wouldn't be doin' that shit in the first place."

There was silence on the other end of the line. Corbett would never cheat on his wife, and though he would never admit it, he did sort of live vicariously through Anthony. He now understood that Anthony had known that all along.

"That's…well,   that's…wow…Anthony…and   she scratched you?"

"Yeah," he laughed. "The bitch scratched me so hard she drew blood. Broke the skin. But what the fuck—no one makes me come like her. *No one*."

"Does your wife know yet?"

"Yeah, she has some ideas, but I know if I have to show her those scratch marks on my back, there's no lying my way out of that one."

"No kidding," said Corbett as he shook his head.

"So I was so flustered I lost my phone, and I couldn't find your cell anywhere."

"You just lost it?"

Anthony sighed. "Yes, I lost it." he said sarcastically. "It ended up in the ocean, and by the time I found it, the saltwater had fried the thing."

"Don't you have a backup service? I mean, you are a government employee."

"Those fucks at the DEA are so corrupt. I wouldn't trust them to not give the backup contract so some back-alley people that fucked it up anyway."

"I know it's so corrupt," replied Corbett. "That's why I left to start Omicrone. I like being neutral. Like Switzerland."

"Eh, I wouldn't be so easy on yourself," responded Anthony. "You're not really Switzerland. I don't see any skiing or chocolate or fancy little knives coming out of Omicrone. You're more like the guy on the street I ask for directions, who then promises to make me more lost unless I pay him. You're a shake-down artist. Don't think I don't know that, Corb."

"Well, at least I'm not actively making the people lost who ask me for directions like you are."

"Maybe not," said Anthony. "I'm just being a little more upfront about who I am and what I do."

"Fair enough. I'll let you know when we start consulting on sex addiction."

"Very funny, Corb."

"So your phone wasn't backed up?"

"Yeah, well I thought I had done it, but I never set it up correctly, so all the time I thought it was backing up, it wasn't. And trust me I tried."

"You tried?"

"One of my wife's friends, Lily or Lila or something like that. Her kid sells salvage electronics online to pay for his video game habit. Little freak sits inside his room for twenty hours at a time with headphones on and a big projection monitor. Real nut case. But he literally buys stuff for pennies, and then picks out the pieces of electronics that work, and sells them for parts. Kid's a genius, but no social skills."

"I know someone like that," said Corbett.

"Well *he* couldn't fix it. That's when I knew I was in trouble. He told me there was good news and bad news. The bad news was that the memory was fried and there was no way to get the data off the phone, and it was lost forever. The good news was that he'd give me ten bucks for the phone."

"Great news."

"Yeah," said Anthony. "I told the little shit to keep it, gratis, as long as he promised not to shoot me when he grew up. Probably made a C-note selling it broken. I'm glad I could support his little first-person-shooter habit."

"'Tis the way of the world. So what's going on?"

"Oh. Well, I know that you're the man with the plan. You always know what's up."

"Well, after I retired from government work I've kept a lot of my contacts, if that's what you mean."

"That's a pretty early retirement, Corb."

"I wanted better things for myself, and government work…it's rewarding, but it has a lot of rules."

"Be straight with me for a minute Corbett."

"Okay."

186

"I want to know what you've heard about Durham Pharmaceuticals."

"Durham? I've heard lots of things. Omicrone doesn't specifically consult to them, but I have some contacts that work closely with their office in Germany."

"And?"

"And what?"

"And what have you heard about what's happening in their office in Germany?"

"Don't you know anyone over at Food and Drug, Tony?"

"Now why would I need to know anyone over at Food and Drug if you've been my boy since we worked on that thing when we first met? Without me, you would *never* have gotten the exposure you did. And since then I didn't ask you for anything. Nothing. You made a name for yourself. You started your own little thing. And I decided to stay put."

"And I respect your choice, and mine. What about it?"

"All I'm saying is," said Anthony, "You could help me out with something here. You don't have to think about it like you owe me a favor for helping you make a name for yourself and then start Omicrone, and be flying all over the place to meet with dignitaries and be invited to fancy cocktail parties. Just call it professional courtesy. Maybe I don't have your charisma. Maybe I'm just lazy. In either case, I need a favor."

"Tony, you and I both know I owe you. This isn't a chit you have to call in. You can just ask me what you want and I'll help you. No questions asked. We've known each other a *long* time. What is it?"

There was a sigh on the other side of the line.

"What've you heard about Durham Pharma, Corbett."

"Off the record?" asked Corbett.

"It's all off the record. That's why I called your cell."

"Off the record, my contact tells me that their lab is working on some secret compound that the American office has plausible deniability around. A heavy-duty fast-acting plant-based organic hallucinogen it's studying in ways we've never seen before outside of science fiction. For all intents and purposes, it does not exist."

"Oh, Corbett, *it exists*."

187

"Believe me, Tony, it *doesn't*,"

"Believe *me*, Corbett. *It does*."

"The reason it does *not* exist, Tony, is because of the way it's being handled. It's eyes only. The only reason I'm even talking to you is because it's *you*."

"I understand that. We're in the same business. I know about this compound too. It's called '5,6,7.' Chemical name is '5,6,7-trimethoxy-dmt'."

"That's right!" Corbett sounded surprised.

"Don't sound so surprised. We're the DEA. We know about this stuff."

"Well, how do you know about it?"

"Hey. I asked *you* for the favor."

Corbett was frowning on the other side of the phone.

"I'll tell you what I know when you tell me what you know. One hand washes the other," said Corbett. "What's going on at your end?"

"Okay. I don't mind going first. I can tell you that there was a young man named Shola Oma, a Venezuelan here on a student visa. I can tell you that he had enrolled at one of the schools in the California University system, and then he dropped out and disappeared after a semester. He popped up on the radar again when he tried to order some very specialized laboratory equipment at one of our online dummy corporations. Usually, the people we catch in that net are the meth cooks, and they usually just get turned over to local law enforcement. But this guy, he was born in Venezuela, then came here as a student. Sound like a meth cook to you?"

"Absolutely not."

"Right. So, turns out our boy Shola here is actually cooking up yaje for Berkeley hippies."

"Yaje? That's the same thing as ayahuasca, right?"

"Yes. Vine of the soul. Orally-active DMT. Hallucinogenic soup. Usually served to you by some priest with crazy face paint and lip piercings."

"Glad you kept up on all your chemistry."

"Honestly Corb, I don't know a whole lot about the chemistry. But I know enough. Shola's cooking up batches of real traditional yaje. Now, that stuff's like crystal meth—all the ingredients are legal. It's just the act of cooking the brew that's illegal. It turns out he wasn't much good to us. He only brewed small portions, didn't even make that much money, and was selling it basically on the street to these hippies we don't give two shits about. They're pacifists, you know. They're not blowing up houses. They're not killing kids. They're burnouts. Useless. The whole thing was actually kind of disappointing. It was kind of like catching a blue lobster in the trap and being all excited and you think it's worth extra and everything 'cause it looks so different from everything else you've caught. But then when you boil him up he tastes exactly the same. Disappointing."

"I would say he's more like those Portugese fisherman who caught the Coelecanth," shot in Corbett.

"The seal-a-what?"

"The Coelecanth? It's this extinct fish. Well, they thought it was extinct until they caught a live one. Then they started catching more."

He heard a pause on the other end of the line.

"Well, how can it be extinct if they caught one?"

Anthony sounded annoyed. Corbett frowned to himself. Oh my goodness, he thought. I've turned into Josh, stopping the conversation for a stupid point. He picked up right away.

"Exactly," said Corbett, "Fish, lobster, whatever. I didn't mean to interrupt you. What happened with Shola?"

"Well, he turned out to be useless. We don't even prosecute those ayahuasca people. Most of them are dudes you would never even see. They don't rock the boat. We don't make any points for throwing them in the can. Most of them make hemp jewelry, or medieval chain mail, or sew clothes, or do some other sort of menial job. They're off the grid anyway. They live on communes with microbuses. There's no reason why the state should give 'um three hots and a cot and free cable. We usually wave our arms and shout and scare 'um, and they shit a brick and slink quietly away into the background. And quite frankly, their drug doesn't kill people and wreck people's lives like the meth. It's honestly the lowest priority. But Shola, we could do a lot with him on account of his being a foreigner. We had leverage."

189

"Well, what did you find out?" asked Corbett.

"Well, we found out that in addition to the yaje precursors and admixtures that we had heard of, he had imported a large quantity of this plant that was called Virola sophismata."

"I don't know that name. I mean, I've heard of the genus Virola, but not Virola sophismata."

"Well you're a step ahead of *me*. I had to look that one up."

"I remember," said Corbett. "Virola species are the ones used in the hallucinogenic snuffs of the Amazonian shamans. I think it's called 'epeña' or 'epaña' or something like that."

"Wow, Corb. I'm impressed. If you don't mind me asking, how do you know about that? That's way off my radar."

"I did a lot of reading of Sasha Shulgin's work when I was younger."

"Oh. Whatever. Well, anyway, it turns out that this Virola sophismata is the natural plant precursor for a DMT analog. Your little chemical called…"

"5,6,7." Corbett smiled.

"Right. 5,6,7. So, this South American guy's last shipment into the country before we bagged him was this plant Virola sophismata. I tell him I need to know where it went. We're going to deport him anyway, since his visa's expired. I'm just making it so that he doesn't have to serve time here. Just get out of my country, you know?"

"I hear you."

"Well, turns out that it goes to some guy whose roommate is a grad student in a neuroscience lab. The trail ends there. When we go try to find out some more information, we get a huge amount of pushback."

"What do you mean, pushback?"

"Well, the neuroscience lab is run by a guy named Pickering. Real piece of work. I swear to God, Corbett, this guy is the cow that starts the stampede. He starts yelling at my agent about fascism and corporate capitalism, and he'd rather get arrested than tell my guy anything, and all this, and we hadn't even told him why we were there! Nothing at all about 5,6,7! I swear to God we just said hello and showed him a badge. Can you believe it? I mean, yells at my guy and doesn't even know what he wants?"

"Well, there are those anti-government types, Tony. They do exist. And you're probably more likely to find them in an academic job at a liberal university."

"Liberal?" asked Anthony. "Corb, the guy's a freakin' Communist. We didn't get *any* information. Then my office gets a call from the Chancellor's office telling us that we don't have the right to bother their professors who are busy working, and we should address our queries to *their* office. And then you know that's going to be a shitshow. A whole pile of bureaucracy and lawyers, and throw in some extra firepower from the fucking law students who are smart enough to be rocket scientists and who hate government. For all I know, they'd use this as some sort of faggot-ass teachable moment, and have a whole law class just try to fuck us. It would be open season on the DEA. Just a total clusterfuck. And you and I are both in with the CALPERS people, so it looks really bad for us from all directions. I called our guy off. We know where the stuff ended up. It's in that lab. Case closed in my book."

"So that's what you know about 5,6,7, Tony?" There was a pause.

"All I want to share about right now."

"But you started asking me about Durham Pharmaceuticals," said Corbett.

"Right. I started asking *you* about Durham, not 5,6,7. Tell me what you know."

"Well," began Corbett, "One of my contacts, a German national, let me in on some information. He said that Durham is working on a researching a new chemical, and all he would tell me is that it's called 5,6,7 and that it doesn't exist. He says that the German government has an unnamed operative that works inside of Durham and gathers information."

"Now *that*, I didn't know," confessed Anthony.

"Well, Tony, I mean, it's a huge privately-held company. There's a lot of economic risk for the government there and they deal with a lot of systemic risk too. Just because they've been successful doesn't mean that one misstep and the release of something like a Vioxx wouldn't seriously impede the whole

191

region's profitability—they're a big employer. I believe their involvement is purely to protect financial interests, not anything more sinister. They're European. Totally different paradigm."

"Fair enough. You always so believe in humanity you little shit. Go on."

"Well, it turns out that they're working on this 5,6,7 chemical, which was sourced from the Amazon rainforest. But, apparently, instead of extracting and purifying it from plant precursors, they're synthesizing it from scratch on a molecular level. They're reverse engineering it, so to speak. They started producing it."

"And?"

"And, my contact tells me that they've made quite a bit of the stuff."

"And?"

"And, he tells me that they're getting it into this country using a system of phony DEA control numbers that someone they have working at the DEA created from scratch, and manually entered into the computer that shouldn't be there. So, they'll be importing this chemical here *legally* by saying that it's a harmless one. And then anyone in any law enforcement capacity that looks it up will check the number, and it'll check out. They'll be able to get a whole ton of this stuff into the country to the Durham headquarters this way. It's an incredibly safe and efficient ruse. Instead of having to import plant material from outside the country that's bulky and raises red flags, they're just importing the actual illegal chemical, and circumventing those issues altogether by using someone on the inside to mislabel it."

"And?"

"And all they have to do is run their trials and get it okayed for mass production."

"Mass production?" asked Anthony.

"Yeah. Mass production. This is apparently an expensive drug to make, but it's a good research chemical for them at Durham."

"But what if mass production isn't the endgame? What if FDA approval isn't what they're looking for?"

"Well, Tony, I think I know where you're going with this, but Durham is a very well-respected firm. I mean, I know for a fact that they make Duscantia. It's a migraine medicine. My cousin takes it and she says it's the only thing that works for her because she's allergic to Imitrex. They make Gestacin. This is a respectable company that's really, *really* mainstream. I mean, I understand your position, but I'm telling you they don't want *anything* illegal or scandalous attached to their name. They make plenty of money on these good, time-tested drugs they sell. I know there's a really fine line between a lot of the illegal drugs and the research chemicals, but this is the first I've heard of anything these guys are not doing exactly by the book. I'm not sure if I feel you're taking this the right way. It doesn't necessarily mean that they're trying to do something criminal just because *you* happen to be in law enforcement."

"Corbett, do you remember that quote from *Batman Begins*? The one I've repeated for you many times?"

"I know which one you're talking about, I just don't remember it word for word."

"*Criminals thrive on the indulgence of society's understanding.* Liam Neeson's character says it to Christian Bale. I have a copy of it on my desk next to the monitor on the left."

"Yeah, you tell that one to me a lot. But I don't see it that way. *If* my guy is telling me the truth, there's still a very good chance that this is just a rumor, a story planted purposefully as an internal test at the company to root out a malicious employee, or even a group of employees trying to sabotage Durham internally. Government operatives or not. There's a ton of money invested in their pipeline. Or it could be something cooked up by the Germans and their intelligence to see how the information spreads over to the States—a kind of diagnostic self-test. I mean, this is an enormous multi-national company. I just don't necessarily believe everything I hear. And in my line of work, I have to be very careful to sift through what comes across my desk, and not be too quick to accept its veracity."

"But what does your *gut* tell you?" asked Anthony.

"Honestly, Tony. Occam's Razor. The simplest explanation. My guess is that it's not just a planted story intended by the company as a self-test. Possible, but not likely. More likely, it sounds more like Durham may have just passed a cop on the highway driving sixty-five, and they're stepping on the gas a little bit, pushing it to eighty-five or ninety for a short period, and betting there isn't another cop on the road for at least a little while. And they're doing it to make a short-term bet that their company can move faster than a large bureaucracy trying to regulate them. Honestly, big pharma's a really cutthroat marketplace. I really think they may be bending a few rules in order to get moving on some testing quicker than they could by following the specific legal protocols. I think they're doing that in order to get a jump on the competition in the market of a new class of drugs that we thought, until now, was simply science fiction."

"And?"

"And, I am not necessarily saying they're doing anything wrong. I mean, if they're making use of their being a multinational corporation to sidestep the rules and regulations in any of the countries they do business in, they just joined a pretty huge club that's much more universal than pharma. And I believe sometimes these drug companies get held to a different standard because they're marketing products that we actually put into our bodies. But, my personal opinion about this is that your agency and the FDA are kind of complicit, since you set up protocols that are hard to maneuver around. I mean, you loosen emissions standards a little, you get much more fuel efficient cars. You loosen them too much and you have *really* efficient cars, but the thousands of protesting hippies camping in the streets and holding up signs to save the polar bears and endangered beetles clog the roads so you can't drive at all. It's a balance, you know. Durham is tipping the lever a bit—not more than a commercial airliner banks, but enough to try to beat some competitors out of the gate with what promises to be a new watershed in understanding our brains."

"And?"

"And what? That's all I know. That's all I think. That's what I know about Durham and 5,6,7," said Corbett.

There was a long pause.

"Corbett. How long have you known me?"

194

"I don't know, Tony. Maybe eleven, twelve years?"

"Yeah. About that. You've watched me go through two wives and three mistresses."

"Yeah," Corbett laughed. "I have."

"You've never judged me."

"Never. Not my place to judge."

"Judgment is mine sayeth the Lord," said Anthony.

"Yes. Yes, it is. Wow. Scripture."

"Corbett, I may be in need of your services."

"Well, you know I'm always willing to help a friend, Tony."

"No, I mean, I may want to hire Omicrone to formally consult for me."

"For you personally?"

"Yes. For me personally. You knew a lot of information that I didn't."

"Well...likewise."

"But I'm DEA, Corbett. *Active* DEA. We're the ones in charge of knowing about this stuff. You...you get to decide what you want to know."

"Go on..."

"I just think that you might be missing the boat with this one, Corbett."

"How so?"

"Have you ever considered the possibility that 5,6,7 was never going to get through clinical trials, and the company knows this, and that those were just going to be a way for it to be tested on humans, in terms of dosage and efficacy. And instead, it was just going to end up being the next designer drug, the next club drug, to hit the scene? That it was never going to pass muster, never get okayed for production? And that maybe, just *maybe*, the DEA's role here was going to be to kind of let it happen, because of some of the particular details of how this drug works?"

"I had not," replied Corbett. "Honestly, Anthony, I don't typically think that way. I don't know a ton of neuroscience, and I don't want to. I usually give the company the benefit of the doubt. Most of my prior work has been in the Middle East, where the ease of information is not as great as it is here. Here, there's almost too much information."

"Well Corbett, I'm using this call as a way to formally ask for Omicrone's services. I want you to consult for me. You're like having a huge periscope. And not like the one I have." Both of the men laughed. "I mean, you have a different purview than I do. I have a lot of juice here. But not out there. You dig?"

"I dig. You want my services. What kind of term?"

"Until you retire."

"For life?"

"For life."

"Wow," said Corbett. "That's a long time. And you're going to pay me the standard rate?"

"I'll pay a thirty percent premium. But you deal only with me, and no one else."

"Fair enough. And what do you want me to do, specifically?"

"I want you to keep your eyes and ears open. And I want you to tell me what you see and hear. That's all. Only about 5,6,7."

"That's all?"

"That's all."

"Okay," said Corbett. "This has been a nice surprise. I mean, we still have some I's to dot and T's to cross…"

"We'll write something up. But next time we meet. You'll get paid by one of the DEA dummy companies. All above board. Audit-proof. There are some paperwork issues I have to work out before I see you next time. But it'll be soon."

"Tony, I just need to ask you one thing."

"What's that Corb?"

"Are you going rogue, or is what you're doing sanctioned by the DEA?"

"I don't believe I have to disclose that to my consultant. But if you hear anything on the topic of my compliance or my rogueness, do be sure to keep me abreast."

"But Tony, you *are* the one at the DEA who entered the fake control numbers into the computer system to allow Durham to illicitly import 5,6,7?"

Anthony paused and inhaled.

"Why else would I call you?"

Corbett exhaled slowly.

"Happy to have you onboard, Tony."

"Happy to be Omicrone's newest client. I'll call you soon." Click.

* * *

David looked into the refrigerator for a snack, saw a yogurt, and reached for it. When he picked it up, the side was split open and pinkish goop shot in between his thumb and index finger and began dripping down his hand. Disgusting, thought Dave, as he looked around for a dish towel. You would think the kids who bag at the grocery store wouldn't throw everything in so sloppily. It's their only job.

While he was reaching for a towel to wipe off his hands, he tried to drop the damaged yogurt cup into the trash can under the sink, but it hit the rim and splashed yogurt all over the floor. He decided to pull the whole thing out to clean it. Allison's gonna' kill me if she sees that mess, he thought.

He pulled the trash bag out, and saw a tiny piece of paper stuck to the outside. For some reason he pulled it off—it was a piece of a prescription label that had been ripped off the bottle. He could read part of his step-daughter's name, and then the drug name Levonorgestrel. He knew what that was, and he couldn't believe it. He shouted up to his wife.

"Allison!"

There was a muffled answer. She was on her computer. He thought it might be easier to just send her an email instead of talking with her in person—their communication had just been breaking down as her drinking had increased. But this made him angry.

"Allison, quit drinking and come down here."

She appeared on the stairs a moment later, swaying as she made her way down to the kitchen. He didn't need to be near her to know that she stunk like booze.

"What is it, Dave? I'm busy." She leaned back and forth on unsteady legs.

"Do you know what this is?" he asked as he showed her the prescription label.

"Trash?" she said and looked at his eyes, waiting for him to laugh. He didn't.

"No. It's a prescription for our daughter. Plan B. The morning after pill. Emergency contraception." He glared at her.

"I know what it is," she said, her body now tensing up.

"I thought she didn't have a boyfriend."

"She doesn't. Listen, we didn't want to talk to you about this. We both thought that you would get upset." She could see David winding up.

"I *am* upset. Abortion is *murder*! Just because I'm not out there on the street protesting or killing doctors doesn't mean I support *Roe v. Wade* and this country's liberal agenda."

"Now you see, this is exactly what I knew would happen." She pushed past him to the refrigerator and poured herself a glass of wine. He was too angry to harangue her about the alcohol.

"So, you kept this from me?"

"David…"

"Don't 'David' me, Allison. We're not supposed to have secrets like this. When we got married, we got married in the Church. You hadn't been married before. I loved that you kept her and tried to raise her on your own. I thought that abortion was one of the topics we agreed on."

"We do agree, honey."

"Well, I don't believe in emergency contraception. I'm not stupid enough to think that people are just going to wait until they're married to have sex, but abortion is different."

"Honey, I don't believe that pill is the same as an abortion."

"Allison. It's an abortive. It's an abortifacient. By definition, that's what it *does*. It causes life to cease. Life that begins at conception."

"I think it's a little more complicated than that, David," said Allison, her eyes narrowing.

"And what's that supposed to mean?"

"Honestly?" she asked.

"Honestly."

198

"It's complicated," she said, and drank the whole glass of wine in one gulp. She looked at him, just begging him to get angry about the wine, but he wouldn't take the bait. He truly wanted to hear what she was going to say.

"How about I'll let you talk, and I'll just listen," he said. "I say, 'life begins at conception.' I thought we agreed on that simple statement. Now I find out we don't. How is conception 'complicated,' exactly?"

"We do agree, but I believe that life begins at implantation, not conception. And your daughter agrees with me. It's a bit of a nuanced position. We've spoken about it."

"A nuanced position? What are you, a politician?"

"No. Our daughter and I agree."

"You've spoken about it? Or you let her change your mind?"

"She didn't change anything. And yes, we spoke at length. A few years ago, she asked me what I thought about all this. Her friends were having sex. It was a complicated time. When she asked me what I thought, I told her it wasn't about what I believed. I told her it was about her finding her own path. A few weeks later, she told me she had reached an understanding. She told me that she believed in God, and that it was God's will whether or not a sperm and an egg got together and formed another human being. That it had to be God's will, because there were so many sperm, and just a single egg. But she also told me that she learned in school that many times a sperm and an egg get together, and something isn't right, and the body just flushes the fertilized egg out during the period. The body can do that naturally, and it does it about half the time the sperm and egg meet. And she believes that if God doesn't want that child, it gets flushed out of her body."

"But this isn't God. This is her. *She* is taking that pill to cause that to happen."

"David, if the fertilized egg doesn't implant, it's not viable. A fetus, a child, a new being cannot be life until it's connected to its mother and begins the process of growing. Until the embryo implants, it's not a child. It's not a life. Life begins at implantation. Not conception. There's a little window of time in between there for a few days. And the Plan B just makes sure that the little zygote doesn't implant, and it gets flushed out like half the fertilized eggs do without taking the drug. If causing a fertilized egg not to implant, and then not become a fetus, is murder, than every woman is an abortion machine since it happens so often. That's God's way."

David paused. He was dumbstruck, but could see in his wife's eyes that she was serious. The woman who had always insisted she was pro-life just snuck in a little curveball. And he thought she only pitched fastballs. And he swung and missed.

"You really believe this."

"I do."

"Why did you never tell me this?"

"It never came up." David was pensive for a moment. Allison refilled her wine. He didn't even notice. He was too caught up in the realization that his marriage was falling apart, and that he didn't even recognize the person standing next to him as his wife. After staring into space for a moment, he continued.

"Life begins at implantation? It doesn't even sound right."

"I know. It sounds like Souplantation. Life begins at the salad bar."

David laughed. "I liked that place." He went and wrapped his arms around Allison, trying to feign a sense of love, intimacy, and belonging. When he did, he could smell the booze on her mouth, and he felt nothing. It was like hugging a dummy, or a sack of flour. She was vacant, devoid of a life force. All of a sudden he was incredibly sad—he just wanted to have a normal, happy life. His thanks for working to bring home a fat paycheck and the long hours and the tough decisions was a wife who smelled like a winery, a wife who stayed upstairs on her computer because otherwise she was so drunk she couldn't make it up the stairs at night. He was silent, and very sad. All he wanted was a marriage like they used to have, and instead, he was married to a drunk. A drunk who apparently was changing her supposedly deep-rooted morality as she slid further into her disease.

"Honey?" Allison said as she left his embrace. "Are you there?"

"Yeah, I'm here," David replied. "I guess I like, 'life begins at conception' better. It just sounds better."

"I agree it sounds better. But I just think it's not that simple. I truly believe that life begins at implantation. As a woman. As a man, you couldn't possibly understand."

David was dumbstruck. Now he just felt insulted. She wasn't really talking about biology—it was semantics. He had no idea what to do with this relationship with her.

"Honey," said David. "I..."

"I'm sorry. I was just trying to make the case that things are more complex than they look at first glance. I do believe, though, that life begins at implantation."

"You really believe that?"

"Really."

"Wow. That's a lot to think about."

"David. Honey. You have a pee-pee, so you don't have to worry about these things at all! So just worry about your little pee-pee, and not about our little coochies. Okay?"

David looked at her confusedly. She smiled and almost stumbled as she turned and headed back upstairs to sit alone at her machine.

"It's not little," he said as she walked away. She didn't reply. "I said it's not little!" he shouted up the stairs. He heard the door shut, stared at the broken yogurt cup and the trash, and felt as close as he'd ever been to crying over his marriage.

*   *   *

Morgan couldn't believe that Brian had the guts to come into the store. She can't believe she could've slept with him. Slimy, nasty, sleazy, horrible, Brian. He was the first man she had ever been with. He wore too much cologne, and ran a shady used car lot. He was an addict. He made his money buying the shitboxes at the auction that no one else wanted, the donation cars and the dangerous ones with bad axles, sticky calipers, and bad racks. He had his cousin buying used odometers on eBay that he'd swap out. Honda Accord with 257k becomes Honda Accord with 154k. The out-of-state cars didn't have the same reciprocity over emissions records, and other ways that the states tried to keep track of people like Brian. He used an out-of-state wholesale plate to wash titles and make odometer discrepancies disappear. He was as shady as they came.

She still remembered lying in bed next to him. He was explaining to her exactly how the salvage process worked. A car would get in a pretty bad accident and get totaled out by insurance. Then, his friend at the boneyard would get him the parts off of other cars in the yard, his cousin would slap it together, take the salvage title to Maine and register the car, sell it back to Brian, who re-registered the car in Connecticut. All gone salvage title. He did this to hundreds of cars, on top of the hundreds that got their odometers turned back.

"But don't you ever feel guilty?" she asked him when they were in bed.

"Why?"

"Well, you know. It's not a safe car. Someone could get hurt. Or killed."

"It's not like that."

"What do you mean? Why not?" she asked him, unable to understand.

"If you're gonna' get in an accident, it's an accident. That's why they call it that. I don't have any responsibility in that."

"But you sold them the fucked up car."

"Who cares? It's not my problem. Once it leaves my hands, all bets are off."

"But you have to have some sort of accountability, Brian," she said.

"Listen. Morgan. You remember when I got that DUI and they made me go to classes?"

"How could I forget," she replied. "I drove you around all over the place. And don't tell me you learned anything there. You still drive around drunk all the time!"

"No, Morgan, I don't drive drunk, only buzzed." Brian grinned from ear to ear.

"Brian, I swear to God you're an idiot," shot back Morgan.

"After I got that DUI," he continued, "I had to go to these alcohol ed classes, but they also made me go to a bunch of AA meetings. And at those meetings, there were some *fucked up*

202

people, let me tell you. But at those meetings, they talked about how everyone has a God, but if you don't want to call him God, you can just say 'Higher Power,' which just means a power greater than you that isn't you."

"Brian, there are so very many things that are powers greater than you that are not you," replied Morgan in disgust.

"No, listen. So they said that everyone has a Higher Power of their understanding, and that every person has their own path and their own conversation with that God of their understanding." Brian was excited.

"So?"

"So, if I sell someone a car, and then they get in an accident and get hurt, that's part of their Higher Power's plan for them. If it's meant to be, it's meant to be, and there's nothing I can do to stop it."

"*But you caused it to happen!*" she said.

"*No I didn't!* If their God didn't want it to happen, then their God wouldn't have let them buy the car from me in the first place. Not my fault."

Morgan looked at him for a long time. He was sitting there smiling, grinning like an idiot. He really believed this line of rationalizing bullshit he was feeding himself. What a sick dude. She was appalled by his moral relativism.

She snapped out of that nightmare. He was still in the store. She had literally gone and hid in the back room until he left. She had brought the next newsletter she had gotten from The New Liberty Church and had been reading the main article.

The Invention of Zero: The Nautilus, the Fractal God, and Manifest Destiny

The name of the first nuclear-powered submarine was no mistake. The Nautilus had its own nuclear reactor onboard, a fission reactor that slammed atoms into each other and destroyed matter in a rather orderly fashion, intending to heat up water to turn turbines and generate electricity to power large motors, and push the huge tube through the depths of the ocean. Its job: to protect American interests from a strategic defense point of view, and break records for staying underwater.

But more interesting is, why the name, the "nautilus." The nautilus shell is the easily recognized spiral shape, which is a representation of the Golden Mean, the Fibonacci sequence, and the same way evergreens and ferns and every other thing grows. And the Golden Mean, the ratio of the length of sides on the Golden Rectangle, has been studied for years by mathematicians. It's about the same ratio as a widescreen television, such that if one were to draw one vertical line in the rectangle to create a square inside, the ratio of the remaining rectangle is the same as the first. This Golden Mean, this nautilus, is also the shape of the cochlea in the inner ear, a set of tiny internal nautilus shells in our own heads, helping us decipher our world around us.

They should have called the U.S.S. Nautilus the U.S.S. Cochlea, as it was in charge of hearing with sonar all around itself for the good of our nation…

Morgan was having a hard time following the article—she couldn't focus today. She wanted to see Laida, who'd been on a shopping trip for about a week. She peeked around the corner and saw that Brian was still in there talking to Mike. Why won't he just leave, she said to herself.

She couldn't stop thinking about Laida. It was almost obsession. She wanted her—no doubt. No one knew at the store. She hadn't told anyone else. But she had made peace with whatever sort of sexual hang-ups she had. She never thought she could be with a woman, but she felt like she had never really known that transwomen existed. It was as if she were always taught that there were two choices: be with a man, or be with a woman. She had never considered the third option: man's body for sex, but without all the douchebaggery of any man she'd ever come in contact with, and then woman's brain for talking and stuff. Her eyes skimmed along and moved toward the bottom of the article.

…This idea of manifest destiny that was so prevalent in the early American world of pushing the frontier to its limits is not a new one. Just like our original American ancestors asserted themselves and believed that they were chosen to inhabit the whole country and to colonize the West, we see this theme repeated throughout human history.

This idea that the Earth does not belong to people, but to the animals and plants that inhabit it, is incredibly rational. And then we add this mushroom, which needed a way to expand its mycelium from a distant planet to ours. We see how the mushroom sent these little spores in every direction, an amazing climax, an amazing explosion of genetic material off of its home planet, and some of those spores reached earth.

And then the hunter-gatherer apes ate the mushroom (which needed only animal excrement to grow after surviving the conditions of interstellar space) and it incorporated itself into our DNA. A virus. Replicating in the ape's brain, increasing the number of serotonin receptors that worked ever-so-well with its psilocybin. And slowly but surely, like a runaway train gaining speed, the ape became human. Then, that human believed itself to be a ghost in a shell, a spirit in a body, something both divine and very mortal all at once. And so the spirit, our spirit, came to colonize the earth with these terrestrial flesh and blood human vehicles to create a new world for itself.

Like the founding of Israel in the Bible with the Jews defeating the Caananites (read: the original inhabitants of Earth) with the power of Yhwh, we see how we humans have conquered the Earth with the power of the mushroom. It is that force bringing us closer and closer to thinking and moving in unison, as it shores up its mental connections and continues to perfect its physical transportation routes all over the globe. Soon the planet, this new planet of our symbiosis with our physical flesh and the great mushroom hypermind conducting the every shred of our reality, with every firing of every neuron in every brain in the whole world like a grand and perfect conductor, able to hear every note of a multi-billion person symphony.

It's turning our planet into a self-reflecting entity of pure love. Our manifest destiny continues to be repeated, another iteration of the same fractal. The same fractal that is winding down as the world gets smaller and smaller. As the communication speed, information retrieval speed, and productivity reaches infinite levels, we find that we are simply looking at this backwards. We are not heading toward infinity.

Infinity is conceptual. We are heading toward something concrete. The end of privacy. The end of time. The end of government in any form we understand. The end of autonomy. But we're not headed toward zero.

Zero is a placeholder. It's an invention. It didn't exist until humans created it as a placeholder to make mathematical calculations easier. Because in reality, there is no nothingness, ever. There is only feeling disconnected from others. But there is no nothingness, there is no nothing. So then, if we are not heading toward infinity, but we are headed into its opposite, where are we going? To One. Not Zero.

Unity. Not a singularity. A unity. And that is why zero does not exist, and neither does infinity. There is only one. The consciousness. The cloud and the land coalescing, but not with a lightning strike, from afar, creating bits of glass out of sand, and huge amounts of voltage and amperage and loud thunderous explosions. Unity. Oneness. Never zero. Never infinite. Perfection. We are moving deep into the inner ear now. Deep into the nautilus. The farther we go in, the more we know we can never leave. But we must remember that we are not lost, and we will not die. We need only trust in the light. We are never alone.

"You're boyfriend's gone!" yelled Mike from the front of the store.

I'm never alone, she thought. I'm always surrounded by idiots.

"Shut up, Mike!" she yelled. She folded up the newsletter and emerged into the store.

"You watch your mouth, Missy."

Just as she got back to her area, her phone vibrated. It was a text from Laida saying she was on her way to the store. She got excited. Her face got flushed. She had to say something to someone.

"Mike, Laida and Danny are coming down in a little bit."

"Don't think so, Morgan. I already met Danny V. yesterday."

"Yesterday? I didn't see them yesterday." Morgan got anxious. How had she missed Laida coming in? Why wouldn't she have said anything? What was wrong?

206

"I didn't say I met that tranny, young lady. Just Danny V."

"But were they here?" Morgan asked, with persistence. Mike was immediately suspicious that the girl too apathetic to get up and answer the phone six feet away from her suddenly cared so much about those two junkies. He sent out a feeler bet.

"Tell me the truth, Miss Chandler. Have you got something going on the side with Danny?"

Morgan was *really* taken aback.

"*Wha—at?*" She couldn't believe that he actually thought she would sleep with that guy. Ugh, just disgusting all around. Unless he meant side *business*. In either case, her unadulterated response had answered Mike's question. He picked up where he'd left off.

"I already met Danny over at Buddy's. He already got his cash. He's out shopping again. Why did you just say they were coming?"

Morgan didn't understand what was happening. Despite what had happened with Laida, she had never seen the two of them apart from each other. And though Mike only dealt with Danny from a business standpoint, Morgan didn't want to let on anything else. She played it cool.

"Oh. Well, I got a text from Laida telling me she was coming. I just assumed they both were."

"You're texting with her now?" asked Mike.

"Well, yeah."

"Why do you need to see that he/she?"

Morgan paused for just the slightest moment. How do I tell Mike that I made love to her twice that night last week, and then twice again in the morning after holding her all night, and that I didn't want her to leave my bed. But that I'm not gay. I just love this *person*. And not to call her a he/she, or a shemale, or a shim, or a tranny, or a shman, or a ladyboy. She's a woman with a penis. Not a man. And a better lover than you ever could be, Mike. How could she sum all that up and spit it in his cigarette-smoking face? She gave a flat response instead.

"She borrowed one of my South Park box sets and was supposed to give it back to me."

Mike knew she was lying. The delivery was all wrong. But he didn't want to get involved. Though he loved Morgan like a daughter, he didn't really have to do the heavy lifting a dad would have to do, nor did he want to know her business with Laida. Still, it intrigued him. It was the first time in his life he'd seen a sparkle in Morgan's eyes. About anything. He decided it was safer to just be dismissive.

"I don't know why you don't just turn in those box sets to sell, and just watch the shows online like everybody else. Then maybe you could buy *me* lunch once in awhile!" He went in the office and lit a cigarette.

"Stop telling me what to do. You're such a loser, Mike."

"You're right, honey, I'm a loser," he said. "Now why don't you keep quiet and paint your nails while I sit in here and count piles of money." He shut the office door.

"Ugh! I hate you!" He didn't respond.

She immediately texted Laida: "what's up?"

She didn't respond. Morgan was worried. What had happened? Was it her? What was going on with all this? Had that time they'd spent together meant nothing? Was she playing games with her? What on Earth was going on? Before her mind got carried away with too many conjectures, Laida walked in the door. She looked different, somehow. Warmer. She immediately looked at Morgan. Morgan could tell something was different, but nothing was wrong. She approached the jewelry counter.

"Morgan. Hi, I just…" Morgan wanted to embrace her.

"Lai. Hi. Just, um, just come around the other side of the counter." Her eyes brightened.

"Is that okay with Mike?"

"Fuck Mike. Come around and sit near me so we don't have to talk over the counter." Laida sat next to Morgan. She was crying within ten seconds.

For the next fifteen minutes or so, Morgan sat in silence while Laida explained that she couldn't run with Danny V. any more. It had nothing to do with him. He hadn't changed, and he never would change. It was all her. She didn't want to shoot up any more. She cried and cried, and explained to Morgan that she was a junkie and addicted to heroin, and that's why she left so early the next day because she was going to be sick if she didn't get high. And she softly cried and apologized that she had lied to her and said that she was only taking Percocet. In reality, she was a junkie. She shot dope. That's what drove everything in her life. And she was so sorry she lied. And she didn't want Morgan to hate her.

"So what made all this happen?" asked Morgan. She was hoping that she knew the answer. Deep down she was selfishly hoping it was her.

"Honestly, Morgan," said Laida as she wiped the tears from her eyes, "I never meant to get hooked on dope. I never wanted that for myself. And then once you get in a routine and pick up a habit, that's all there is. You know? It's your whole world. And I'd just been running for so long. I was tired."

"But why were you doing it? Was it because you hated being a man and wanted to get out of yourself?"

"Honestly. Honestly. That's not the reason. I'd made peace with that a long, long time ago. Yes. I hate my father. I hate my father for not accepting me as the woman that I am. I hate my mother for leaving my father, and I feel like that was somehow my fault. Like, if I were just a regular boy or a regular girl, they would have stayed together. I have a lot of guilt around that."

"No. No. Laida that's not your fault. Parents split up if they need to. And that doesn't matter if you're Larry or Laida."

Laida laughed a little when she heard the name Larry.

"Morgan," said Laida. "I realized something last week. I realized that the reason I was getting high was not because I was uncomfortable with being a woman born a man. I was getting high because I was afraid, so afraid that I was never going to meet anyone that would love me for me. Like, I might find guys that would want to have sex with me because they wanted a tranny sex experience, you know, but that I was always going to be someone's one night stand. Someone's weird, kinky, freaky, perverted sex experience. Like, I've been reduced to my body parts and nothing more. I'm not even a woman that can get pregnant, you know. I'm just worthless." She started crying again.

"No," said Morgan. "That's not it at all. Why would you even think that?" The tears kept pouring down Laida's face.

"Morgan. It's just…it's so simple…" She smiled through tears. "You know that song, it goes, …*the hardest to learn was the least complicated?*" Morgan looked at Laida. Her heart skipped a beat. She knew before she said it.

"Yeah. I actually do." Morgan reached over and touched her hand. Morgan's eyes started welling up with tears.

"Yeah," said Laida, squeezing her hand and looking deep into her eyes. Morgan could feel Laida's energy flow through her hand, down her arm, and right into her chest. Her heart beat the warmth all through her body, and she felt a stirring deep inside herself. *Oh thank God they were okay.* Laida didn't have to say the word "lesbians." Morgan understood. She caught Laida's energy back, and started singing very softly. She didn't even realize she knew the words to the song. They were coming out of some place deep, deep inside of her, and came up so naturally. She felt like the stone that Moses struck. And her water flowed.

Morgan had never sung to anyone. The tears flowed down her cheeks as she kept the melody: "I remember the time when I came so close to you, sent me skippin' my class and running from school. And I bought you that ring 'cause I never was cool. What makes me think I could start clean-slated? The hardest to learn was the least complicated..." Her voice faded to silence.

Their energy was completely intertwined. Morgan could feel Laida's pain. She told her with her mind it was going to be okay, and that she loved her. And they felt each other. And it was good. Neither of them could speak for a minute. They were just amazed that they were together. Finally, Laida spoke.

"I want to be with you. That's why I'm here..." Morgan began to reply. Laida stopped her and held up a finger. "...And I've made peace with what that means. The reason I was getting high was not because I was afraid of being Laida instead of Larry. I'd rather have someone kill me than live life as a man. That choice was simple. I was afraid that I was going to be alone, because no man would ever want me because of my body. I never even considered being with a woman, because to me, being a woman meant being on a man's arm. But after that time I spent with you, I had this moment of clarity. I realized that being a woman was the opposite of that. Being a woman had nothing to do with being on a man's arm. Being on a man's arm was what you did because that's what the man wanted you to do for other men's sake, but that I was the one who got to choose that man in the first place. The choice was mine. That was my power. And then after spending the night with you, I realize that I'm comfortable partnering with a girl too. So, I don't feel like a lesbian or anything. But I want to be with you. If that makes any sense."

"It makes perfect sense, and I want to be with you too," said Morgan. "And I don't feel like a lesbian either. I'm attracted to attractive people. And until now those attractive people have always been men. But the more I've been with men that I've found to be attractive, the more they just turn me off and turn me away. I just think you are so beautiful on the inside, and so hot on the outside, and no one has ever made me feel the way that you do. So, yeah, I want you too."

"Well that's good. That's why you haven't seen me."

"What does that mean?" asked Morgan.

"I went to detox. Four days. To get off the heroin. Now I have to go to the methadone clinic every day to get my dose and I can't miss a dose. And they'll wean me off of it. But I've been clean for a week."

"Oh my God, that's amazing! Congratulations, Lai!" She leaned over and gave her a hug.

"Well, thanks. I just felt like, if I were going to start a relationship with you, I wanted to do it clean. You make me love myself. I want to live when I'm with you. And I don't want that feeling to go away. And after I saw you and went and got high with Danny, it was *so* bad. So. Bad. I couldn't pretend anymore. I just knew that I was just numbing myself so that I couldn't feel because I was so scared and fearful and afraid of being alone. So if that's why I was getting high, I needed to stop. So that's what I did. So I could start a relationship with you."

Morgan looked at her intently. She paused. "This is all really, really new to me. Partnering with another woman."

"Just be you, Morgan, that's who I want. I've never met anyone that makes me feel like you do."

"Me either. You're the forbidden fruit." Saying that made them both smile. Morgan looked around. Mike was in the office with the door closed. There were no customers in the store. Carlo was watching the computer screen, and he was really far away, literally and figuratively. She leaned in and kissed Laida, with every ounce of beauty inside of her that she could muster. Laida bit her lip very softly and sucked on it, and felt the warmth flood down her chest and between her legs. She emitted the smallest little moan, just audible, and the girls parted lips. Morgan glanced quickly back to Carlo. He hadn't moved.

"You're an amazing kisser," whispered Morgan.

"No, you are," replied Laida. They looked deep into each others' eyes, but they both knew that this was not the time or the place for any funny business.

"I missed you," whispered Morgan.

"I missed you too."

"Can we hang out after work?"

"Yes." Morgan brought her voice back up to its normal range.

"So, um, what are you doing for money then, if you're not shopping with Danny V.?"

"Well, I don't know yet. But I started going to twelve-step meetings and the people there told me not to worry, and a lot of the women gave me their phone numbers and told me to call them any time, and that I never had to use again. And they told me that it didn't matter that I didn't have any work right now. The important thing was to change people, places, and things, and to get away from toxic people and any people that use. So, that meant I had to stop running with Danny V., because if I hang out with him, I'll definitely get high again. And the most important thing I can do is not get high any more."

"Wow. That's really intense. I mean, can you smoke pot or drink?"

"No. I can't do *anything*," said Laida.

"Nothing?"

"Nothing. They told me that if I smoke pot, it would just be a substitute for dope, and eventually, I'll just make my way back to my drug of choice. So, no. No drugs, and no drinking."

"Wow," replied Morgan. "That's really intense. I mean, that's actually clean."

"Yeah. Clean."

"How do you feel?"

"I feel *amazing*. I get it now."

212

"Huh. Should *I* stop?" asked Morgan.

"Well, that's up to you. It's your life. There's a real specific reason why I've been getting high for so long. And now that I've recognized it and am dealing with it directly, I can move on and grow. You might not be an addict, and people who are not addicts can start and stop whenever they want. It's not like you're a junkie."

"No, never," she said. Morgan looked with sadness into Laida's eyes. She didn't mean it to come out that way. "How about this, Laida: I just won't smoke pot when I'm around you. Would that be okay?"

"That would be amazing," said Laida. The two women embraced.

"So, what are you driving now?" asked Morgan.

"Well, believe it or not, I didn't think I was going to be able to afford a car, because I didn't have that much money saved up from all the trips. And then this guy at the meeting sold me a little old white Honda Accord for $400."

"Oh my God, his name wasn't Brian Levine, was it?"

"No. His name's Pauly. Pauly D."

"Pauly D.? Like the kid from the *Jersey Shore*? You don't know his last name?"

"Right. It's an anonymous program. So no, I don't."

"Huh. Did he tell you why he sold it to you so cheap?"

"When I asked him why he was selling it, he told me it was his grandmother's and she couldn't drive any more because of her cataracts. He said he didn't want to profit off of people in the program. And he told me he could tell I really needed the car, and that's why he did it. He's been clean ten years. No drugs in ten years."

"Ten years? Is that a joke? Nothing at all? Who's clean for ten years?"

"No, Morgan, he *is*. I'm driving the car right now. It's nice and peppy, and cozy inside. I put little heart seat covers on it. It's cute."

"Wow," replied Morgan. "This is just such a turnaround. I'm really proud of you, Lai." She hugged her again. They heard Michael coughing in the office.

"He smokes a lot of cigarettes," said Laida.

213

"I know. It's like he has a death wish."

Michael emerged from the office and looked like he was ready to leave the store. He had decided a few moments ago that he was better off not saying anything about that sloppy French kiss he witnessed on the video camera that hung in the eye in the sky over the jewelry counter. He rarely watched the monitors, but Morgan had been given specific instructions never to let anyone behind the counter. Instead of coming out and yelling, he had waited, on account of that look that Morgan had in her eyes that he had never seen. He was curious. Seeing that had shaken him up a little bit, which was why he had taken so long to leave the office. He was waiting for Laida to leave so he didn't have to see him/her—he couldn't trust what his reaction was going to be, and he didn't want to embarrass them. He didn't like it when things shook him up, especially right before he was going to play cards. He decided to be polite—an unusual move for him—but only in an unabashed attempt to please the poker gods.

"How are we doing today, ladies?"

"Good," they said in unison. Morgan quickly realized that she wasn't sure if Laida were supposed to be behind the counter. At the first sight of her looking agitated, Michael jumped in.

"No need to change seats ladies. I'm off to go play cards. You can close the store down with Carlo." They glanced over, and Carlo saluted them without removing his eyes from the screen.

"Are you going to Buddy's?" asked Morgan.

"Actually, no. Buddy and I are making a special trip. One of Buddy's friends knows someone named Johnny-O. He runs a big game in Stamford. I've never been down there to their club, but Buddy says there's hedge fund guys and some other suits. He's been there and the action's good. I'm always looking for good action." Laida giggled.

"And what's so funny, Missy?" Michael was being incredibly careful to refer to Laida as a female now that he knew there was something going on with her and Morgan. He didn't want Morgan angry with him, and he didn't want a fight. He still had to process that one. That would be homework.

"Nothing," Laida giggled. "It's just the way you say 'action.'"

"What's wrong with the way I say *action*?"

The girls giggled again. Morgan put in her two cents.

"It's just…Mike, it sounds like you're trolling for hookers or something." She modulated her voice and moved it as low into the male register as she could. "*I'm looking for some action…*" She definitely didn't sound like a man, but it was funny. Laida couldn't stop laughing. She looked at Morgan and laughed harder, thinking about impersonating the Dos Equiis guy on their first date. Morgan looked back at her, thinking about the same thing.

"I'll leave you ladies be. You know what kind of sandwich you need, right? Lettuce alone."

"Ha-ha, very funny Mike," said Morgan. "Why don't you get some new material?"

"Carlo, don't forget to set the alarm," he said as he walked away.

"You got it, boss."

Michael walked out the door and into the world, and the girls looked into each others' eyes and made their own.

The Turn

David was worried. His friend Peter had called him to ask how things were progressing with the company's research on 5,6,7, but the conversation had quickly disintegrated when Pickering happened to mention that there was someone from the government visiting the lab, who had attempted to shake him down for information. He started snooping around and asking questions. David was furious at Peter for his apparent lack of useful information.

"But was he *asking* you about 5,6,7?" David said strongly.

"I told you David, *I don't know*. He wanted access to the graduate lab, and wanted to check on what chemicals we had there. I had no problem telling him to go to hell."

"But was he there because of 5,6,7?" David's adrenaline was up.

"David, I told you, *I never asked him*. We deal with all sorts of chemicals there, and I don't worry about those types of permissions. We have a legal department at the college that has a liaison with the government, and they keep all of our ducks in a row. This visit was totally out of line."

"Peter. You aren't answering my question. Was the agent there because of 5,6,7?"

"David, you aren't listening to me. *I did not ask him*. I would never ask him. I simply explained to him that he didn't have the right to even ask me those questions. That's the truth! He does not have the jurisdiction to even be in my lab. He does not have implied or explicit permission to speak with me. That's the college's policy. And the government knows the college's policy, and this person was trying to skirt the rules."

"But, Peter…"

"Quiet, David! I simply said to him that I would not be a part of his fascist self-reinforcing hegemony, and that I would not answer any of his questions. I told him that if he wanted to ask me anything, he could come back with an arrest warrant. Once he did that, he would be free to detain me, at which point I would retain counsel, invoke my right against self-incrimination, and sit silently until the University came to my aid. At that point, I would be free on bond, and I would sue the government for wrongful arrest, unlawful detention, slander, and intentional infliction of emotional harm, and I would seek damages as yet uncalculated. And I would *still* not say a word. So it was in his best interest to leave. Which he did."

David was speechless. He really did like Peter. Deny 'til you die, without even knowing it. He was a boulder—an immovable object. The amazing part was that because Peter was so interested in fighting *the system* as he interpreted it, he couldn't actually see the individual trees in the forest. It was all just forest to him. But David needed to know about one particular tree in that forest—that lone tree whose fruit he was not supposed to eat—and he needed to know if the government had seen him snipping off a little cutting under cover of darkness.

This conversation was so unnerving to David—it was as if this 5,6,7 side project was becoming his main one. Not only was it becoming his main project, it was becoming his only project. Travel had happened to slow down, and he realized that the rest of his reporting work that he thought filled days could actually be completed in a couple hours. It was the first thing on his mind when he woke up. It was the last thing he thought of when he fell asleep next to his comatose wife passed out from the booze. His step-daughter wasn't talking to him any more—she was miffed. This new compound and his communications with the German office and the planning and the hedging were all threatening to engulf him. Thank God that he had Peter.

Peter was the best guard dog. In a single breath he not only proclaimed his undying loyalty to David, but he also did so in the best way—under a misplaced notion of it somehow being a matter of principle. David was sad for a moment. He realized

217

that deep down, he knew as soon as Peter had come to him with the 5,6,7 exactly how this would all play out. It was like a poker hand, and it was just one of those hands that played itself. David *knew* that he could manipulate Peter because of his radical left-wing proclivities. The only reason he felt bad was because they'd known each other for so long. And the flop had come perfectly. David took a deep breath.

"Okay. Okay. I understand Peter. Some government guys…"

"One single government agent. A scout, if you will."

"Okay. One lone government agent came to see you. Because you feel so strongly about your particularly broad interpretation of Constitutional rights, you decided to not even find out what the man wanted, but decided it would be an easier tact to simply go on an anti-government tirade to scare the agent away. Does that sound about right?"

"It happens all the time in the animal kingdom, David. The puffer fish inflates to stick out its spines when it feels threatened. An octopus squirts ink to confuse and then hide from a potential predator. These examples are everywhere in Nature. I dug in my toolbox and pulled out some solid material. It felt right."

David chuckled a little. He knew he wasn't getting an answer to his question. He knew the plan. He had designed it. He had his contact, Viens, at the Durham office in Germany working with the DEA directly in a covert way to import the chemical back into America. When Viens asked if it were a problem if this were done in a less than legal way, David told him to do whatever he needed to do, as long as there were no bits of evidence that could link the importation of illegal chemicals to him. He just didn't want to know.

"I understand, Peter. This is just some sort of San Francisco convention of rules of engagement with powerbrokers. You just love a confrontation with an authority figure."

"I do. I really do."

"I know you do. So, was your gut feeling that this agent was there on account of the 5,6,7?" There was a pause and he heard Peter exhale.

"Honestly, David. I don't know. As soon as I saw that laminate and those three letters DEA, I just saw red."

He really is just like a guard dog, thought David. How a man so smart could be so easily fooled...

"Okay. Thanks for letting me know," replied David.

"And how has the research on the compound come along?" asked Peter.

"Good. We've been able to reverse engineer it and synthetically create it, but it's costly, time-consuming, and the chemical process itself apparently utilizes some relatively unstable compounds that break down outside of certain narrow temperature ranges. We're still working on a better method to extract it from the plant material, but it's difficult because it's found in highest concentration in the most delicate parts of the plant, and without having access to a whole lot of the plant, we're kind of muddling through."

"It sounds like you need a greenhouse."

"Well," replied David, "All that's taking place in the German offices for good reason. We're still banging out what's better—synthesis or extraction. It's difficult without an entire team, but this is a very sensitive chemical for a number of reasons."

"Of course," replied Peter. "I'm sorry I couldn't have been more helpful about that little 'visit' I had."

"That's fine Peter. I always appreciate your call."

The two men ended the call and David stood looking at his refrigerator. This was concerning. He had to think this through. Unconsciously, he opened the fridge to grab a snack. He looked in and saw that Allison had finished several boxes of wine in just the last two days. It disgusted him. He called for his wife who was upstairs.

"Allison! Allison!"

He heard a muffled response.

"Allison, come downstairs."

"I'm sorry?" she said as she sauntered down the stairs.

"You know you drank almost all that wine."

"Is this going to be a big argument, David? Because you still haven't brought my car in for service and that light is still blinking. If you want to argue, we can argue about all the things that you said you were going to help me with around the house, and then don't because you go out and play cards with those degenerates."

She might be drinking all the time, but he had to admit she didn't miss much. David got annoyed, but he didn't want to get started with this. He didn't need his escape valve blocked at this point, especially after this new stuff he just heard from Pickering.

"Fine. I won't argue." He bit his lower lip. She was getting more and more distant from him as she slipped deeper and deeper into alcohol addiction. But he caught himself—was that really it? Or was it that his choices of late trying to massage the law and work on 5,6,7 was clouding his judgment? Was that making him focus on the negative parts of his relationship, since it was a secret he couldn't tell his wife about? Was it just another secret that would continue to drive a wedge through his already fragile marriage?

"Just remember things are usually more complicated than they look," began Allison. "You didn't see me drink that wine..."

"Allison, I..."

She walked back upstairs to her computer. He wasn't thinking about her right now, though. He was thinking about Pickering.

Something bothered him about Peter's interaction. That first meeting when they had convened had been off the record. He still remembered it—they were talking about linking people's consciousness together for short periods of time, and he was driving in the car service car with ridiculously high mileage, and the driver was mentioning workers drunk on the assembly line at the Ford plant. No one had known about that meeting. Peter had told his grad students they didn't get government clearance for studying the chemical, and he had insisted that David was the only one that he'd contacted. Clearly, Pickering would never sell him out to the government. David was forced to arrive at the conclusion that this could have only come from inside his own company. Were they watching him?

He shrugged it off. He knew that he was still in charge of the game. It was *his* game, and *he* was calling it. He knew that even if his operation got shut down as the chemical were being imported into the U.S., he could still claim that he had no idea that Durham was doing this. His name was not on anything. He had full deniability. He trusted Pickering with his life—the entry point of the 5,6,7 into his personal pipeline was secure. That man would rather be burned at the stake and die a martyr than break down and cry to the government. The back end was safe. No, it was the front end where there was risk. But he had one more trick up his sleeve.

He knew that even if their government contact at the DEA turned on them, he had one more group that could pick up the slack—his little group of acquaintances (including personal friend and COO, René Boudreau) who ran the huge Family Heritage Fund. That private equity group controlled over $150 billion in assets worldwide. He could sell them all of the work that was done around 5,6,7, and they could set up a new company in an appropriate country to make the stuff. Lord knows, they had contacts.

If the U. S. of A. decided to be a little less Lady Liberty and a little more the World's Policeman, he would call René, but only as a last resort if his back were against the wall. He knew he could have gone to them in the first place, but he knew 5,6,7 needed to be handled by a large pharmaceutical firm to be studied for its maximum efficacy. He was the right man for the job, and his company was the right company for the job. This was a poker hand that was all playing out like it was supposed to. For David, this was not about taking a principled stand. He wanted to make money, to appear successful, to impress his wife, to keep up with the Jones's, and to make his deceased parents proud. He thought that maybe if he were more successful, Allison wouldn't want to drink any more. He was shallow. He didn't think about anything but the money. That's what it was all about for him. Hard work. Well-placed bets on the market. Thoughtful executive decisions. Nothing more.

René was definitely his last choice, but he was glad he *had* a choice. He didn't want to cook his goose on this one. David knew he could technically be found guilty of breaking a boatload of laws. He had intentionally sent an illegal scheduled drug overseas, in order that it be synthesized in large quantities away from the direct purview of the DEA, in order that it be imported back into the country for trials in the U.S. that rested in a legal grey area. In fact, this whole 5,6,7 project seemed to have taken on a life of its own, and didn't even feel under his direct control any more. He felt as if he were watching himself and his own life from outside of his body.

He was now in charge of a classified project in a large multinational corporation, one that if the CEO ever found out about, Herr Koenig would tie around his neck like a millstone and drop him in the Mariana Trench, firing him immediately and publicly with loss of pension and benefits. And this didn't scare him one iota, because he knew if this were the case, he would call his friend René. He would sell René those illegal blueprints to create a chemical that would allow the Family Heritage Fund to make copious amounts of money.

But he wasn't worried about any of that. He was a poker player. That was the low-probability event. The one-outer—when his opponent only has one card that can save him. David wasn't drawing dead. He still had outs. He liked his positioning. René was just a hedge bet, a side bet, not the main pot. A credit default swap. A term life insurance policy.

The only thing he didn't grasp was why they were talking to Pickering. It was probably nothing. He always cried wolf. Such a Democrat. David decided he wouldn't overreact to that news, and put it in its place where it belonged. This was why he worked as part of a team. And Pickering was not on his team. He was just the water boy. But David was getting thirsty.

"Allison, is there any more wine?"

She didn't answer. He opened the fridge and saw the one box left in there. He picked it up—it was very light. He pushed the button and one last glass trickled out. He didn't feel like flattening the box and hiding it. His wife was a drunk. And suffering.

He stared at the glass of wine for a long time.

"Bottoms up," he said, as he threw his hand back.

*   *   *

222

Josh had dozed off after his eyes got tired from surfing the web—his sleep was interrupted when the doorbell rang and the mail carrier left a package at his door. He had been thinking back to that horrible twelve-day stretch of time at school when he couldn't sleep, no matter how hard he tried, and how much better he felt now after cutting back on his drug regimen. He still remembered his psychotic thoughts as if it had happened yesterday—he always found that fascinating that replaying an experience in his consciousness could be almost exactly like the first time it happened. He'd believed he was in a movie. He remembered asking himself a string of questions as he sat looking out his window at the other people walking by as the thoughts flowed out of his rapidly-spinning sleep-deprived brain:

Was this planet he was walking on poisonous? Was this some sort of *Twelve-Monkeys*-esque nightmare scenario where he was some sort of prisoner being sent to the ruins of the surface to inspect these people he was seeing? Were his keepers just using his brain like a two-way radio, seeing out of the cameras in his eyes to take stock of these aliens that had colonized Earth? The Earth that they had somehow destroyed? Or was he just walking through a virtual replica of the Earth, suspended in time immediately before it was destroyed with the press of a button, trying to figure out how *not* to blow it up? Who was holding him captive? Was he born enslaved? Then why did all these aliens look so much like us? Did they clone us? Or were they just spirit beings moving like light, a wave and a particle simultaneously changing form and function to illuminate us for the sacks of flesh flour that we are? Was he being filmed now?

He'd finally made the decision to go the infirmary, but even in the doctor's office, his mental state was falling apart. The questions flowed once more:

Was he not actually seeing a doctor, but learning to heal himself? Would just physically seeing the doctor be enough to heal him? Was the exact specific image that made up what his brain perceived as the doctor's form actually his prescription? Was this the promise of future medicine? Once we had invented time travel in the future, wouldn't the Josh from the future have already told the doctor what to say to him? Why didn't he already know what the doctor would say to him? The door opened.

"Hello, Mr. Grenier. I'm Dr. Ladd. Why don't you come inside with me."

Josh had followed him through the door. There were pictures of skeletons and of the human bodies. They sat facing each other, the doctor looking at him with concern.

"What seems to be the trouble?" He had a folder in his hand, and Josh had decided that whatever was going on in the deeper background processes in his mind had to pause for the time being. He chose his words carefully and spoke slowly.

"I haven't been able to sleep. I'm really stressed out. Do you think you could give me an Ambien or something?" He paused. "Just so that I can rest?"

Dr. Ladd looked over his glasses at Josh. "Is there any particular reason you're not sleeping?"

"No reason. Stressed I guess. Exams coming up."

The doctor's brow went up. "You're just stressed out about your classes? Any class in particular?"

He couldn't remember the last class he'd attended. He couldn't even think of the name of one of his classes.

"Honestly, I just need to sleep."

Doctor Ladd sighed. "Have you taken anything recently that might be affecting your sleep? I've seen it all, Josh." The doctor smiled kindly. The cloud of craziness around Josh's head seemed to have some breaks in it. He did some quick mental calculations.

"I don't know. What do you mean?"

"Well, I'm just worried that you might have taken some drugs, and unless you tell me what you've been taking, I can't really help you. Do you understand?"

Josh did. His brain started spinning. He couldn't tell the doctor the kinds of drugs he was taking. They'd commit him. Or lock him in jail. Josh said nothing.

"I'm looking at a campus police report here, Josh. From your freshman year. Do you know what I'm talking about?"

His engine spun wildly. He tried to shift out of neutral but he couldn't get the clutch disc to grab the pressure plate. The smell of burning clutch with the engine wide open. He licked his lips but couldn't speak. The doctor continued.

"It says here that they found you in the middle of the night wandering around in one of the buildings barefoot, and that you were not responsive. They told you that if you didn't speak to them they were going to take you to the town jail. You then were put in a cell in the town jail, at which point you proceeded to strip off your clothes and put them in the toilet, repeatedly flushing the toilet full of clothes, until the guard came over when the water was running all over the floor. At which point you told him you were trying to escape by flushing yourself down the toilet, clothes first."

Josh half-remembered that night. He saw the stainless steel toilet with no seat. He didn't remember that part of the story, but he had been told that several times afterward. The doctor continued.

"It says in the report that you told them you had taken a substance called 'alpha chloralose,' which is, if I'm not mistaken, a tranquilizer designed for large birds. I don't even know where you get it from. I've never seen or read about a human being ingesting it in all my years as an intern or as a physician. And then it says here that you were never formally charged—apparently you have someone pretty important looking out for you, because someone called in a favor, and you were given a warning and told to see a physician. Josh, I don't know where you got this goose tranquilizer, but it indicates to me that you're past the experimentation phase. You may be just a plain old drug addict."

Of course he was a drug addict, Josh thought. But this doctor had no idea what it was like to be him. He was unique. He was special. He needed this stuff because he couldn't look at the darkness that was inside of him. He was never a destructive sort of person. He was at Williams after all, and he always reminded himself that he was at the number one liberal arts college in America, the greatest country in the world. He didn't want to die. He wanted to live. He wanted to build. He wanted to protect people's right to alter their consciousness as they saw fit. That's why he was going to make the church. That's why he was going to influence public policy with his views. He was going to teach these other people and show them he was smarter than them—they needed their right to get high protected before the government took it away. And Josh was willing to be their bellwether. He was willing to work within the system to design a church to do it. Why didn't Dr. Ladd understand this?

This doctor's visit was cutting into his time. He just wanted to get back to his projects. He was just about ready to plant the next harvest of phalaris grass to begin the next DMT extraction. Something in his brain could just not release that image of the DMT. He could see it, that caramelized sugar on top of a crème brûlée, that burnt plastic smell, liquefying and vaporizing in the pipe, burning his lungs, exhaling the smoke and watching reality melt and disappear into a red and green pixilated hyperspace of timeless, shapeless, pure energy. Yhwh Himself. Josh had a second of peace. He looked at Dr. Ladd.

"Can I tell you the truth?"

"Of course," said the Doctor.

"It's like, I feel like when we sleep, our soul leaves our body and flies around in the air at the speed of light to this secret special spot on the Earth, where it goes down a little tube with everyone else's souls, like a soul highway. And it downloads our experiences into the big computer that is the Gaian hypermind, that is this planet, this Earth, and then the Earth uploads our instructions for the next day and our soul flies back into our brains, and then we wake up. And we're all doing this, every day and every night, as part of this big plan for the Earth. And I can't sleep. And I'm afraid my soul will never be able to find that spot again. And I'm so worried that I've been cut off, you know. Like the Earth is rejecting my soul from going home. But I haven't hurt myself or anyone else. I just don't know why the Earth won't let me come home. I don't know what to do."

He had sat and sobbed quietly while Dr. Ladd called for an ambulance.

And Josh was back, staring at the cardboard box that had just arrived. It was heavier than he thought it would be, and opened it carefully. He had finally located a relatively affordable copy of Johnathan Ott's *Pharmacotheon* on, of all places, Amazon.com. He thought that was so ironic—he was buying a book explaining the nuances of the known entheogenic plant-

226

teachers from the Amazonian rainforest, and had purchased it from an online site called Amazon.com. He decided that his next project would be to enter, by hand, a fairly long list of psychoactive compounds in the rear of that book into his protected chemical list. He hadn't felt like writing another newsletter yet. His stress level had been rising.

The book was out-of-print: some even banned it or called it dangerous. It was a comprehensive collection, a compendium of all of the known data on intoxicating tryptamines. Josh loved its density and its copious references. He had already added every chemical to his website to be protected by the church that was known to be psychoactive, so it seemed as if the next step would be to add every chemical from *Pharmacotheon* that was potentially hallucinogenic but not studied in humans.

He started entering the data in list form. When he typed in "5,6,7-trimethoxy-dmt," he didn't note it as any different from any other alkaloid: he was just transcribing others' research. He uploaded the list to the web.

*   *   *

The flop had come queen of diamonds, queen of spades, five of diamonds. There was a pre-flop raise to seventy, which was pretty standard in the 5-10, and three players in: Greek Timmy, David Evans, and in his first visit to the club, Mike Mazzone. After Buddy introduced Michael to everyone, he had made himself right at home and started smoking up a storm. They all thought Michael was a really likeable guy—a man's man. They loved his calm demeanor and cool delivery, and he had great stories. But right now he was quiet. Deep in thought, playing poker.

Mike was first to act, but not the raiser, who was Greek Timmy, who had been making some wild bets in a very lively 5-10. He checked to David. Dave seemed like a good guy to Mike, and a strong player. He already had gotten the vibe off of him that he was a consistent winner and played solid poker. The Greek was definitely the wildcard. David surveyed everything and checked. The Greek checked.

The turn card was the jack of clubs. Mike looked down at his King-Queen offsuit. He didn't like where this was headed. He surveyed how much everyone had in front of them. He flopped three queens with a king kicker and checked out of position on the flop. Now, even though no one had bet, he didn't like the two diamonds, he didn't like the jack, and he didn't like the crazy Greek last to act. He counted out a bet of $250 and threw the chips. He eyed David.

David was thinking. He looked at the Greek's chipstack: he was light, maybe $1500 in front of him. David was sure he was going to raise Michael's bet, it was just a matter of how much he wanted to put in. David slid $1000 in a neat stack to the bet line. Timmy didn't even wait. He said "all-in" and slid his chips. Michael, who had watched David's bet and understood what he was doing, said he called, as did David. There was a little over $5000 in the pot with no more betting.

"You wanna' show?" asked the dealer, this goofy looking kid named Keith. "Or you wanna' wait for the river card."

"I show," said Timmy. He flipped over the king of diamonds with the ten of diamonds.

Mike swallowed. That was worse than he thought. Ace-queen he could accept. It would be a cooler, but he could accept it. He put Timmy on king-queen, or even pocket tens. Seeing king ten of diamonds made Michael worry. He didn't like that. His exterior was still, but on the inside he was fuming. The Greek had a lot of outs. Any diamond for the flush, any ace, or any nine for the straight. That was a lot of outs. What was even more a worry was that David hadn't turned over his cards. He could have hit the boat on the flop with pocket fives, or on the turn with pocket jacks. Or he could have queen jack and hit a boat. But he wasn't showing his cards yet.

The river bricked out. Four of clubs. Timmy's face turned red. He walked away over to the couch and just sat down quietly. He'd taken a lot of heat lately and was just on a losing streak. He waved his hand up and said he was out. Michael looked at David.

"Whatcha' holdin', Big Pharma?" Michael laughed at David. Dave smiled. He liked Michael, first time meeting him. And Mike had already nicknamed him.

"I don't know Pawn Star, what do you have?"

"I have a feeling that name's not gonna' stick." He was smiling at David, still trying to read him after the hand so he would have his number if he ever played him again.

David flipped over king-queen offsuit. Michael laughed sharply and flipped over the same hand. David laughed.

"Split pot. Trip queens," said Keith. Keith robotically started splitting the pot.

"You had me scared there, Big Pharma. I thought you might've boated up."

"If I had boated up, I would have raised to $750 instead of $1000 so I could re-pop you."

"I kind of guessed that. It's predictable play, but good poker."

"Thanks, Mike," he said, counting his chips. He thought back to what they were discussing earlier. He wanted to pick up the conversation they were having before that hand.

"Hey Mike..."

"Yeah?"

"You know, I've been thinking a lot about what you said. I may need to stop and see you. I mean, why should I pay full price for electronics when you have things for so much less?"

"Because the shit is stolen," piped in Carrick, who was sitting on the couch. He had already blown his wad in the 2-5 earlier and was watching football and waiting for some late-night hot wings to get delivered.

Michael's eyes got big and he shot a glance over to the couch, but he couldn't see who was there.

"You got somethin' to say tough guy? Come over here and talk about it."

"Hey, hey," said David to Michael, "That's just Carrie. He's a drunk and he doesn't know what he's talking about. We don't need to make a thing of it."

Michael glanced over at Buddy, who was talking shop with Johnny-O. He caught his glance, made sure Michael knew he was seen and heard, and went back to his conversation. Buddy had told him on the ride down that he knew Johnny-O. from a long way back when they both made book, and he told Michael that as long as he didn't wave his piece around or get in

229

a fight, they could stop down from time to time and skim a little off the top from these fucks in the 5-10. Michael was a little torn about what to do. So much of his rapport was about being the alpha dog, that when he was challenged in a new social situation, he had to walk that fine line between saving face and not upsetting the house. He wished that Carrie would come over and man up, but the fact that he didn't gave Mike some power.

"It doesn't matter if the shit's stolen. I don't break any laws. People come into the store and sign a piece of paper that says they hold legal title to the goods. If they want to steal shit and then lie about it to me, then they're wrong, not me."

"But Mike, I mean, if you know it's stolen, then that's wrong. Isn't that simple?"

"It's not that simple, Dave."

David looked at him. God, he thought, he sounds like my wife. His tone begged for his response.

"Okay. Why isn't it simple?"

"How can you prove to me that something's stolen? When the person you claim stole it comes in and signs a piece of paper saying that they didn't steal it? That *is* the proof."

"But they're just lying."

"Prove it. Prove they're lying."

"Well, I can't prove it. But they're lying," said Dave.

"Well, if you can't prove they're lying, then you can't prove it's stolen."

"Okay, I understand your point, but let's try using induction instead of deduction."

"Induction? You going to put me in the hall of fame, or make my wife have a baby early?" The other guys laughed. Michael was the life of the party.

David initially thought that Mike was just another slimy guido, but it was becoming clear from his interaction that while he was a little rough around the edges, his mind was sharp and crisp. He waited for the laughter to subside.

"No," said David. "How about thinking about it this way. A guy comes in with a brand new, I don't know, what do people bring in?"

"For the sake of example?" said Mike. "Okay. A Kitchenaid."

230

"Like, a mixer?"

Michael nodded.

"People pawn mixers?" David asked.

"We can only take them new because of health code stuff. But the professional ones are $300 retail. If you're interested, I'll let you have one for $150."

"Huh," replied David. "You know my wife was actually bothering me for another one of those. She loaned hers to her cousin and never got it back, and now it's this big thing, and...well, maybe I do want a Kitchenaid. Do you have all the different colors?"

"Red, white, black. I don't think they make the pink one any more. Just take your pick."

"Huh. I actually will probably end up taking one of those from you. Anyway, stop tempting me. Just stop it."

"What the fuck, stop it. I just offered you something you need at a $150 savings and you're telling me to fuck off?"

"I'm sorry, Mike. You're actually a really nice guy. I've just never met a pawnbroker before," said David.

"Not too many in your little suburban cookie-cutter neighborhood? Let me guess. A lot of white picket fences and stone walls?"

"Actually, there *are* a lot stone fences," replied David.

"What the fuck is a stone fence?" asked Carrick, from the couch.

"Well," said David, "A stone fence is like a stone wall..."

"But it has no mortar." Michael finished his sentence. David looked incredibly surprised that Michael knew that tidbit. He always pictured a pawnbroker to be, unsophisticated somehow.

"Yeah, that's absolutely right. How, um...how did you know that?" asked David.

"Know what? The difference between a stone wall and a stone fence? I don't know. When the guy was putting in the stone lions at the driveway to my house, we had a conversation. Hooked him up with a nice Murano vase. Old Italian guy talked my ear off."

"You have stone lions in front of your driveway?" David looked at Michael quizzically.

"You don't?" Michael paused with a deadpan expression. He let the weight of his comment sink in. "Anyway, so you were saying. A guy brings in a brand new Kitchenaid. And…"

This guy's confident as shit, thought David. He intentionally derailed my train of thought when I'm trying to question the legitimacy of his business. He then offers to sell me something at a significant discount, and when I protest, he seals the deal, and then allows me to continue arguing against him. Hot shit.

"Okay. So, a guy brings in a brand new Kitchenaid. Where did he get it?"

"I don't know. Maybe he got it as a gift." Michael pulled on his cigarette.

"Is the guy single?" asked David "Because I can tell you right now only people who bake use those. And guys that live in a house usually are married. What if he brings in two, or three, or four?" David twirled his wedding band around on his finger.

"Maybe he gets a lot of gifts. Got lots of friends that don't talk to each other to make sure they didn't all give him the same thing." Mike chuckled.

"Seriously, though."

"Seriously?"

"How would you answer that question to someone in a governmental capacity?"

"Well, David, I would tell anyone that needed that level of detail and who wanted to scrutinize my business to that point, that most likely this unlucky fellow had maxed out the cash advance portion of his credit card, and had purchased the item brand new from the store for $300, knowing that we would give him $100 cash on the spot today for that item. Whether or not he was ever going to pay off that $300 he just ran up on his card is out of my view. If the guy declares bankruptcy or defaults, that's something you need to take up with banking regulators. How's that, Mr. Evans? I mean, Big Pharma? Professional enough for you?"

Mike laughed and lit another cigarette. He raised his fingers and motioned to Buddy he wanted to stay four or five more minutes. Buddy nodded and kept talking to Johnny-O. in the corner in hushed tones.

"Well, while I believe that to be a good yarn, Mr. Mazzone, you are not expecting me to believe that with the volume of people coming in every day, enough to support a whole store, that everyone is simply maxing out their credit cards? I mean, if that were really true, that would show up in other ways. The metrics just don't work. I don't buy it."

"Prove to me that it's not true," said Mike, grinning.

"Well, I can't. I can't. But it can't *be*. I mean, it just can't."

"Well Big Pharma, it looks like you're batting zero. You couldn't prove that my merch is stolen. You can't prove the customers are lying. And you can't prove they're not just maxing out their credit cards and taking the cash, or that they're pawning gifts. I have to say, I honestly only exist as a business because of you."

"I'm sorry?" David was taken aback.

"Because you don't cure drug addicts. You keep them sick. Whether they really are boosting or not, you'd have to be high to sell a $300 item for $100. That's crazy! No, Big Pharma. It's you. Your company has us by the balls. Coming and going. And keeping us sick while we're here."

"That's not fair, Michael. Our top-selling drug is Duscantia. It's a migraine headache medicine. We're not making people sick. We're helping them."

"But it's your industry, David. Your industry got challenged with curing drug addicts, and what do you come up with? Methadone? The junkies hate methadone so much they want to do smack again. Or they take half and sell half, all at the taxpayers' expense. It's genius. But not only that. It's like a self-reinforcing downward spiral. And big pharma makes more money by keeping addicts sick instead of treating the root cause, because then they can continue to make more money on a sick person than a well person. Face it, David, you don't want people to die. You just want them to have just enough diseases that they require as many of your services for as long as possible. That's a sick business, bro. Fuck that. I'm happy pawning. And the junkies coming to see me, are only here because your company and all the ones like your company don't give a shit about us. Only money. You and me, we're the same. We're both in the

233

same business of fucking drug addicts. I'm just more upfront about it."

Michael let all that sink in. He didn't mean to challenge David too much—he just knew the dude could take it. He was a good player.

"Hey Keith," said Michael. "This is my last hand. Then I need a rack." Keith busied himself with the cards.

"You're all right, Michael," said David. "I wish that I could agree with everything that you said, but you know I can't. But it really was nice to meet you though. A true pleasure. And I might take you up on that mixer."

"Honestly, Pharma, you're a better poker player than a debater. We'll see each other again, I'm pretty sure, when Buddy feels like driving with me all the way here." Mike looked down at his hand. Ten four suited. He threw them into the muck and got up to leave.

David looked down at his hand. Pocket aces. Huh. He was surprised. First time he'd had those all night. The action went around pre-flop while Michael was cashing out. When he came back, there was seventy-five dollars in the pot and David was in the hand with one caller. He glanced up at Michael.

"David, I knew I liked you when we chopped up the Greek's money. We fucked him good. I knew you were my boy. So, you call me if you need anything. *Anything. You understand, Pharma?* You call me. Here's my card."

"I will," said David. Mike threw his business card on to the table right as Keith laid out the cards for the flop. David saw the glossy business card and finished reading the large print, "Mike Mazzone, Premium Pawn" at the same time Keith had spread open the five, six, and seven of clubs. In sequence. David inhaled sharply. He didn't remember if he said, "Shit."

It took David a second to focus on what was going on. The guy to his left had checked and it was his action. He knew he had pocket aces. It was just surreal. Sitting there at the table. The first time he'd had aces all night. Right as Michael was leaving. If you need anything, here's my card…and there it was, the 5,6,7, numerically laid out in front of him. He couldn't stop staring at those cards. 5,6,7. Plain as day. He felt as if he were in a dream space. And the only thing between him and the 5,6,7 was the card that read "Mike Mazzone." And he was holding bullets. He didn't speak for a minute. He was taking it all in. The moment was just too overwhelming. Few moments in his life were ever that potent. Finally, Keith chimed it.

"If you want to check it down, Mr. Evans, that's okay. You're still eligible for the jackpot."

"I'm sorry, what?" David was confused. Befuddled.

"The jackpot. If you make a straight flush you automatically win $250. You can check it down if you want and still be eligible if one of you hits it."

"That's fine, I check," said David.

They ended up checking it down. David's aces held up, and they were pushing the pot toward him when he saw the door open and Michael leave with Buddy. Something was happening to him. He started thinking about the future. He had some very rash thoughts.

These coincidences were too much. He thought back to meeting Josh and him saying 5,6,7 twice. Then the Mexican man holding the sign about 5 appetizers for $6 til 7pm. And now, the cards. The cards were the last straw—he was definitely supposed to meet Michael. His mind drifted. What if things went south with Viens, and he got fired, and he ended up selling the 5,6,7 blueprints to Réné's people? What had he become? And these numbers just mocking him like this? Or was it God? That complex being he'd never really understood and paid lip service to without ever really thinking too much about his faith? Were those cards God speaking to him? Reminding him of the number of the train he was on right now? That train set in motion by his own hand, and now traveling much faster than he ever thought possible? Hurtling toward what?

He shook himself back into reality. He was a businessman, an executive VP of sales for a multinational pharmaceutical firm. His phone was full of C-level contacts from across the nation. He was at the top of his field and at the peak of his earnings power. The only reason he was even hanging out in this hole-in-the-wall underground poker club is because he wanted to get away from his wife, whose alcoholism was pushing him farther and farther out of his own home.

Maybe Michael had a point. Maybe his company was to blame. Maybe he wasn't putting the time into his marriage he should have been because of all the travel and the meetings. Maybe he was trying to keep his relationship healthy by trying to keep her alcoholism contained, instead of attacking the root of the problem and telling her that he was going to leave her unless she went to rehab. But he wasn't going to deal with that now— that was tomorrow's problem. And tonight? He didn't want to stay in that poker room anymore. The five, six, seven of clubs had freaked him out. He needed to get away from the table. He racked up and went to cash out.

Michael's business card went right into his wallet. He never connected well with guys like him—usually it was the people like Josh in the world that gravitated toward him. But there was something he saw in Michael's eyes. It was a twinkle of understanding. He just knew somehow. He knew that he was destined to meet Michael in this off-the-beaten-path underground poker club. It was in the cards.

* * *

Laida was driving her little white Honda over to Morgan's apartment to pick her up so that they could go together to her twelve-step group. She was thinking about what she was going to share about when she got there—she had been finding it very therapeutic to talk about her problems with other people publicly, and to befriend other women. However, she hadn't told any of the people in recovery that she was transgender, and so far as she knew, no one was the wiser. That was very positive in that it gave her a new start, but it meant there were certain subjects she had to keep to herself. The men and women who had been clean for many years had all told her the same thing— you're only as sick as your secrets. She didn't consider it a secret that she'd been born a man: it was just something that was none of anyone's business. Still, she found it easier to stuff those memories than to speak about them.

As she pulled up to a traffic light, she saw that the car in front of her was a Buick like her father's. Almost unconsciously, she lost focus and started remembering riding in that Riviera to go to the movies with him. He took her to watch violent movies made for men. She wouldn't even try to watch. At the end she didn't even pretend. He would be watching the car chases, the bad guys spraying the good guys with bullets, and their responding single shots taking out the aggressors. He cheered when the train hit the car. He cheered when the bad guy's hand got chopped off. And Laida was just watching the women. What were they wearing? How did they keep their hair and makeup so perfect while doing those stunts? Where did they get those clothes? Nice eyelashes. She hated the rides home. She remembered one day when she was thirteen.

"Now, I just don't think that he could have gotten shot in the shoulder like that and then run all that way to go tell her that they were going to blow up the house," her dad said.

"Huh?" Laida responded.

"I mean, I tried running and working out after giving blood."

"That's stupid, Dad." She didn't even know why he was talking to her. He just wanted to connect—to engage his moody and irritable child who seemed to be getting more and more distant and stranger every day.

"No it's not. Some runners go to places like Denver where the air is thinner and there's less oxygen to train for races, so that it's easier for them to run at a normal elevation. That's what the most serious runners do."

"That doesn't mean it's a good idea to give blood and then run."

"Well," he said, "I thought, what's the difference if I go to a higher elevation where there's less oxygen, or run after giving blood so there is less blood in my body to deliver the regular amount of oxygen to my brain? Same thing right?"

"I don't think so, Dad." He could be so stupid.

"Well, you would think it would be."

"I wouldn't think that."

"Well, I can tell you for a fact that it's not the same thing. It's a *way* deeper sort of weakness in your body. Real fatigue. Different than just having it be really humid or with really thin air. I felt like I was going to pass out after three-quarters of a mile! Like, really pass out. Falling down passing out!"

"That's the stupidest thing I've ever heard," she said.

"Larry, it's not stupid. I'm just saying that there's no way he could've run that far after losing the amount of blood he appeared to have lost just on his shirt after getting shot. It's not realistic."

"It's not supposed to be realistic, Dad. It's Hollywood. And don't call me Larry."

"You're my son, Lawrence. I named you that, and that's what I'm going to call you. Now stop it. And did you see that other scene where the car had a dent on the driver door during the car chase, and then a little while later it didn't have the dent. Did you see that? I poked you to tell you to look."

"I felt you poke me. And I didn't appreciate it. And my name isn't Lawrence, it's Laida. And I'm not your son, I'm your daughter."

"We're not doing this again. Why do you have to always ruin a perfectly good night? You're my son, and that's that."

"But, I'm not."

"Don't argue with me, Larry."

"It's Laida."

"Larry, please, I tried to take you to a movie for you to have a good time with me. Just father and son. Do you have to do this every time?"

"Dad, I will never be Larry. I never have been Larry. You named me that, but my name is Laida. It just is. And unless you call me that, I'm not talking any more."

"Larry, I'm not calling you that. You're a boy. Period."

Silence. More silence. Her father finally slammed the dashboard with his palm and made a little dust that had collected rise and fall.

"*Why can't you just be a normal boy?!*" he yelled straight ahead at the open road. He hit the steering wheel with his hand and rubbed his brow and forehead. They both sat in silence until they got home, at which point Laida went into her room and sat crying softly to herself. She stripped off all of her boy clothes and changed to dress as a girl. She put on a pink shirt she'd swiped from her sister, and padded one of her bras with water balloons, and started brushing her hair. She lay on her bed and played some music. The tears dried up. It was a visceral reaction to looking natural. She was doodling and calming down when her father knocked on the door.

"Will you come out and talk to me? I want to apologize." She thought about it. He had never seen her in girls' clothes. Her older sister Nicole had told her to never to do that to him. She was a nurse, and had already moved out and had a job, but she told Laida that would just upset him, and that he was trying his best.

"No, Dad."

"Will you just open the door then? So I can say goodnight?"

"No."

"Please, Larry. I don't want to fight with you." Hearing that name caused her to start crying again. Why wouldn't he call her Laida? Why wouldn't he let her start high school as a girl? In a different town? She would go anywhere, do anything, to be her.

"Don't call me that. My name is Laida!"

"Larry, I..." Her anger took over. Fuck him, she thought. Nicole was wrong. Laida didn't care if she were a nurse. She didn't know what this felt like, to be emotionally abused like this. Maybe if her Dad just saw her like this, he would be able to deal with it better. Maybe he would see that this is what she was supposed to look like, who she was supposed to be. She swung the door open.

Shock couldn't really describe her father's face. It was more confusion, and then his face turned red. She had never seen him like this—it was very scary. He stammered and stuttered, and he couldn't make out a single word. He stared at the lines of the bra and the fake breasts and his eyes got wide. He lunged and her and slapped her across the face.

"Faggot!"

Laida fell to her knees, shocked that he'd hit her. He had *never* hit her. Her father stood above her, shaking.

"You...fucking...little..." His voice shook, and he started to cry. "You're a little faggot. You're a fucking...you're a little fucking...homo. You piece of shit. I didn't raise you like...you...you...I don't...you..." Laida was crying.

"I'm not a faggot," she whispered between coughs and wheezes. The tears were rolling down her face. "I'm a *girl*." She started bawling. Her father looked like he was going to say she wasn't, and instead he just exhaled and turned around crying and walked away. They had never really spoken deeply again after that day.

As she pulled into Morgan's driveway, she wiped the wet corners of her eyes and sniffled. When Morgan got in the car, her face had returned to normal, and she explained to her that they were running late and had missed the first five minutes of the meeting already. After they'd parked at the church and hurried in, the girls quietly took their seats as the others were clapping at the introduction of the speaker.

"Hi, my name is Rollo and I'm an addict."

"Hi, Rollo," the group replied in unison.

"Is he the group leader?" whispered Morgan to Laida. She was very confused. She'd offered to go to a twelve-step meeting with Laida to see what this recovery thing was all about, but it seemed like Greek to her. When the two of them had walked in, this guy with prison tats had hugged them. Morgan was repulsed, but Laida went right up and hugged him and so she did the same. He said, "Welcome."

"We can't talk during the meeting," Laida whispered back.

Their relationship was about a month old, and they had become inseparable. Morgan hadn't wanted to go to those meetings with Laida, but curiosity really had gotten the better of her. Laida said this was a good one because it was a speaker meeting.

"But is he?" she whispered louder. One of the older women looked up and shot her a glance that made it clear that she needed to be quiet. She took the hint. Rollo continued.

"I'm standing in front of you today by the grace of God and everyone in these rooms in order that I may share my experience, strength, and hope. By some miracle, I just celebrated ten years free from all drugs and alcohol, and in what was almost harder, I haven't picked up a cigarette in five years.

But we're not going to talk about that today. The topic is unmanageability, and I'm going to try to stay on topic. It's really synchronous, too, how things happen. I really do see God in everything. Like, I don't need to go to a church to know that God exists. I just look at the highway. Here we are, four lanes of us all driving eighty miles an hour inches away from each other, and yet there aren't massive deadly pileups all the time. It just doesn't happen. We're connected together somehow, and that's God to me. Or when I look in my three-year-old daughter's eyes. That's God looking back. And God can take away my unmanageability. I just have to ask.

So, I was saying it was synchronous. I was thinking about what I was going to talk about tonight. And my wife gave me a grocery list to stop at the store before the meeting, and she gave me a little Coinstar receipt with the list and told me not to forget to use that when I paid. And it…it just reminded me of that whole life I had before I met her. And how grateful I am that my wife and my daughter have never seen me high or drunk, and they never need to know that man.

So it reminded me about a story from when I was younger, that Coinstar receipt. And it totally goes with the subject matter. So, you know, I'm an addict. And that means I'm always looking for a way to scam, or skim off the top, or do anything where I can make a quick buck. I mean, I was always looking to hustle. Always looking to score. Never trying to be productive, never trying to, or willing to work hard. I felt as if all work just interfered with my using.

So, I was hard up for cash one night, and when I was searching through some old boxes for something to pawn, I came across a little stash of Canadian money. It wasn't a lot. A couple dollars in coins. I just figured it would be a pain in the ass to mix them in to my change. Oh yeah, I should mention that this was back in the day nobody wanted Canadian money because it wasn't worth anything.

So anyway, I thought, maybe it would be faster to just go to the store and dump those into the Coinstar machine and take the slip and get the money. And I could go to that little neighborhood grocery store. Oh yeah, I forgot, I used to go there and steal thirty-packs of beer. Wow, that was so long ago. Anyway, I decided to dump the coins into the machine. What was the worst thing that could happen?

Well, I tried the quarters first. The machine just ate them. I got nothing back. That kind of pissed me off. Then I tried the dimes. Same thing. Gone. Now I was pissed. The machine took some of the nickels, and spit some of them out. The ones it spit out I couldn't figure out why it did, but it wouldn't take them. Anyway, the machine took all the pennies. All of them. Even the ones with like, twenty edges. So that was cool. I cashed out the slip and grabbed a thirty-pack too.

So, while I was getting wasted on the Busch, I started thinking, and I hatched this scheme. So, I called some Canadian banks just over the U.S. border in Sherbrooke, about a six-hour drive from here. I told them I was an American coin collector and I was looking for lot of Canadian pennies. They asked me how much. I said $1500 Canadian. One bank said I needed an account there. One said they couldn't get that many. And the other said come tomorrow.

So, I guess I need to clarify. At that point in time, the exchange rate was that $1 American purchased $1.50 Canadian. So, I was going to take the $1000 check I'd just gotten from my grandmother, cash it, take the money up to Canada, and bring home $1500 in Canadian money. Then, I was going to take that $1500 and dump them into Coinstar machines to get the full amount less their fee and put the extra in my pocket.

So, I told them I'd be up the next day. I planned out a route by looking for Coinstar locations between here and Vermont, and had a little map planned out. I didn't just want to dump all the pennies into one machine. I mean, I figured that would be kind of suspicious. So, I planned to dump them off in about ten different stores.

I drove my old station wagon all the way up to Sherbrooke, met with the woman at the bank who was super nice and really perky. They let me use their handtruck to load my car. Oh, so if you didn't know, when pennies come in bulk, they come in $25 bricks. Each brick is about the size of a regular brick, but weighs a lot more. And $1500 in pennies is a *lot* of bricks. So many bricks that my car was just so far weighed down in the back that I wasn't sure if the shocks were going to hold up.

After I crossed the border, my first stop was the package store. I was so happy. I had made it across the border. Time to celebrate! So, I bought a plastic squeeze bottle of rum, and then started sucking down the rum while I unwrapped the pennies from their wrappers with my free hand and threw them into a bucket. And all of this while I'm cruising down I-91. I mean, it's ridiculous. Really ridiculous. I'm literally driving with my knee and unwrapping all these rolls of Canadian pennies. The floor of the car was full of empty wrappers. And I'm getting drunk.

I stopped at all the places on my map. I dumped off the pennies in each one of the Coinstar machines and got the receipts and cashed them in at each store. It took me all day. But, remember I started with $1000. That became $1500 Canadian. There were 9% in fees. That's $135, and about $60 in gas. So I cleared $300 for the day. And I got wasted. And I drove to Canada and back. I was so psyched. I just drove around all day and made $300 and got drunk. But the worst part about it was…"

Rollo was still talking but Morgan just had to get up. She walked out the back door, with Laida looking a little nervous and embarrassed, but following closely behind. They didn't speak until they got outside.

"Laida," Morgan said, "I just can't do this. These people are just too crazy. I couldn't listen any more. I mean, that's just so *pathetic*, I just…I just had no idea how to process that. Seriously, I smoke weed. I get that. But it doesn't run my life. These people are nuts."

"But Morgan," she replied, "I *am* these people. I mean, that wasn't my exact story, but the things I used to do were just as crazy. I mean, I came out as a transgender woman to the whole court in Hartford in order to get out of a drug charge."

"Seriously?"

"Yeah. Seriously. I'm *sick*. I need these meetings."

"But you're not sick. You're not like those people in there. Did you see those people? That guy you hugged when we came in? He was covered in prison tats and had a pirate hooker on his arm. How can you hug him?"

"Well, Morgan, it's…"

"And that other guy, Jon or Don or whatever? He had teardrop tattoos and white power ink. I mean, this isn't safe. Those people are dangerous. You don't belong here."

The two of them got into Laida's white Honda and she fired up the little four-cylinder.

"If I'm going to stay clean, I have to come here. I want to stay clean so that we can have a relationship. Don't come with me then. But don't get jealous of the time I spend with these people. It's my medicine. It's the same as chemo or dialysis. It's medicine for my condition, and I make the best of it."

"I'm just worried about your safety, Lai. I mean, you're a transwoman. You never know who's nuts in here. They all seem nuts."

"Morgan, I'm fine."

"No, Lai, it's not fine. I worry about your safety. These people are animals. If they find out you weren't born a girl, they might want to hurt you, you know, because they don't understand. I just want you to be safe."

"Morgan, I'm safe. I love you."

"I love you too."

They kissed and she put the car in gear to head back to Morgan's apartment.

*　　*　　*

"Philip, get in here." Anthony Clark dropped his phone loudly. He had just re-read the report on Ric Lenz and was incredibly frustrated. "Troubled," was a better word.

Over the past few years he was working with others in his office to nab a Cambodian national named Ti Phan. Phan had entered the country illegally, and ran a piece of the Cambodian mob that moved heroin into the country and then used a complex distribution network to get his drugs on the streets. They were very sophisticated technically—the DEA had an incredibly hard time getting any decent information from their phones and their computers. What's worse, it was an incredibly tight community, and everyone knew each other. It took years to get an operative in. Even then, not only would their agent have to be Cambodian, but if he spoke the wrong dialect, couldn't trace back his family tree, or were too Westernized, these guys would sniff him out and he would end up in pieces on little sticks being sold in Chinatown as teriyaki beef.

244

They had pictures, they knew his whereabouts, sometimes, and they had some passing evidence of loansharking and racketeering around the names of some of his associates, sometimes, but there was nothing they could ever do to pin him to the actual narcotics trafficking. Unlike a lot of his contemporaries, Phan also seemed to be able to outlive so many of his fallen Asian gangbanger brethren when they perished in so much gun violence in the territorial warfare his office was covertly in charge of creating. Anthony was at the end of his rope. He couldn't send in an agent directly to kill Phan. He couldn't kill him indirectly by poking the beehive. He could never find a direct link to him touching the drugs. But he was definitely the target. No doubt.

They got the smallest of breaks two years ago when one of Phan's associates got a flat tire in a delivery van on the interstate. A man named Rithy Taing. Anthony would never forget that name. Rithy was driving his old delivery van when he had a sidewall blowout on one of the rear drive wheels. In an attempt to not have to stop on the highway (and apparently, to avoid dealing with local law enforcement) he kept driving to try to make it off the next exit. After the tire shredded off, he continued driving on the rim. Still, he didn't make it to the exit before he snapped one of the studs and lost the wheel. Immobilized, he was in the breakdown lane taking out a full-size spare from the back of the van. Rithy was attempting to jack up the van before the wheel had even cooled down.

A state worker in an orange pickup truck named Tate Wilson had watched the whole thing, and pulled up behind Rithy with his blinkers on in an attempt to block his vehicle from being inadvertently hit. In a statement to the police, Wilson detailed his interaction with Rithy, who spoke very broken English. Tate said he explained to Rithy that he had just avoided a very serious accident, and asked him if he were aware that his wheel had just left a huge slice in the pavement. Tate also said he'd never seen a man change a tire that fast outside of a pit in NASCAR, and that he'd used heavy duty gloves that were for carrying refrigerated items to change the wheel when the whole thing had to be hundreds of degrees from all the heat as it sparked its way across the pavement.

The state police didn't even have time to respond—they were busy with a fatal accident on the other side of the highway a couple miles up, and when Tate called them about this one and they found out the driver was okay, they told Tate to just wait with him until his vehicle could operate again. The only piece of useful information they got was when Tate told Rithy that the cops couldn't come because they were very busy. Once he said that, the Cambodian's face lightened, and he explained he was fine.

Tate asked him if he wanted help, but Rithy said no. Tate asked him where he was going in such a hurry, and he responded "to Peace Pagoda" to "pick up his son." By the time Tate had picked up the huge pieces of rubber left on the road from the blowout, the van had driven delicately away on four studs instead of five. In the police report, Wilson had never gotten the license plate or license number, but he'd gotten the man's name, Rithy Taing.

Once the police report got filed, Rithy's name got flagged in the DEA computers. He was a known associate of Phan's. Owing money to the mob, he was paying off his debt by making deliveries of Phan's heroin with his wholesale Asian food trucks. Anthony had never even tried to bring in this Rithy and question him. They had never had any luck that way. But one of his agents interviewed Tate Wilson, who confirmed the report, and what he and Rithy had spoken about. He even showed the agent the marks on the highway. (Tate would have taken all day with the DEA—even though he smoked reefer, he was getting paid time-and-a-half to come in on his day off to discuss a person who he described to his girlfriend as "an international criminal.")

Since then Anthony had been watching the Peace Pagoda. But very, very, covertly. This was a touchy national security matter—he knew from his briefings that the religious community that lived there had been granted asylum after being persecuted for their beliefs. These people had been granted relief from a government back in their home nation that sought to kill them and invade their privacy. For obvious reasons, this was not the best place for a DEA raid, and it was an incredibly safe place for Phan to store his drugs. Anthony had already been sternly warned by the brass that he was under no circumstances to go in

246

there until he could prove that Phan *and* the drugs were *both* there. Despite his protests that this was hampering their investigation, Anthony found out through the grapevine that their deputy director's son had married a Buddhist woman and had converted. This was going to be a lost cause.

And that's where he stood with Phan. That prick was a thorn in his side, a constant reminder of his need for vigilance, and concrete proof that the forces of evil would continue to multiply without a concerted effort against them. This is why he was leaning so hard on this new information about blogger Ric Lenz—if someone else did the legwork, it would be incredibly easy for him to commandeer the research, slap his own name on it, and deliver a drug kingpin dead or alive to smiling superiors. And now *this* report. Philip sprinted into his office.

"What is it, Tony?"

"Shut the door. Sit."

"Is everything okay?"

"I just need to go over some things with you to make sure that I understand this report correctly."

"Oh, that's fine." Philip relaxed in his chair. There were a lot of things that scared him about his boss, but inaccuracy in his reports was never something that worried him. He prided himself on always being on point.

"So, what you're saying is that this guy, Ric Lenz, who was blogging about Peace Pagoda, has no connection to Phan, any of Phan's associates, and most likely does not know who Phan is at all. Is that correct?"

"Yes, Tony. It's all right there. The team searched everything and cross-checked everything. We were very thorough."

"That I believe. I've seen your record collection. Meticulous."

"Alphabetical by artist name and then by release date. Everything is mint, or mint minus."

"Well, Philip, the vinyl *does* just sound better."

"It does. I don't think Edison would have liked digital music. I mean, a song isn't a song. It's just an incredibly long string of zeroes and ones. It's just an incredibly large number. That's no longer art. It's something, different…"

"Anyway, back to this report," said Anthony. Philip sat upright in his chair. "Did we actually get on to his computer, or are these just pieces that he actually published to the web?"

"Yeah, we installed some programs on there to make a clone of his hard drive over here. We have everything that he does. But I can tell you with certainty that he did not go to Peace Pagoda to find Phan."

"Yes. Yes, I got that. Go on."

"Apparently, he was looking for this individual, 'Josh Grenier.' He had scanned in a receipt with the man's signature on it. That was *definitely* the target of his informal investigation."

"Well, Philip, in your opinion, do you believe this Josh character should be the target of *our* investigation?"

"Well, certainly not for trafficking heroin, but I believe he would be a useful person for our office to watch. I don't know if you saw, but I prepared a little dossier, more of a primer, actually, on Josh. He's only twenty years old. Now, this is Josh Jr., not Josh Sr. The old man's actually ours for a few more years."

"Yes, Philip, it took me a minute, but it did click. He was the one who was driving marijuana in antique dressers across the country for the Albanian mob."

"Right. Actually, in their statement, I believe that that the local law enforcement said he was using armoires, not dressers."

"Okay, Philip. *Armoires*. Not dressers. But we're on the same page here."

"Absolutely," responded Philip. "Josh, Sr. is in the federal pen for trafficking marijuana. And, with no father figure to guide him, Josh Jr. has started a little website. You saw some of the panels there in the dossier."

"More like a primer, Philip," replied Anthony with sarcastic disgust.

"Yes, well, Sir, I am sorry about the truncated report on Josh Grenier. To be fair, I thought I was supposed to be prepping you on Ric Lenz."

"Fare is what you pay to ride the bus," replied Anthony dryly. "Can you have more of a write-up for me on this Grenier kid? By the looks of this website, we may have accidentally stepped in a pretty big pile of shit."

"You mean, maybe *my* team stepped in a pile of shit? Helping you chase Phan? Your white whale?"

"Hey. If you're digging for gold and you find silver, do you just leave it there? California might be the Golden State, but Nevada's the Silver State, and I sure as shit like hitting Vegas. You know what I'm thinking, right Philip?"

"Not really, Tony," he said as he exhaled slowly.

"I'm thinking that the next time the brass gets on me about not delivering Phan to them, I'm going to hand them over ten or twenty or a hundred or however many people we can flip off this kid's client list and tell them a hundred small fish still makes for a good meal. Buys me some more time with this slanty-eyed piece of shit."

"I don't know if that's the right, um, naming standards for the, um, Asians, uh…"

"Oh shut up, Phil. I just want you thinking of ways to pressure the young Grenier."

"Well, I wasn't thinking that Tony, but I'm thinking that now. When do you need a dossier on Josh Jr.?"

"Yesterday."

"Understood."

"And Philip?"

"Yes?"

"Is this website live?"

"Yeah. Just type in thenewlibertychurch.org and see what happens."

"How did we never flag this?"

"Because the kid's a *geek*. Goes to Williams College. Wrote the computer code himself, from scratch. By hand. That's why we never saw it. You see, almost everybody uses software to publish to the web, and as part of the license agreement that they click to use that software, you know, the box no one reads? Well the program kind of flags everything and creates a summary of terms we used to call 'meta tags.' Of course now, the programs…"

"Get to the point, Philip."

"Sorry. Because he didn't use a software program, and he generated the code by hand, our computers didn't pick it up. That's fucking brilliant. I mean, he's smart enough to write in computer code, which means he might be smart enough to know how we track stuff too. Plus he used all of the full chemical names of research compounds rather than slang or shortened names. And nothing on there is technically illegal, even though we could nail anyone with almost any of these chemicals with the Analog Act."

"Thank God for that one, huh," said Anthony. "I mean, if they ever decided not to roll over and they put up a fight, we'd bury them under a pile of litigation with so many motions it would make their heads spin. No one touching these types of chemicals has the bankroll to fight us, or the principled position to do anything other than be nuisances. It's all leverage."

"I'm going to get back to work," said Philip. He'd heard Anthony sermocinize more times than he cared to count. Plus, there was a rare vinyl recording he was watching on eBay that ended in a few minutes.

"Okay, Philip. I'm fired up now. I'll talk to you later."

As soon as the door closed Anthony's brow furrowed. He went on the church's website and he had to re-read it several times to make sure that he was understanding what he was seeing. He hit shift-refresh. And there it was, plain as day. On a list of protected chemicals. "5,6,7-trimethoxy-dmt." How the fuck did that end up there? Was Viens trying to fuck him? Was Durham trying to fuck him?

Anthony had only signed off on those phony control numbers to import the 5,6,7 into the country because he owed Viens a favor. He had copies of all the documents on his computer, where he agreed to import the chemical and mislabel it in exchange for copies of all the data collected by Durham with respect to the compound, including details around its extraction and synthesis. He was not telling his supervisors about the project. If Viens flinched, he would hang him out to dry, hand over the docs, and claim he was running a covert operation on an American living in Germany and trying to important an illegal analog. Major points. If Viens were good to him, he would have leverage against Durham when their American office

250

ever tried to do anything with the compound, since it had not been patented nor made exclusive with their firm in any way. It wasn't blackmail. It was business. In either case, Anthony was going to come out on top. He had all the evidence on his home laptop whose wireless switch was permanently off, and that never went near the internet.

But why on earth did this kid Josh Grenier have the name of a research chemical in full view of the public on a non-profit website claiming it would protect its use from future legislation? Was this kid nuts? And how on earth did he even hear of it? He whipped out his phone.

"Thank you for calling Omicrone..."

Shit, he thought. I called the work number. He hated phones.

"Just put me through to Corbett."

"I'm sorry, Sir, but Mr. Reynolds is in a meeting right now."

"Well, tell him that Anthony Clark needs to speak with him right away."

"I understand you, Mr. Clark, it's just that he's in a meeting."

"Fine. I'll call his cell then."

"I can take a message if..."

Anthony hung up. He smacked his phone on the desk. Then he smacked it again. It still worked. Resilient pieces of electronics. Those fucking Chinese can do something right, he thought. He calmed down. He was going to call Corbett—that's what he was paying for. But none of this was sitting right. He was troubled. Very troubled.

The River

David was not happy with the email he'd just gotten on the Durham intranet. He read it again. "David. It's Viens. We need to talk NOW. No Skype. No email. Will call shortly on burn-a-cell. Please pick up the phone when I call."

He was kind of frozen, actually. He had no idea what to make of this. He knew that it had to be about 5,6,7—this was his little partner in crime reaching out—and he knew it couldn't be good. Whenever someone wanted to communicate on a disposable phone, it meant they wanted no record of the call. Nothing cached in a database on a server in New Zealand for future use. A burn-a-cell. His phone rang, a number he had never seen before on the caller ID. He had to answer.

"Viens? Is that you?"

"Yes. David. How are you?"

"What's wrong?"

"We have a problem."

"How big of a problem?"

"Manageable. But bad."

"Tell me what's going on, Viens." David's heart was in his throat. He wasn't sure if his foray into the underworld was going as well as he'd hoped. This was truly a slippery slope.

"Well, a lot has happened since we talked last, and I can't talk to you on email any more. They're watching me."

"Who's watching you?"

"Durham. Well, not exactly. Listen, David, you don't think I'm crazy, right?"

"Not at all." David remembered when he first met Viens. They had both just started with the company and it was David's first trip to Germany. They went out on the town together. It was *awesome*. They'd been friends ever since. "You're one of the sanest people I know. What's happening over there?"

"It's complicated, David."

David inhaled. Again with this complicated business, he thought. Enough. First Pickering is overreacting because someone from the government visited the campus. Now his good friend Viens sounds like a paranoid schizophrenic having an episode. Why did he always have to be the strong one? The one to have to calm everyone else down and say that the sky wasn't falling? He needed more patience.

"It can't be *that* complicated," replied David. "Just relax and start from the beginning."

"Okay. Well, my computer froze the other day. I was trying to install a Flash update and it just froze. I restarted it. Tried again. Froze again. I figured it was some kind of software glitch. I didn't really need the Flash update. Anyway, I had loaned my tablet to Lucy, so I figured I'd bring the laptop home and use that. Long story short, I happened to have a few friends over that night, and one of them is really good with computers. I tell him about the problem. He looks at the computer, and tells me it has a virus. I tell him no way. He says way."

"Did it have a virus?"

"Well. Yes and no. So he calls a friend of his and while he's on the phone, the two geeks are gabbing back and forth. Techie shit. He types a little, talks a little, types some more. All of a sudden he goes, 'aaaaaaaaah.' And looks up at me. He says, 'Someone at the company installed this program on the machine. For whatever reason it was causing the Flash update to crash because it was causing an error that would never correct itself, because this program was using some of the memory and CPU in a stealth way...' He went on and on."

"And?"

"And, someone's been watching me. At *our* company."

"That's ridiculous. Durham believes so strongly in personal freedom that they don't even drug test their employees. No way are they reading our emails and spying. It's not possible. Allowing personal freedom is what the company's all about. It's antithetical to the whole mission of the corporation. I don't believe it."

David chuckled to himself. He thought about it though—everyone handles stress differently. He went and blew off steam at the poker club. Maybe Viens turned inward and had panic attacks like this when he was stressed out. David made a mental note to talk to him about some healthier stress releases when he was feeling better. For now, he was just going to let him tell the story so he would stop being so upset.

"I'm telling you, David, someone is watching my computer."

"Who? Who exactly is watching your computer?"

"My friend didn't know. When he tried to locate where the spyware was on the hard drive and make a copy of the program, it deleted itself. He got a little bit of the code, though, before that happened. And get this. He says it's the German government. He didn't have enough code to know what the program was exactly, but he said his friend was positive."

"That's the most ridiculous thing I've ever heard."

"No, David, you don't understand. This is the *truth*." Viens' voice quivered. David caught it. He changed his tone abruptly.

"How do you know?" asked David.

"My friend took the small amount of the code he was able to grab out of the cache before the program destroyed itself and posted it on a hacker website. Within minutes there was a whole thread…" He trailed off.

"Are you there?" he asked. David heard crying on the other end of the line. "Shit," said David. He didn't mean to make the man cry.

"David, I saved the thread, but I didn't even have to. I don't want to tell you where it is because I don't want you accessing that website in case anyone else is monitoring that. But I printed it out." Viens was sobbing. David bit his lip.

"What does the printout say?"

"The printout says that about a dozen hackers all over the world independently verified that based on the program that made it, and the formatting of the code that it was the German government. It was definitely *not* another hacker. They all agreed—all twelve of these crazy kooks who do this for fun. This wasn't a joke. This wasn't a test. It was government. They said it *stunk* of government. On my laptop!" Viens began sobbing, loudly.

"Holy shit!" David was shocked. He didn't know what to do. Hearing another man cry just stopped him dead in his tracks. And his partner...

"Holy shit is right." Viens pulled himself together. "So, I ask my friend what happened, and he said the program was designed to delete itself if it were detected, but nothing else on my hard drive, just itself. He said he had no idea what the people were looking for, but he said they would probably know that I deleted it. The good news was that they would probably just think it was the installing that particular Flash update that caused it."

"Holy shit!"

"Holy shit is right!"

"Well, were they watching just you, or is it everyone?"

"That's a good question, and I don't know the answer. I can tell you that my friend is a really smart guy. He said that in order to get that program on to my machine, because we have a dedicated line and a firewall, the person would have to be working at Durham and physically have *put* it on my machine. Do you know what that means, David? That someone from the German government is working at Durham!"

"Like, an employee?"

"Yes! There's a German government operative at Durham! And that person has probably seen all of my notes about 5,6,7!"

David exhaled sharply. "Shit," he said under his breath.

"I know. Shit."

"Do you think they know about me?" asked David.

"They shouldn't. The only person they know about is my contact at the DEA. But he's in your jurisdiction. And if he tries to find *you*..."

"Shit. Viens. I know I told you I didn't want to know anything so that I could have full deniability if this ever imploded, but can we talk about that now?"

"We can talk about whatever you want, David. I'm just totally freaking out right now. What do you want to know?"

"How are you getting the 5,6,7 into the States?"

"Oh, well that's easy," said Viens. He stopped sniffling. "I have a contact named Anthony Clark at the DEA. Real piece of work. He owed me a favor and I called it in. He's pretty high up in the agency. He created phony DEA control numbers from scratch. It's like counterfeiting money perfectly. He got me these electronic control numbers, so we ship the 5,6,7 and it's marked as something generic. When customs runs the numbers, they go straight to the DEA database and it checks out and comes back clean and they wave it through. It never sees a scanner, a handler, or a TSA employee. It's pre-cleared. It's perfect."

"Why would this Anthony Clark do that for you?"

"Do you really want to know?"

"Kind of. I'm running this and now that you're letting me know the details I didn't want to know to begin with, I think I need all of them."

He heard Viens take a deep breath on the other end of the line.

"I was young and stupid. And if it all happened again I would never have let this go on. But it did. I was in Vegas for a conference, and one of my friends who lived out there told me about these sex parties they have."

"Sex parties?" David was in way over his head.

"Yeah. They have them all over the country. You know, hook up with strangers who are into the same stuff you are. Anyway, I'm at this sex party and I meet Anthony. You never know where they're going to be. They're run by these people who are like the people who run the Rainbow gathering, you know?"

"The Rainbow Gathering? I have no idea what that is either." Swing and a miss for David.

"Geez, David, there's so much we need to catch you up on. And I thought I was out of it after leaving the States to take this job. The Rainbow Gathering's where all the hippies get together once a year, like, out West. They kind of collectively make a decision of where to set up camp. Anyway, the people who sponsor the sex parties kind of decide where to have them.

They have real estate all over the place. So, they let you know where you're meeting in a text, and you go to like, a random door with a particular symbol on it, and there's a party. You know, BYOB, but they have baskets of condoms and lube and stuff."

"Are you serious?"

"Yeah. You've never been?"

"No. No, I've never *been*."

"Anyways, there are all sorts of little 'rooms' set up and cordoned off with curtains. There are swings and toys. Bondage stuff. You name it. And people are doing all sorts of things. Living out their fantasies in real life. Anyway, I meet Anthony because we're both checking out the same girl. And I'll always remember, he looked right at me. 'You wanna' double-team her?' he said. 'If you do, I want the front. She is *hot*.' And I was like, no. Well. I watched. And David, he raped this girl. He *raped* her. She didn't want him. He held her down, he covered her mouth, and he raped her. He fucking raped her."

"Holy shit," replied David softly. He was thinking about his step-daughter and how he just wanted to protect her so badly from the world.

"Yeah. Well, it became a problem. The girl ended up going to the cops. It was a *thing*. And his credentials weren't getting him out of it. The girl's uncle was an assistant D.A."

"And?"

"I alibied him. I told the cops he was with me walking on the strip during the time the girl claimed to be raped, and that we'd met at the conference. That alibi kept this out of his house and his work. He told me he was DEA, and that I could call in a favor when I needed one."

"You let him rape the girl?"

"Well, like I said, I was young. I didn't understand."

"Wow. Wow. Viens, I'm sorry."

"No need to be sorry. I've made peace with that. I do a lot of volunteer and charity work. I'm fine. But anyway, I had Anthony's number. And I called in the favor. And he helped me."

"Well what about the rape? Can you use that against him?"

"The statute of limitations just ran out."

"Wow. That's insane."

"I know. Insane." Viens sighed. "No one knows about that, David. But it felt good to come clean to you. I've been carrying that around for a long time."

"I understand. Wow. That's...I..." David did not want to be this guy's shrink. He tried to bring it back around to the business at hand. "Okay. Okay. So, you don't have any leverage on this Anthony Clark. He's just doing you a favor."

"Right."

"So he could turn on *you*?"

"Well, I don't think he would do that. Not just because he likes me and owed me that favor, but because our ankles are already kind of tied together. He can't really take me out without taking himself out, because I'm here in Germany. It's much more likely that he would try to sniff you out. He doesn't know you exist yet. But he's government. He has different sorts of means at his disposal."

"Yes, yes he does." David was deep in thought. "Well, could you use any of the 5,6,7 stuff as leverage with him? I mean, don't you have copies of your agreement for the control numbers?"

"Well, yes, but that's dangerous."

"Why is that dangerous?"

"Well, I have to cover *my* ass, right?"

"Shit, Viens, what did *you* do?"

"Well, as part of my arrangement with him, I promised him copies of all the research on the 5,6,7 in exchange for those numbers."

"Why would you *do* that?" David was *very* angry. This ship needed to have no holes in it to make this journey without sinking to the ocean floor.

"Relax. David. I'm not an idiot. I didn't give him *that* information. I gave him the stuff on DP-153407. It's just mislabeled. Exactly what he's doing for me. He's not getting a shred of information on 5,6,7. He sold me counterfeit DEA control numbers, and I paid in counterfeit chemistry diagrams."

David resumed his usual demeanor. He'd picked his team well—Viens had done well. They were still running the show.

He was proud of his partner's acumen. They were in charge of this. It was still his game.

"That's pretty smart, Viens. What if he checks those diagrams?"

"Are you kidding me? The guy at the DEA that I met at a sex party? David, this guy is an ape. He's muscle. He's a meathead. He doesn't know anything about CAS numbers, let alone how to read chemistry diagrams. He's only holding that information for leverage over me in case I don't do what he wants. That's the only reason."

"So you never gave him any real information about 5,6,7?"

"Absolutely not," replied Viens.

The one thing that Viens did not disclose was that he had, in fact, saved copies of all of their research as leverage in case David turned on *him*, and tried to pin this on him and get him fired from Durham. He had a contact high up in a white supremacist group who had already shown interest in the marketability of a brand new club drug. He told them it would be the next Ecstasy: better than MDMA. But, like David with the private equity fund, he didn't want to sell out to the Neo-Nazis unless it meant it were the only way to save his own ass. He would never leave himself without an out, and telling that to David would compromise his exit strategy in case of a fire. All he needed was one exit, a window even, to get out that building filling with gas that he and David were both standing in, if his friend ever decided to strike a match.

"So, can we get copies of all those documents? Documents that would incriminate Anthony? Couldn't we use those as leverage?"

"Well, that would be extremely difficult," said Viens.

"Why? You just told me you know hackers. Get dirt on the guy. If this is a money issue I don't mind ponying up."

"It's not a money issue, David. This guy Anthony isn't stupid. I asked him this same question. Remember, he thinks he has the *real chemical blueprints* to the next big thing. I asked him how I could be sure that no one would steal them from *him*, which would compromise the whole operation."

"And?"

"And he stores the docs on a computer. A laptop. And it's not connected to the internet. It never is, and never will be. He has it for that reason. It's like a safe for information. We can't hack it. We'd need a copy of that hard drive to have enough evidence to incriminate him if he tried to screw with us."

"You're sure this laptop exists?" David's mind was racing. His motor was redlining.

"Absolutely. It's in his home."

"Do we need the actual computer, or just a copy of the drive?"

"Well, we need a copy of the drive. I wouldn't want to be holding on to a laptop computer that belonged to a DEA agent who was looking for it." He paused. "Oh my God! David! You're going to *steal* it?" There was a long pause.

David's breathing was even. He was calm. He was an executive. He had to make executive decisions. This is why he earned the big salary. Why he drove the nice car. Why they lived in a nice home. This was where the rubber met the road. He calmly looked at what was happening. His German counterpart was compromised, and through no fault of his. If an operative in the German government knew the game, anyone in the American government could catch wind of the same information. And if this Anthony Clark were such a scumbag that he raped girls on business trips, then he's probably the kind of guy that has enemies in his office, enemies who would be trying to take him down. And he would be looking to save his own ass. It didn't matter if he had bad information. It wasn't about the information—it was about the leverage the information provided.

David closed his eyes and took it all in. He saw it just like a virtual flowchart. He understood. This dirty government agent was going to be looking for him. Him. David Evans. And if he did that, and he found him, it would ensure he was going to be fired. Jailed, even, if they wanted to make a federal case out of it. And they could—they *were* the Feds. Plausible deniability was quickly evaporating. He had to be step ahead of Agent Clark. If he had evidence of Clark's complicity, Clark couldn't turn him in. He needed that computer. He knew what he needed to do.

"Viens. That information you gave him on the DP-153407."

"Yes."

"Let's say he doesn't know what it is, but if a medical professional or an expert witness or a judge ever saw it, would it matter if it were marked 5,6,7 and were actually DP-153407? Would that mean anything? Is that, like, a technicality that would foil a lawsuit?"

"I don't know what kind of lawsuit you're talking about, David. But I can tell you that conspiracy to commit a crime usually carries a nearly identical penalty to actually doing it in any sort of criminal case. And in a civil situation, the malfeasance is apparent whether or not the chemical diagrams lack real accuracy. I'm not the only person this man has had dealings with. Those docs on Anthony's computer prove he's a criminal. Beyond any doubt."

"You're sure?"

"One hundred percent."

"OK, then. I'll take care of it."

"You'll take care of it? Just like that?"

"Viens, remember when I told you to get the 5,6,7 into the country and be light on the details?"

"Yes?"

"Well, I'm going to buy a little insurance policy and get a copy of that hard drive." David paused. "And I'm going to be light on details."

"Fair enough. If we need to talk, I'll use the cell. I believe in you, David."

"Thanks for the heads up."

The men disconnected. Viens rubbed his eyes. He wondered how he even got involved with all this. He knew David wouldn't throw him under the bus. He didn't even want to think about that meeting with the white supremacists, though. He hoped it would never have to come to that.

David could still see that moment from only a short time ago—it was the most flawless moment of clarity, the strongest impression of a perfect universe he'd ever had. It was emblazoned on his mind like Moses seeing the burning bush— there was the 5,6,7, and the person's name who was directly between himself and the numbers. Laid out graphically in

261

Technicolor. He pulled out the business card and started dialing. He heard a kind of whiny, nasally, female voice.

"Premium Pawn. Morgan speaking."

"Mike Mazzone please."

"Hold please."

* * *

"Josh, it's Corbett. We need to talk."

"What's up?"

"Well, remember when you came to me with this church idea? And I told you I thought it was a good idea?"

"Yes."

"You know I didn't think it was a good idea, right?"

"But you said…"

"I said I thought it was a good idea, but not because I think everyone should go around taking potent drugs."

"Then why did you say it?"

Corbett sighed. He had to tell Josh the truth.

"Josh, to be frank, I've felt bad every time I think about your dad. He shouldn't be in jail."

"Well fuck you, Corbett. You didn't do anything to get him out."

"It's out of my hands, Josh. They asked him to name names. He refused. They threw the book at him."

"You and I both know that if he ratted on the Albanians they'd have killed him over a game of Barboot and thrown his body in a dumpster. They paid my mom and me instead for him being put away. He didn't have a choice. But you could've helped."

"Josh, like I said, there was nothing I could do."

"I can accept that, Mr. Reynolds. But he'll be out soon. You don't understand—he doesn't get me. You get me more than he does."

"I do understand, Josh. I thought the church was a good project for you because it was a way for you to work out some of your feelings. It would keep you occupied while your father was away, and it made for a complicated enough independent project

262

that would challenge you while you were at school. And I took a look at the website. It looks great."

"Thank you."

"You're welcome."

"So, you're just saying that it was a good idea because it would keep me busy. Like a cat condo or a hamster wheel? Not because you believe in what I'm doing?"

"Josh, you're not following. I run a consulting firm. My job is to learn about my clients' needs, the landscape for their field, and help them navigate through problems. It doesn't mean that I would agree with everything every one of them does."

"Okay. So, what's the problem?"

"Well, Josh, one of my clients asked about your website. Specifically."

"He asked about me personally?"

"Well, not you by name, but your work."

"Wow. I mean, that's awesome."

"Well, it's not necessarily *awesome*, it's…"

"Was he asking you just about my church? You know there are others out there, like a church for the followers of the hallucinogenic toad, and another one for some snuffs, and…"

"Josh, this is actually not a good situation. I thought you were going to be flying under the radar, but apparently it looks like you've broken out and the air traffic controllers see you now."

"Well that's good. Maybe I'll get a better job offer."

"Oh yeah. I saw something about that on your Facebook. You didn't say where the offer was from."

"This guy David Evans. The company is called Durham. They make pharmaceuticals. But maybe your client could make me a better offer, you know. I don't necessarily want to work for pharma."

Corbett was silent. This was just too outrageous. Anthony was paying for him to learn what he knew about 5,6,7, a chemical being made by a company called Durham, who just happened to be looking to hire Josh. Did Durham know what Josh was up to? Was he part of their plan? Anthony had called him because Josh had posted the name of their secret research chemical on the website. Was Durham using Josh as live bait to see if the government would take a bite? Corbett needed to know Josh's role in all this.

"Well, Josh, you know I can't disclose who my client is. But I can tell you that others definitely know who you are now on account of the church website."

"That's good. I believe in what I'm doing. I'm forcing a dialogue. Entheogenic plants have a special relationship with humans. And I'm just trying to make that information more available. I'm the next generation of a McKenna or a Shulgin or a Leary or an Ott. I'm those guys in a world made much smaller on account of technology."

Smaller world didn't even describe, thought Corbett. He needed to know if Durham knew about the church.

"Josh. Your job offer from Durham. Do they know that you run this website on the side?"

Josh laughed.

"No way! This is extracurricular. I covered my tracks pretty well. Someone would basically have to work for the government to be able to figure out who I am. I mean, I'm not saying I'm a hacker or anything, but no one without professional experience with computer security would be able to figure out that this site was put up by me."

"You need to shut it down, Josh."

"No way! What do you mean, shut it down? You want me to put it out like a campfire? No way, Corbett. I have a couple hundred people that signed up. My mailing list is getting bigger and bigger and I'm writing articles and I like what I'm doing."

"Josh, you don't understand. This is going to get out of hand. Just take it down."

"No! Corbett, why are you being like this? I mean, I want to do this."

"I understand that Josh. I'm just not sure if you realize what you're up against."

"I don't think you know how much I believe in myself, Corbett. I will *not* shut it down."

Corbett sighed. Josh had no idea what he was getting himself into. As soon as he listed the name of that chemical on his website, he had already set off a chain reaction that would eventually blow up in his face regardless. But Corbett had been in the field for a long time. He knew that this was not the time to ask where he had gotten that information. He didn't need to alarm Josh.

"Josh, just be careful."

"I will be, Corbett."

"Josh, you know I've always looked out for you, like a son."

"Yeah."

"Well, remember when your dad didn't sell out the Albanians?"

"Yeah."

"You may not be so lucky. Keep that list of your church's membership in a lock box. You may need that as a bargaining chip."

"Corbett, I…"

"Don't say anything, Josh. Just one time. Listen to me. *Something's coming down the pike.* Just make a copy of your records and have them available. If you won't shut it down by choice, it might happen coercively. So, just be cool, and keep good records. I believe in you."

There was a pause.

"Thank you, Corbett."

"Behave, Josh."

Click.

*   *   *

"Thanks for meeting me at Johnny-O's, Mike. I didn't really know where else to go."

"That's fine, Pharma. Listen, I got your number when I first played with you at the table. You're in trouble. I could see it then, and I see it now. It's in your eyes. It's the fear of not having enough fear for the shitshow you're facing. I know that look."

"Really? You could read all that in me?"

"Reading people's what I do. All day long."

"What do you mean?"

"I mean that all day long I sit in a store and arbitrarily decide what to pay people for the shit they bring me. It's a joke. I sit back, judge how desperate they are, and how much I can make off of them. You? I had you pegged when you walked into Johnny-O's. You're dealing with some shit, man. I don't know if I can help."

"I hope you can. My back's against a wall."

"Uh-huh. I got that. Whatta' ya' need? I don't touch drugs. You need a piece, right?"

"No!" replied David, startled. What had he gotten himself into? "No, I don't need a gun."

"I just figured you needed, like, a nice gun or somethin'."

"You could get me a gun?"

"You want a filed-off serial number? A silencer? What?"

"No. No, I'm sorry Mike. I'm nervous. I hate guns. I have a daughter."

"That's cool." Mike's demeanor didn't change.

"I need a job done."

"Pharma! I'm not a hitman!" Mike started laughing and lit a cigarette. "Is that what you think I am? Some sort of gangbanger?"

"No! No. Sorry. Mike, I'm just nervous."

"You met me at an illegal poker club. There's nothing to be nervous about. Just tell me what you need, and I'll find you a person."

"Wait, what do you mean?" David was *so* nervous.

"David. David Evans. You're a VP at Durham Pharmaceuticals. I run a pawnshop. That's all. My name's Mike Mazzone, and I run Premium Pawn. That's all anyone ever needs to know. And David, you are not the only corporate VP I know, either. Do you know why they call people like me a fence?"

David shook his head. "No. Why?"

"Because I'm the fence between the regular world and the underworld. I have one foot in each. You, you're a square. You're up there in the regular world, the above ground. You have your little golf clubs and piano recitals and your goddamn circle jerks and I don't give a shit what you do. But I have contacts in the underworld. People that you would never even see. These people are my friends, my associates. That's what I do. I watch the bridge, the door, between those two worlds. And I take a little toll at each end. And my kids are going to use that

266

money to go to college and get jobs in *your* world, and they will never have to do what I do for work. We have the same visions for our kids. You feel me?"

"I totally feel you, Mike."

"Good. I guessed you needed a gun because that's what most square guys like you want."

"Really?"

"Really. Usually, they have some naggy bitch of a wife that has 'um by the balls and won't let them have a gun because it's unsafe, and guns kill people, and blah, blah, blah. And the wives are smart, you know? So there's no way you're getting your pistol permit through without her seein', because she's home before you getting the mail. And you're not going to be able to take a whole day off and take the class without lying to her, and you know you'll get caught. And most guys like you, they just hide the gun in their safe anyway, and just open the door and look at it every now and then. Or they want to be able to flash it when they're at the club or whatever. So that's what I guessed you wanted."

"It's an honest mistake, I guess," replied David. "I actually don't want a gun at all. I hate violence."

"Good, me too." Michael smiled like the Cheshire Cat.

"I need something stolen."

"Now you're speaking my language."

"Well, I…"

"Now wait a second, David. How do you know I'm not a cop?"

"Wait?" David got extremely flustered. "Are you a *cop*?"

"No. I'm not a cop. In fact I hate the fuckers. But what I'm doing is showing you that you expose yourself too much. So from this point on, you don't say anything to anybody. I want to know as little as possible. I just need to ask you a few questions, and I'll figure out who to hook you up with."

"So, you're not going to help me directly?"

"I'm helping you right now."

"But why am I paying you if you're not going to do the job?" asked David.

"I *am* doing the job. The job is to hook you up with the man who will get what you need." Michael stared at David. Poker without the cards. "What do you need to steal? A car?"

"A laptop computer."

"Well, that's easier than a car."

"It's inside a house."

"That's a little harder."

"It's inside a house of someone who's pretty, um, *powerful*."

"Powerful? Dave, a house is a house. What the fuck does he do?"

"He works for the government. Feds."

Michael took a long pull on his cigarette. He exhaled slowly, half coming out his mouth, half out his nose.

"There's only one guy I can send you to for that. And he's expensive."

"Money isn't a huge issue."

"I know that."

"Michael, you're really doing me a solid."

"I know that too." Michael put out his cigarette. "Listen, this guy's name is Sammy. He's gonna' call your cell, and tell you to meet him somewhere to talk. He likes the casino, so you might be driving. I'm going to give him your number and explain the situation. Sammy and I go way back. When I got pinched back in the day, we were in the joint together."

"You were in jail?"

"Ancient history, David. Fifteen years ago. Just a misunderstanding. Young and stupid. But Sammy's your man. I just have a couple more questions."

"Go ahead." David was already feeling better.

"You need the computer. Anything else in the guy's house? I mean, he's going to have to make this look like a burglary. He can't just take the laptop."

"Actually Mike, I need to amend something. I don't even want the computer."

"Wait, now you *don't* want the computer? What the fuck are we talking about then?"

"No, I mean, I just want what's *on* the computer. I need Sammy to just take a little flash drive and copy the hard drive. I don't even need the machine."

Michael lit another cigarette and pulled hard on it.

"David, let me explain something to you. I don't know shit about computers. I got a girl at the store that comes in and fixes mine when it's broken. Sammy's gonna' steal that computer. What you're just saying to me is that you don't want it coming back to you, so you don't want to be in possession of the hardware. Is that right?"

"Well, yes."

"Okay, so, I'll tell Sammy to make a copy of the hard drive, and he can sell the laptop and any jewelry or whatever he takes out of there to the junkies. But you'll get your flash drive. That sound good?"

"Yes. That's what I want." David felt a wave of relief. He had executed the difficult decision. This is what he did it for— the confidence of knowing he made a move and would not go back on it.

"Okay," said Mike. "Write down the address for me so I can tell Sammy."

David paused. "I…" he said.

"Pharma, listen to me. You can trust me. We both know Johnny-O. You did the right thing coming to me. You deal with Sammy because I tell Sammy you're all right. Otherwise, you only ever deal with me. No one else. Someone else talks to you and you don't like their looks, or what they're asking you, you call my cell. You understand? I'll always answer. If I can't talk, I'll tell you I'm at my kid's baseball game or whatever, but I'll be there for you."

David scribbled down Anthony's address. He handed the paper to Mike and looked a little concerned. He began. "I…" Mike cut him off.

"I'll burn the paper when I'm done. I'm a pro. Stop worrying."

"Okay," said David. "This is all just new territory for me. I just never thought things would come to this. Sorry, Mike, you're all right."

269

"Hey David, I don't think the pilgrims ever thought it would come to sailing all the way across the ocean either. But it came to that. Shit happens. Sammy's gonna' take care of you. He's the best in the business."

"Thanks, Mike."

"You came with cash?"

"Five large." David handed Michael a business envelope stuffed full of hundreds.

"Pleasure doing business, friend."

"Likewise."

"You just bought half my seat into the Main Event. You comin' out to Vegas in July?"

"Mike, if I get through this, I'll get you a suite wherever you want for the month."

"Nice. I'm gonna' hold you to that. Just remember, if you sit down at the table with the sharks, and you look around the table and you can't figure out who the fish is, you're the fish. Got it?"

"Got it."

"Don't lose sight of why you sat at the table. Get that money and get out."

If only it were that easy, thought David. If only it were that easy.

*　*　*

The text David got wasn't especially ominous. "9pm Mohegan Sun. Sky casino high-limit dice pit. Red hat, Raiders sweatshirt."

He had left plenty of time to park and get there, and he had a lot of cash on him. He navigated through the maze inside of Mohegan Sun to find where Sammy was standing, but when he got there he knew he had found the right guy. He was black and weighed about 300 pounds, wearing the clothing that Michael had said he would be. Sammy knew it was him as soon as he was within his view. He subtly motioned his head to David to come over to the craps table. The pit boss immediately greeted him.

"Hello, Sir. Can I have your card?"

270

"I don't have one," David replied.

"Well that's okay. I'll take your license and we'll make you one."

"Okay." David handed over his identification.

"Is this address current?"

"Yep."

"Okay, she'll be right back with that. How much would you like to buy in for?" David looked at Sammy. Sammy put up two fingers and scratched his chest.

"Two thousand."

"Great."

David pulled out twenty one-hundred dollar bills from his moneyclip. He didn't use the money he'd brought for Sammy, which was in his jacket pocket zipped up. The pit boss unfolded each bill and laid them out for the cameras. While this was happening, Sammy started talking softly to David.

"You shoot craps?"

"No," replied David. He wasn't sure how he'd gotten himself into this.

"Just bet the minimum on Come. Don't touch the bet unless they push it to you when you win. Then you bet the minimum again. If you lose, bet it again. Understand?"

"Yes."

They were still counting out the money, and the supervisor come over and nodded to the pit boss when the chips went out. A woman brought back his license and a brand new Mohegan Sun card. Then a waitress came up to David.

"What are you drinking, Sir?"

"I'll have a Jack and coke," he said.

She turned to Sammy.

"Another Corona for you?" Sammy nodded. David had no idea what was going on in the game, but he just watched. Occasionally, when things got noisy around them, Sammy would speak to him, just bits and pieces.

"Mike says you're good people. But there's a problem."

"What's the problem?"

"Underground utilities." Sammy motioned to one of the two black women behind him. She had a gold sequined purse on

271

her lap. He whispered to her and she walked away. The other stayed behind him, talking on the phone.

"I'm sorry?"

"It's 50k, not 30k."

"What? I don't have that."

"Relax, kid. You can pay me the other twenty later when I give you the drive."

David was agitated at the change in price, but it helped to hear Sammy say that about the drive. Michael had apparently filled him in on everything.

"Why is it more?"

Sammy looked back and forth. He looked back at the other woman.

"Rhonda," he said. She looked up. "You sit tight until my boy here comes back."

"Mm-hmm," she said, and went back down to her phone.

"Floyd?" he said to the pit boss.

"Yes, Samuel?"

"Get me and my friend here lammers. We're gonna' stop over at the Wolf Club for a minute and grab some shrimp."

"We can bring you some food, Sir, if you'd like."

"Nah, it's cool, Floyd. I need a little exercise."

"Whatever you like." The pit boss pointed across the room, snapped his fingers, then grabbed two clear chip protectors and placed them over the chip stacks while he typed into a nearby computer.

Sammy lumbered off and motioned for David to come with him, who followed him out of the dice pit and into the crowd. Sammy never looked at David when he spoke—he was always looking around and scanning the people around him. They still managed to have a fairly normal conversation.

"It's fifty. This whole neighborhood has underground wiring. We can't just knock out a transformer or snap a breaker to knock out the power. I needed to bring on another guy that digs. And he's expensive. Top notch dude. But costs extra."

"You're going to cut the power to his house?" David was incredulous. He didn't know what to say. Sammy shot him a disgusted look and spoke very deliberately.

"Don't look at what the doctor's doin' when he slices you open. Just count backwards from ten and fall asleep. You got it?"

David was offput by this man. He didn't know how to read him. He was just flat.

"Got it."

"So, thirty now. Twenty more when I hand you the drive."

"I don't want the computer, just what's on it."

"Oh, I got that. Mikey told me. I feel you, white man. You don't want to get dirty. Don't worry. This job ain't too hard…"

"But you…"

"Don't worry about what I said. Give me a couple days. I'll text you after I copy the thing. I'll have a flash drive for you. I'm not keeping a copy. I don't give a shit what's on this dude's computer. Kiddy porn or whateva'. I don't wanna' know. I get in, and I get out like an Army Ranger. You feel me?"

"Yeah. I feel you." Sammy made David really feel like a square.

"When I tell you it's done, you come and meet me in the same exact place. And our business'll be done. Now, see the Wolf Club lounge up there?" Sammy pointed and David nodded. "Tameka is waiting over by the entrance. You saw her before at the dice pit. She has the shiny purse. You saw that purse, right?"

"Yeah."

"We're gonna' walk up there together. You're going to hand that brown bag of hundreds you got to Tameka, and then me and Tameka are going to go in and grab a bite. Rhonda is still back at the pit by your chips. Go back there and tell the pit boss you want to cash out. He'll color you up, and Rhonda will walk you over to the cage so that you can cash out. We cool?"

"Yeah. Pleasure, Sammy."

David did as he was told and waited by the phone for the next three days.

All-In

"They fucking stole my computer!" Anthony was livid as he was speaking with the police officer in his living room.

"Just calm down, Mr. Clark," said the officer.

"Isn't there anything you can do? Put me through to the fucking Chief or something."

The officer looked at Anthony. He knew him, but Anthony didn't know that. They'd had domestic calls over the years to this house. The cops knew that Anthony was rough with his women, but on account of him being DEA, they never much bothered him. The cop taking his statement now, though, had a sister who was a victim of domestic violence. He hated guys like Anthony.

"Sir, we're doing everything we can. But I gotta' be straight with you here. These guys were pros. They cut the power from an underground junction box to disable security, and it was worth it. I mean, if what you're telling me is accurate, they probably got away with gold coins and diamonds worth almost 50k on the street. They probably just grabbed the computer because it was just sitting there."

Anthony wasn't entirely sure of that. He had bragged to quite a few people during different moments of various levels of intoxication that he had copies of all sorts of documents that gave him leverage over others for criminal behavior. Of course, revealing many of those misdeeds would also implicate him, but it was always the leverage, the threat of force rather than the force itself, that moved mountains.

"Either way, I want to talk to your supervisor. These scumbags stole almost 50k in precious stones and gold coins and I want them held accountable."

"Anthony, do you have riders on your insurance for them?"

"Of course."

"Then this is all basically a formality. You're creating a document with me here that shows that you were the victim of a crime. And trust me, you were. That's not being disputed. And we don't know they were targeting you specifically. This is a nice block. When they hit that box, they knocked out the power to your whole street. Just because they hit you first didn't mean that you were the only target. They might've gotten spooked by something and were gonna' wipe out a few others here. Lots of big, secluded houses here, empty all day without a good view of the road."

"How did they even do this?"

"It looks like they had to be posing as a private construction crew. They had digging equipment. I've heard of this m.o. before. Not in our town, but this is a crew. They'll eventually get caught, but I wouldn't hold out too much hope on getting any of your stuff back. Let insurance replace it, and maybe we'll get lucky."

Anthony was actually pretty confident that whoever had the computer did not target his machine as what they were looking for—the value of jewelry and gold coins that were stolen *was* about 50k. Even if the person or people who stole his gold tried to access the machine, he had some pretty sophisticated data encryption on there that would ward off anyone but the most seasoned computer expert.

"We might be in luck," said Anthony.

"Now why do you say that?" asked the officer.

"Well, I installed a special program on that computer. That's my spare home machine—it never leaves my house and was never intended to go online. As an added measure of security, as soon as someone plugs in that machine and it accesses the internet, the program basically sends out a beacon telling me where it is. So, if whoever broke into my house is dumb enough to turn on that machine and try to go online, we can nail the pricks who stole it."

"We might be in luck then, Anthony," said the officer.

"Let's hope these pricks turn it on," he said, licking his lips. He didn't think he'd ever been this angry—it'd taken him a long time to come across those coins. That tennis bracelet and opera length diamond chain belonged to his wife, two apologies for two different extramarital trysts. The only way he could be any madder is if he found out that whoever did this wasn't after the gold, but was after the computer. He didn't know what he would do if they were trying to find those documents to try and ruin his career. If someone did that, he thought, whoever broke into my home was going to die an early death.

*   *   *

Laida got out of her twelve-step meeting. She'd been going to the same ones now for a little while and was getting to know the girls in the different groups. She was excited—a couple of the young women had invited her to go out for coffee after the meeting. She knew Morgan didn't like her going out with "those people" as she called them, but she was just doing what she was told, and was trying to recover from the disease of addiction. She followed the others to a little dingy coffee shop just around the corner from the church where they held their meeting.

As soon as they walked in the waitress just pointed them over to the large table in the side room—the members of their group had been going there and socializing in a sober environment for years. She walked slowly with the pack of young men and women boisterously making their way through the diner. She passed a group of white teenagers wearing black shirts and baggy black cargo pants sitting with a just a pot of coffee, not talking and staring at each other. One of them caught Laida's eyes as she walked across with her recovery friends. He started to move in the booth towards the aisle to engage her. Her friend Amber saw this horrible grubby kid who was surely ready to attempt to flirt with Laida, and stepped in front of her and up to the boy.

276

"Do you know her?"

The teen mumbled something Amber couldn't hear. Standing between the boy and Laida, she pushed Laida past him with the rest of the group.

"Well keep it that way," she said as she joined the rest of her friends. Laida put down her things and then excused herself to go to the restroom. As she walked down, she saw that the young man had not stopped looking at her the whole time. He was *creepy*—he looked at her as if they'd known each other a long time, but he was not familiar. Laida's mental Rolodex spun rapidly, but she had never seen him or met him as a girl, or as a boy. She was walking toward his table again to get to the bathroom on the other side—Laida could have changed her route and walked all the way around, but she didn't. She had made a conscious decision not to live in a fear-based reality. She had been indoctrinated that fear and faith did not live in the same house, and she had faith in her Higher Power that she could stay free from heroin one day at a time.

As she walked toward the booth, the young man jumped out and faced her. He flipped a knife out of his pocket and said, "I knew it was you. I've been waiting for you." He stabbed the blade deep into Laida's side. She fell to the floor in horror, and in a flash of red, passed out.

*   *   *

"Degan," said Mike, "What's happenin' my man?"

"My *boy*. How's it goin', kid?" Degan walked loosely into the store, long, lanky arms at his side.

Mike came from around the pawn counter and saw that in the hand opposite him the young man was carrying a laptop computer.

"Haven't seen you. Things okay?"

"Yeah, Mike. Need to make a sale."

"Okay. Carlo?!" he yelled across the store.

Degan held up the nondescript laptop.

"Mikey. Can't have this one in the book."

Michael looked at him quizzically. He didn't want this to go where he already thought it had gone.

277

"Is that…"

"From a mutual friend. Sammy."

"You brought that *here*? You fucking shithead!" Mike didn't raise his voice but was livid.

"Can we talk, uh…" Degan motioned to the back room.

The wheels in Mike's brain were already spinning. He was going to need to erase the data on the cameras. The cameras had seen his old friend come in with that laptop. It was already being recorded to the DVR. He didn't have plausible deniability if anyone came there looking for that machine. Would it be better to just erase all the feeds from a particular time stamp? Or would anyone investigating be able to prove he intended to hide something? Did the Chinese place still have that little camera outside their building next door? Was that a good enough camera to make out Degan from across the parking lot? How much doubt was reasonable? He needed to call Lexi. He dialed her number.

"I'm calling Sammy in a minute," said Michael, glaring at Degan. "What the fuck are you thinking?"

"Yo, Mike, that house was a federal agent's." Michael held up his finger and spoke into the phone.

"Lexi. Where are you…?" There was a pause and he held his finger up to Degan. "Well get down here right now. No stopping for coffee. *Now.*" His tone was extremely clear as he clicked off his phone.

"Mikey, I…"

"Shut the fuck up, Degan. Before I call Sammy, tell me what the fuck happened."

"I have a message from Sammy. He said fuck the rest of the money that Dave owes him—he never wants to see that dude again. He said there was plenty of other shit in there. More than he'd expected. But that he didn't want to have to meet David. He's afraid of heat, Mike. He said they just got out of there before shit went bad."

Mike was pensive. Sammy hadn't really done anything *too* wrong. He had just given the machine to Michael instead of meeting up with David to square up. Michael just hated that Degan had brought it to *him*. I mean, he thought, I guess he has no choice. He spoke deliberately.

"Degan, you put me in a pretty awkward position. I don't want that thing here."

"Neither do I, man." He was animated.

"No. You don't get it. This thing's fucking kryptonite. It's fucking radioactive. It's fucking *uranium*. I can't have it here. The problem is, the camera has you coming in the store and holding a laptop."

"What do you want me to do?"

Michael thought about it. It was not a good situation any way he could spin it. The law required that every time people came and sold things to the pawn shop, they were required to sign the book saying that they held title to the goods, and provide identification, and the item would then be logged, and that log sent to the police. The penalties for taking in an item without logging it in the book were a $25,000 fine and/or six months in jail, along with any other penalties the district attorney decided to slap on. If you took something in and didn't write it in the book, you were through. Mike knew that.

He didn't know what to do. First he thought it could look like Degan had come in to sell the computer and then he left it for no monetary consideration, but he didn't think a jury'd buy that. I mean, their logs they sent to the police had dozens of laptops purchased not working but just for parts for small sums of money. No, if Degan left the store without that machine, it would be implied that a sale occurred. And he had to keep the tape rolling. Mike licked his lips.

"You mind if I have you sign the book as someone else?"

Degan wasn't following. He looked confused and kept this dumb look on his face. He didn't see what Mike was getting at.

"Like, just scribble down a signature, and we'll log you in the computer as someone in the joint right now."

"Oh," said Degan. He understood. "That's cool. Just want no heat."

"Yeah, no heat. It's just a clerical error on our part. You're protected. You and I know I can't put you in the book. No connection to you. None to Sammy."

"What about the laptop? You gonna' finish this?"

"I'm on it. Got a girl that fixes my computer. She's gonna' come down and copy the hard drive right now for you to take, and then she's gonna' rip the machine down to parts and sell it."

Degan looked at him incredulously.

"They strip 'um and sell 'um for parts," said Mike. "It's like what we used to do with the Caddys."

"I feel you. Worth more in pieces. You got someone who does that?"

"Yeah. Five years she's been helpin' me. All the machines come in that are stolen and the files are locked, whatever, she can't break in, she breaks 'um down into parts and sells the laptop parts online."

"Serious?" asked Degan.

"You should see her. She's got little screwdrivers and everything."

"Yo, I don't wanna' know nothin' about no little tools."

The two men laughed.

"She'll be down in a couple minutes," said Mike. "She should be able to copy the drive pretty quick, then we'll run it back to Sammy."

"No way," Degan stood up. "I've never seen Sammy like that. Fear of *God* was in him, Mike. Said he never wants to see your boy Dave again. You do it and handle it. I'm not going back to Sammy with anything but some Mohegan Sun chips."

He got up to go. Michael knew he couldn't stop it. He handed him a couple C-notes for coming down, half-embraced him, and watched him leave. His attention was fully focused on that computer. He stared at it sitting there like it was one of Jack Hanna's animals—he didn't quite know what to do with it, and he was afraid of it getting loose in his store. He continued to stare at it. Just as he went to call Lexi again, she walked in.

"Come here," he said.

"Hello to you too, Mike," she responded. "What's this…"

"Not today, Lexi. Listen to me." He handed her the laptop, and she went to flip it open.

"Don't even open it!" he said, slamming it closed. Lexi had never seen him like this. He wasn't being cool.

"Mike, I…"

"Lexi. Look at me and don't say anything. You need to take this machine and get it out of the store."

"Is it hot?"

"*Fucking five alarms*," said Mike as he looked her in the eyes. Lexi smiled—the energy was almost sexual.

"Got it. How much is it?"

"It's fucking free, Lexi. But you need to take it now and go. You need to copy the hard drive. It might be password protected or whatever. Just work your magic. Fuck. I don't care. Rip the drive out of the thing. That's all I want. You keep the rest. Anything with a serial number, you put in the trash. Sell anything else you want."

"Okay. You want the actual laptop drive? I mean, they're internal so you have to be careful handling them. I could take it out of the caddy and put it in an anti-static bag, I guess, just…"

"Lexi. Take the computer and go. Copy the hard drive. Bring me a copy on one of those little cards or drives or whatever. If I knew how to do it, I'd do it myself. Don't be nosy. You understand? Just do your thing. I'm giving you the rest of the machine as payment—the screen's gotta' be worth at least a C-note."

"More, probably. It's pretty high-end. I understand. I'll call you when it's done."

She flounced out the door. Michael switched gears and turned once more to the phone. When he called, all he got was David's machine.

"David, Mike. Little change of plans, no big deal. You're going to meet me at the club instead of meeting Sammy at the casino. I'll see you there tonight at seven." He popped a breath strip in his mouth and waited for Lexi.

*   *   *

Alexis had never seen Michael that worked up. She'd been doing business with him for years, and they had slowly built up a very high level of trust. It took a long time for them to know each other well enough to engage in borderline illegal, and then fully illegal activities.

Lexi had a system. Many of the computers that would come into the pawn shop were stolen. The store would take the machines, and then if the "owner" didn't know the password to get on the machine, they could totally squeeze the jerk on the price because everyone knew what was happening. Then, Mike would call Alexis. He thought what she did was magic. In reality, it wasn't that hard. Boot the machine in safe mode to get around the passwords. Boot the machine from a disc to get around the passwords. Pop the drive out and attach it with a USB to a desktop, erase all the data, reformat, add a pirated copy of Windows, update and/or download drivers, activate, and voilà! Perfectly working computer to resell. It could always be done—it was just a question of how much time it was going to take. It was a very rare situation when Alexis couldn't figure out how to work on these machines—she was raised working on computers.

Recently, she found that a lot of the machines that came in had just huge quantities of digital music on them. She had built herself quite the free music library by copying the songs she liked off of different units. It definitely wasn't piracy—these were songs on a machine that she had legally obtained at a legal business. In any case, she had amassed a very large library of songs, and loved flipping through all sorts of different genres.

Finding a back door into this computer to circumvent the password was easy, but when she went to copy the drive she saw that a lot of the files were hidden, and a lot were encrypted. She had a program on a different laptop that would unlock those files, but she decided it was just going to be easier to just download a copy of the program from a mirror, since the whole machine was getting torn apart anyway. That's the moment she noticed that the machine hadn't automatically connected to her wireless network. She looked around for the cause of the problem, and enabled the wireless card. The machine connected to the internet, and she downloaded the program and began copying the drive.

The unmarked car was at her door in twenty minutes.

*　*　*

282

The heavyset woman was crying softly at the table, puffy red eyes flooded with tears, alone except for a box of Kleenex one of the officers had left for her. She had stopped looking up every time she thought she heard the door open—she was waiting for the detective to come back after going to fetch some paperwork. She tried to compose herself when he returned.

"Mrs. Palmer, I just got the report from the psychologist on Casey. I just need to ask you again, has he ever acted like this before? Has he ever been violent?"

"No, no, no," she sobbed. "Casey is such a good boy. He would never do anything. Never..." She broke down and couldn't speak.

The officer felt for her—he saw this sort of thing all the time. It was a terrible feeling to know that your offspring was capable of something horrible and vicious. It shook parents to the core.

"Ma'am, that might have been true before, but he just stabbed a girl. In a restaurant. Twenty people saw him do it. He's never had a history of violence?"

"No. Never." Casey's mother tried to pull herself together. This just all seemed like a dream. A nightmare. She never believed she would have gotten a call from the police saying to come down to the station and that her son was in custody. She'd raised him right. She raised him to be a gentleman. Stabbed someone? She couldn't handle this.

"I have to ask you something here, Ma'am. And I'm not trying to intrude. I'm just trying to figure out a motive. Before the psychologist spoke to him, I just thought this was random, but...well...has your son ever had any, you know, sexual problems? Was he ever a victim of abuse?"

She started sobbing again.

"No! What kind of a mother do you think I am? Casey has been such a wonderful boy, such a bright child, straight A's until just recently. He doesn't have any sexual issues!"

"Well, does he have a girlfriend?"

"Well, no."

"A boyfriend?"

She started crying again.

"He's only sixteen. He's not gay. He had a girlfriend, but they broke up about four or five months ago, and since then, well, he's been kind of depressed. I just thought he'd pull himself out of it. But he's been getting worse. With those clothes he's been wearing…" She broke down again.

"Well, Ma'am. There's a bit of a complication. The girl's still in ICU. I don't know if she's going to be okay or not yet."

"Oh. God…"

"And apparently, she's, uh, she's, um, a, um, a, a, pre-operative transsexual."

Casey's mother looked back at the officer, confused.

"Like, a transvestite?" What's next, she thought. Just take me now, God, she said to herself.

"No, ma'am. Some people say transgender. But, um, a transsexual. Living full-time as a female. Looks like a female. Breast surgery. Makeup. Womens clothes. She's a female and all. Just, with a, uh, you know." He pointed at his crotch. "We didn't know until the doctors told us when they, uh, well, when they cut her clothes off."

She was beside herself. Her son stabbed a he/she?

"Well, I mean, did he know her?" she asked. "Did he know she was a, uh, a he/she?"

The officer was embarrassed.

"Well, that's just it. *We* didn't even know until the docs told us. She doesn't look like a, um, you know, a, um, drag queen or anything. She looks just like a regular girl, you know. I looked at her myself, personally, and I'm telling you, I had no idea. I'm just asking, because there are, you know, enhanced criminal penalties if this was, you know, a, um, a hate crime. Transgenders are protected, you know. Like, if you stabbed a blind person or an old man. So, we're just wondering how he knew that she was transgender and we didn't. Were they ever, uh, *involved*?"

"No! My son would never be hanging around with people like her."

He only stabs them, the officer thought.

"Well, Ma'am, why don't you take a look at the transcript of Casey speaking with the psychologist. That's what I left to go get."

He handed over a piece of paper to her. He watched her alternately cry and attempt to hold back tears:

Casey: Yeah. I met the devil. He was white. Like me. With a pointy chin, but not in a Satan sort of way. In a WASPY way. A bold chin. He told me his whole purpose was to do nothing, and coerce others around him to do nothing too.

Police: You met the devil? In person? Or when you were asleep?

Casey: When I'm in bed.

Police: Sleeping in bed?

Casey: I don't really sleep.

Police: You don't sleep at all?

Casey: Well, I fall asleep, but every night I have this recurring dream. I'm a guard at what looks like a gate. At this gate where people come in who have been dreaming for the night.

Police: You don't sleep?

Casey: Not really. I'm awake on that side, and asleep on this side.

Police: No. You're awake now.

Casey: Prove it.

Police: Excuse me?

Casey: I'm awake on that side and asleep here. I go through the motions. But every night is the same. If every night is the same, and every day is different, and discombobulated, and doesn't make any sense, doesn't it only seem logical that the daytime is my dream state and the nighttime in my bed is my awake state where I'm actually doing something?

Police: But what are you doing all night when you're sleeping?

Casey: I told you. I don't sleep. I work.

Police: What's your work?

Casey: I'm a guard at a gate. Other people in that dreamspace have been dreaming. They've been partying, hanging out with different people, having a grand old time. I am the one who helps direct them into these little chutes.

Police: Chutes?

Casey: Yes. The people come in six at a time. Six men, Six women, six men, six women, over and over and over again all night. My job is to close the gate behind them after we get six inside in a line. They come in like cows.

Police: Then what happens to the people in these chutes?

Casey: Another person comes and puts what looks like a hood on the people. Inside the hood is a soft LCD screen that shows the person a movie about evolution, how everything works together, a little pep talk to remind them what life is like, and to remind them that everything is going to be okay. They get moved along with their hoods on, down a little path, at which point their necks get put into these little holders while they're watching the movie. Then, a laser comes and lops off the heads with the hoods on them. Those get dumped to the left so that the hoods get washed. The bodies get dumped to the other side to be liquefied.

Police: And you see this happen?

Casey: Every night when I go to bed. I go to work. I have a hard time communicating there. It apparently seems like my job is that I'm paying off some sort of debt to the devil, which is why I'm working there.

Police: Then why did you stab the victim?

Casey: Because I recognized him.

Police: You mean you recognized her.

Casey: No. I recognized *him*.

Police: You knew that she was a transsexual woman—a natal male who had transitioned to female.

Casey: What you're born is what you are. That doesn't matter to me.

Police: Explain that. Why doesn't that matter? You stabbed a young woman.

Casey: Every night I would see him in the crowd. There are lots and lots of people working at different gates, but once you've been there for awhile, you start to recognize people. Whenever he came to my gate, there would always be confusion. He would say, I'm a girl. And I would say no you're not. And then I would put him in with the men.

Police: So, you're saying that every night, you see a crowd of people that you direct into these chutes to get killed?

Casey: Well, not killed. You see, that's their dreamspace. They're dreaming, and when it's time for them to wake up, they

286

get herded over to me. You're there too. You just don't remember. I mean, it's like everyone on the whole planet.

Police: And you see this every night.

Casey: Yes. And I'd seen that guy before. He caused a problem. A few times, he got belligerent and argued, and they ended up sending him with the drug addicts to be liquefied.

Police: I'm sorry, the drug addicts?

Casey: Yeah. When the addicts come to the chute, the ones that have been getting high instead of sleeping, we put them into a big chamber in a big group for them to be destroyed. We don't spend time sorting them by sex to give them the right movie to watch. They don't get a bedtime story. It's just lights out.

Police: Go on.

Casey: Well, after that happened a few times he would just submit and be put with the men.

Police: You can tell the difference?

Casey: Always.

Police: And you always put her with the men?

Casey: Yes. Then, I was working and he wised up. He said, put me in alone. I said no one has ever asked to have that done before. Ending someone's dream feels just like dying to them—they don't know they're just going to wake up. They're just scared. That's why there's that movie for them to watch. You know, most people don't want to die alone. If there are other actual people there, it's easier for them to accept somehow. A lot of the people I see who are done dreaming, and are ready to go back to their bodies…they all hold hands at a certain part of the movie.

Police: Did you put her in alone?

Casey: Yes. I put him in alone.

Police: And what happened next?

Casey: I wasn't supposed to do that. It's a waste of the other five spots. It's inefficiency. It was a blip. As soon as it happened, I "woke up" as you would say.

Police: And then what happened?

Casey: That next day, I went and played some video games, then my friends and I went out for some coffee, and I saw him.

Police: Just like that?

Casey: Just like that. And I stabbed him. He had held up the line over and over and over and over again. I finally did what he wanted and put him in alone, so that he wouldn't be counted as a male. You don't understand. I can't put him with the females. He's not a female.

Police: The woman you stabbed is a female.

Casey: He's not. I had never seen him on this side before. And after that happened, I knew what I had to do.

Police: What do you think will happen to you tonight when you go to bed?

Casey: I'm going to get a promotion.

Mrs. Palmer couldn't read any more. She pushed the paper over to the policeman and cried and cried until she couldn't shed another tear.

"I'm very, very sorry, Ma'am. I know this is very troubling. We're doing everything we can to help."

"What's...what's going to happen to my son?"

"Well, he's going to be sent to an inpatient psych ward. We don't want to keep him here because we don't want him to hurt himself. He seems very calm and docile, though. He's not fighting us. We just need your help."

"Anything."

"Well, has anything like this ever happened before? Has he ever had a psychotic break?"

"No."

"Do you have any incidence of mental illness in your family?"

"Just my post-partum." She sniffled.

"Does he take any medications?"

"No. He's strong and healthy."

"What about illicit substances? You mentioned he used to be a straight-A student. What happened?"

The woman's eyes welled up with tears. She had already foreseen where this was all going, but she didn't want to believe it. He'd started hanging around with those druggie kids. He wouldn't talk to her. He'd lock himself in his room for hours with music pounding. And he'd gotten this strange newsletter coming to the house. She pulled the paper out of her purse.

288

"He was getting this," she said and handed it to the officer. She was still sobbing.

"The New Liberty Church? What the heck is that?" The officer's eyes were skimming the page.

"I found it in his room," she said. "I don't like to snoop around, but he was starting to scare me a little. We were going to have an appointment with the therapist next week."

The officer's eyes kept skimming the page. He excused himself and took the paper with him. The woman sat at the table and wondered why God was punishing her like this—she had raised her son so well. She had taken him to church, and had him volunteer. He had a job. He played sports. He was kind, and fun to talk to. When he got moody, she just thought it was a combination of breaking up with his girlfriend and hormones. She thought it was just a phase. And then it got worse. And when she found that pamphlet, it scared her half to death. That's what made her schedule the therapy appointment. She had gone to the website—drugs as religious sacraments? Mushrooms and fractals and Easter Island? This was insane. What next? Crop circles? Stonehenge? She knew this was trouble, and she hoped her boy hadn't bought into that drivel. The officer came back in.

"They're going to move him to the psych ward now, Ma'am. He'll be handcuffed. You can't talk to him, but you can come separately. They're going to run some tox screens on him for some of these chemicals on this website."

"You've heard of this church?"

"No, Ma'am, not this one. But we definitely deal with people like this. Trying to hide behind the First Amendment while they poison people's minds with this trash. Telling them to get high. Trust me, we get OD's from dope, and people have heart attacks from smoking crack. But when people take these crazy drugs, they end up doing crazy things. Like stab people and say the devil told them to do it. This isn't the first time I've seen people taking these sorts of drugs, but I can tell you things are looking just a little bit better for Casey."

"They are? What do you mean?"

"Well, I mean, you told me Casey was a straight-A student, right?"

"Yes. He was involved in his church. He loved his family. He excelled in math."

"Right. He was a good kid. So, when a good kid just starts all of a sudden behaving badly, it's usually drug-related. If we test him and he's got these wacky drugs in him that this church is telling him to take…"

"But I don't know if he got them from the church…"

"Don't worry, Ma'am. That doesn't matter. I already have my partner making a call to the Feds. They're going to find out who's behind this website and bring them in wherever he lives for questioning. If your Casey stabbed someone because of the crap he was taught to put in his body from that website, the D.A.'s going to put Casey in a hospital where he belongs, and throw the book at this church, if you can call it that. I feel like I'm blaspheming even using that word here."

"So, it's going to be okay?" She saw her first glimmer of hope.

"Well, we don't know if she's out of the woods yet. She's still in ICU. But if someone else was telling your son it was okay to get high with these weird chemicals that scrambled his brain? You read that interview—Casey said some crazy things. If someone else directed him to take that crap, they're the ones responsible."

She started to feel a slight relief. She didn't even know where it came from, but was combined with a long, slow exhale.

"What's the girl's name that he hurt?"

"Laida."

"Well, I'm going to say a prayer for her."

"That's very sweet of you, Ma'am."

"And what about Casey's friends? Did either of them know anything about this church?"

"Yes. We're already photocopying that newsletter, and the officers in the area are going to be looking at it and cross-referencing any other cases they've had lately involving any of the chemicals on this site. It's going out to all of the officers."

"Are you going to find the people responsible?"

"That's what we do, Ma'am. And the Feds are working on it right now too."

"I want to know who these people are that have ruined my son's life. I want to know who put up this awful website telling him to get high. I want them held responsible for ruining Casey's future."

"We're working as fast as we can."

*   *   *

Alexis was not talking. No way, no way. She didn't think Michael would actually have her killed if she ever flipped on him—she thought most of that was just guys puffing out their chests. But she'd remembered some earlier conversations she'd had with Michael. He told her that in their business, sometimes you had to take a pinch. If the cops ever arrested you, you were never to tell them anything. Ever. At all. He told her he would always do the same, as would anyone else he did real business with.

"The only way they really make their cases is if you confess," he'd taught her. "The whole point of detaining you is so that they can threaten you with a much worse punishment than they would ever give you, and tell you that's what they're going to do if you don't cooperate."

"But what if they do that? What if they charge me with some horrible crime?" she'd asked.

"They won't do it. They just *say* they will. They read you to see how scared you are, and they try to put more and more fear in you until you confess. You see, once they have that confession, they can do whatever they want to you. But if you don't confess? If you stay completely silent and say not a word until they put you on the stand at trial when you plead the Fifth? If you do that, they have to collect all the data themselves, organize it into a case, get witness statements, they have to do a jury selection, there are lawyers and motions. It costs them a *lot* of money. And then they have to convince a group of your peers that there was no reasonable doubt you did the crime. If you keep your mouth shut, do you know how hard that is to do? It's damn near impossible. With the right defense lawyer? It *is* impossible."

"So, should I just tell them I want to talk to a lawyer?"

"No! Then it just goes to the D.A. And plus, that lawyer's going to cost a lot. No, the lawyer's the last resort. You never tell them you want a lawyer. It makes you look guilty. Keep playing with them and pretend to be working with them, but just don't tell them anything."

"So they'd be arresting me to get information?"

"Sort of. They'd be arresting you in order to try and make a deal with you. Just remember, if this ever happens to you— these people are not your friends. And you don't deal with people who are not your friends."

"What about you? Do they bother you, Mike?"

"No. I got pinched fifteen years ago, a long time before I had the store. Since then, not once. I have a relationship with the cops now."

"Well, what about me? Would they ever come after me?"

"They might. But don't worry. Don't sell anyone out. They'll never make a case against you unless you do."

That conversation was being replayed in her head on a loop. They had been holding her in an interrogation room at the local police station, and had told her nothing. They had, as yet, refused to tell her even why she was there. The detective finally walked in.

"You're going to go to jail," he said gruffly.

What, no hello, she thought. She decided she was going to act just like she thought Michael would want her to.

"Excuse me?"

"Do you know why you're here?" he asked her.

"You banged down my door and dragged me into a piece of shit cop SUV."

The officer was not amused by her lip.

"That computer you were working on when we picked you up was stolen out of the home of a federal employee. It's federal property. Where did you buy it?"

"You don't think I'm the one who broke in and stole it?" she asked him sarcastically. He wasn't expecting that response.

"Should we be looking at you for that?"

"Well, the fact that you're assuming that I bought it rather than stole it means you don't really have any case against me." She was very satisfied with her first salvo.

She's a bitch, thought the officer. Cocky and smart. Time to knock her down a notch.

"We know you didn't steal it. At the time it was stolen, your credit card was swiped *by you* and signed for *by you* at a store miles away from the robbery, and you were on the store's surveillance camera. We know you didn't steal it. But we want to know why you have it."

Shit, she thought. These guys were much more thorough and much faster than Michael had characterized them.

"I don't know what you're talking about."

"That's okay. We're holding you for possession of stolen goods. We have all day and some of the next to detain you before we decide to charge you with anything else. As we speak, they're running your credit cards to see where you were, and your cell records to see who you called and when, and what towers you were near."

"You can't do that! That's a violation of my rights!" She was starting to get nervous.

"We *can*."

"You need a judge for that! You'll never get a warrant to do that! There are no exigent circumstances." She was breathing heavily.

"That's smart, Ms. Rini. You must have watched a lot of *Law and Order*. Except this isn't New York's finest. You were in possession of federal property. That means federal rules. Federal court. Federal jail. And you *are* going there."

"And why are you saying that?" Her face was getting flushed and the back of her neck was getting sweaty.

"Because, if you don't tell us what we want to know, we're sending you away for the max."

It's just like what Michael said, she thought. She calmed down a moment and actually breathed a sigh of relief. Michael had prepared her for this moment. She had been trained. She was so happy that she'd asked Michael so long ago what to do if she got pinched.

"I don't feel like saying anything else, but I don't mind sitting here with you." She conspicuously did not ask for counsel, and smiled at the man in front of her.

"That's fine. That's your right. But let me be very direct with you: your cooperation is not necessary, but it can't hurt. Do you really not think we're going to figure out where you got it from? Once we run your cards and your phone? We'll know exactly where you've been since the robbery occurred. Throw in some red light cameras and it's just a matter of time."

She did the math quickly. They were going to know it came from the pawn shop. She remembered there was a light right by the store that said "traffic signals photo enforced." She cringed every time she sailed through a yellow. Then she thought about it. What if they saw that? And they could probably subpoena the camera footage from the pawn shop. She knew Michael had cameras in there to watch for thieves that recorded to a DVR. There was a tape of her going into the store and walking out with that computer. Would they be able to prove it was *that* computer? Was that what reasonable doubt meant? Could she bank her freedom on that small of an amount of reasonable doubt? But then, how had they even found her and banged on her door? They knew way too much. This game was *much* harder than Michael made it seem.

"I'll tell you, but I want immunity."

"Immunity from what?"

"I don't want to be prosecuted."

"Ms. Rini, this isn't a movie. This is real life. There's no immunity. You have federal property in your house, and it looked like you were copying data off the machine. If you didn't steal it, then you're definitely complicit in a number of other crimes."

"I don't want to go to jail."

"I can understand that. Tell me where it came from."

"I can't."

"Then don't. Take the heat yourself. But I'm telling you. Someone broke into someone's home to take that machine. It wasn't something someone walked out of a Walmart with. You're in way over your head. Just tell me where you got it so we can speed up this investigation. If you help us, we treat you right. If you try to slow us down, we're going to lock you up."

Lexi wanted to cry. She would *never* show this man her tears. She thought it through. They were going to figure out it came from Michael. Michael would understand. It was her only choice. She licked her lips.

"Premium Pawn. Mike Mazzone," she spoke softly.

She heard a door distantly shut. She hadn't realized others had been watching her.

"Thank you. We'll bring him in. Once he corroborates that, you're going to be free to go."

He left the room and left her alone.

What have I done, Alexis thought.

* * *

David did *not* like what he saw. The doors to the pawnshop were closed and locked, the lights were off, and there was a handwritten sign in Sharpie marker on the door that read "temporarily closed." Carlo was standing out front, alone, smoking a cigarette.

"Where's Michael?" asked David, jumping out of his Mercedes.

"Store's closed early today," said Carlo.

"I've been calling his cell and he's not picking up. I need to speak with him right away," said David.

"He left for the day."

"What's your name?"

"Carlo Bisi," he said, and held out his hand.

"Carlo, David Evans," he said shaking Carlo's hand. "Listen, I play cards with Mike down at Johnny-O's. He tried to schedule a meeting tonight at seven, and I was calling him because my mother-in-law's coming over for dinner tonight, and I was going to have to reschedule. And he hasn't been picking up his phone. Can you pass that message along to him?"

"I don't think he's going to make that meeting," said Carlo.

"Well, I still need to talk to him," said David.

"Yeah," snickered Carlo. "I understand that."

"Well, maybe he lost his cell or left it in the car or something." David didn't want to pay any heed to the silent alarms slowly going off up and down his spinal cord. "Do you have his home number?"

295

Carlo looked at David. Nice suit. Nice car. Michael had never mentioned him. But he had his cell number and was supposed to meet him.

"Cops came and picked him up," said Carlo matter-of-factly. He didn't seem to know anything more than that, and he didn't know David.

"What?"

"He's in lockup," laughed Carlo. "They don't let you have a phone in the can."

"He was arrested?"

"Yeah. They picked him up a little while ago."

"Did they say what it was about?"

"I don't know. I heard them talking about stolen goods, which doesn't make any sense, you know? We do everything by the book, and turn over the lists of what we buy to the cops. They were looking for something though, something *really* valuable. I don't think we had it here though. They took him away in cuffs."

"Jesus," inhaled David. He knew immediately. It was the computer. It had to be. Michael had called him earlier in the day to tell him he wasn't meeting Sammy at the casino, but Mike at the club. And since that message he hadn't answered his phone. And David had called him every ten minutes since. Then his heart froze. What if the cops were checking Michael's phone? They would see his number on there.

What if Mike ratted him out? What if Mike told the cops that David had orchestrated the whole thing? How was he going to get out of *that*? It was a terrible feeling—he knew this was his fault. How could he explain away those repeated calls to Michael if the cops questioned him? What was he thinking, taking that chemical from Peter and then trying to work on it secretly? Why did he ever think that would even work? He couldn't have just turned it over to his superiors? Why didn't he do that? He thought about it. He did it because he wanted to sin. Pride. He had too much of that. He thought he was smarter than everyone else, and that he could do this better. Greed. He wanted that money—his salary and bonus was not enough. He wanted more. He was *choosing* to sin. And people were falling all around him.

Carlo saw the fear on his face and tried to calm him down by just speaking.

"I know, right? I'm just out here waiting for him to get released. Telling everyone who stops by we closed early."

"So you had no idea what's going on?"

Carlo's eyes narrowed. He had spoken to one of the policemen that he'd known personally for years. He had told Carlo that this was about a piece of missing federal property. Carlo didn't have to be a genius to know it was the computer that Degan had brought in. And Mike knew that it was hot, and had him sign a fake name in the book. God bless Mike, he thought. He was a lot of things, but he was not a rat. He'd never say anything to bust anybody. He'd take the fall himself.

"Not really," said Carlo to David. "Whatever the cops were looking for, though. They were making a federal case about it..."

David's face turned white. This was all going to be over. The other shoe was going to drop. He was going to get a call at home or work, or maybe the agents would just show up, unannounced. Mike was going to sell him out for that machine, and he was going to be jailed and fired. He had been running for so long toward the underworld, he'd forgotten that he had made these choices. He intended to deceive others around him. He was responsible for that. He felt sick to his stomach. Carlo picked up on his body language.

"Don't worry, Chief. Michael won't tell those damn cops a thing—if he ever rats, he loses all his street cred. He'd be out of business. They'll arrest him, he'll fuck with them for a little while, and then he'll post bail and the store'll open tomorrow."

David looked exactly the same. This man has no idea, he thought. "Carlo, I..."

"If you think *he's* got it bad, *forget* it. Morgan, the girl who works here? Well she just found out when the cops came here that someone stabbed her girlfriend last night."

"Your employee was stabbed?"

"No, not Morgan. *Her girlfriend*. This woman Laida. And get this. This is the most fucked up part. The kid that stabbed her? He was on some crazy drugs that he'd heard about in some

297

nutjob's newsletter. The same newsletter that *Morgan* was getting at the store."

"Wait. What?"

"That's insane, right? Morgan is getting this newsletter at the store about some church that protects people's 'right to get high.' Then some nutjob takes those very drugs, and stabs her girlfriend. She's in the fucking hospital! You can't make that stuff up!"

"Huh," said David. He was still very distant. "You wouldn't happen to have a copy of that newsletter, would you?"

"Yeah, I got one. Come inside the store." Carlo loved meeting new people, especially when he was wearing the boss's shoes. He was so sick of always playing second violin. He felt like showing off.

Carlo opened the door and let David in. He went into Michael's office and into the incoming mail slot.

"For some reason," said Carlo, "When the cops came, they took the copy of this newsletter that Morgan had left out on the counter. They had all kind of gathered around it and made a couple calls, and then took it. We had a newer one in the mail pile. Can you imagine? The kid who stabbed her was on the drugs in that newsletter. I mean, what are the odds?"

He handed it to David, who skimmed the main article entitled "The Invention of Zero: The Nautilus, The Fractal God, and Manifest Destiny." When he saw the author's initials "J.G." his antennae stood straight up. His eyes stopped midway down the page.

...They should have called the U.S.S. Nautilus the U.S.S. Cochlea, as it was in charge of hearing with sonar all around itself for the good of our nation. However, we still fail to understand why blind people can hear better than those gifted by sight—when missing one of those basic faculties, the brain is able to turn up the volume so to speak on the ones it still possesses. This begs the question as to why the brain itself cannot just turn these senses up on its own, in fully-functioning healthy people. It comes back to the fundamental question I ask every new person I meet: Do you believe that you are the same as everyone else, or incredibly different?...

David inhaled sharply. He'd remembered Josh asking him that exact question the second time they'd met at the poker club. The night he'd given Josh his business card. The night he'd gotten the idea in his head to use Josh's brainpower like a giant battery to add thrust to his work on 5,6,7. Could "J.G." really be Josh Grenier? What were the odds of that being true? He skimmed a little farther down in the article.

...It's simply because our brains are not designed to work in such a way to be able to interpret the fractal God. It's why we need the psychedelic: we need the intermediary between the human brain and the divine mind to be able to understand the fractal God. The Bible does a good job of introducing it, but verbal communication can only do so much justice. We see how Yhwh works indirectly: the wind, the light, a massless but incredibly powerful force that uses people to show others how to live best, and then move the hands of prophets to pen the stories of others to help us interpret our world. And sadly, we cannot even understand the thrust of this book.

For example, the story of David, the cornerstone of the House of David, the beginning of the lineage of Jesus Christ, gets reduced to a boy killing the giant Goliath with a slingshot. When David was king of the Jews, he committed adultery with Bathsheba, conceived a son, then sent her husband Uriah into battle on the front lines so that he'd be killed to cover his indiscretion. The meaning of the story is lost—that if one trusts in Yhwh, there is nothing to fear, and all can be forgiven...

David dropped the paper on the floor. He'd never fainted. He didn't, but he put his hand down on the counter to steady himself. It's Josh Grenier.

"Are you all right" asked Carlo.

David's mouth was dry. He licked his lips and could not feel any wetness. He felt like he had lost his breath, his spirit. Finally he collected himself enough to speak.

"Just tired. I didn't sleep a lot last night. Tell Mike to call me. He's got my number."

David could hardly remember stumbling out the front door. He sat in his Mercedes, just looking at his hands. They were dirty, no matter how hard he washed them.

He closed his eyes. He saw the whole thing graphically. How amazing was God, this God whom he pretended to pay homage to at church, but was usually just staring off into space thinking about the pipeline?

He had been handed the 5,6,7: the genetic blueprint for the forbidden fruit. Almost as if it were inherent to the thing, he was immediately tempted to hide it from others, and get greedy and work in his own self interest. And at an illegal gambling hall, he met a young man who, unbeknownst to him, was working on an extracurricular project to keep chemicals just like the one he was working on legal. Without knowing that, he had been drawn to him, instinctively, and attempted to dupe him into using his brainpower to help him monetize the tree of knowledge.

And what had he gotten? What was the result of his trying to harness Josh's mental acuity to research the chemical? He got an answer to the research: Josh had told people to use drugs like 5,6,7, and the end result was that a teenager his daughter's age had gone crazy and stabbed a girl. How much clearer could God be?

Then he thought about Josh talking to him in the poker club that day when he found out his dad was in jail. Josh had told him, "The story of David is a story of forgiveness. He was kind of an asshole before he straightened out." He remembered the whole story. And he realized right there—God had been testing his faith all along.

He made a promise to God, right there in his Benz. God, he said in his mind, if I ever get out of this mess, I promise that I will never do anything like this again. I won't break any laws. I won't be greedy. I won't be proud. And I'll stop playing cards to get away from the house. I'm going to talk to Allison and tell her that I think she's an alcoholic, and I can't stand seeing her kill herself slowly like this, and I'm going to take her to rehab and try to mend our marriage.

David inhaled deeply. He hoped God had heard him.

* * *

300

"So, Geronimo, that's about all I know," said Michael.

"It's Giordano, Mike."

"I'm sorry. Giordano. That's how I ended up having that computer in the store. And that's why Morgan's girlfriend is in the hospital. I know it sounds crazy. But it's the truth."

"It actually sounds like the truth," said the detective.

"Really?" said Michael. "You believe me?"

"You can't make that stuff up," he said. "Whenever I hear someone say, 'what are the odds?' I know I'm on the right track."

"And what about me?" asked Michael.

"Depends," said Giordano. "Are you willing to pay a fine to make this all go away?"

"Yes," said Michael, swallowing loudly.

"I can work with that," said the detective. "I can work with that."

Shuffle

Laida recovered from her injuries, except for a small scar that the doctor said, "no one would ever see unless she were wearing a bikini." She said later on that she wished Casey had stabbed her in the breast, so she could have redone her implants and gotten them bigger. After having been shown the interview between Casey and the police psychologist, Laida decided that she would not press charges if the young man got help for his drug problem, which he did. She was incredibly disturbed by the fact that he somehow knew that she was transgender without ever having met her, but living in recovery from addiction, she had been learning that the universe was incredibly beautiful and remarkably intelligent. She realized if she dwelled on the negatives instead of the positives, she would go back to using heroin and slowly killing herself, and she wanted to live, to love, and to be loved. She and Morgan continue to grow closer.

Anthony was indicted by a federal grand jury on a laundry list of corruption and bribery charges. He was remanded to a federal correctional facility while he awaits trial. As a result of the investigation into his dishonest dealings, the DEA was able to answer questions surrounding many apparent accounting irregularities, which ended up being much more sinister. While he was being held, he found out through networks in prison who the criminals were that most likely burglarized his home, but found himself powerless to act. When he contacted one of his best friends on the outside who worked at the agency and still agreed to take his call, Anthony was informed that the documents seized on his computer implicated a number of other agents, and formal investigations had been launched into many of his colleagues. Because of this, he learned that his reputation had been ruined, his career was finished, and he should consider himself lucky to still be alive.

Josh was quickly found, and detained. He called Omicrone, and Corbett worked out a deal with the Feds: he would turn over the rolls of his church membership (around 200 people), as well as all of the IP addresses of the individuals who accessed the website. In exchange, he would not be prosecuted for any criminal wrongdoing, provided he attended twelve-step meetings and met with a counselor. While he resented that all of his work about creating the church website was now taken down from the internet and was in the possession of the federal government, Corbett advised him that maybe he should write a fictional account of creating the church and then sell the book. He told Josh he'd make the same amount of money (probably more) than if he continued to grow his church's membership, and that the book detailing his escapades would be something his father could be very proud of when he would be shortly released. Not only that, Corbett reminded him that if he produced something for more mainstream of an audience, it would actually inform a greater number of people about humanity's ever-changing relationship with entheogens.

Michael paid a substantial fine—one that cleaned out almost all the tax-free cash in his safe—and was put on probation. A few weeks after all this went down, he received a letter from Anthony Clark in federal prison telling him that he knew who Michael was, and as soon as his name was cleared in court, he would be out of prison and intent upon tying up some loose ends. At last check, Michael had told Lexi that he wasn't scared of that joker, but there was a new sign hanging in the door of Premium Pawn. It read: "If it's hot, don't bring it in here." He still went with Buddy to play poker at the club, trying to skim a little from the fish that swam in from time to time, but he definitely watched his back. Though he earned his street cred from not ratting out anyone involved in the store, after that sign went up outside, the pawn shop was never the same.

Remarkably, David completely avoided repercussions. Because Sammy got spooked and the laptop ended up at Lexi's home instead of in David's hands, the Feds detained Anthony before anyone at the DEA found out David's identity as the Durham employee at the other end of the line. On top of that, Viens said that while he was positive the German government had their research, he was never confronted or accused of anything criminal, and so he decided to proceed as if the project never existed. David was never privy to the private transcript that showed Casey using drugs like 5,6,7: a radically altered consciousness that confused waking and dreaming, and allowed Casey to know things about Laida that were simply impossible to know.

He thought that just maybe the 5,6,7 was the fruit of the tree of knowledge, and this was why God tucked the chemical away in a special tree in a special place in a special Amazon jungle far, far away from our stone fences. He attributed avoiding being fired and jailed to the prayers he made to God in his car: he kept the promises he made during that watershed moment, embraced his redemption, brought his wife to treatment for alcoholism, and continues to strengthen the love in his marriage.